DEAD BEES & DRAGONFLIES

A Novel

By

Michael E. Leishear

Sally!
Who would thought
I'd ever do something like
this! I hope you enjoy
the story. Best of luck)

ISBN 0-7414-2356-1

Published by:

INFINITY
PUBLISHING.COM

1094 New DeHaven Street, Suite 100
West Conshohocken, PA 19428-2713
Info@buybooksontheweb.com
www.buybooksontheweb.com
Toll-free (877) BUY BOOK
Local Phone (610) 941-9999
Fax (610) 941-9959

Printed in the United States of America

Printed on Recycled Paper

Published January 2005

ACKNOWLEDGMENTS

My mentor, Robert Gover, deserves a special thank you for 'showing me the way.' Brian thanks for your contribution. Linda and Amy I love you both.

Mom, thanks for bringing me into this world and getting me to adulthood.

DEDICATION

The bulbs of fall respond to the warming soil of spring. The dormancy of winter ends with the colorful flourish of new blooms.

Mother greets each new arrival with the giddiness of a child on Christmas morning.

As spring melds into summer a parade of perennials takes the places of the withering tulips and daffodils. There is color in every corner of her yard, both front and back.

Mother's gardens flourish, but her proudest achievement of flowering majesty are her children.

Within each of us she planted the seeds with which we landscape our own lives. Our pain from each fall, each scrape, each cut is felt by mother.

Mom, you have always been there to nurture the tiny wounds of childhood and the gaping gashes of our adulthood.

Where would we be without you?

I love you mom.

PART ONE

Jane's skin tingled under the intense July sun. She had a perfect view of her two children at play across the street. She sought relief from the stress of her disintegrating marriage. Constant anxiety had reduced her stomach into a knot of twisted nerves. Jane's fear had become part of her, like an arm or leg. Most of her waking hours were spent trying to remember happier times.

One of those times was sixteen-years ago. Rob's application to the Bureau had been accepted. The day after graduating from the FBI Academy he received assignment to the New York field office as a Special Agent. He insisted on getting married right away. They found a J.P. and tied the knot later that day.

*****

Jane had greeted the news of Rob's assignment to New York with mixed emotions. Part of her would miss the mother she'd never been away from. Another part of her looked forward to the adventure. They were leaving the familiarity of D.C. for the excitement of the big city. Jane would miss her mother, Martha Higdon. Robert couldn't wait to get away from his mother, Hilda Webster.

Jane went home to break the news to her mother and pack.

"Jane, why did you have to get married so quick?"

"Mother, Rob has to be in New York tomorrow. We didn't want to wait."

"Why did you have to marry him? Charles Blankenship has been after you for months."

"Rob is older and more settled than Charles. Besides, I love him."

"What about his mother. She and I don't get along."

"Mother, that was years ago. Surely Mrs. Webster has gotten over it?"

"I don't think she's the kind that forgets anything."

"Now that Rob and I are married, I'm sure she'll come around."

"For the sake of your marriage, I hope you're right."

*****

Rob was sitting in his office, thinking about the night before. *How can I lose control like that? That's what my mother used to do. I don't want to be like her. Her way did work with me. Then why do I hate her? I don't want my boys to hate me. It's my duty to discipline them when they disobey. My dad wasn't around to help me. Dad, I wish you were here. Why doesn't Jane understand? I didn't want to hit her. She shouldn't interfere. I need a drink. I'll go to the Slipper for lunch.*

He thought of what his mother said when he married Jane.

"Why did you have to marry that Higdon woman's daughter?"

"I have to be in New York tomorrow."

"So, what does that have to do with you getting married?"

"I told the Bureau I was getting married. I thought it would improve my chances of getting hired."

"How could you be so stupid?"

"The Bureau wants married men. I know I could probably do better, but she'll make a good wife. At least we should have good looking kids."

"You know what I think of her mother. The daughter can't be too much different."

There was no love lost between Martha Higdon and Rob. He knew she didn't approve of him. His mother's reaction gave him doubts about his decision. *Is Jane going to turn out to be a pain in the ass, like her mother? It's too late to worry about it now.*

*****

Jane couldn't remember seeing Rob any happier. The promotion had him smiling constantly. Rob's was a rising star. He was everything the Bureau looked for. He was a responsible family man, the perfect Bureau man.

Jane's only real concern about moving back to D.C. was living near Hilda. Visits home seemed to affect Rob negatively. What would a steady dose of Hilda do? After ten years her relationship with Hilda had not improved. Jane bent over backward trying to please her. Nothing worked. She didn't want to spoil Rob's moment, so she put on a happy face.

That was six years ago. Since that time, things had gotten worse. Rob was turning into Hilda. His drinking was getting out of control. The more he drank, the meaner he got. What saddened her the most was the change in her boys. They vanished each night when Rob got home.

The beatings started when Robert realized his yelling wasn't intimidating enough. The thick leather belt was impossible to tune out. Jane's efforts at protection were puny at best, such as last night.

Try as she would, Jane couldn't stay his arm as Rob lashed the boys with the belt driving them to the floor. Jane rushed to stop him but was slapped to the floor as well. All she could do was curl up with the boys, offering what protection she could. The belt was indiscriminant.

Jane wasn't watching the children now. Her eyes were shut tight. She shook her head trying to force the thoughts from her mind. They wouldn't go away. She was all set to tell Rob about her pregnancy last night. She was too busy getting beaten to the floor with her boys. Jane needed to summon her reserve of courage. Jane wondered if her unborn child felt her fear. *I have to tell him I'm pregnant.*

Being the devout Catholic, Robert didn't believe in the use of 'devices.' Jane knew he would blame her for getting pregnant…for her carelessness. Nothing was ever Robert Misner's fault.

There were times when Robert reminded her of the man she married. He became that man again around Mark or 'The Scorch,' as Rob called him. Singed eyebrows from the previous year's birthday candles prompted the nickname. The toddler drew out the best in Robert. During those times Jane realized she still loved him.

They had been in their new house about a month. Jane's warm smile and friendly manner allowed her to make friends easily. Louise Scolnik, the neighbor across the street, became Jane's best friend. She was amazed at how fast Louise learned to read her moods. Rob's outbursts were becoming the talk of the neighborhood. During this morning's chat over coffee, Jane accepted her friend's offer to watch Scorch and Nicole.

"Jane you look awful!"

"Gee, thanks a lot!"

"Honey, that's a real shiner! It didn't look that bad last night. What happened? He didn't hit you again?"

"Louise, if you don't mind, I really don't feel like talking about it."

"I'll tell you what! Why don't you spend some time by yourself this morning while I take your two home with me?"

"That's nice of you Louise, but I don't know."

"Sure you do! Looks to me like you need some time to sort things out. Lonnie's been wanting them to come over anyway."

"You're sure it's no trouble?"

"Nonsense!"

Two hours went by before Jane knew it. She left her cleaning to go back out. She couldn't believe it was 1952. The children were still at it. She thought, *where do they get their energy,* as she sat to watch them.

So far, Robert had not touched Mark or Nicole, five. She doubted Robert would lay a hand on his Scorch. Nicole was another matter. That morning she caught her little girl making faces in the mirror.

"Nicki, haven't I told you not to stand on the furniture?"

"I'm sorry mommy, I was looking in the mirror."

"I see. What are you looking at?"

"I'm trying to make myself pretty."

"Don't you think you're already pretty?"

"No."

"Why not, sweetie?"

"Daddy never looks at me. He thinks I'm ugly."

"Nicki, he doesn't think you're ugly. Your daddy loves you!"

"Why is he mean to me?"

"Honey, he's not mean to you. Why would you say that?"

"He never says nice things to me. He plays with Mark, but not me."

"That's because Mark is the baby now. When you were the baby, he played with you all the time."

"I don't remember."

"You were little then, but he did."

"He did?"

"Yes honey, he did. I'll tell you what! You and I will make your daddy some cookies this afternoon. Would you like that?"

"What kind of cookies?"

"Your daddy's favorite."

"Chocolate chip?"

"That's right."

"Oh goody, when can we start?"

"This afternoon, after you and your little brother get back from playing with Lonnie."

At least the boys knew where they stood with their father. Rob's indifference to his daughter was far worse than the sting of any belt. In fact, Jane thought the belt might be kinder.

One of the few times Robert acknowledged Nicki was when he made her Mark's protector. Jane remembered the day well; it was Mark's first day home. The little girl's chest filled with pride at hearing her father's words.

"Nicki, I'm putting you in charge of your little brother's safety. Can you do that for daddy?"

"I'm a big girl daddy! I can do that!"

Jane was still trying to work things out in her mind.

Somehow, I need to get through to him. I guess it's partly my fault, but he's never acknowledged raping me. We both know that's the night Nicki was conceived. Maybe if I forgive him, he'll treat Nicki better. I just can't find it in my heart to forgive him, especially after last night.

Jane's attentions went back to the children. The Scorch was pretending to be a vicious bear, chasing the other two. They ran round and round Louise's circular flowerbed. The Scorch was growling and slicing the air with his tiny claw-like hands. His barrel chest and hair that went where it wanted, gave him the appearance of a little bear.

"Me catch you Lonnie and Nicki. Me gonna eat you all up…grrrrrr!"

The sight of Mark's pursuit of the others started Jane's laughter. It mixed with that of the children, echoing through the air. This was the tonic she needed. Her stomach still cramped but not from nerves. In her mind, the Scorch represented life in its purest form, laughter and happiness. He filled her heart with a big dose of both. Jane knew she should get back to her housework, but couldn't make herself break away.

"Oh no, look out Lonnie, here comes the bear! Run, run before he eats you up!"

The children ran for their lives from the vicious bear. Louise was in a similar state as Jane. Old 'toothless,' as the children called her, was leaning on her rake absorbed by the chase. Jane counted herself lucky to have such a friend. As if on cue, Louise spread her mouth in a huge toothless smile.

The children changed gears and were now running through the freshly raked grass clippings. Anyone else might be angry, but Louise just smiled. She took up her rake and began repairing the destruction. Jane watched Nicole pick up a rake, working side by side with her 'mama Louise.'

Jane could feel her friend's disappointment at not being able to have more children. Louise always wanted a daughter. That explained her attachment to Nicole. Jane was pleased to see Nicole return the affection. Whoever said imitation is the highest form of flattery had to be right. Nicole copied everything Louise did.

Louise and Jane were the same age. Without her teeth, Louise looked much older. Conversely the avalanche of brown curls resting on Jane's bare shoulders, made her look ten years younger. Jane's yellow sundress also accentuated the curves that were still in the right places. The two women may have looked totally different from one another, but they were of like mind; they both put their children first.

The boys were flat on their backs, pointing at the sky. Louise and Nicole continued their raking, but Jane thought she could hear Louise muttering.

"Poor dear, poor dear, that man just doesn't know what he has."

Jane saw she wasn't the only one curious about what Louise was saying to herself. Nicole stopped her raking and looked up at Louise with a puzzled expression.

"What, momma Louise?"

"Nicki, I forgot all about you being there. Look at those piles! Who taught you to rake grass that way? Those are the most perfect piles I've ever seen. I swear they are!"

"Momma Louise, it's not nice to swear."

"Sweetheart, I wasn't swearing."

"But you said swear! Isn't that swearing?"

"Not at all darlin'. Swearin' is when someone cusses."

"What is cusses?"

"Cusses, I mean cussing is swearing, you know, bad words."

"What bad words?"

"Honey, why don't you ask your mommy when you get home?"

Louise's expression told the story. Jane empathized with her. She could tell her friend was under siege by a barrage of questions. *Louise, I know that look. I know your head must be pounding.* Nicole went back to making her neat, little piles of grass. Louise retreated to a more distant part of her yard.

Jane loved the smell of freshly cut grass. Years from now that fragrance would remind her of this moment of happiness.

The two boys had been rolling on the ground. Clippings clung to their play clothes. Nicole raised her voice in protest as they rolled through her handiwork. Soon she abandoned her task and started chasing them with armloads of grass. Jane knew she would play havoc getting the stains out of their clothes. *Maybe if I close my eyes, this day will last forever.*

Her thoughts went back to Robert.

Last night was bad. He started in on the boys as soon as he got home. Jane could see what was coming. She decided to make a stand no matter how afraid she was.

"Rob, please, not tonight. The boys will do a better job tomorrow, won't you boys?"

Bruce was always the spokesman when it came to facing the music.

"Yes sir, Freddy and I will get up extra early tomorrow. We'll do a better job, I promise."

"See Rob, they're sorry. I'll make sure they do a better job."

"I have a father's duty to discipline my sons! They have to learn to do as they are told the first time! Jane, get out of the way!"

"Rob, please, I have something important to tell you!"

"So is this!"

The impact of his hand spun Jane around before she hit the floor.

He had never hit her before. He began lashing the boys. Dazed, Jane crawled to the boys. They all hunkered together on the floor. The belt was indiscriminant. Jane got to her hands and knees, pleading with Robert to stop.

They had forgotten about the little ones. She noticed Mark and Nicole staring up at their father. The expression on their faces was pure horror. Rob must have seen them also as he hesitated.

"Robert! Please stop! Look at your son! Nicole, take your little brother upstairs! Robert?"

He was poised to strike again, but didn't. The brass buckle swayed above his head. Five pairs of eyes were transfixed to its hypnotizing dance. Like a metronome, it kept cadence with the moment. A look of anguish registered on Rob's face, as he looked down on his Scorch.

Nicole pulled at Mark's hand, but the little boy wasn't moving. His eyes drew a line from the dangling buckle to his father's contorted face. Father's and son's eyes locked onto each other. Rob's widened at the look of pure hate he saw. Before Jane could speak, Robert looked at her and dropped the belt. He hung his head, as he turned to leave. One look from the Scorch had defeated him.

Picking up his hat, he went to the door. Before leaving, he looked at his family again. Windows rattled and pictures fell from the wall, as Robert slammed the front door. A gentle knock followed, breaking Jane's trance. She opened the door and saw a friendly face.

"What on earth is with your man? He about ran over me getting to his car! Oh my goodness, your face! What happened?"

Jane broke down. Through the sobs, she told Louise what happened.

"You mean he hit you with his fist?"

"No, no, with the back of his hand. It didn't hurt, as much as it...hurt."

"Your dress is torn! Jane, you're bleeding! That's not all he hit you with, is it?"

"I guess that's from the belt. I was trying to protect the boys."

A look of pure disgust registered on Louise's face, as she responded.

"What kind of man does something like this?"

Jane felt the friendly warmth of Louise's hands on hers, as they sat on the couch.

"I wish I knew what's happened to him. He never used to be like this."

"You're not the only one that's gone through this."

"You mean Emil…"

"Yes honey, Emil. How do you think old toothless became toothless?"

"I had no idea."

"As you well know, it's not something you want the world to know about."

"Louise, I would never say a word to anyone."

"I know you won't. Listen, you call me next time and I'll come running."

"I can't ask you to do that. Besides, he'd just go into a bigger rage after you left. I have to get through to him somehow. I don't know what to do."

"You can always call the police."

"I can't do that. He could lose his job. Where would we be if he lost his job?"

"You can get a divorce."

"I'm a housewife. What am I trained for? How would I live?"

"Your no good husband would have to support you, that's how."

"You don't understand, I'd be afraid to be on my own. Besides, I still love Rob. He's just under a lot of pressure."

"I think you're dreamin' honey, but there's always hope."

"Yes, there is."

Neither woman spoke. Jane's head rested on her friend's shoulder. Louise put her arm around Jane's shoulder for comfort. Jane decided to unburden her mind. She sat up straight, looking into Louise's concerned eyes.

"Louise, I need to tell you something that I'm afraid to tell Rob."

"What is it, darlin'?"

Jane took a deep breath and whispered the words.

"I'm pregnant."

"I knew there was something bothering you!"

"You did?"

"You found out about a week ago, didn't you?"

"Yes, last Tuesday."

"You haven't been yourself...too quiet."

"Rob has said he doesn't want any more children. Given the way he's been...I'm afraid to tell him. What should I do?"

"Maybe if Rob knew, he'd ease up some. Either way, waiting will only make it worse. It's better to tell him and get it over with."

"I was all set to tell him last night and then this happened."

Jane put her fingers over the welt.

"You're not telling me everything. There's more."

"I've had awful cramps the last few days. I didn't feel this way with the others."

"Cramps?"

"They're very painful. Its like being kicked in the stomach."

"Have you been to see Doc Sterns?"

"He'll just lecture me on how hard I work and tell me to take it easy."

"That's crapola and you know it. Come on and I'll drive you right now. I'm sure he'll squeeze you in. I'll call Judy. She'll watch our brood while we're gone."

"I don't have an appointment."

"Are you kidding me? YOU don't need one. That old man has got the biggest crush on you. He'd drop everything if YOU stopped in!"

"I feel okay now, besides, I have to start thinking about what to fix Rob for dinner. Maybe I'll call him for an appointment tomorrow."

"You do that, you hear!"

"Okay, you can take me tomorrow."

That was yesterday. For now she'd enjoy her children. She still had a few hours before her appointment with Doctor Sterns. Jane did feel somewhat better for having shared her secret with Louise. She was determined to break the news to Rob tonight. *I have to tell him. How will he react? He'll explode, that's how. Wouldn't it be wonderful if he were actually happy about it? He won't be. I have to tell him anyway.*

The cramps had returned. It was another hour until her appointment. *Maybe I should have Louise take me now.* Jane rocked back and forth in quiet desperation.

*****

Nicole remembered the laundry on the clothesline. She promised her mother she would bring it in. Brushing the loose grass from her peddle-pushers, she started for the street. A familiar voice echoed from behind her.

"Nicki, me go with you!"

"No Mark, I have to bring the laundry in."

"Me wanna help. Take me."

"You play with Lonnie. I'll be back in a few minutes."

Nicki thought of the promise to her father. She didn't want to leave her brother but saw her mother watching him. She looked both ways and crossed the street. Safely in her own yard, she went to the back.

"Nicki, where are you going?"

"I have to finish taking down the clothes."

"Sweetie, you can do that later. Go back over to Lonnie's and finish playing."

"I don't want daddy to be mad at me."

Jane picked up the sound of anguish in her daughter's voice. That helped answer one of her questions.

"Okay, if that's what you want to do. Come here and give your mommy a kiss."

Nicki ran to her mother and kissed her on the cheek.

"I love you mommy."

"I love you too sweetie, now hurry up so you can go back to playing with your little brother."

Nicole disappeared around the corner of the house.

I'm only going to be gone for a little while. Mark will be okay. Nicole loved helping her mommy with chores. She couldn't reach the clothesline without the use of her stool. As she moved down the line, the basket and stool moved with her.

Most of the time Mark would try to help her. Nicki thought of how her brother would stand under the line with his arms spread apart. He tried catching the clothes as they fell to the basket below. Nicole wanted to finish and go back across the street. She didn't feel right leaving him over there.

As Nicole worked, she thought about the night before. Seeing her big brothers get spanked was nothing new. She'd never seen her mommy get hit before. She was afraid her daddy was going to hurt her. All she could think about was the sound the belt made when it hit Bruce and Freddy…smack, smack, smack.

The sound reverberated in her head. She wondered why Bruce never cried. Nicole knew it had to hurt. She decided Freddy wasn't as brave as Bruce, because he always cried. She concluded; the best way to keep from getting spanked, was to finish her chores and stay away from her daddy.

*****

Bruce had accepted the previous night's beating with stoic dignity. His father was very much on his mind this day.

"Man Freddy, I'm tired of getting my ass kicked by the old man because of you!"

"What do you mean, man?"

"You know damn well what I mean. You didn't do what he told you to do, so I got whipped for it."

"What are you talking about man, I got whipped too. Besides, you were supposed to help me."

"Yeah, but I always get it first. By the time he gets to you, he's worn out. Plus, you cry like a little baby."

"How come you don't cry? That belt hurts like Hell."

"I used to cry. I think he likes to make us cry. You ever notice how he gets that sick smile on his face when you start crying?"

"How can I see his face while he's whipping my ass? Jeezy peezy Bruce, are you dumb or something?"

"I think he enjoys seeing us cry. He's not going to see me cry anymore!"

"If you can take it, so can I."

"Come on Freddy, you're not filling your bucket enough. I'm carrying twice as much water as you!"

"This bucket is heavy as Hell, man. It's hurting my fingers."

"Aw, poor little baby. You want me to get you a rattle, so you can suck your thumb?"

"Why don't you shut your mouth?"

"Why don't you try and make me, you little dweeb."

"How much more water do we have to carry?"

"That's a dumb ass question, even for you. We gotta water the whole goddamn garden and we're not even halfway done."

"Why can't we have a hose like anyone else, instead of having to lug this water from home plate to second each trip?"

"Cause he's a cheap, mean bastard and wants us to suffer, okay!"

"You're right, he's a cheap, mean bastard."

"I don't know about you, but I'm not missing my ball game this afternoon because of this stupid garden."

"Hey Freddy, I have a game just like you, so you're not going anywhere until this is done, or I'll kick your ass worse than the old man ever did, you hear me?"

"Yeah, yeah, yeah, I hear you, queer bait."

Watering the garden was at least a two-hour job. Afterwards the boy's arms were too tired to hold above their heads.

"Hey Bruce, our sister has decided to do something for a change."

"Yeah, I see, I wonder where the little brat is?"

"I'm sure he's having a great old time, playing with the kid across the street."

"One of these days he's gonna have to bust his little ass, just like us."

"Yeah, he better enjoy his fun now, while he can."

"You're not kiddin', little brother."

*****

The Scorch had just picked himself off the ground for the millionth time. He and Lonnie had been lying on their backs, looking at the puffy clouds.

"Lonnie, look, that one looks like Smokey! Me gonna see him tomorrow, at the zoo!"

Scorch loved Smokey the Bear. Jane read him the story at least once a day. He always cried when she got to the part about Smokey's mama dying in the forest fire. The smile always returned with the cub's rescue. Scorch especially liked the part where Smokey came to live at the National Zoo. Jane was planning a trip to the zoo for the next day. The Scorch couldn't wait to see his favorite animal in real life. He went around the house singing the song over and over.

"Smokey the bear, Smokey the bear, growlin' and a prowlin' and a sniffin' the air. He can smell a fire, before it starts to flame, that's why they call him Smokey, that is how he got his name."

It was hard for anyone not used to his speech to make out the actual words. He had the tune down to a tee.

Everything was spinning, as Scorch tried to get up. Staring at clouds always made him dizzy. As he tried to get up again, he saw a yellow flower and plucked it up.

"Lonnie, look at my pretty lellow flower. Me going to give it to my mommy."

The Scorch could see his mother sitting on the porch across the street. Jane waved at him, as he held the blossom up. She couldn't make out what he was holding. His excitement was unmistakable.

"Mommy, mommy, see my pretty flower!"

Scorch's feet found the graveled surface of Horseshoe Drive.

*****

From the corner of her eye, Jane was aware of the big green car making its turn. She knew it was the Layton boy, from around the curve. Jane had seen him many times before. *What a hunk that Jimmy Layton is! I bet he has a dozen girls after him. If I were sixteen I'd be after him too.*

Jane's reverie was interrupted by the laughter of her little boy. The Scorch had stumbled his way toward her. Jane could see Louise still raking. Her friend was unaware the Scorch was about to cross the street. One minute Jane was at the height of happiness. A split second later, her whole world changed.

*****

The girls stood in line for Jimmy Layton. He was the coolest cat at Maplesville High's class of '53. He called his wheels "The Green Hornet." It took Jimmy two years of saving to buy the car. The Hornet needed lots of work. Jimmy was his father's son, good with his hands.

Jimmy bought the 1937 Ford Coupe from a nearby junkyard. His uncle Harry owned an auto body shop at Tyson's Corner. That's where Jimmy brought it back to life. The final touch was the bright yellow fuzzy dice, hanging from the rearview mirror. Mr. Layton heard the excited calls of his son.

"Dad, dad! Come check out the Hornet! I got her started and doesn't she sound cool?"

"She's beautiful, Jimmy! It reminds me of my first car. Let's go for a spin."

"You got it pop! Where to?"

"Anywhere you want son, you're driving."

Jimmy looked over to his father while driving and sat as straight as possible. At seventeen, he was almost as tall as his father. Mr. Layton was powerfully built through the shoulders and chest. He carried himself with the confidence of someone who could handle any physical threat. Jimmy idolized his dad.

One day, men will look up to me the way they do my dad.

The next hour was spent in silence, between the two, as they cruised the streets of Maplesville. Words were not needed to express feelings. Before they knew it, the ride was another memory, as they sat with the rest of the family, eating dinner.

Jimmy loved his wheels. The Hornet was a mean, mean driving machine. He and his buddies would cruise the drive-in, at Lee Highway, for chicks on the weekends. These nocturnal excursions always seemed to produce positive results. Chicks loved to be seen in the Hornet. The girls compared notes about their experiences with Jimmy. The 'make out' sessions with Jimmy at Black Pond took on mythical proportions.

Jimmy had dreams of one day being an architect. He loved building things. He knew his father could never afford college. Jimmy labored at several part-time jobs, saving his money. The oldest of seven children, Jimmy was mature for his years. He knew what he wanted and was willing to work hard to attain it.

The thermometer was up to 95. The humidity made the heat even more oppressive. Jimmy had been working at the Haskins dairy farm. Of all his side jobs, he considered baling hay the ultimate drudgery. The only positive was the money, five bucks for the day, plus lunch. He was now on his way home.

His upper torso was sweaty and covered with hay chaff. All of the windows in the Hornet were open, including the vents. Jimmy was doing a no-no, steering the car one-handed. His left arm rested on the door. He thought the breeze on his bare skin would cool him off. Nothing seemed to give him relief from the heat.

The white T-shirt he had worn that day had long since been removed, soaked with the efforts of his labor. The upholstery of his seat acted like a blotter. Jimmy knew there would be sweat stains on his seat, but he didn't care.

All I want to do is get home and find a way to cool off. I could strip down to my underwear and sit in the deep part of the creek. That would feel great. There's one problem with that; my little brothers and sisters will splash around me. No, I just want to relax by myself for a while. I wonder if mom has fresh lemons for lemonade. That's it, that's what I'll do! I'll get a nice tall glass of mom's lemonade and sit under the walnut tree in back. It's always cool under that tree.

"Come on Hornet, let's get home!"

Happy with his solution, Jimmy smiled as he steered the Hornet toward home.

*****

Rising, Jane yelled at Scorch to stay where he was. She started running toward him, screaming for him to stop.

"Mark! Mark! Stay there, don't move!"

He was giggling, while holding something up. He didn't pay any attention to his mother's pleas and continued on.

"Honey, mommy will come and get you. STAY THERE! STAY THERE! NO! NO! STOP, STOP, OH GOD PLEASE STOP, MY BABY!!!"

*****

Jimmy caught movement from the corner of his eye.

"What the…"

The Hornet had just made its way onto the home stretch. There was a sudden movement in front of the car. As he passed the first house on the left, Jimmy saw a woman running toward him. She was screaming something. He barely had time to think.

"What was that?"

All of his previous thoughts vanished with the sound of a thump. His physical misery was gone in a flicker. He had run over something…or someone.

"Oh my God! What was that? I hit something!"

Rubber squealed, as the Hornet's tires fought the gravel. His foot was frozen to the brake pedal. Jimmy's eyes were big with fear. His arms locked at the elbows as he gripped the wheel.

*****

Jane ran as fast as she could. Mark was in the middle of the road. The car kept coming. She realized Jimmy didn't see her little boy. Jane's heart was in her throat. Screams erupted from her mouth. The unimaginable was about to happen...*WHUMP!*

Jane had just gotten to the edge of the road when the car ran over Scorch. She felt the breeze of its passing and gave chase. Something was rolling behind in a kind of disjointed manner. It was her baby!

Still running behind the car Jane tried, but could not catch up to the bundle. It trailed the car, as if being pulled. She would almost get to it, reach down and grab air. Finally the bundle came to a stop with the sound of screeching tires. Jane could finally reach the bundle. She tenderly gathered it in her arms.

His tiny claw hands and the hair that went where it wanted, was covered in a crimson horror. She held the bundle of bloody rags that was her little boy. Her yellow sundress was smeared with gore, as she clutched Mark to her breast.

His right fist dangled lifelessly, but was still holding something. Jane noticed the brightness of the freshly picked dandelion, unmolested by the carnage. The mother stood there, alternating her stare from the weed, to the formless frame of her little boy.

*****

Bruce raised his head when he heard the screeching of tires.

"Freddy, what was that? Come on!"

The brothers heard the scream. They dropped their buckets and ran from the back yard to the street as fast as they could. As he ran past Nicole, Bruce yelled for her to follow. She jumped from her stool and ran after the boys. The three children saw their mother standing in the middle of the street holding something...it was their little brother.

Nicole's stare was fixed on the bloody bundle in her mother's arms. Her lower lip began quivering. A flood of tears sprung from her blue eyes. She looked to her mother for reassurance, but got none. She wanted to speak, but couldn't. Only small gasps escaped her mouth. Finally, she found her voice.

"Mommy, is my little brother hurt bad?"

As if an alarm went off inside her brain, she remembered the promise to her father. *I'll take good care of my little brother, daddy, I'm a big girl!*

Something else crept into her mind...the belt. Nicole remembered the sound it made...*smack, smack,* and *smack!* The sounds reverberated in her mind and suddenly she could think of nothing else. *What will daddy do to me?*

Nicole bit her quivering lip. Her mother was in another place, unable to help. Her little brother wasn't moving. His arms and legs were scraped and bleeding from countless cuts and abrasions. The thought he may be dead, overcame her. The words tumbled from her mouth.

"Mommy, mommy, is my little brother alive?"

There was no answer to her desperate question. Nicole hugged one of her mother's legs. A sudden breeze caused the sundress to billow around the little girl, spreading some of its slickness on her. There was no response to her repeated question. Her crying turned to wailing when her face became smeared with blood. She repeated over and over again.

"Is he alive? Is he alive?"

His sister's crying got Bruce's attention. He knelt beside her.

"Nicki, come here. Let mom be for now. Mark will be okay. I can see him breathing. He's a tough little guy. The ambulance will be here soon and the doctors will fix him up, you'll see, he'll be okay. Show mom how brave her little girl is, okay?"

Bruce lied to her. Mark's body looked just like the cat he had seen hit by a car last summer, mangled beyond recognition. He thought about his catechism and heaven, wondering if there really was such a place.

Her breath was still labored, but Nicole found reassurance from her big brother. She loved him for that. She put her arms around his neck. For the first time, in a very long time, Bruce could feel the wetness of his own tears. He didn't try to hide them, as he held onto his little sister.

Freddy stood there...alone. He always seemed to be the one left out, forgotten. He needed reassurance too, but had no one to hold onto. He stepped over to his siblings and put both arms around them. He saw his big brother's tears. His own welled in his eyes. Freddy looked over to Jimmy and realized where he was needed.

*****

Jimmy finally emerged from the Hornet. He wanted to say something, but didn't know what. He looked down and saw a boy of about ten, staring at him. He recognized the boy as Freddy Misner. Freddy tried to hold Jimmy's stare. The dark orbs bored through Freddy. He knew he'd never forget that look.

Freddy wanted more than anything to comfort Jimmy. Every kid on the block wanted to be Jimmy Layton. They all looked up to him. Freddy was sure Jimmy didn't even know he was alive...until now.

"Jimmy, it's not your fault."

The teenager looked down at the boy.

"It is my fault. I was the one driving. If I'd been paying attention, this wouldn't have happened!"

No one knew who called for the ambulance, but the sirens were getting closer. Soon, the flashing lights of the Maplesville rescue squad could be seen turning the corner. The attendant was trying to get through to Jane. Her despondency was a wall between them. She pulled away as he tried taking the Scorch from her.

"Ma'am, we've got to get him to the hospital. Let me take him. You can ride in the back. We need to go!

Jane was starting to come around.

"Is my little boy breathing?"

Jane's mind wouldn't let her think of the word she dreaded most…dead.

"Ma'am, I don't know, we need to go. Please give him to me."

Jane thought the young man looked like a child himself. His words soothed her. The green cursive letters over the left breast pocket spelled his name. Jane offered Mark's limp body to Albert. Albert took Mark. Jane climbed in the back and the ambulance sped away.

Louise was herding the rest of the children toward her car. No one noticed the county cruiser that had arrived behind the ambulance. A nod of the officer's head told the woman it was okay to take the children. The officer approached Jimmy.

"Son, are you okay?"

Jimmy heard the officer, but his attention was riveted on the yellow flower that fell from the little boy's hand.

"Son, can you hear me? Are you hurt?"

Having picked up the flower, Jimmy turned it over in his fingers.

Jimmy saw his father pull up. Jimmy's eyes fell to the officer's hand on his shoulder and then to his approaching father.

"What's going on here officer? Turn loose of my son!"

Jimmy knew how strong his father was. The officer found out first hand as he felt the grip on his arm.

"Sir, I'm just trying to get to your son. Can you talk to him?"

"Jimmy, are you hurt?"

The sound of his father's voice broke Jimmy's stupor. He felt his dad's reassuring embrace. Jimmy told his father the story between heaving sobs.

"Dad, I hit a little boy."

Holding on to Jimmy, Mr. Layton looked over to the officer for some clarification.

"Officer?"

"Sir, we haven't been able to get anything from your son yet. The ambulance left five minutes ago with the boy and his mother. We don't know how the little boy is. I've been waiting for your son to steady himself, so I can ask him some questions."

Jimmy looked up at his dad.

"Jimmy, it's going to be okay. Take a deep breath, easy now, breathe, breathe."

Jimmy took some deep breaths and slowly calmed himself. By this time, two other squad cars arrived. The police measured skid marks and took pictures from every angle. One of the officers was interviewing a few of the bystanders. Jimmy was calm enough to answer questions, while clutching the tiny flower.

"Mr. Layton, I've got everything I need right now. Why don't you take Jimmy home? Once he's settled down, bring him to the station for a statement. This was just an unfortunate accident."

"Thanks officer, I'll take him home. Come on Jimmy get in my car. I'll drive you home. We can come back for the Hornet later."

"Dad, could you take my keys? I don't think I ever want to drive that car again."

"Sure son, but you'll feel differently in a few days. This wasn't your fault. Come on son, let's go home and see your mother."

"Dad, you don't understand! I wasn't paying attention to the road, like you taught me. I had my mind on something besides my driving."

Jim stuttered, as tears formed again.

"Dad, I need to know what happens to the little boy. Take me to the hospital, please?"

"Don't you want to go home and clean up?"

Jim's determination was evident.

"Okay Jimmy. Let's tell your mother where we're going, then we'll go to the hospital."

*****

Rob had the events of the prior night on his mind. So far, he hadn't gotten any work done. He needed a diversion, something to get last night off his mind. *I got it! I'll go see Brandi. She's never failed to make me feel better.*

The Silver Slipper wasn't a place where the patrons actually acknowledged each other. The place was dark, but Rob could see her seated at the bar, a cigarette in one hand, a Tom Collins in the other. She saw him and made for one of the back rooms. Their pleasantries would be exchanged behind the small curtained room.

"I didn't expect to see you until tomorrow."

"I've had a rough day at the office."

"Let me see if I can get you relaxed."

Brandi sat on his lap and worked at him through the thin material of her silk panties. Nothing happened. She bent down to kiss him. He didn't respond with his usual fervor. His groping was even insincere.

"Baby, what's wrong?"

"I've got problems at home."

"Tell me about them. Maybe doctor Brandi can help."

She took Rob by the penis and worked it until it was semi-hard. Brandi mounted him again, gyrating her hips and pressing her breasts into his chest…no response.

"Baby, you're not turning queer on me, are you?"

"What kind of goddamned comment is that?"

Robert abruptly stood, almost spilling the stripper to the floor.

"Watch it mister! You may get away with treating your little wife that way but I'll cut your balls off!"

Robert glared over her. He reached into his wallet and pulled out a five. He crumpled it up and threw it at her as he left. He went for a walk around the Monument grounds before going back to the office. When he got to his desk, his intercom was buzzing.

"Mr. Misner, your wife is on the phone."

I may as well get it over with. Damn it, I didn't want to hit her. She shouldn't have gotten in the way.

"Did she say what she wanted?"

"No, but she sounds very upset."

Robert didn't know what to say. He sat at his desk not answering his secretary. *Of course she's upset, you stupid bitch. I hit her.*

"Mr. Misner, are you there? Your wife is frantic, something about your son being in the hospital. Mr. Misner, she's on line two."

His son was hurt! Which one?

"Jane, who's hurt?"

"Thank God you're there. You have to come, now!"

"Calm down, Jane. Tell me who is hurt!"

"Mark was hit by a car and...Robert, Robert, are you there? Rob!"

As Robert ran from the office, he yelled at his secretary.

"My boy has been hit by a car! I don't know when I'll be back!"

Lunchtime traffic was light. Washington was not the congested metropolis New York was; even so, the roads were pitifully insufficient to carry local traffic. His mind filled with visions of his Scorch. He couldn't forget the hate in his son's eyes the night before.

Rob was laying on the horn, willing the cars to part in front of him. All of the roads in and out of town were two lanes. The gawking tourists made driving miserable. They were easy to pick out. He had an urge to start shooting them with his .38. Steering and honking, honking and yelling, Robert was out of control.

"Move, goddamn it, move! Get the hell out of the way!"

He felt uneasy about Jane. He didn't mean to hit her. She got in the way. Things between them were getting worse. They argued all of the time. Most of the arguments were over money. A growing number, however, were over her increasing interference.

Robert relied on Brandi more all the time, to relieve his tension. Today was the first time she failed him. He'd met her several years ago. Rob remembered the exact night. It was the night Clifton died. Brandi was the first. Well, the first since coming back to DC. There were others in New York.

Women helped him deal with the many frustrations in his life. He was always more tolerant at home on days he went to the Slipper. *Relieving my sexual anxiety makes me a better husband and father.* The confessional was a convenient means of getting rid of any guilt.

He had just crossed the Key Bridge, into Arlington. He made the right on Wilson Blvd. *It won't be long now. I should be there in ten minutes. Damn it woman, get the hell out of my way!* Robert kept his hand on the horn as cars parted before him. *She didn't tell me who hit him. Who hit my boy? Whoever did it is going to pay!*

Robert's head was out the window. He was screaming like a man possessed.

"Bitch, get out of my way! Drive your goddamn car! Move, move!"

Twenty minutes after leaving the office, he stopped his car in front of the emergency entrance. Running into the hospital, he yelled at an elderly volunteer manning the desk.

"Where's my son? Where's my Scorch?"

Robert got a puzzled stare back in return.

"I'm Mr. Misner. My son was brought in here a little while ago. You know, Mark Misner, the little boy hit by the car. Where is he?"

"Oh, of course. They bought him in about an hour ago. He's in exam room number three."

Robert heard the last words as he ran for the exam rooms. He saw Jane standing in the middle of the room. Louise and the kids were with her.

"How is he? Is he alive?"

All Jane could do is nod up and down. She appeared to be in shock. Jane moved closer to Robert putting her arms around him. She buried her face in the wetness of his shirt.

"Rob, I'm so glad you're here! It was awful! He's a mess! One minute he was rolling on the ground with Lonnie, the next he was hit by the car and rolling after it! I picked him up and thought he was dead! He wasn't moving…and the blood! I can't get the way he looked out of my head! There was so much blood! Oh Rob, he can't be dead! My little boy can't be dead!"

"Calm down and tell me what happened, exactly. I have to know who hit my son...whose fault it is."

Jane took her arms away and clutched her abdomen. Her next words came out with great effort.

"Don't...you want to...know about your...son first?"

Jane exhaled deeply, fighting the intense pain. She bit into her lower lip. Suddenly she remembered the missed appointment with Doctor Sterns. She felt something warm and sticky on her legs. Fresh blood was creating a pool around her feet. Jane sank into its warmth and passed out.

Robert's eyes went wide as he saw blood pooling around his wife.

"Somebody, come quickly!"

Robert huddled over Jane. Louise had been trying to keep the kids busy. Everyone gathered around her. Louise ran for a doctor. An instant later, she returned. The nurse knew in an instant, the hospital had another emergency. Jane regained consciousness as they hefted her to a gurney. Robert heard her babbling something about a baby as they rolled her away. Robert thought she meant the Scorch.

He looked at Louise with a question on his face. Louise understood his confusion.

"Jane is pregnant. She didn't want to tell you because she was afraid to. Robert Misner, you are a miserable sort. You don't deserve that woman, or these kids for that matter!"

Louise was in his face. Robert was not used to being confronted in this manner. He gathered himself and responded.

"Afraid of me? I'm her husband. Why would she be afraid of me?"

"Robert, you're a fool! You beat your wife and kids. Do you think they love you for that?

"I'm the head of the house. I work hard to support them. All I ask is that they do what I tell them. It's my duty, as their father, to discipline them when they disobey me."

"They're not your slaves, Robert! Jane is no child! Look what you did to her!"

"That was an accident. She got in the way."

"She was trying to protect her children from a wild man."

"I warned her not to interfere!"

"No man has a right to do what you've done to your family! You should be ashamed!"

Louise stood her ground in front of Robert, her bony finger thrust into his chest with each point. Robert wanted to grab the offending digit and snap it off. He decided to change gears and play the role of the concerned husband and father. Besides, he needed her help with the kids. *The only way I'm going to get this bitch off my back is let her think she's won this battle.*

He sagged into a chair, staring at his feet. When he raised his head, the defiant look was gone. Replacing it was a mask of confusion.

"What do I do?"

He could see the effect on Louise, as her face softened. Rob felt her hand patting his shoulder, as she replied.

"Your children need you. I'm going to look for someone to tell us what's going on. Here comes your son."

I'd have to agree with her there. They do need me. Without me, they'd grow to be soft and weak. I know my way is best. They'll be strong men, able to stand on their own, because of me. They'll thank me later.

Bruce stepped up to his father. He'd been a pillar of strength for his brother and sister. Seeing his mother collapse in a puddle of blood scared him. The thirteen-year olds resolve needed bolstering. Appraising his son, Robert could see himself. He remembered, many years ago when his father collapsed in the living room while moving furniture. He remembered how empty he felt. *I wonder if Bruce feels that. He is strong. I've done that.* Bruce was the first to speak.

"Dad, what happened to mom?"

"Son, I don't know what's wrong with her. Mrs. Scolnik is trying to find out."

"I heard Mrs. Scolnik say mom was pregnant."

"Yeah, I guess she was."

"Why was she bleeding like that?"

Robert was tired of being on the defensive, first with Louise and now with a thirteen-year old boy.

"Bruce, I don't know!"

The loudness of his voice got the attention of others in the waiting room. He gave them a furtive look and lowered his voice, as he continued with Bruce.

"I'm sure the doctors will know something soon. In the meantime, we have to wait."

Robert was mainly concerned about his Scorch. Everyone else seemed more interested in his wife. He wasn't worried about her. She shouldn't have let herself get pregnant in the first place.

"Did you see the accident?"

"No sir. Freddy and me were weeding and watering like you told us. We ran to the street when we heard mom screaming."

"How did the Scorch look?"

"There was a lot of blood. He didn't look like he was breathing."

"Who hit him?"

"Jimmy Layton was driving that big green car of his."

"Was he speeding?"

Robert's voice was starting to rise with his frustration. All Bruce could do was shake his head in answer.

"I don't know, dad. We were in the back."

Robert saw Louise walking toward them and gave his instructions to Bruce.

"Bruce, get your brother and sister ready to go home. I'm going to ask Mrs. Scolnik to let you stay with her for a couple of days."

Bruce was glad for a reason to get away from his father. Louise approached Robert.

"They won't tell me anything. I'm not a family member."

"I'm sure they'll come out when they have some news. Louise, would you do me a favor and take the kids home with you?"

"Of course they can stay with me. You'll call me when you hear something?"

"I'll call when I hear something."

"Be sure you do."

"I'll call as soon as I can."

Louise got the children together and started for the exit. Bruce kept looking back until they disappeared from Robert's view. Rob sat down and waited. He hadn't realized how big Bruce had gotten. *Why is he so obstinate? He refuses to be broken. I know the whippings hurt him. Why doesn't he cry? If he just cried once, I wouldn't beat him so hard. He makes me so angry.*

Robert saw the similarities between Bruce and himself. He wondered if his son hated him, like he hated his mother. He watched his father collapse and die on the living room floor. *Was Jane going to die, or the Scorch? At least Bruce had his brother and sister for support.*

Rob had no one but himself. His wife and children stuck together. He only had his mother...and a stripper. Neither was the nurturing kind. *Maybe I am too hard on them. After all, I don't know any other way. No! My way is the right way. I turned out fine and so will they.*

He wondered what life would have been like, had his father lived. Jane reminded him of his father. Over the years, Robert learned to deplore the weakness he saw in his father. Jane had the same weakness. He wasn't about to let that infect his children. He was determined to control his family. This conclusion had a calming affect on him, as he leaned back into the softness of the couch.

After a while, one of the doctors came out.

"Mr. Misner, I'm Doctor Taylor. I've been with your little boy."

"How's my son?"

"I wish I had better news. It doesn't look good. His injuries are...extensive. We'll know more when we see the x-rays. I'll send someone out as soon as we have more information. There's a chapel across the hall, if you'd like to wait there."

The doctor turned to leave, but Robert caught his sleeve.

"Doctor! What about my wife?"

"Your wife? I don't know anything about Mrs. Misner. I've been tending to your son."

Robert was used to being in control. The waiting had taken a toll on his patience. He snapped back at the doctor.

"What kind of hospital is this? She collapsed in a bloody heap right over there!"

"Mr. Misner, calm down. I know you've got a lot on your mind. No one told me about your wife. I'll check. Have a seat."

Doctor Taylor came back a few moments later.

"Mr. Misner, your wife is in serious condition. She lost the little girl, along with a lot of blood. We have the bleeding under control. We've also given her a sedative, so she can rest."

This is exactly what was wrong with his marriage. Jane kept things from him, like this pregnancy. *She had no right to keep that from me! How did she think she was going to hide that? Maybe she was afraid to tell me because it wasn't mine?* Robert knew the doctor was waiting for some kind of response. He also knew he should look concerned.

"When can I see her?"

"Later, after she has a chance to rest. Undoubtedly, the stress from seeing your little boy hit by that car triggered it."

"It?"

"The miscarriage."

"Oh yes, undoubtedly."

"We'll let you know when you can see her. Why don't you wait in the chapel?"

"Okay, come get me when she wakes."

Robert paused in the chapel's doorway. *This isn't a Catholic chapel. There are no confessionals. I need to talk with Father Podgurski.* He sat in the front pew looking up at the cross, aware his devotional posture was a veneer.

Where did it go wrong? Why does she keep things from me? Who has she been screwing?

He knelt there for what seemed like days. His mind drifted back to another time in search of the answers to his questions.

Unbeknownst to Robert, Jane was in a similar mental state. She was caught between two realities, past and present. Each of them went on their own journey, seeking an answer to the same question; where did it all go wrong?

PART TWO

In 1946 Maplesville, Virginia's population was 1,143. The Maples family settled the area in the early 1700's. Back then the settlement was home to the first County seat. During an Indian attack, the courthouse was burned to the ground. The new county seat was moved to Fairfax. Time stood still for Maplesville thereafter.

The main drag was arched by hundred-year old sugar maples. Over time a few of the trees succumbed to disease. These few were a pittance compared to the toll progress would claim. A five and dime, Wright & Hunts anchored the north end of town. On the south end was Willy's Market. In the middle was a smattering of Victorian styled homes with their pristine yards.

In the spring, red, white and yellow climbers adorned the picket fences along Maple Avenue. Breezes from the spreading canopy carried their sweet scent. Entire families strolled beneath the coolness of the trees. Autumns attracted Sunday drivers from all around the Washington area. Maplesville was the new home to Robert Misner and his family.

Their brown brick bungalow sat on thirteen acres of rolling Virginia countryside south of town. Large craggy hardwoods lined 300 yards of gravel driveway terminating at the house. This setting was the antithesis of Flushing, where neighbors could hear every whisper. Here there were no neighbors in sight. The only thing Jane disliked more than the isolation was the fact Hilda owned the house.

Hilda's weekly intrusions were beginning to take their toll on Jane. Jane and Rob rarely argued, but were in the midst of one now.

"Rob, do we have to live in her house? Why can't we find an apartment instead?"

"Jane, we've been over this. Why can't you look at the good side?"

"It's still your mother's house. She's driving me crazy. Can't we find some place else?"

"I don't need this, Jane. I'm under enough pressure from the promotion."

"I'm all alone here."

"You have the boys. Besides, it's a lot more peaceful than the city. You can have your gardens and I can have my bird dogs."

"You think more of your dogs than me."

"Jane, why are you being so contrary? I thought we agreed to live here for a few years."

"That was before I realized how alone I am."

"Luke Selmer says the place to meet other housewives is at Willy's. I bet you haven't even tried that yet?"

"I haven't, you're right."

"I'll walk there with you on Saturday. We'll introduce ourselves to the neighborhood. It'll be great, you'll see!"

"The boys do seem to like it here."

"Are you kidding? They love it! The nearest tree in Flushing was four blocks away. They have thirteen acres of open fields, woods and even a stream to swim in."

"I suppose you're right. I've never seen them this happy."

"I know you miss your friends. Give it time; you'll make new ones. Besides, did you ever think you'd have this many gardens?"

"They're your mother's gardens."

"She said you could do whatever you want with them. All she ever grew was weeds."

"It's still not the same."

"Why are you so worried about my mother? Why can't you give her a chance?"

"Robert, I've tried for ten years. She hates me."

"I'll admit she can be a pain, but Hell, she lives all the way in DC."

"We've been in the house for two weeks and she's already been here four times."

"Let's not go there. Martha has been here for almost a whole week."

"She's helping me get things organized."

"My mother offered to help with that. Maybe you two would have bonded by working together."

"You know our mothers can't be in the same room."

"Martha could have stayed home. I still say you'd be closer to my mother now, had you let her help you with the house."

"I could say the same about my mother. You've never gone out of your way to improve your relationship with her."

Robert knew he couldn't win this one.

"She hasn't liked me from the moment we met."

"I can't argue that. How would you like to be renting from my mother?"

"Martha doesn't own a house, so what's the point?"

"The point is; if this was reversed, you wouldn't like it either."

"You've got me there. Right now, this is the best I can do. Be patient. In a couple of years, we'll buy our own house."

"I just wanted you to know how I feel."

"I know how you feel. Please try to get along with mother."

"It seems like I'm the one that's been doing all the trying."

*****

Hilda's house was furnished. What furniture they owned in New York was either sold or given to friends.

"Rob, not being able to afford our own home is one thing. But why do we have to live with her ugly furniture?"

"I've already told you. I'm trying to save our extra money so we can buy our own house. I wish you'd stop your complaining."

"I can't stand her meddling. Have you heard her latest? She expects me to put brown paper on the floor, so we don't soil her rugs. She even bought the paper."

"You know she uses paper on her floors. She's not asking us to do anything she doesn't do."

"Rob, she wouldn't leave until I put the paper down."

"Mother likes things neat. The house and everything in it does belong to her."

"That's exactly why I didn't want to live here."

"Jane, we've been over this a dozen times. I don't want to hear it anymore."

"The paper is dangerous! Bruce slipped this morning and hit his head. He could have been seriously hurt."

"Was he running through the house?"

"Well, yes, he was. But how are you going to keep a seven-year old from running around?"

"My job is to support this family. Your's is to keep them in tow. I don't think I'm asking for much. Keep the goddamn paper down like she wants!"

"At least talk to her about it. Will you do that much?"

"It won't do any good. Put up with it for a couple of months. When my raise takes effect, we'll buy rugs."

"Do you mean it?"

"If it gets you off my back, then it's a small price to pay."

"Let's go shopping tonight!"

"Jane, I said a couple of months."

"You'll change your mind in a couple of months."

"No I won't. Besides, we're a little short in the checking account right now."

"How can that be? You make more money now than you ever did."

"Our expenses are higher. There's no subway here, remember? I had to buy a car. Then there's gas, parking."

"You told me expenses would be the same as in New York. That's the reason for living here. You said we could get a car with the money we'd save on rent. What other expenses do we have?"

"I have to dress better. You're forgetting the Director is just down the hall from my office. I had to buy a couple of new suits."

"There's nothing wrong with your old suits."

"Who is making the money around here…you?"

"You know I'm not. For one thing, you won't let me work."

"That's right! Supporting a family is the man's job. The man also makes the financial decisions, so quit asking me how I spend my money!"

"The boys need clothes. They barely have one pair of pants between them. I haven't bought a new dress in over four years. Don't you think we deserve some new clothes from time to time?"

"When the boys get ready to start school, you can get them new clothes. Anyway, I don't hear them complaining."

"They're not but…"

"Good!"

Jane knew she should have stopped with the carpets. Lately, her happy times never seemed to last long. She retreated to her sanctuary. Jane closed the door to the little room she used for sewing. She sat at her machine, mulling over her situation. *What is Rob doing with the money? I'll have to find a way to make some extra money without him knowing about it.*

The squeaking screen door broke her concentration. She peered out the little window overlooking the driveway. Rob was getting something from the trunk of his car. As Jane thought of the possibilities, her excitement grew. Her doldrums were temporarily forgotten, as she hurried to the kitchen to see what he had.

Rob waited until he heard the door to her sewing room shut. In his haste to go to the car, he forgot about the squeaking screen door. He hesitated, watching for Jane's appearance in the hallway. *Maybe she didn't hear.*

Rob went to the car, opened the trunk and took the box out. The door squeaked again as he entered the kitchen. This time, Jane was waiting for him with an anxious look on her face.

"What's in the box?"

Rob knew his answer would sound feeble, but his mind refused to come up with anything better.

"Just something I picked up the other day."

"Is it something for me?"

"No Jane, it's not for you."

"It must be for Freddy. I was going to remind you about his birthday next week. Is that the bat he's been asking for?"

"If you must know, it's a new shotgun for me."

"A shotgun! Why do you need another shotgun?"

"I put it on layaway last month."

"That doesn't answer my question. Why?"

Rob was getting irritated with Jane's questions. There was something else beginning to bother him about Jane; her growing rebelliousness. His response was curt.

"Because, I work my ass off and I wanted it!"

"You seem to think you're the only one in this family that needs anything! No wonder we don't have any money! You spend it on yourself!"

"Buying a shotgun isn't going to kill us! I work hard! What do you do all day but sit around? It's my money and I'll spend it any damn way I want!"

"Your money! Do you think I enjoy scrubbing and cleaning? Who do you think does the laundry and ironing, your mother?"

"Leave my mother out of this!"

"I'll bet you asked her opinion about buying the gun."

"She didn't think it would do any harm!"

"You did! I can't believe you, Rob! She knew we'd argue over this? Don't you see this is just another way for her to mettle?"

"Shut up about my mother! You have no idea what you're talking about! I'm not listening to any more of this! I'm going out! Don't wait up for me!"

"Fine, I'll leave a pillow and blanket on the couch! Don't let the door hit your backside on the way out!"

While preparing dinner for the boys, she thought of her mother-in-law. *Score one for Hilda.*

Robert had only been gone a few minutes when Bruce ran into the kitchen from outside.

"Mom, where's Dad, isn't he going to eat dinner?"

"No Bruce, he's gone out for awhile."

"I wanted to show him the rope swing we hung over the creek."

"Well honey, you'll have to show him some other time, maybe tomorrow."

Jane could see Bruce's disappointment as he went back outside. She knew Rob missed another opportunity to share something with his son. *Rob, your sons are growing up fast. One of these days they won't have time for you. Why can't you think of them? I can do without things, but they need their father.*

She realized Rob grew up solely under Hilda's influence. She understood the void left by his father's passing. Her father died when she was little, too. *I'll talk to him when he's in a better mood.*

*****

Robert walked through the back entrance of the Maplesville Bar & Grill. His drinking cronies had a head start on him. He'd be playing catch up. Rob sat next to Luke Selmer, the Maplesville Police Chief. Whip Maples was regaling all with another tale of his sexual prowess.

Rob heard Whip's story many times. He envied Whip's freedom. As the last male heir, Whip inherited all of the Maple family's holdings. Not blessed with enormous intelligence, Whip had no viable means of supporting himself. Whenever he needed more money, he simply sold a few more acres.

Rob loved Whip's philosophy. If it couldn't be eaten, shot or screwed, why bother? His reputation with the ladies around town kept the grapevine humming.

"Hey Rob, over here! We've got a cold one waiting for you."

Rob took a long swig from the cold Hamm's. He could see Whip was on a roll.

"Have another fight with your wife?"

"Whip, why don't you mind your own business?"

"Boys, Rob here is what you call henpecked."

Whip's comment drew laughter from the others. Rob was in no mood to put up with Whip Maple's sarcasm.

"Whip, how would you like to be eating this bottle?"

Whip didn't sense Rob's dark mood and persisted with his jibing.

"Rob, your wife is about the prettiest thing I ever saw! I can think of better things to do with her than fight."

Rob got to his feet and took a step toward Whip. He had the empty beer bottle clenched in his right fist.

"Shut your goddamn mouth!"

"Come on Rob, I'm just having some fun with you. You know I don't mean nothing by it! Drink up and lets have another."

Rob felt a big hand on his shoulder. Luke Selmer, the sheriff of Maplesville, decided it was time to intervene.

"Rob, you know old Whip is just being himself. He doesn't mean anything by it. Sit down and let's have another beer."

"I'm not in the mood for his bullshit tonight, Luke."

"Okay Rob. Whip, back off on our friend, here."

Everything settled down as the men entered into a long discussion about ungrateful women. Drinking made Rob horny. All he could think about was getting home and satisfying his lustful needs. As far as he was concerned, this was his world and everyone else was just taking up space.

Rob thought about how good her body felt beneath his as he drove home. He liked the control he had over her during sex. Jane was at her most submissive during those times. He knew what she wanted and he planned on giving it to her.

Rob pulled into the driveway, but there were no lights on outside. Angered, he fumbled for the right key. Once in the house, he stumbled through the darkness to the bedroom.

He could make out her curves beneath the thin sheet. His ardor was reaching a crescendo as he tugged at the sheet. His uncoordinated ministrations woke her up.

"Rob, what are you doing? I told you, you're not sleeping in here tonight. I left bedclothes for you in the living room. Stop that, I'm not in the mood. Rob, I said no, not tonight, leave me alone."

"You're my wife. You can't refuse me!"

"No Rob, you're drunk. We'll do this when you're…No Rob, oh God no please, not this way!"

Even drunk, he was too strong for her. As Rob had his way, he mistook Jane's writhing beneath him for passion. After only a few minutes, Rob was completely spent. Jane was desperate to get away from him. She was trapped under his sleeping body. It took all of her effort to pull herself from under him.

The tiled floor of the bathroom felt cool under her feet. Was she dreaming, or did her husband just rape her? Jane looked in the mirror at the tormented reflection and knew it was no dream. She wanted no reminders of this night and did her utmost to wash his seed from her most private parts. Afterward, she retched all over the cool tiles. *What am I going to do? How can I stay in the same house with him after this?*

Jane curled into a ball on the couch. She spent a restless night, entwined in the covers meant for Rob. The next morning, Robert found Jane at her place by the stove.

"Good morning, honey! What's for breakfast?"

"This is for the boys! You can eat downtown!"

Rob wasn't sure he heard her correctly.

"What did you say?"

"I said; I'm not fixing you anything!"

"You better fix my breakfast!"

"Why, you going to rape me again?"

Jane couldn't hold back the tears and started crying uncontrollably.

"What are you talking about? You're my wife. There's no such thing as rape between husband and wife!"

Between sobs Jane replied.

"There is if it's against my will. I can't stand looking at you! Why don't you just leave?"

"All right. I'll get dressed and get the hell out of here!"

On the way to work, Rob tried recalling the events of the previous night. He remembered the sex. Jane seemed to be her usual, compliant self. Outwardly she was prim and proper. Once in bed she rivaled the best New York whore. Could he have mistaken her writhing as something else? *What does it matter? Even if she didn't want to, I have my rights as her husband. Rape! Who's she kidding? She's just mad about the gun.*

*****

Nine months had gone by since that night. Jane was due any day. Swollen as she was, nothing kept her from working. It was getting late in the day and time for her to start dinner. She'd been thinking about fresh green beans from the garden all day. The problem was, she needed salt and pepper. *I suppose Bruce is big enough to cross the road.*

"Bruce, can you come to the kitchen for a minute?"

"I'm coming!"

"Honey, I need some salt and pepper. Are you big enough to go to Willy's by yourself?"

"I can do that."

"Promise you'll look both ways before crossing the road."

"I'll wait until there aren't any cars; just like you do."

"Here's a dollar. Remember, salt and pepper."

"Do you want me to take Freddy?"

"No, Freddy can help me pick the beans."

Jane watched her oldest bolt from the house. *I wish I had his energy.*

Ribbons of brown earth separated the neat rows of beans. Jane surveyed the results of her labor with satisfaction. She took the first few steps into one of the rows. Bending down, she searched through the plants for the most succulent beans. Half way down the row, the first contraction came. *I need to get to the house.*

Jane slowly rose to a standing position. Another contraction hit. She dropped the pan of beans as she clutched her abdomen. Something moist was running down the inside of her thighs. *Oh my God! My water has broken! I've got to get to the phone!*

The contractions seemed to be coming in waves, each new one more intense than the previous. Jane had gone only a few tentative steps when the big one came. She doubled over in pain and slowly sank to the ground. *I'm not going to make it. The baby is coming.* She saw Freddy from the corner of her eye.

She wanted to tell Freddy to fetch his older brother, but she couldn't catch her breath to speak. Jane closed her eyes, trying to block out the pain. It was working. She made it to her knees. Her movements were slow and deliberate. Jane balanced herself on one knee. *If I can only stand, I can get to the phone ... and help.*

The next contraction sent her to the ground for good. The pain was unrelenting. Bean plants she had nurtured from seeds provided a cushion for her body. She knew it wouldn't be long. Her strangled cries came out as hoarse gasps. *Bruce ... Bruce!*

In her pain, Jane forgot about Freddy. She looked up to see her little boy standing next to her prostrate body.

"Freddy, mommy needs your help."

"Are you hurt, mommy?"

"Mommy will be fine. I think the baby is coming. I need you to get Mr. Frazier."

Without a word, Freddy ran down the driveway. Bruce was halfway home, when he saw Freddy running toward him.

Jane held on as long as it took Freddy to disappear. The baby was definitely on its way. The pain made her recall the night of its conception. She hadn't slept with Rob since the night he raped her. The delivery was unexpected just like the rape. Her physical pain now mirrored her mental pain during conception. *Will I ever be able to look at this baby and not think of that awful night?*

The boys ran back to their mother. When they got there, she wasn't alone. Bruce reacted first.

"Mom, are you okay?"

"Boys, say hello to Nicole, your little sister."

One look at her new daughter and the past was forgotten. Her two boys were in awe of the baby. Jane closed her eyes briefly contemplating fate's hand in this game. *I was meant to have this little girl, no matter what the circumstances.* She resolved to put the past behind her, but couldn't get over thinking; *how can something so beautiful be the result of something so horrific, unless it was meant to be? I'm tired of being angry. I hope Nicole has the same affect on Rob.*

*****

Jane lay in her hospital bed. A call was placed to Robert while Jane was getting settled into a room. Nicole was being checked out thoroughly by Doctor Sterns. Exhaustion finally overcame her and she fell asleep.

Rob came panting his way into the room. He stopped short when he saw Jane asleep. *I'll let her sleep for a while yet.* Rob went to the pediatric ward to see his new daughter. *I should feel excitement, but I don't.* The nurse on staff pointed out Nicole to him. All Rob could do was stare blankly at the newborn. Rob saw the nurse and motioned for her to come to him.

"Nurse, I'm going to the cafeteria for a cup of coffee. Could you page me when my wife wakes?"

"Of course Mr. Misner, I'll be happy to do that."

After an hour, Robert heard his name paged over the loud speaker. As he approached her room, he saw she wasn't alone. Her friend, Concha, was with her. He hesitated before entering the room.

"Hi honey, how are you feeling?"

"Like I've been run over by a truck. How do I look?"

"Like you've been run over by a truck."

"Gee, thanks."

"I'm only kidding, Jane."

"I'm just tired, I didn't mean to snap at you, Rob."

Jane decided to put on a happy front for her friend. She didn't want anyone thinking the couple was having problems.

"Do you want to hear how this happened?"

"You bet I do. How did you do it?"

Jane thought, *rape, rape is how it happened!* Jane wanted to tell the world what happened, what kind of man she was married to. She kept those thoughts inside. She told herself, for the sake of the baby, she'd move on and forget about that night. She silently prayed Rob would feel as she did about Nicole. So far, he didn't seem very excited.

"First of all, your boys are heroes. Freddy and Bruce took care of me while Bruce called for the ambulance."

Jane related the details to Rob. He was shaking his head in amazement.

"How long were you in the beans?"

"I don't know. It seemed like a long time. I was resigned to my situation and tried to make the best of it. Once little Nicki decided to come out, it didn't take long."

"Were you in much pain?"

Jane thought; *that's a dumb question, even for him.*

"Robert, I'll tell you what. Take your upper lip between the thumb and index finger of each hand. Make sure you have a strong grip. When you've got a good grip, pull the lip over your head!"

"I guess that was a dumb question. I don't know what I was thinking."

Jane gave Concha a knowing look before responding to Rob.

"You're not a woman, I don't expect you to understand."

"What a story. Wait until I tell everyone at the office. Mr. Hoover will probably want to meet you. Would you like that?"

Jane's answer was more sarcastic than she'd intended.

"Oh yes, I'm sure he would just love to meet me."

Jane finished the thought to herself. *I'll tell the Director what a nice rapist you are. That should help your career.* She called for the nurse to take Nicole. Robert left the room and she gratefully closed her eyes.

*****

By the time Jane woke, she was starving. As was typical with her, the baby's needs came first. The suckling infant was like a salve to the painful memory of her conception. Two days later they were released. Rob pulled into the driveway. Both grandmothers were there.

Rob's stepfather, Clifton was also there. Jane wished her mother had met Mr. Webster first. Hilda didn't deserve such a nice man. Martha would have been a much better fit for Clifton. His warm gentle manner put people at ease. Jane couldn't understand why he would be attracted to Hilda. Clifton was the first to greet them.

"Jane, let me take Nicole while you get out of the car. How are you feeling?"

"I'm feeling much better. Nicki, your grandpa wants to hold you."

Clifton's eyes lit up when as he held the newborn.

"Jane, she's beautiful!"

"Yes, she is."

The grandmothers were standing in line, waiting their turn to hold the baby. Clifton got a cool look from Hilda, as he handed Nicki to Martha.

Robert felt a storm between the grandmothers brewing and made his escape to the living room. He heard his wife's voice trailing him.

"Rob, where are you going?"

"There's a ball game on. I don't want to miss it."

"What about our guests?"

Rob turned.

"What about them?"

"You're being rude."

"Jane, it's just our mothers, for Pete's sake."

"What about Clifton?"

"Clifton, do you want to listen to the game?"

"That would be great, Rob. I'd love to listen to the game with you. The Yanks are in town, right?"

Clifton never quit trying to win Rob over. Rob always resisted his stepfather's efforts. He didn't want Clifton infringing on his father's memory. Rob realized Clifton and his father had a lot in common. Hilda dominated both. The two men were also avid Senator fans. Rob smiled at the thought of his father's obsession with the perennial losers. *I still miss you, Dad. The Senators are still lousy. But I'm sure you know that.*

*****

Robert was only ten when his father died. His father's legacy to him was the love of baseball. They went to see the Senators as often as possible. During Robert's early boyhood in DC, the Senators were the cream of the American League. This was mainly due to the 'Big Train,' Walter Johnson.

Rob remembered 1924. That was the Senator's year. They'd won the World Series. The following year his dad died. Young Robert wanted the Senators to win for his dad. They lost the 1925 Series to the Pirates in six games. Robert never forgave them. He also became a Yankee fan for the rest of his life. He quit going to games until Clifton came along.

Clifton started seeing Rob's mother shortly after his father's death. Robert did everything he could to annoy Clifton. Rooting for the Yankees achieved that. Clifton wouldn't replace his father. Rob knew his mother was furious with him over his treatment of Clifton.

"Robert, why can't you be nicer to Mr. Webster?"

"I don't like him."

"He's never done anything to you! I want you to be nice to him. I'm tired of the way you treat him."

"If you want to roll around on the basement floor with him, I don't care. Don't expect me to like him just because you do."

"Roll around…well…when did you…"

"Why are you so surprised? I've been watching you since the first week Dad died!"

Hilda smacked him three times before he was able to flee.

"Why you little…" SMACK, SMACK, SMACK!

Robert ran to his room and blocked the door with his dresser. He ignored her screaming and banging until she tired of it and left. He could still feel the stings from her open palm. He missed his father. *Why did you have to die Dad?*

*****

Clifton cleared his throat ending Rob's reminiscing.

"Rob, you look like you're daydreaming. I get it! The Nats are beating your Yanks, so now you're not interested in the game."

"It's only the fifth inning! Do you really think they can hold a two run lead for four more innings?"

Robert was starting to get into the game, which provided a needed distraction. He was having a hard time accepting Nicole. Jane quit having sex with him after that night. The baby would be a constant reminder he didn't need. Rob sensed someone behind him. It was Hilda.

"Robert, I told you to keep paper on the rugs! Clifton had to do it for you!"

Rob tried to imagine Clifton bent over the three-foot wide roll of heavy paper. He envisioned him rolling out the paper and following behind in a crab-like fashion.

"Jane doesn't like it."

"I don't care what she likes or doesn't like. This is my house, my carpet! You're just renting, so you'll do what I want!"

Robert got a glimpse of Clifton rising from his chair. One look from Hilda and Clifton sat back down. Robert hoped Clifton would show some backbone, but knew that was wishful thinking. The old man went back to the game. Hilda stayed her course.

"What are the winter rugs still doing on the floor? You should have rolled them up long ago and put the summer rugs down! How many times must I tell you? If you're going to live in my house, you will take care of my things! You haven't changed a bit! You're still lazy! Get off your duff and change these rugs!"

"Mother, can't this wait? This is Jane's first day back with Nicole. I'm sure she doesn't feel like putting up with a bunch of commotion."

"That's always been your problem! You're just like your father was, always making excuses!"

Robert used to live with this kind of abuse everyday. He knew what Clifton went through. Robert knew his mother thrived on intimidation. As his mother railed on over the carpets, Robert saw Martha enter the room.

"Hilda, you're the one that's never changed! You're still the same mean, vindictive, old woman you've always been. Clifton, you and Rob listen to your game. I'm not letting anyone ruin my daughter's first day back with my granddaughter."

Martha's head was inclined in a posture of defiance.

"Robert, are you going to let her talk to me like that?"

"Mother, Martha has a point. There're too many people around here now. I'll do the rugs tomorrow."

Martha wasn't done yet.

"Hilda, does your son pay you rent?"

"Of course he does! You don't think I'd let him live in my house rent free?"

"I'm sure you wouldn't. People might think you were a caring mother. My point is, Robert pays rent. Did he sign a lease?"

Rob could see the confusion crease his mother's face. Hilda was no match for Martha. Hilda looked around for support. None was given. Robert knew he and Clifton would pay later, but for now, he was enjoying the show.

"That lease is just a formality!"

"Hilda, would you say a lease is a legal document?"

"Of course."

"Is there anything in the lease that says he has to change rugs and put paper down?"

"There is something about paying for damages."

"The rugs Hilda, is there a clause that SPECIFICALLY mentions them?"

"No, but he knows what I want!"

"So, if it's not in the lease, how can you make these silly demands?"

"He's not just a renter, he's my son."

"Is Robert on time each month?"

"Of course he is, he's no deadbeat! He knows I depend on the income from this house. I could have gotten another fifty dollars a month from someone else, but I let him have it."

"We all know when George died he left you in excellent financial condition, so it's not the money. It is nice that you think your son's worth fifty dollars. Would you make a stranger cover the furniture and rugs?"

"Of course not, who would ever rent it!"

"Don't you think it is worth fifty dollars per month having someone live here that you know will take care of everything?"

"Well, yes, I guess it is."

"Well, there you have it. You not only have a free caretaker at your disposal, he pays almost full rent on top of it! Why don't you leave the men alone?"

Robert enjoyed the look of helplessness on his mother's face. He added his own comment.

"Mother, why can't you be nice for a change?"

"I'm nice all right! Nice and fed up with being treated disrespectfully! Clifton, we're leaving!"

The pained look on the old man's face told Robert the ride home would be a long one.

"Rob, I'm sorry. I'll try to talk some sense into your mother."

Robert looked at Clifton as if for the first time. He was able to accept the man for himself rather than his father's replacement. He felt bad for him. Hilda's temper exploded.

"What do you mean talk sense into me? Clifton Webster, how dare you imply I'm being unreasonable, I never! When we get home, you can change OUR rugs! You can also rearrange the furniture!"

"Mother, Clifton treats you like a queen. All you do is make his life miserable. You treated my father the same way! It's your fault he died! You had him moving furniture too!"

Hilda was caught by surprise by her son's outburst. She was not accustomed to it. He'd never talked to her that way before. With added vehemence, she turned to Martha.

"See what you've done? My own son has turned against me! I hope it makes you happy!"

Martha was unmoved by the reproach. There was a trace of humor in her voice as she replied.

"As a matter of fact, it does. It's nice to see your son take up for his family for a change."

Robert didn't appreciate Martha's comment. It was time to change sides.

"Martha, you have a lot of nerve criticizing my mother. You've never offered to help with anything. At least my mother provided a place for us to live when we needed one."

"That's right; I don't feel it is my place to take over your responsibilities. Jane's brother-in-law, Frank, doesn't need my help. He owns a house and has the same number of children to support. He doesn't run to his mama when he's in trouble."

He didn't like being compared to Frank. Frank had been stationed on the U.S.S. West Virginia during the attack on Pearl. He'd been on disability since.

"Would you have been happy if I got injured in the war?"

"That's not what I'm saying and you know it!"

"I know no such thing. His disability checks don't support that family anyway. Ginny is the one working in that family. Frank could work, if he wanted. He's just lazy."

Rob knew he'd get no disagreement from Martha. He'd heard her say as much when she thought he wasn't around.

"You could have served in the military like other men."

"Martha, I know you're smarter than that. I did more than most during the war. I was busy catching spies. How do you think I got my promotion?"

"With all that money you make, you'd think you could provide better for your family."

"I've had enough of this! You have a choice. You can keep your comments to yourself, or get your ass on the bus back to Langley Park."

Hilda gave her son a prideful look. Jane passed her mother in the hallway as she came into the room to put an end to what was becoming a free-for-all. Martha did an about-face and followed her.

"All of you stop it! I can't stand listening to this anymore!"

"Dear, I'm just defending you against…this woman. I thought her yelling would disturb you and the baby."

"Mother, I'm used to it. I'll deal with it on my own. I don't need you to fight my battles. She's not going to change so why bother."

Jane turned her attention to Hilda.

"Hilda, I'm sick of your meddling ways."

Hilda looked at Jane, dumbfounded.

"How dare you talk to me like that! You wouldn't have a bed to sleep on if it weren't for me!"

"Fine, take your damn furniture with you. Take the rugs too!"

Jane had Hilda on the ropes. Hilda could only offer a feeble reply.

"Of all the ungrateful…"

"Not ungrateful, just fed up. I didn't want to move into this house. I wanted an apartment of our own. But Rob insisted on living here, so he could have his precious hunting dogs. If strangers were your renters, I dare say you would treat them better than your own family."

"You're not MY family. You were my son's choice, not mine."

Jane noticed Bruce taking it all in and nodded to him.

"Bruce, take your brother and go outside to play."

Bruce took Freddy by the arm and went outside. When the children were out of earshot, Jane continued.

"That's a fine thing to say in front of your grandchildren. Since we disgust you so much, why don't you leave?"

"Clifton, we ARE leaving! I'm not going to put up with this treatment."

Jane turned on her heel and headed for the porch swing. As she sat with her new daughter, Hilda stormed past, with Clifton in tow.

Clifton stopped, patted Jane on the arm and kissed his grandchild's forehead.

"It'll be all right, Jane."

"I'm sorry you're leaving, Clifton. I hoped today would be different, for a change."

Before Clifton could respond, they heard Hilda's voice ring out.

"Clifton, are you coming?"

"I'm on my way, dear."

Jane slid over to make room for Martha. They watched in silence as the car pulled out.

"Well mom, all we need now is to have Robert leave."

"That would be nice, dear."

The squeaking of the screen door announced Robert's presence.

"I better follow them home. I have a feeling Clifton is going to pay for all of this. I'm not sure how long I'll be."

Robert left without another word. Jane enjoyed the quiet with her mother. They were content to watch the antics of the two boys, while they raced to the rope swing. Jane wondered what her boys thought of all the arguing. What kind of affect did it have on them?

"Janey, what are those two little rascals doing?"

"Looks like their taking their clothes off. Whoa, there goes another shirt!

"I wish I could spend more time with you and the kids."

"Mom you can come visit anytime you want. You're always welcome here, you know that."

"No honey, I'm not and you know it. My visits always seem to get Robert going. It's better if I only visit every now and then."

"Momma, that's not fair. I'm going to talk to Robert about this. You don't cause near the trouble Hilda does and she's here all the time."

"I don't understand how you can love a man like that."

"Mom, I'm going to tell you something, but you have to promise not to get worked up."

"What is it, then I'll tell you whether I'll get worked up?"

"No, you have to promise first."

"Okay, I promise. What is it?"

Jane told her mother about Robert coming home drunk and raping her.

"Jane! I want you to go inside and pack bags for you and the kids. You're going home with me! How can you stand looking at that man?"

"I can't do that. I know I should hate him for what he did. I've told myself to forget it happened, but I can't get it out of my mind. I know this will sound strange, but I still love Rob. Besides, I have the kids to think about. How would I support them? We need him."

"You were a good secretary before getting married. You shouldn't have any trouble getting a good job. With child support and alimony, you'll do fine."

"Who will watch the kids?"

"I'll help with that, if it gets you away from him."

"I'll think about it. I'm so confused about Rob. Sometimes I see the man I married. At other times, he's like a stranger."

"I'm worried about you and the kids. What if he gets violent with the children? Look how he yells at you. It makes me sick. You need to leave him."

"Mom, the kids need their father, I can't leave him."

Jane and Martha watched the boys take turns swinging from the rope into the creek. Before they knew it, two hours went by and it was time to fix dinner. Jane called the boys in. Freddy yelled from the creek.

"Awe Mom, can't we play for another half hour?"

"No Freddy, it's time to come in."

"How about two more turns?"

"No more turns!"

Jane laughed at her mother's embarrassment as the boys made their way to the shed dressed only in their soaking skivvies.

"Jane, what are those boys doing? They better put their clothes on. They're making a spectacle of themselves!"

"No one is going to see them. If you haven't noticed, we're in the middle of nowhere."

"I can see they're little, little, uh…"

"Peenies mother, teeny little peenies."

"Well! I'm not staying out here! That's embarrassing!"

Martha went into the house, leaving Jane on the porch. The boys were chattering back and forth. Jane could hear them clearly as they talked.

"Freddy, do you like grandmother Webster?"

"She's mean. She makes us work all the time."

"Bruce, how about granny Martha?"

"Granny Martha is like Mom. She's nice, I wish we got to see her more. I don't think Dad likes her."

As the boys climbed the porch steps, Jane thought, *from the mouths of babes.* The boys peeled off their soaking underwear. Jane wrapped their nakedness with a towel. She saw the boys smile at the empty driveway.

*****

Robert enjoyed being alone in his car. It helped him sort through problems. Listening to the ballgame with Clifton reminded Rob of his father. *Dad, now I understand what she put you through. I see her through a man's eyes. I miss listening to the Senators games with you. Clifton and I did that today. He's a lot like you. Why does he let mother walk all over him? Why did you let her treat you that way?*

He was crossing Chain Bridge, into DC. He strained to look out his window over the railing. He could barely see the rocky features of the Potomac as he crossed over to Canal Rd. *Dad, remember the first time you took me fishing? I'll never forget it. You took me right under this very bridge. The herring were running. I was five. You gave me a bamboo pole. You showed me how to swing the line out and jerk it back. Sometimes the treble hook would snag more than one fish. That was a great day. Maybe I'll take the boys down to the river next spring, when the herring make their run.*

Rob saw Clifton making the left at Arizona Ave. The light was red when Rob got to it. *I'll never forgive Mother for the way she treated you. I guess I've got some of you and her in me. I like playing ball with my boys. They're going to be good...better than I was. I can pass your love of baseball on to them, as well as your love of the outdoors. As much as I hate Mother...I know you don't want to hear that but it's true, she did bring me up to be strong and self-reliant. I owe it to my boys to do the same.*

He didn't remember making the left at Nebraska. Robert was now turning onto Fessenden St. He could see his mother's brick colonial on the right. The thoughts of his father left him as he saw Hilda unlock her front door and wait.

Robert hesitated before getting out of the car. *Look at her. She looks like a volcano ready to explode. Clifton and I are in for a long evening.* Seeing his mother with Clifton triggered an old memory.

*****

As he entered the kitchen for an after school snack, Robert heard moaning. It seemed to be coming from the basement. He called for his mother thinking she may be hurt. There was no response. He didn't know what an orgasm was, but Hilda was working up to one. He moved down the first few basement steps and saw them through the railing. Each was oblivious to his presence. His mother's legs were wrapped around Mr. Webster. Her hands clawed at his head, which was buried between her exposed breasts.

Robert knew he should leave, but was mesmerized. His mother's moans became pants, as if she had just run a long distance. The expression on her face gave her the appearance of being almost...beautiful. He had never thought of his mother that way before. Her face was normally contorted in an expression of perpetual anger. One last long gasp and her rapturous moment ended. He scrambled up the stairs before he was noticed.

Watching his mother in the midst of sexual climax became young Robert's favorite pastime. Those were times of discovery. Mainly the discovery of the pleasure his left hand gave him. Robert dreamed of the day he would experience real sex for the first time. The ten-year old became obsessed with those thoughts. Age only made Robert's desires stronger.

*****

Rob became aware of someone rapping on the passenger window. He knew who it was. As he followed his mother into the house, Clifton was already struggling with furniture.

"Mother, I see you didn't waste any time."

"You know we like to move things around."

"This heavy work isn't good for Clifton."

"You worry too much. He's as strong as a horse."

"Your horse needs some help. Let me help you with that, Clifton."

His mother's only contribution was beating the rugs with an old straw broom. Robert could tell she enjoyed it. The thought of Hilda madly swinging the broom never failed to amuse him. This day, she took to the job with uncommon vigor. Everyone in DC, but Hilda Webster, owned a vacuum cleaner.

After beating the rugs, they had to be removed from the line, rolled and hauled up to the attic. The replacement rugs were then brought down where the beating process was repeated before they were put down. There were two main floors in the house, plus a finished basement. Each floor had rugs. This meant some of the rugs had to be carried up and down three flights of stairs.

By the time the men hauled the last rug up, they were both panting with exhaustion. When they got to the top step, both collapsed in a heap of abused muscles. Robert looked at the older man.

"Clifton, you look pale. Let's sit here and get our breath before we go downstairs."

"That sounds good. Once I get my breath, I'll be fine."

"Clifton?"

"Yeah, Rob."

"Why do you put up with her? I mean, she's my mother, but she is an incredible bitch. Why do you do it?"

"Rob, she's my wife. I don't want you calling her that."

"You're right, it won't happen again…at least in your presence."

Clifton smiled, enjoying the first real moment they ever had.

"You and I never could quite hit it off, could we? The loss of your father must have been hard on you. My father lived a long life. I'm not sure how I would have reacted, if put in your place. I can understand your resentment at that age."

"You're right on the money."

"Believe it or not; I love your mother. There's a side to her you've never seen."

Robert gave him a cryptic smile.

"I'm not so sure about that, Clifton. I know there is more to my mother."

"I'd like to be friends, Rob. Can we be friends?"

"Sure Clifton, we can be friends."

When the old man's eyes began to water, Rob put a hand on his shoulder for reassurance. Rob got up to leave before Clifton got embarrassed.

"I better get going. I need to make a stop by the office before I go home."

Rob's last vision of Clifton was of him crying.

Robert parked his car at about 6pm. As he walked to the office, he kept thinking about the 'Silver Slipper.' A friend told him about it earlier. He hadn't had sex in a long time. *I'll see what this place has to offer.*

It was about 6:15 when the elevator doors to the fourth floor opened. Rob almost ran into his boss, Gordon Starling.

"Rob, what are you doing in here? I thought you'd be home with your new baby. Boy or girl?"

"We had a little girl. Her name is Nicole Marie."

"A girl, that's great! How is Jane faring?"

"Considering she gave birth in the middle of the green beans, she's doing fine."

"Giving birth in the garden! That's one of the most remarkable things I've ever heard of."

"It is amazing. My oldest son, Bruce, called for the ambulance."

"You must be proud of him. Rob, don't stay here too long. You should be home with your family. That's where I'm headed."

"I had a couple things to do, then I'll head home."

"Have a good weekend, Rob."

"Thanks boss, you too."

Rob entered the office. He sat in his lumpy chair and took the bottle of Old Crow from his lower right hand drawer. After taking a long pull, he lit up a Chesterfield and leaned back. This was the most relaxed he'd been all day. The bottle of Old Crow was half empty when he put it back. Its warmth relaxed him like it always did. He lit up a third smoke.

Rob prepared himself for what was to come. He'd been with other women many times when they lived in New York. It helped him keep his sanity. Married life was too hum-drum for him. Since moving back to DC, he'd refrained from extra-curricular activity. He was focused on his new job and didn't need complications. *How was I to know my wife would quit having sex with me?* His frustrations with Jane were building. He was ready to explode. It worked before and will work again.

Rob went to the door. He stopped short and went back to the desk. He'd almost forgotten the condoms. He reached in the drawer, retrieving the three-pack of Trojans. Under his breath, he cursed his wife. *Damn you Jane! See what you've done.*

The 'Silver Slipper' was only a block or so from the office. It was supposed to be more than just a strip joint. Word was, a guy could get laid for the right price. Robert's steps were brisk as he thought of what was in store for him.

The place was crowded with men looking for what they lacked at home. The girls hustled drinks, while parading around in their see through attire. *Look at these women. Corbin Larson was right.* "I'm getting laid tonight!" Robert voiced those thoughts a little too loudly. He didn't see the tall brunette standing behind him.

"I, for one, think you might get lucky."

One of the most seductive women he had ever seen, took a long drag on her cigarette. Rob watched her mouth suck in the smoke.

"Oh baby, I think I'm in love."

"You're just in lust, honey. My name is Brandi and ooooh, I am sooo randy!"

"I'm Rob and I got just what a randy Brandi needs. See right here baby, it's all ready for you."

The prostitute took Rob's hand and placed it on her breast. He worked on one nipple at a time as they sat in a dark corner. After they finished a couple of drinks, Brandi's head went under the table. Her warm mouth engulfed him. Rob's expression was rapturous. Just before the moment of truth, she stopped. Her head popped back up, while his hands stayed busy.

"Did you like that, honey?"

"You didn't finish me off! Why are we wasting time here? I've got a nice big back seat in my car!"

"There's plenty of time for that, besides, don't I get a tip for being so nice to you?"

"A tip, oh yeah, I remember now."

"Baby, a sexy man like you must get around? You don't think a drink is enough for all of that pleasure, do you? You treat me right and I guarantee you'll be happy."

Rob knew he was in the hands of a seasoned expert. Brandi knew just how far to take him. Each episode under the table was good for a fiver. There seemed to be no end to it, but Rob was powerless in her hands. His lust for this vixen was stronger than his will power. Finally, Brandi stood, holding her hand out.

"What now? I've already given you fifty bucks!"

"Oh baby, I've never had a man turn me on like this. I just have to have you inside me. Don't you want to fuck me?"

He'd already spent more than he planned on, but he found himself lost in the seductive sway of Brandi's hips as she led him to a small room in the back.

*****

Each evening around seven-thirty Clifton would retreat to the sanctuary of his wing chair. Here he would read the evening paper and enjoy his pipe. The 'Cherry' blend tobacco filled the house with its sweetness. Tonight was different. Tonight he felt the beginnings of a new relationship with Rob. He felt almost content as he packed the pipe.

This old chair feels good. There's nothing like a pipe and paper to help a man forget his problems. I'm tired. These old bones ache. I can't seem to catch my breath. So much for my quiet time, here she comes. What now? I guess I better get up and see, but my breath. Oooh! My chest...the pain...I can't...

Clifton tried to get up but sank back into the chair. As Hilda approached, she saw the last wisps of smoke exiting his open mouth. Clifton would never have to move another stick of furniture, or haul another rug.

*****

Robert felt good about himself. Alone, in the car, he anticipated his next trip to the Silver Slipper. *Oh Brandi! I haven't had a blowjob in...well, not since I got married. Baby you have found a customer for life. Jane could hump my ass off every night for the rest of my life, but I'd still come back for more of that. Jane never did like playing the mouth organ. I need to come up with a reason for being so late, hmmm, oh shit, I'll just tell her I went to the office and worked. Jane is naïve. She'll believe anything I tell her.*

Thirty minutes later, Rob pulled into his driveway. The night was mild, but Robert looked as though he had just left a sauna. As he paced around in the driveway, thinking about his dalliance with the luscious Brandi, the backdoor opened and there she was...tall, brunette and...untouchable.

"Where have you been? Your mother has been calling. She's frantic! Clifton's dead! She said you were on your way home. Where did you go? I even called the grill to see if you had stopped there. No one had seen you!"

"Wait, wait a minute, go back! You said Clifton is dead? I just left him a few hours ago. He can't be dead! What happened?"

"It was next to impossible for me to get information from your mother; she was hysterical. She said he went to his easy chair to read and have a smoke after dinner. She went in to do some darning and found him motionless. She shook him, but he didn't respond; that's when she called. That's all I know. You need to go back. I've packed some things. I'm going with you."

"What did the rescue squad say when they got there?"

"She never mentioned that. I assume they took him. I'll get the baby."

"That's not going to work. For all we know he could still be in the chair. I better go by myself. There's no place for the baby at her house. Besides, the baby will just create more confusion. It's better you stay home."

"You're right, I wasn't thinking. My mother will be leaving the day after tomorrow, bring Hilda here. She can stay with us for a couple of weeks."

"Are you sure about that? You better think about it some more."

"No, Robert, really, it's okay. She shouldn't be alone."

"I'll tell her. I don't think she'll take us up on it though. Hell, she won't even say thank you for offering."

Jane thought to herself; *As much as I dislike her, we're all she has. She shouldn't be alone, but did I have to volunteer for TWO WEEKS? Jane, you idiot!*

Jane didn't share her husband's optimism. Hilda would see this as her golden opportunity to make her life miserable. How could she pass on that?

Robert couldn't get Brandi off of his mind. She smelled of nicotine, booze and sex. He was already planning his next visit when he turned onto Fessenden Street for the second time that night. He was all his mother had left. He wondered if he would survive her. When he pulled up in front of her house, she was sitting on the stoop.

"Robert, what took you so long? I've been waiting here for over four hours. Clifton is still in his chair!"

"Mother! You haven't called the ambulance yet?"

"I didn't know what to do. Poor Clifton! I have no one but you Robby! What am I going to do? Why did he have to die and leave me alone?"

"You'll not get sympathy from me."

"What kind of thing is that to say?"

"This makes the second husband you've gone through. You know damn well why he's dead! You killed him! You knew Clifton's heart was bad. Did you think all that heavy work was good for him?"

"He never complained. He enjoyed helping me around here."

"Enjoyed it! You never gave the man a minute's worth of peace. I'm never rolling up another rug. I'm letting Jane go out tomorrow and buy our own."

Hilda started crying. Rob knew the tactic. He could expect a heavy dose of guilt. He called for a rescue squad. Twenty minutes later Clifton was being delivered to the mortuary. Robert looked for some sign of remorse. Her only lament was how lonely she'd be.

Three days later Clifton was buried at Fort Lincoln Cemetery. Robert got to thinking about his own death and wondered how many would show up for his funeral. Clifton didn't have any relatives of his own. Hilda saw to it he didn't have many friends either.

Jane sat next to Hilda with an arm around her. Hilda had her face buried into Jane's shoulder, playing the grieving widow. Robert wasn't buying any of it. He couldn't figure his wife out. There was more to her than met the eye.

Robert was not looking forward to the next couple of weeks. With Hilda in the house, his life would be miserable. He decided to spend extra time away from home. *Let Jane take care of her. We'll see how much compassion Jane has after two weeks. If nothing else, it should be entertaining.*

*****

Jane was feeling closed in. School was starting in a few days. The boys needed new clothes. Jane needed a break from Hilda. Her two-week visit turned into four. She showed no sign of leaving. Something had to give.

"Hilda, would you mind if I left the boys with you for a few hours?"

"Why? Where are you going?"

"School starts on Monday and I haven't been shopping yet."

"I suppose you blame me for that."

"Of course not."

"I don't baby sit. Why don't you call your mother?"

"That's ridiculous! You know Mother doesn't have a car. It's an hour's bus ride from Langley Park. Besides, you're here."

"I said I'm not baby sitting."

"They're your grandchildren!"

"I'm too ridiculous to watch them!"

"You know what; forget it! I'll take them with me!"

"You don't trust me with my grandchildren?"

"You just said... I give up! I've done everything I can think of to make you feel welcome. All you've done is complain."

"I've pulled my weight!"

"Really! What have you done to make this easier?"

"I've helped around the house. I did the dishes last night."

"And I thanked you at least five times. When have you thanked me for anything?"

"I'm a guest in this house."

"That's my point."

"You're just like your ungrateful mother!"

"I'll take that as a compliment. My mother's a wonderful person. My father died and left her nothing. She had to go to work and raise two girls by herself. Rob's father died and left you a bundle. At least my mother worked for what little she had."

"I knew you were just like your mother. I allowed her to live in one of my apartments when she had no place to go."

"I remember that apartment. You charged her double what it was worth."

"I had a right to make a profit. I had to pay the upkeep on the building."

"Upkeep? There were big chunks of plaster hanging from the ceiling, plus the heat never worked."

"I had the boiler fixed at great expense."

"Yeah, only after Mother got the rest of the residents to sign a complaint."

"So, you admit she was ungrateful. After I had it fixed, she moved out without any notice! What do you have to say about that?"

"My sister developed pneumonia from that drafty slum you call an apartment."

"Slum! I suppose you think this is a slum?"

Hilda gestured with her eyes around the house.

"Not at all. This is a prison."

"I warned Robert about you. He wouldn't listen. He said he had to get married in order to get that job."

"You're lying."

"It's true. Ask him."

"You're a vindictive, miserable old woman."

At five-foot seven, Jane towered over Hilda. She took a couple of steps forward. Hilda was surprised by Jane's boldness and retreated slightly.

"You can't talk to me that way! I'll tell my son!"

"You'll have to do it from your house."

"What do you mean by that?"

"I'm calling a cab. You're leaving!"

"You can't kick me out of my own house!"

Jane took another menacing step. Hilda packed and was gone shortly thereafter.

Robert got home around seven.

"Mother called and said you threatened her!"

"I think you know better than that."

"What happened?"

"You should have asked that first."

"She chewed on my ear for an hour. I'm not in the best mood. Tell me what happened!"

"Your mother is mean and spiteful."

"What else is new?"

"I'm so happy you understand. She also told me why you were in such a hurry to marry me."

"She did what?"

"You heard me."

"You can't pay any attention to what she says."

"I know how she is. I'm not so sure about you."

"I've had a long day. I'm going to the Tavern. We'll talk about this later."

*****

Squirrels scampered around the property collecting acorns. The vibrant colors of the leaves were fading to rusty brown. Sweaters were donned for protection against autumn's chill. Hunting season was nigh. Rob was infused with excitement. This year he would introduce his sons to the hunt.

Rob was in the middle of showing Freddy how to groom Duke when the phone rang.

"Give me the brush, Freddy. Let me show you how to do it. Make long strokes, like this. See how 'ol Duke just lets me brush him. See how he closes his eyes, almost like he's saying oh that feels good!"

On the fifth ring, Jane called to Rob from her tulip bed.

"Rob, aren't you going to answer that?"

"Just let the damn thing ring. I know who it is. I don't want to be bothered right now."

"Rob, you know she'll let the phone ring and ring. You're better off talking to her and getting it over with."

"You're right, I'll get it."

Jane hadn't seen Freddy this excited about anything since Christmas. All he talked about was going hunting with his dad. Robert spent too little time with his sons. Jane hated seeing anything cut it short.

"Freddy, hold Duke's collar while I get the phone."

Rob's jaw clenched as he answered.

"Robby, I need you over here immediately!"

"Mother, I'm busy. What's so important that I have to drop what I'm doing this minute?"

"Don't take that tone with me, Robert! I need you to help me with something."

"But Mother, I have plans today."

"What I need from you won't take long. You can go back to your precious plans afterward.

"I'm not moving anything."

"You don't care about your poor mother. It's been lonely without Clifton. What would you know about that? You have your family. I hope you never have to be alone like this."

"Mother, I realize you're lonely, but I can't be there every minute of the day."

"I'm not asking you to be here every minute! You aren't a bit concerned that there has been a strange man looming outside, looking through my windows!"

"Who's watching through the window?"

"Some man!"

"Was he standing in front of the window, or on the sidewalk?"

"What difference does that make? I tell you a strange man is staring at my house and you're not the least concerned!"

"Mother, a second ago you said he was looking through your windows. Was he staring at the house, or waiting for a bus?"

"Why are you asking all of these questions? I don't know! What difference does it make? I'm frightened!"

"For all you know Mother, he may have been waiting for the bus. Is the man still there?"

"No, he's not still there!"

"Then what are you so upset about?"

"He might come back and break into the house."

"That sounds crazy. You're being paranoid."

"I am not crazy and I am not imagining anything!"

"Mother, you're worried about nothing."

"Nothing! You call my safety nothing! You DON'T care anything about me after all! Well, you go about your business. Don't worry about your mother....click!"

"Mother, mother! Oh shit, goddamn it!"

Robert went back outside. Freddy hadn't moved. Duke was leaning against the six-year old enjoying the attention. Rob sat on the stump next to Freddy and scratched Duke's muzzle. Jane stopped her work when Rob returned.

"Who was on the phone, Rob?"

"Who do you think?"

"What is it this time?"

"She's convinced someone is watching her through the windows. The old lady won't even walk to the corner for bread, for fear of being attacked. I don't know what I'm going to do with her. This has got to stop!"

As Robert sat on the stump, he noticed Jane stooped over the garden. Her lightweight dress rode high on her thighs as she planted her bulbs. The outdoors brought out her beauty. Jane was in her element. He imagined taking her right where she was. He imagined his hands sliding up her dress, parting her legs...the phone rang again.

"Don't get up, I'll get it. I know who it is. Freddy hold onto him until I get back."

Rob came right out.

"Your mother?"

"I have to go. She's screaming about strangers."

"I thought you were going to run the dogs with the boys."

"I won't have time. I've got to go. Don't wait dinner for me."

"Why don't you think about hiring a live in companion?"

"That'll be the day. Who would want to be with her all day? Their skin would have to be tougher than rawhide. It's a good idea, but there's no way she'd allow a stranger in her house. I better get going."

Robert returned to the dog.

"I'll finish brushing you later Duke ol' boy. Oh yeah, you're a good-looking boy, yes. You love me don't you, boy? It's nice to know someone does. I'll see you later, boy. Get in there now, gooood boy!"

Robert didn't get to spend nearly enough time with his dogs. He appreciated their unwavering devotion to him. If Jane gave him half of that devotion, he wouldn't have to screw every whore in D.C. *One good thing about whores; they don't give me any shit. Anyone of them will screw me blind for twenty dollars and my sweet little wife; it's your fucking fault.* He had to admit, none of them excited him like his wife could.

Robert went in for his keys and checked his wallet. *Hmm, I need some more cash.* Trips to his mother's were always followed by a visit with Brandi. Rob opened the checkbook, finding the balance woefully low. *Damn, if I go see Brandi tonight, I won't have enough money for lunch the rest of the week. Payday is a week away. I haven't paid the bills yet. Aw, screw it! I need some relaxation.*

Rob's craving for sex and booze was starting to run his life. The money situation was getting serious. He could only afford to give Jane twenty dollars a week. *Well, twenty dollars a week is equal to four blowjobs; serves her right. I'd never have been driven to this if she'd performed her wifely duty.*

*****

The next morning Rob was in a hurry to get to work. He almost forgot to give the boys their daily directive.

"Bruce! Bruce, I'm calling you son, get in here!"

"Yes sir."

"Don't forget to clean the dog pens this afternoon. You remember how I told you to do it?"

"Yes sir. Dig a two foot hole down by the creek and dump the poop into it."

"And...?"

"Oh yeah, sprinkle some of the white stuff on it. What is that stuff?"

"Limestone powder; it kills the odor. You don't want your yard smelling like dog poop, do you?"

"I guess not."

"You guess not what?"

"I guess not...sir."

"That's better. Always show men proper respect son, especially your father, understand?"

"Yes sir."

"Do a good job, because I'm going to inspect your work when I get home."

"Yes sir, Freddy and me will do a good job."

Rob looked on his son with approval while thinking; *my boys have it a lot easier than I had it. I got smacked every time I did something Mother didn't like.* He picked up his keys and left for work.

Later that day, Rob was mulling over his relationship with Sheila Santini, one of his more recent hires. They were to rendezvous at her place, after work. This would make the third Monday in a row for Rob. Even though they went out of their way not to act suspiciously, there was still talk around the water cooler.

Unconsciously, Rob opened his right hand desk drawer and reached for the bottle of Old Crow. It was empty. *Damn, I just bought that bottle. I'll have to stop by Stan's at lunch and get another.*

Rob started chasing young office girls as a means of relieving the stress off his finances. Sheila was the latest. Rob found new pleasure in robbing young women of their virginity. His expensive forays to the 'Silver Slipper' were less frequent. For now, he needed a fresh bottle.

As Rob stepped into the hallway, he almost ran his boss over.

"Whoops, sorry boss, I didn't see you."

"Rob, do you have a minute? I'd like to talk to you in my office."

"Sure, I was just on my way to the drug store to get some aspirin for this headache."

"Rob, we need to talk about what's going on with you."

"Going on? What do you mean? I'm perfectly fine, nothing is going on."

Robert was on the verge of panic.

"There must be, Rob. You're not the same person you were six months ago. Where do you go in the middle of the day? I was trying to find you yesterday. No one knew where you were. Your work has slipped, badly. Another thing; the office grapevine has you chasing young skirts around the office. I call that something, don't you?"

Robert's ego wasn't ready for this. He viewed himself as indispensable. Rob broke eye contact as his confidence faltered. *Does he know about Sheila? Maybe he's only fishing.*

"Boss, I don't know what to say. I've always given my best. About yesterday, my mother called and needed me. Ever since Clifton died, I've been worried about her. I'm sorry for not telling Miss Cassidy where I was, but I was in a hurry."

Robert knew Gordon was no fool. Would he take the bait about his mother?

"Why didn't you tell me about your mother? I lost my father a couple of years ago. I certainly appreciate what she's going through. It's a very difficult adjustment. Do you need to take some time off?"

This was perfect. Rob could now play the martyr.

"Thanks, boss, but that won't be necessary. I appreciate your concern. I stop by her house on the way home every night. She does seem to be getting better."

"Rob, you've always been a valuable member of the team. In light of the problem with your mother, I'll lighten up on you. But I do need to know one thing."

"What's that, boss?"

"Rob, quit calling me boss. It's condescending and I don't like it."

"Sure boss…er Mr. Starling whatever you say, sir."

"Don't go overboard, Rob. Give me a straight answer. Are these rumors true?"

"Mr. Starling, I have no idea what you are referring to. I'm a happily married man, with three children."

"Don't pretend you haven't heard the rumors. Where there's smoke, there's fire."

"I've heard them and I assure you they're not true!"

Robert's response was short on conviction. Gordon's wrinkled brow didn't go unnoticed.

"You can assure me? Mr. Misner, I can assure you; if I find out different, I'll have you busted to field agent at the biggest shit hole available. I don't care if your mother does need you. Is that understood?"

"Yes sir, I understand."

"No, I don't think you do! You're not some kid fresh out of the academy. This is serious! If you don't treat it as such, you'll be looking for a career somewhere else! Now do you understand?"

"Yes, sir."

"All right then. You can get back to work."

Robert closed his door. He opened the drawer, but forgot the bottle was empty. He needed a clear head for the thinking he had to do. *The prick actually threatened to fire me.*

*****

Robert followed Sheila to her apartment after work. He struggled to come up with a plan. An idea suddenly came to him. Rob's mind was busy as he sat on Sheila's couch.

"Rob, are you all right?"

"Of course baby, I'm fine."

Sheila knew what he needed. She made her way to the couch undoing one button of her blouse at a time. She hiked her skirt up, exposing the paleness of her thighs as she straddled his lap. Rob felt himself grow hard, as he placed his hands on her hips.

Their movement was synchronized and slow at first, but gained momentum. Their mouths met in a long, deep kiss. Rob's hands slid over her shoulders to the bra's clasp. Sheila's breasts were free of their confinement and swayed seductively with the rhythmic rocking of her hips.

Rob lifted her from his lap, laying her on the couch. He undid his pants, as he stood over her. She parted her legs, pleasuring herself with her fingers. Rob went to his knees. Sheila moaned softly as he penetrated her.

"Robby you're an animal. Oh yes, yes, that feels so good."

Rob exploded his seed within her. When they were done, he broke the news.

"Baby, that was the last time we can do this, unfortunately."

"What do you mean the last time?"

"Starling is suspicious, if we get caught, it would mean both of our jobs. We're going to have to lay low until this blows over."

"Robby, how long?"

"At least a few months."

"How can I go to work everyday and know I can't have you?"

"That's a good point. It's going to be even harder for me, baby. How can I go without this body for three months?"

Rob playfully tweaked an erect nipple.

"What can we do, Robby?"

"I think I've come up with a solution. I can transfer you to another department. That should end the gossip."

"Rob I couldn't stand not being near you everyday, but if you think that's best?"

"Do you have a better idea? Once the rumors die down, we can pick up where we left off."

"You mean with these?"

Sheila cupped her size 38 D's in each hand tracing her fingers around her areolas. Robert's face got lost in the fleshy softness, as he came to life again.

"Hmm baby, one more time for old time's sake."

*****

While their father was getting his rocks off, Bruce and Freddy were addressing the task at hand.

"Freddy, where's the shovel?"

"What shovel?"

"The shovel for the poop."

"I don't know."

"We need the shovel for the poop."

"I don't know where it is."

The boys looked all over the yard but came up empty. Bruce remembered the little shovel by the fireplace.

"Freddy, go get that small shovel by the fireplace."

Freddy returned a moment later.

"I found this little broom too!"

"You did something smart for a change. You hold the shovel and I'll sweep the poop into it."

Ten minutes later Bruce proudly surveyed their work.

"That wasn't hard. Oh, I almost forgot. I found the big shovel."

"Where was it?"

"Leaning against the house."

"Take these back to the fireplace and I'll go bury the poop."

By the time Freddy returned, Bruce was done.

*****

Jane had gotten used to not getting phone calls from her habitually late husband. She had his warmed up dinner almost ready as he got home. She noticed his mood immediately. She felt a sense of dread as soon as he stepped into the kitchen.

"Did you stop by your mother's?"

"No, why?"

"You don't seem to be in the best of moods tonight."

"I had a bad day. Where's my dinner, I'm starved?"

"Rob, how am I supposed to know when to have it ready for you? You come home at a different hour every night."

"My dinner should be ready when I walk through the door!"

"If you called, I'd know when to start it."

"That's no excuse!"

"Why do you have to yell at me? I haven't had the best day either."

"I'll yell if I want! The problem with you is, there is no one here to supervise you."

"What are you talking about? I've never heard of a housewife supervisor. Are you suggesting your mother come back?"

Jane's attempted humor failed.

"I don't think that's funny! I'm going to read the paper. Call me when dinner is ready!"

Not a minute went by before Jane heard him calling.

"Jane! Come in here!"

"Rob, do you want to eat or not? Can't it wait?"

"No, something smells in here! What did you do in here today?"

"Smells, what are you talking about? I cleaned thoroughly in the living room this morning."

Jane turned the burners down and went into the living room.

"It does smell! Whew, what is that? It almost smells like...dog poop?"

"Were the dogs in here today? Did they crap in the house?"

"You know I can't stand the smell of those animals. The last thing I would ever do is let them in my clean house."

Rob walked around the living room. He sniffed, trying to detect the source of the odor. As he got closer to the fireplace he bent down. The scoop he used for the ashes had fallen down.

"Holy shit!"

"What is it?"

"Look at this! It's got shit all over it! Where are the boys?"

Jane saw what he was talking about. There was only one way poop could wind up on the scoop. Jane gulped hard when she saw the look on his face.

"Boys, get in here!"

Rob dwarfed his sons as he stood over them while holding up the scoop.

"Bruce, did you use this to clean the pen today?"

"I couldn't find the big shovel."

"Answer my question, boy!"

"Yes sir, we did. Freddy held the shovel and I used the little broom to sweep the poop up."

"The little broom?"

Robert bent down and found the brush caked with excrement. Jane sensed something bad was about to happen. She shrunk back while Rob unbuckled his belt. He pulled it free in one swift motion.

"Robert! Don't you dare hit them with that!"

She stood between her husband and sons like a she-bear, defending cubs. Robert put his hand on her shoulder and shoved her to the floor. Jane saw the fearful look on Bruce's face. She was frozen in place. At the age of nine, Bruce got his first whipping.

Jane's horror grew with each swing of Robert's arm. She rose to her feet, lunging for his arm, but was repelled again. Jane pleaded for Rob to stop.

"Rob, stop hitting him! He's bleeding!"

"Stop your interfering! I have a right to discipline my son!"

"You have no right to beat him like this!"

Again, Jane went for the belt and again, Rob shoved her to the floor. On the tenth lash, she succeeded in getting between her husband and son. She pushed Bruce out of Rob's reach.

"Boy, come back here, I'm not done with you!"

Jane saw that Freddy was glued in place; his eyes registered terror.

"Bruce, take Freddy with you, quickly!"

Robert glared at Jane, as he started to raise the belt to strike her.

"You have no right to interfere!"

"Are you going to hit me now? Rob, are you insane?"

"He will learn to listen, or pay the consequences!"

"Consequences? Bruce is nine years old! How could you do such a vile thing to your own son?"

Rob's eyes bore into Jane's. She froze in fear, expecting to feel the sting of his belt.

"He's not hurt. I got much worse than that when I was his age. It just made me stronger."

Rob lowered his arm, to Jane's relief. After threading his belt back through his pants, he took the soiled instruments outside for cleaning. As he passed Jane, he held them up, as if to confirm justification for the beating. Jane was overcome with sadness and relief at Rob's leaving.

She went to the boy's room and slowly opened the door. Freddy was curled up in the corner. Bruce sat on the edge of his bed, wiping at his tears.

"Are you okay, honey?"

"Why did he have to whip me? I didn't mean to hurt anything."

"Honey, I don't know. Can I get you anything?"

"No! I hate him!"

"You don't mean that."

"Yes I do!"

"Are you sure I can't get you something?"

"I just want to be alone."

"Okay, sweetie. Freddy and I will be in the sewing room."

Freddy hadn't moved from the corner. He was still huddled into a tight ball. Jane would never forget the look on his face, as he blurted out.

"I don't want to go out there!"

"It'll be all right, Freddy."

"Mommy, I'm scared!"

Bruce had always seemed to be older than his years. He forgot about his humiliation, as he placed a comforting arm around his little brother.

"He can stay with me, Mom."

Jane felt a surge of pride. She gave them a reassuring smile before leaving.

"I'll be in the sewing room if you need me."

She could smell the rancid odor of his cigarette, as she left the boy's room. Fear and anger battled one another within her. Jane stopped in mid-stride when she heard Robert demanding his dinner.

"When's my dinner going to be ready?"

Rob showed no signs of remorse. He was like a stranger. All Jane could do was stare at the twisted expression on his face. Her words wanted to explode from her mouth, but were caught in her throat. She had never witnessed such a brutal act, let alone been the victim of one. Jane went into her sanctuary, slammed and locked the door behind her.

Rob went into a rage.

"I said, when is my dinner going to be ready?"

Rob was filled with a feeling of power. It was exhilarating. His children would learn to respect him. If that lesson was harsh at times, so be it. Rob would gain their respect through fear, Jane included. *Maybe she'll be more compliant if she fears for the boys.*

Rob stood outside the locked door and pounded. The hinges shook with the force.

"Where's my dinner? Unlock this door!"

There was no answer from within the small room, as Jane cowered behind the door.

"All right then. I'm going out!"

As he went to his car, another idea came to mind. *After I eat, I'll stop by the Slipper for some desert.*

Jane heard the back door slam. She sat at her sewing machine, thinking about what happened and how she could keep it from happening again.

*****

Jane discovered ways of supplementing her allowance. She found Robert's wallet on the floor one morning. It was thick with cash. She lightened the load by two tens and a five. *What are you doing with all of this, while we have nothing?* If Rob ever missed the cash, he never mentioned it. Every other week or so Jane would liberate an extra ten to twenty dollars.

Sewing for her friends became another means for Jane to make money. Willy's market was her conduit for finding business. Willy also became a source for extra income. He heard how good Jane's canned fruits and vegetables were. One day, while Jane was in, he made his offer.

"Mrs. Misner, I have a proposition for you."

"What might that be, Willy?"

"I've heard from some of your friends how good your canned fruits are."

"The garden and fruit trees keep me pretty busy. It's a real shame; most of the stuff just rots before I can get to it."

"How would you like to make some extra money?"

"What do you have in mind, Mr. Frazier?"

"We could sell your canned goods in the store and split the proceeds fifty-fifty."

"My husband wouldn't like me doing that."

"It'll be our secret. How about it?"

"I could certainly use the extra money, okay, it's a deal."

Jane worked the garden with a new purpose. Fruit wasn't left to rot on the ground, either. The savings account she opened was the first step toward her independence. Earning her own money gave her confidence she never experienced.

Willy provided Jane with ample boxes. Every few days, Jane would load up the wagon and go to Willy's. One late summer afternoon, she was packing boxes and heard footsteps on the porch. Much to her surprise, it was her mother.

"Mother, I'm so happy to see you. Why didn't you tell me you were coming for a visit?"

"I wanted to surprise you. What are you doing with all of that canned fruit?"

"I'm so happy to see you! I was getting ready to go to Willy's."

"Willy's?"

"I've never told you about Willy's, have I?"

"I don't believe so, dear. What is it?"

"It's the little country store across from our drive."

"You mean that dilapidated old house at the bus stop?"

"That's the one."

"What's all this about?"

Martha motioned to the boxes Jane was stuffing with mason jars of fruit and vegetables.

"Oh, yes, this. Willy and I are kind of in a partnership."

"A partnership?"

"Yes, Willy and I split the sale fifty-fifty."

"I have to see this."

"You'll love this place. Wait until you meet Calvin and Henry."

"Who are they?"

"A couple of country gentleman."

"Do they work at the store?"

"No. They sit around on the big burlap bags of stock feed in the front of the store, playing gin all day."

"Why would they do that, for heavens sake?"

"They have nothing else to do. They're very entertaining. I think they have a crush on me."

"Really? Why do you think that?"

"They race each other to the door when they see me coming. I pretend not to notice their fawning stares. They're cute old gentlemen. I have a feeling they're going to like you."

"No! Don't they have wives?"

"Widowers."

"Both of them?"

"Yep."

"Oh my."

Bruce and Freddy pulled Nicole in the wagon. Jane and Martha lagged behind slightly while they talked. Jane waited for the right time to tell her mother about the beating the night before.

"Jane, you look worried, what's wrong?"

"Mother, I'm glad you're here. I was going to call you."

"What's he done now?"

Jane spared no details.

"I knew that man was wrong for you. How can a father beat his children?"

"Mother, he reminds me more and more of Hilda every day. I don't know what to do."

"Why don't you and the boys stay with me until you sort this out?"

Jane walked the last few feet to the end of their driveway. The children waited before crossing. She could see the expectant look on her mother's face. Jane didn't know how to answer her. They crossed 123 to the gravel parking lot.

A smile came to Jane's face as she saw the Shiflette brothers through the rusty screening of Willy's front door. She could hear Willy's voice as she stepped onto the porch.

"Mother, let's continue this later."

"You can count on that, Jane."

As they approached Willy's porch, Jane could hear his voice.

"Hey Calvin, Henry, here comes Mrs. Misner."

Jane heard the resultant scramble of feet over the plank floor, as she winked at her mother. Both women tried to stifle their laughter. They could hear the brothers' verbal sparring, as the door opened from within.

"Get out of my way Henry, you decrepit old fart, I got up first!"

"I got my hand on the door first and I ain't lettin' go any time soon. You might as well sit back down on that bag of sweet feed and take your turn. I'll be opening the door for the little lady this time!"

"Not ifin I have anything to say on it!

Jane saw that Henry was not about to let his older brother open the door. This was a privilege that came with snagging the seat nearest the door.

Calvin was the first to react to Willy's announcement of Jane's approach. Not to be outdone by his older brother, Henry was able to squeeze between Calvin and the door. They struggled against each other's lanky frames for leverage. Henry won out and gallantly held the door open for Jane and her entourage.

Jane didn't receive the normal greeting. The brothers were too busy gawking at Martha as she sauntered past them. Calvin and Henry bowed in unison as they spoke.

"Afternoon ma'am, who's this vision of loveliness with you today."

"I'd like you to meet my mother, Martha Higdon. Mother this is Calvin and Henry Shiflette."

Henry stood at the door, slicking back his few wispy strands of hair.

Calvin answered.

"Pleased to make your acquaintance ma'am. You'll have to excuse my runt of a little brother, he's a might slow witted."

"Runt, slow witted! You're a good one to talk. At least I made it to the sixth grade. I'm also a lot better lookin than you, ain't that so Miss Jane?"

Jane could tell by Martha's expression that she was being thoroughly entertained.

"Henry, I'd be hard pressed to choose between the two of you. You're both so big and strong."

"Awe Miss Jane, you're bein' too nice. Me and Calvin are just two old country boys makin do with what the good lord give us."

"Henry, you're being too modest. Why, any woman would be fortunate to snag either one of you. Don't you agree, Mother?"

Both brothers turned expectantly to Martha.

"Why yes, either one of you two distinguished gentlemen would be a fine catch for any woman."

Calvin and Henry weren't used to such directness from a woman. They shuffled in place as they guffawed at each other. Calvin was the first to gain his composure.

"Mrs. Higdon, your husband sure is a lucky man."

"Thank you very much Mr. Shiflette, but I've been widowed for over twenty years now."

"Ma'am, I'm real sorry to hear that. I thought…you know, the ring and all…"

"Oh, you saw my ring and thought I was married. Since my husband died, I've never taken it off."

"He was still a lucky man. Now that we've had the pleasure of meeting you, one of our questions has been answered."

"What question is that Mr. Shiflette?"

"Now we know where your daughter gets her good looks."

Martha couldn't hide the blush. Jane had never seen her mother at a loss for words. Jane fixed each with a warm smile. She could see her mother was too overcome with embarrassment to answer.

"What a sweet thing to say. Wasn't that a sweet thing for Henry to say Mother?"

Martha pretended to be looking around the store. She was finally able to speak as she turned back to the brothers and said;

"That was a very nice thing to say. Thank you very much for the compliment."

"Aw shucks ma'am, don't mention it."

Jane stepped up to the counter where Willy had been taking it all in. He nodded toward the brothers, as they continued fawning over Martha.

"I think those two like your mother."

"I think Mother likes them, too. She's never experienced anything like this before."

"I just hope the boys don't scare her away permanently."

Jane decided to rescue Martha.

"Mother, come here, I'd like you to meet Mr. Frazier."

After the introductions, Jane had difficulty getting Willy's attention again. It seemed the Shiflette brothers weren't the only ones interested in Martha.

"Willy, can I give you my order now?"

Jane looked at her mother and decided Willy's attentions were not unwelcome. Jane had to repeat herself, to get Willy's attention.

"Mr. Frazier. I need some things."

"Oh, I'm sorry, Mrs. Misner, what can I get for you today. Wait a minute! Let's see if I can guess. Hmmm, I've got it, two quarts of milk, two loaves of bread, a bag of flour and some baby food. Am I right?"

"Willy, you're amazing! But you missed one thing."

"Aw dang it, I must be loosin' my touch."

"I need a spool of red thread. Oh, and a couple jars of prunes."

Nicole crinkled her nose at the mention of the prunes.

"Mrs. Misner, I don't think little Nicole likes prunes."

Jane was holding Nicole, who leaned over to Willy with her arms stretched toward him.

"You want to help me, Nicki?"

"Me go with you, grandpa Willy."

Jane knew Willy liked having Nicole around. He always lavished her with attention...something her father seldom did. Jane wondered why Willy never married. He was excellent with children. Jane noticed Martha's eyes never left Willy as he disappeared with Nicole down the aisles of goods behind the counter.

"Mother? Mother?"

"Oh Jane, yes, what is it?"

"How do you like Willy's?"

"He's fine, oh, I mean the store is fine."

Jane smiled to herself. A thought came to her. *I wonder if I'll see more of Mama now that she's met Willy.*

Willy returned with Nicole on his shoulders. He placed the goods on the counter, never once taking his eyes away from Martha.

"Mrs. Misner, we found everything you asked for, didn't we Nicki?"

Willy had placed a box of shotgun shells on the counter with the other purchases.

"I didn't ask for those, Willy."

"Your husband ordered these a couple of weeks ago. They came in yesterday."

Jane felt like telling Willy to keep them. The shells were nothing but a painful reminder of the past.

"I'll give them to him. Go ahead and put them on my bill."

"He paid for them. Speaking of the bill, I owe you money. I sold everything you brought in last time. Do you have any of those canned peaches left?"

"I've got plenty of everything. You sold all thirty-six jars?"

"There's nothing left."

"How many jars do you want?"

"I'll take whatever you can spare. Everyone has been asking where I got them."

"You haven't told anyone they came from me have you?"

"No ma'am, I haven't. I'll keep that between you and me."

"Thanks, Willy."

"Let me add all this up. I'll get those two old buzzards to load up your wagon."

This last statement got the attention of the brothers who had settled back into their game of gin. Calvin was not going to let Willy's comment go without retort.

"Just who you calling an old buzzard? We ain't no older than you, you old geezer!"

"Calvin, if you don't want to help these lovely ladies with their packages…"

Henry was chomping at the bit to get his two cents in.

"Calvin, you are an old buzzard. Willy, it would be my pleasure to help these two visions of loveliness with their poke."

This started a whole new argument between the brothers as they approached the counter to haul Jane's purchases to the wagon. Once they went outside, Willy resumed his ciphering.

"Okay, where was I?"

He reached into the pocket of his apron, retrieving the nub of a pencil. He had written down all of the items in his notebook and started adding. This was all of the bookkeeping he required.

"Let me see what we have here? Two loaves of bread at twenty-three cents each, two quarts of milk for twenty-eight cents apiece, five pounds of flour for forty-five cents and a spool of red thread for ten cents. I almost forgot the four jars of prunes for my little princess here. Let's see that will be...two dollars and twelve cents. I owe you four dollars and fifty cents for the canned goods. That leaves a balance of two dollars and thirty-eight cents. Here you go Mrs. Misner."

Jane extended her hand and gratefully accepted the money. The two women gathered the children and made for the door, which was being held open by Calvin this time.

"Thank you, Willy. We'll see you in a couple of days."

Jane turned to leave, letting her mother exit first with the children. The Shiflette brothers bowed to the women as they left. The shotgun shells triggered a memory Jane tried hard to forget. She walked in silence as they crossed 123. Jane knew Martha was dying to speak.

"Can you tell me why it's necessary for you to sell canned goods?"

"I need the money."

"Doesn't Rob give you money to buy groceries?"

"He gives me twenty dollars a week."

"Is that all?"

"He says I should be able to manage on that."

"What is he thinking of? Doesn't he know how much it costs to feed and clothe a wife and three children?"

"He thinks twenty-dollars should do it."

"Does he know you have to supplement your allowance this way?

"No, he doesn't mother, and don't tell him either. I know you. You'll want to lecture him about it."

"If I weren't a woman, I'd do more than lecture him."

"Mother, I'd appreciate you not saying anything to him."

"Someone should beat some sense into him."

"Mother, please?"

"Okay, okay, have it your way. I won't say anything to the man. All I'm saying is someone needs to drive some sense into him."

Martha spent the rest of the afternoon with Jane. She was gone when Rob got home. Her visit gave Jane a chance to unload some of her burden. She wanted Martha to stay for a couple of days, but realized Robert would give her all kinds of grief later. Martha knew it too, making it more difficult to leave.

*****

Jane knew it was only a matter of time before Freddy would feel the bite of his father's belt. It happened on a Saturday, while she was at Willy's. She left the boys with Rob. Jane was approaching the porch when she heard Freddy's screams. Upon entering the house, she saw Rob standing over Freddy, holding the belt.

"I see you've introduced Freddy to your belt."

"They're going to learn to do what I tell them."

"Sometimes I wonder who you are!"

Jane had seen the empty bottle of Old Crow on the end table. She had a good idea where Rob was headed, as he brushed past and left the house. Her main concern was Freddy. She hesitated opening the door to the boys' room, when she heard their muffled voices.

"He didn't smack you more than three times, you got nothing to cry about."

Between sniffs and heaves of breath, Freddy replied.

"Why does he have to use a belt? Other kids get spanked, but not with a belt. Joey Burkes father just uses his hand."

"You're lucky. He usually hits me six or seven times."

"You're bigger than me. When I get big like you, he'll hit me just as much. Why does he hit us?"

"I don't know, Freddy. He's mean."

"I hate him!"

"You better not let Mom hear you say that."

"Well, I do. Why does Mom let him hit us?"

"I don't know, maybe she's afraid too."

Jane understood at that moment her two boys had a common bond. She could hear the hate in their voices as they talked about their father. Now more than ever, she had to find a way to get through to Robert. She would have to stand up to him.

*****

Weeks later Jane was in the kitchen when Robert came in from the garden.

"Jane, if you keep canning everything I won't have fresh produce for my friends."

"I don't care about your cronies. They're not the ones slaving in that garden everyday."

"I pay for everything around here. I have a right to whatever I want from the garden."

"You just want to show off. I bet you even tell everybody you're the gardener."

"You wouldn't know how to grow a garden if it wasn't for me."

"You're really full of yourself. The boys and I ARE the ones doing the growing. When was the last time you set foot in the garden?"

"I'm busy earning a living. Gardening is the least you can do to help out. I'm the head of this house. If I want to take everything you've grown, I will."

"You will not!"

"What did you say?"

"I said, like hell you will! I spend hours over the stove canning. You're not going to give it all away."

Robert went into the pantry and came out with a box full of beans, tomatoes and corn.

"Where are all those jars of jelly and canned fruit?"

As soon as she saw him go into the pantry Jane started to panic. She knew he would wonder what happened to the canned fruits and jellies.

"I...I sold them to Mr. Frazier."

"You did what?"

"I sold a couple of dozen jars to Mr. Frazier."

"Why would you do that, for Christ's sake?"

"Robert, I'd like to see you run this family on twenty dollars a week."

"You mean you did it for the money?"

"Of course."

"That stops immediately. People will think I can't support my family."

Jane's ire was rising.

"If you spent less on shells and shotguns, you could give me more than twenty dollars a week!"

"I don't want you selling anymore stuff to that fat son-of-a-bitch, you understand?"

"Why don't you tell him that to his face. You're nice enough when you want something from him."

"I forbid you to continue with this."

"Fine Robert, if that's what you want. I'll never can another vegetable, or work another minute in that garden. If you want to give produce away, you'll have to grow the garden!"

*****

It was a crisp, fall day and Jane was late getting her tulip and daffodil bulbs planted. The sky was slate gray. Snow in late November was improbable, but not unheard of. She had been stooped over the flowerbed trying without much success, to plant her bulbs. The ground was near frozen and she gave up the effort. The snow started coming down at 7:30pm.

The next morning the boys were the first up.

"Bruce, come and look out the window! It's snowing like sixty out! You think we'll have school?"

"Man I hope not. We can have a ball sledding on the hill."

Robert left for work extra early that morning. He figured on gaining points by showing up for work when most would stay home. Jane turned on the radio, listening for school closings. St. Peter's was closed. The boys ran into the kitchen in various states of dress. Jane had hot bowls of oatmeal and buttered toast ready for them. They wolfed down their breakfast, finished getting bundled up and shot out of the house.

There was a stand of pine trees on the property. Each year the family made their way to a tree that had been singled out for Christmas. The boys had come in for dinner after being out all day. Robert hadn't gotten home, so Jane fed the boys and waited. The boys were getting anxious and wanted to get the tree.

"Mom, can't we get the tree without him?"

"Let's give him another fifteen minutes."

Fifteen minutes turned into a half hour.

"Come on Mom, he's not gonna make it."

"Okay Freddy, we'll go. Get the lantern from the shed and make sure it has plenty of kerosene."

Freddy came into the house a few minutes later ready to go. "Okay, Mom, we're ready!"

"Boys, I can't walk in all of that snow, especially with Nicole."

"Mom, we thought about that. Freddy and I can pull you and Nicki on the sled."

"I'm not so sure that will work, boys. The snow is awful deep. The sled will just sink."

"Me and Freddy will be in front, pulling with the dogs. We'll tramp a path through it. That should make it easier for the sled."

"Let's try it and see."

Jane bundled Nicole up in layer after layer of clothing. The little girl resembled a ball when she was done. All the clothes made Nicki's arms stick almost straight out. The boys wore their wool hats, earmuffs and scarves. Four pairs of socks kept their feet warm inside the galoshes they wore. Pant legs were tucked into their boots to provide additional warmth. Each had on leather jackets with a sweater underneath.

Jane put on several pairs of socks as well, along with her wool coat and knit hat. When the hat was pulled over her ears, her dark brown hair framed cheeks made rosy by the cold air. She let both dogs out. The boys tied them to the front of the sled. Each boy took a collar. Duke and Pat pulled the sled with little effort.

"Mom, look at the dogs run through the snow! Don't they look funny?"

The dogs were breaking a trail in snow up to their bellies. They moved through it like rabbits. The darkness was filled with their excited barking.

"Bruce, don't let them get away from you."

Freddy was barely able to keep up with the dogs and kept falling down.

"Mom, I can't keep up with Bruce, he's taller."

"That's okay, Freddy. You'll catch up to him one of these days."

"I can do anything Bruce can do!"

With that, Freddy tripled his efforts at keeping up with his brother.

Jane sat toward the back of the sled with her feet on the wooden steering bar. She placed Nicole between her legs. The dogs kicked up large clumps of snow, which pelted the passengers.

The snow on the hill was packed from the day's sledding. No longer having to break trail, the dogs outpaced the boys. Jane and Nicole were on a runaway sled. They crested the hill and disappeared. Bruce and Freddy ran to catch up but couldn't. They could hear the screams of their mother and sister as the sled sped down the steep hill. They both yelled after it.

"Hang on Mom, we're coming."

Jane knew what was going to happen. She put both arms around Nicki as the sled streaked past the dogs.

"Oh no, here we go Nicki, I'll hold on to you! Don't worry, ooooooh here we go!"

The boys stood, watching the sled's progress from the top of the hill.

"Come on Freddy, let's catch the sled!"

"I'll beat you down to the bottom!"

"You're dreamin', you little twerp!"

The boys tumbled their way down the hill. They collapsed in a heap next to their mother, sister and dogs. They were all covered with snow from head to toe. The light from the lantern cast a bright yellow glow from where Bruce placed it at the top of the hill. Tree limbs weighted with snow touched the ground. Jane and Nicole made snow angels, as the boys romped with the dogs.

Another yellow glow from the hilltop got Jane's attention. Robert was home.

*****

Robert had targeted his new conquest. Red heads had always fascinated him. Sandy Wilson had dark auburn hair and eyes the color of expensive emeralds. His plans, in her regard, were still in the planning stage. It was too soon to make his first move.

Jane was on Rob's mind more and more. It had been a couple of years since they last had sex. Even though he persisted at renewing their physical intimacy, she was adept at avoiding his efforts. As he drove home, he made a decision. Somehow, some way, Jane would resume her wifely duties.

Rob heard the commotion as he got out of the car. He went into the shed and retrieved a lantern. As he walked toward the laughter, he saw the other lantern on top of the hill. He followed the beacon. Silhouetted against the whiteness of the snow was his wife.

A feeling of loneliness overcame him. He really did love his family. He felt a need to be a part of their fun. He set his lantern next to the other and started his careful decent. Before he knew it, he was on his backside sliding out of control. Rob's hands grappled for purchase, but to no avail. His laughter was genuine and without effort.

Jane stood over her husband as his laughter slowly died.

"What took you so long getting home?"

"Traffic, I see you started without me."

"You know how these boys are? There was no holding them back any longer."

"I got home as fast as I could. I don't see a tree."

Jane hadn't noticed the odor of cheap perfume on Rob's clothes for a while. She suspected, for some time, Rob found comfort in the company of other women. It gave her pause, knowing their relationship had come to this.

Recognizing their master, the dogs charged Robert, knocking him back to the ground. He fell into the snow. The dogs went at him from two sides with their wet tongues.

"Boys, come over and get the dogs, I can't get up."

Bruce and Freddy each grabbed a collar and were pulled into a pile of arms and legs with their father. The three started throwing snow on one another. A melee ensued. Jane had trouble remembering the last time her husband frolicked with Bruce and Freddy. The snow seemed to bring out the little boy in him.

Jane's mind wandered briefly. She felt something cold on her neck. She had become the target for the snowballs. She picked Nicole up and tried to escape the onslaught. There was no escape.

For a time, it seemed the snow washed away the past. The freshness of the outdoors awakened emotions that had been dormant. *Why can't he be this way all of the time?*

They never looked for a tree. Instead, exhausted, they returned to the house. The dogs were even allowed to go in. They peeled layer after wet layer of clothing off. The boys got a fire going under the kettle of soup Jane made earlier. The big cast iron kettle hung from a tripod over the flames. The scene would have made the perfect Christmas card. Everyone was huddled together in front of a roaring fire, listening to Bing on a seventy-eight.

The children went to bed while Robert and Jane sat in front of the fire. A nervous silence separated them. Robert couldn't take his eyes from her. He thought of the decision he'd made on the way home. He felt his excitement growing, as he stared intently at her. She never could hold that stare long. He was rewarded for his effort, as Jane turned her blushing face away.

Robert sensed something different about his wife. Her defenses were relaxed. All he could think about was how beautiful she was. She seemed open and inviting for the first time in over two years. Robert knew his wife had intense needs too. It had been two years since that night. Robert continued to test the water.

"Jane, can I get you something?"

"I'm fine, thank you. Rob?"

"Yes?"

"Why can't everyday be like this?"

"What do you mean?"

"You were so much fun out there. It reminded me of when we were first married. I haven't seen you romp with the boys in…well, a long time. It made me happy to see that."

I've got her now. She wants me.

"I know I've been difficult to live with. The pressures at work have been unbelievable. I can't tell you why I've acted the way I have. Something inside takes control and I lose my temper. I'll try to do better from now on."

"I should have never made a big deal about the stupid shotgun."

"I shouldn't have been sneaky about it."

"That was the problem. You felt you had to keep it from me. You knew I'd react that way. I've thought about this a lot. This whole mess has been my fault."

Rob inched closer to Jane, taking her hands in his.

"Before I fell on my butt and slid down that hill, I was thinking about how much I missed having fun with you and the kids. I've missed you. I'm still very much in love with you. Is there any hope that you could still love me?"

"You haven't talked like this in a long time. Do you really mean it?"

"I mean it, with all of my heart."

Their coupling was more ardent than it had ever been. Jane received her husband with a hunger she had never known. All of the past ugliness was forgotten, as they lay entwined before the fire, husband and wife. Jane wished for a baby from this union. It would help heal old wounds.

*****

Nicki seemed to be obsessed with her mother's swollen belly. At every opportunity she moved her hands over it, feeling for movement.

"Ooooh Mommy! Is that my baby sister?"

"Yes, put your hand riiiight here. Oh! Feel that? Did you feel it?"

"My little sister is waking up from her nap."

"Nicki, it might not be a little girl."

"I wanna a little sister."

"What if it's a little brother?"

"Hmmm, I guess I could play with a little brother. Can I show my little brother how to garden?"

"Of course honey, you can be his teacher. But it might be a little girl."

*****

Jane and Doc Sterns got to the hospital at the same time.

"Where's Rob?"

"He's on his way."

"Somebody needs to talk to that man about his timing. We need to get you ready. When did your water break?

"Just before we got here."

"We don't have a minute to lose. Nurse! Get Mrs. Misner ready. Her little one is ready for action."

They rushed Jane to the delivery room. It didn't take long for things to escalate.

"Nurse! Help me here, quickly! Oh my! That smell is enough to wrinkle a dead man's nose, whew! We need to get this little guy turned around. I don't think we can take another one of those."

"You're a slippery one! I've gotcha now! There's the head! Look out, here it comes, one last big push Jane, come on, give me a big grunt! Good girl, that's it! There, it's a boy, Jane!"

His first utterance to the world at large was a Bronx cheer. As if in punishment for this odoriferous act, the doctor gave his fanny a couple of good whacks. The pungency of his little fart was still in the air as he screamed against the doctor's assault. Noses were still crinkled as a nurse voiced everyone's thoughts.

"Whew, that was nasty!"

The laughter was contagious. Mark Misner had arrived. At eight pounds and fourteen ounces he looked like a wrinkled bowling ball. His mother's expression said it all; *this is the most beautiful baby in the world.* His screaming stopped the moment he was placed in his mother's arms.

*****

Robert invited Sandy to lunch to welcome her aboard. He kept a nervous vigil over the time. Service had been slow at the restaurant and they returned later than normal. Miss Cassidy was waiting for him. Robert tried getting her moved to another department, but without success. She'd been in the department for twenty-years. He knew where Gordon got his information.

Rob started inviting new hires to lunch within their first week of work. He did this for the ugly girls too. His openness about this new practice, helped deflect suspicions concerning his intentions.

"Mr. Misner, it looks like you've missed another one."

"You mean…"

"A neighbor called just a half-hour ago. She was taking Jane to the hospital. You better leave right now."

Robert didn't waste another word as he turned and made for the door. He got to the hospital too late. Jane had given up waiting and gone to sleep. Robert went to check out his new son. They agreed to name him Mark after Jane's father. Robert couldn't keep the smile from his face.

The time had come to bring his wife and new son home. Nicole had been complaining of an upset stomach the entire trip. Freddy was in the back seat picking on her as usual. Robert was about to tell them to keep quiet when he heard Freddy.

"Oh man! Nicole!"

"What's going on back there?"

"Nicole threw up all over me!"

"Nicole, why didn't you say you felt sick?"

Robert's patience was all but gone. He adjusted his mirror, so he could see them in the back seat. They both saw the look in his eyes through the mirror and got quiet. Nicole was afraid to answer.

"Nicole, I said why didn't you say something?"

"My stomach hurt."

"Answer my question young lady or I'll blister your little fanny!"

She thought of the spankings her brothers got. Her father's threat petrified her. Bruce turned in his seat and inspected the damage. He replied for his little sister.

"Dad, you know how she gets car sick."

Freddy couldn't keep quiet about it.

"Yeah, the little brat upchucked all over me and it stinks!"

"Bruce, when we get to the hospital, I want you to clean up this mess. Go to one of the bathrooms and get some wet paper towels. Leave the windows down. Freddy, take your sister into the bathroom and get yourselves cleaned up."

"Yes sir."

Freddy sat there with vomit all over his jacket. He rolled down the window on his side. Robert didn't object, as he was about to gag himself. Keeping his right hand on the wheel he rolled his window down.

"Bruce, roll your window down too. We need to air this car out."

They endured the cold air for another fifteen minutes. They pulled into the parking lot and jumped out. Robert left Bruce in charge as he went to get his wife and new son. Shortly thereafter the children got their first look at their baby brother.

Jane turned the corner to see her children waiting. She couldn't contain her excitement.

"Hi kids! Come over and see your new baby brother."

*****

One week went by to find Robert with Sandy at the Ambassador for the second time. This time, Rob had more than lunch on his mind. Robert had established the Ambassador as his home away from home. The dining room personnel knew him by name. He could tell Sandy was impressed by his notoriety.

"Mr. Misner, thank you for taking me out for my birthday. Two lunches in one week; you're going to spoil me."

"Don't mention it, Sandy. I enjoy getting to know all of the employees I hire."

"I don't understand how you knew it was my birthday?"

"I was a Special Agent. It's also on your application."

"How silly of me, of course it is."

This was part two of his plan. Robert found Sandy Wilson to be impressionable. The really young ones always were. Today Rob would put his plan into high gear.

"Mr. Misner, you seem a little sad. Is there anything wrong?"

"Does it show that much?"

"Is there something I can do?"

"Sandy, please call me Rob, we're not in the office now."

"Okay…Rob. We can do this another time if you're not feeling up to it."

"That's sweet of you, Sandy, but I don't mind. In fact, it's good to have some company at a time like this."

Rob was good at releasing tears at the right moment. Before he finished his sentence, one trickled down his cheek.

"Oh Mr. Mi, er Rob, you're crying. You poor man! What is it?"

"I don't want to burden you with my problems, Sandy."

"Please Rob, I don't mind. Sometimes we all need a sympathetic shoulder. All of my friends say I'm a good listener."

"It's funny, I haven't known you very long but I get that from you, too. I should keep this to myself, it's very personal."

"Rob, you look like you need to talk to someone. I won't say a word to anyone, I promise."

"I don't know how to begin."

Robert opened up the tear ducts a little more.

"Go ahead, you poor man."

Sandy moved over to his side of the booth and put her arm around him for consolation.

"It's my wife."

"You're wife? Is she sick?"

"Two days after coming home from the hospital with our new son, I found out she'd been seeing someone else."

With this, Rob put a hand over his face to conceal the anguish.

"That's awful! Are you sure? I mean couldn't you be mistaken?"

"One of my friends in Maplesville saw her leave the MI with a strange man."

"The MI. What's the MI?"

"I'm sorry, the local no tell motel; the Maplesville Inn."

"Your wife must be crazy. Playing around on a good looking man like you."

"You're just trying to make me feel better."

Sandy inched closer to Robert and put her other arm around him.

"No, I'm not. You're one of the most handsome men I've ever met. A lot of the girls have a big crush on you."

"Now I know you're fibbing. Sandy you're sweet for saying that, but you're just a child. What would your father think if he could hear you talking like that?"

"My father? I'm a twenty-two year old woman and my father has nothing to say about what I do. In fact…"

Sandy pulled Rob's face to hers and kissed him hard on the mouth. Robert didn't touch her. He let her arms embrace him. He feigned shock as their lips parted. Her whisper was barely audible.

"Is that the kiss of a little girl?"

Robert looked down at her, brushing stray strands of red hair away from her eyes and kissed her forehead.

"We better get back to the office."

"Rob, I'm sorry. I didn't mean to…I mean…"

"Sandy, it's all right, really. I know you were just trying to make me feel better. But I better get you back, before I decide to take advantage of you."

"I wouldn't mind if you did."

"Sure you would, plus, I'd hate myself in the morning."

"But your wife is cheating on you!"

"I have to think of the children, not myself."

"Your wife is out of her mind."

Robert kept his distance from Sandy for a week. The time was right for him to play his trump card. One night Rob stayed well back of his fellow workers as they hurried from the building. He watched as the parking lot emptied, leaving only Sandy behind with a car that wouldn't start. Rob started for his car, pretending not to notice the girl. Seeing Rob, she popped out of her car and asked him for help.

"Rob, my car won't start. Can you take a look at it for me?"

"Sure Sandy, pull the hood latch."

Rob raised the hood, pretending to know what he was doing as he banged around the engine compartment.

"Okay, try and start it."

There was nothing. Of course, Rob knew there wouldn't be. He paid the attendant five dollars to loosen one of the sparkplug wires.

"Try it again."

This time the engine came to life.

"Thank you so much. I don't know what I would have done without you."

"I'm sure someone else would have been able to help you."

"But someone else didn't, you did."

"How far do you have to go?"

"To Arlington."

"Can you get one of your friends to follow you home in case you have any trouble?"

This last statement was well timed, as the parking lot was just about empty.

"Do you think I'll have more trouble?"

"I don't think so, but cars can be very temperamental machines. You never know. Besides, it's getting dark out. I'd hate to see you stranded on Shirley Highway."

"I never thought of that."

Robert looked at his watch and made a turn as if he was leaving, but added over his shoulder.

"It'll be all right. I doubt you'll have any problems. I'll see you tomorrow."

"Rob! Wait, wait a minute! Now I'm scared! I know this is a big favor, but could you follow me home."

"I don't suppose that will take me too far out of my way."

"Thank you, Rob! I really appreciate it."

Both cars pulled into the high-rise parking lot. Robert rolled his window down as Sandy got out of her car. She came over to his open window.

"Rob, I don't know how to thank you."

Robert yawned, putting his hand over his mouth he replied,

"Wow, I must be tired. I haven't been getting much sleep lately. I better stop by the Mighty Mo and get a cup of coffee before I go home. I was glad to help you, Sandy. Have a nice night."

Robert's car started easing from its parking space. Sandy held up her hand for him to stop.

"Robert Misner, you get out of that car and I'll make you a cup of coffee. After all, it's the least I can do for taking you out of your way."

"Sandy, that's really not necessary. I'll be fine."

This time, the yawn was much longer. He rubbed his eyes for effect.

"Nonsense! Look how tired you are. Now, get out of that car and I'll make you the best cup of coffee you ever had."

Robert entered the apartment behind her. She took his coat and disappeared into the kitchen. He made himself comfortable and waited. He heard the sound of pots rattling and then the click-clack of high heels on the wood floor. Ten minutes went by.

"Do you need some help?"

The answer came from down the hall.

"No Rob, I have it under control. I'll be right out."

"Okay."

"I'm coming."

He picked up a magazine. Sandy returned a moment later wearing nothing. She said;

"I have a better idea."

"I can see that!"

She was beautiful. Rob reached for her arm, pulling her to him. It was obvious that Sandy wasn't new to this. They ignored the whistling coffee pot.

Robert drove home, feeling good about himself. *Information gathering, planning and flawless execution are the three elements to a successful operation. I'll have to use this one again.* His relationships with women from the office never were meant to last more than a couple of months.

Robert would start looking for Sandy's replacement in a couple of weeks. The old cheating wife story worked well. Breaking it off would be easy. All he'd have to do is tell Sandy he was going to give his wife another chance…for the kids' sake.

*****

Finally, Rob gave permission to Jane to start house shopping. Jane combed through the paper everyday. Every house she picked, Rob nixed. Jane wondered if he was serious about getting a house. She was beginning to think this was his way of pacifying her. She was disappointed he didn't share her excitement.

Jane found what she thought was the perfect house. It was a three bedroom colonial near Tyson's Corner. She liked the quaintness of Tyson's Corner. It boasted two country stores, Brownsteins and Zirkles. Except for the meat locker and two gas stations, the Haskins Farm dominated the remaining acreage.

The house met all of Rob's requirements, if only he'd look at it. The yard included a small orchard with several varieties of fruit trees. There was an enormous locus tree perfect for her boys, along with an open area suitable for a large vegetable garden.

Rob agreed to meet the real estate agent with Jane.

"Rob, there it is; Horseshoe Drive, turn right. See it, the first one on the left; isn't it beautiful!"

Rob pulled in front of the house. The agent waited on the front porch, as the couple got out of the car.

"Mr. and Mrs. Misner, I'm happy you made it."

Rob didn't bother with niceties. He didn't like salesmen and felt no need to be congenial. His terse reply came in the form of a question.

"What are they asking?"

"Mr. Misner, don't you want to see it first?"

"If it's too much, I won't look at all, so let's cut through the crap, shall we?"

"Of course, the owner is asking $12,000."

"Twelve thousand dollars! That's way too high."

"The house is priced about a thousand below market. The owner got transferred and has to sell."

"If he has to sell, he'll take less."

"Mr. Misner, he won't come down any further. He priced it low to sell it quickly. Why don't you and your wife take a look around? I have another couple coming for a look shortly."

Jane got a panicked look on her face as she turned to Rob.

"Rob, I don't want to lose the house to someone else!"

Rob wasn't going to make this easy on her.

"Jane, I thought you said the property was landscaped? All I see is a lot of grass and some fruit trees."

"It'll be beautiful Rob. I already know where I'll plant flower gardens and shrubs."

"This is going to cost a bundle to landscape."

The agent was bluffing about the other party. Robert noticed his nervousness when he started to balk. Robert knew he had him. *This guy doesn't know whom he's dealing with.*

"But sir, most people do their own landscaping anyway. Isn't that part of the fun in moving into a new house? If you don't like cutting grass, I can recommend a couple of neighborhood boys."

"Fun! Who said anything about having fun? I'm doing this to shut my wife up."

"Mr. Yancy, that's not true. Rob is just pulling your leg, aren't you honey?"

"I think Mr. Yancy knows who will be making this decision. Don't you, Yancy?"

"Of course Mr. Misner, you are."

"That's right. If you want to make a sale, you'll convince them to lower the price."

"Sir, I've already explained. The owner isn't willing…"

"Come on now! Who in the Hell do you think you're dealing with? Give me the name of the owner and I'll talk to him."

"That's not possible, he's been transferred overseas."

"How were you going to finalize the contract if he's not around?"

"His wife has Power of Attorney until he returns from Korea."

"A military man, eh?"

"Yes sir, Gunnery Sergeant Marvin Hill is a Marine."

"Hill, my son plays little league with a kid by that name."

The agent saw a ray of hope.

"Mrs. Hill and her son are going to live with her parents until her husband returns."

Rob didn't want it getting around town that he was a push over for a sad story. He kept pressing the agent on the price.

"I don't want to take advantage of a woman, especially with her husband off to war, but I have my own family to consider."

"Mr. Misner, they're not building new houses these days on two acre plots. You're lucky if you get a half acre."

"Rob, he's right. Look how big the yard is. You'll have plenty of room for your dogs."

Jane had planned on doing a little selling of her own and knew just what Rob would respond to.

"Tell the seller I won't give more than $11,500 take it or leave it."

It was spring of 1951 when the Misners moved into the house. Jane's enthusiasm was diminished by Robert's attitude. Since Mark's birth, his behavior reverted to that of the past. It started with yelling, then swats with his open hand. Jane knew the belt would be next. She also started checking his clothes for those tell tale odors. She was sure something was amiss. Their sex became more infrequent. That wasn't like Rob.

*****

Baseball season was approaching. His sons had proven their talent the previous year. Little League coaches fought over which team Bruce and Freddy would play on.

Robert basked in the glow of their notoriety and pushed them relentlessly. An evening didn't go by that Robert didn't take the boys in the backyard to practice. He knew their abilities were far greater than his at the same age. He couldn't help be a little jealous.

Rob's practices weren't fun. He was intolerant of any lapses of concentration.

"Goddamn it Bruce, how many times do I have to show you how to swing?"

Robert stormed up to his son and smacked him in the head with his glove while grabbing the bat. The glove hit Bruce in the eye. Bruce put his hand up to the eye and rubbed it.

"Ow! You hit me in the eye. I can't open it."

"Quit being a baby. Watch how I swing again. Freddy, pay attention, this is for you too."

"Hold the bat up and step into the ball as you swing. Swing level, not up. Quit rubbing your eye."

"I told you, it hurts. I can't open it."

"Don't talk back to me or I'll give you something to cry about."

"I'm not crying."

"I said don't talk back to me again!"

Robert hit Bruce across the other side of his face with his open hand bringing a welt to his left cheek. Every time they practiced with their father one of them got hit for not performing up to snuff. Rob attributed this tactic to their improvement. Despite these experiences, the boys still loved playing ball.

Not even the delectable Brandi could keep Rob away from his sons' ball games. He loved sitting in the stands gloating over their accomplishments. No sooner had Rob walked in the front door, than he yelled upstairs for the boys.

"Get down here boys, we're going to be late for the game!"

The boys were putting on their uniforms while they talked.

"Bruce, I think I liked it better when he left us alone."

"Yeah, I know what you mean. I never know what to expect anymore. Come on let's get ready, we don't want him having a heart attack cause we're late."

"Wouldn't that be great? All of our problems would be over."

"With our luck, he'll live forever."

"Boys, get a move on, we're gonna be late, let's go!"

"Yes sir, we're coming!"

Everyone piled into the car. On the way, Robert issued directives for yard work after the game.

"Freddy, when we get home you need to finish painting the shutters. Bruce, I want you scraping and sanding the back porch so we can paint it tomorrow."

Jane's irritation with Rob had reached its limit.

"Robert, why do you have to push them so hard? Why can't the boys have some time to themselves?"

"Look Jane, you're the one that's been after me to paint the house. Well, we're painting. Don't you want to be proud of the way it looks?"

"Of course I do, but…"

"But nothing! Once we're done with all the work, the boys will have plenty of time to have fun."

"That's fine Rob, but you've been working them non-stop. The only break they get is when they have a ball game."

"It is not, is it boys? Don't I take you out to the field every night to practice?"

"Yes, sir."

"Practice! Is that what you call it? You work them harder at practice than you do around the house."

"They know if they want to be the best, they have to work hard, right boys?"

"Yes, sir."

"Besides, they enjoy the time with their old man, right boys?"

"Yes, sir."

"See Jane, as usual you don't know what you're talking about."

"Forget I said anything, there's no talking to you."

*****

By 1952, they had been in the house for a year. Robert was driven to have the nicest yard in the neighborhood. The boys toiled endlessly to that end. If their work didn't stand up to Rob's scrutiny, they were punished. Most of the time a strong tongue-lashing was all they received. The heavy belt was only used on special occasions.

Jane confided with her new friend across the street, Louise Scolnik, whenever the stress seemed intolerable. Jane thought things would improve once they got their own house. If anything, things were worse. Robert was obsessed with the house. His temper would explode into screaming fits if things weren't perfect. Jane knew the neighbors got an earful.

Jane had Louise over for their morning coffee. The conversation centered on their kids. Bruce and Freddy had come in for a glass of cold water.

"Boys, are you finished with the pruning already?"

"Mom, Freddy and I have been at it for over an hour and it's too hot. Can we finish tomorrow?"

"What about the watering? You know how your father is about watering the garden?"

"Come on Mom, it's too hot. We watered yesterday. Why do we have to do it today?"

"Because, your father said so."

"Mom, can't you talk to him. We never have any time to do stuff with our friends."

"Finish the weeding today and do the watering tomorrow."

The boys returned to their drudgery.

"Janey girl, I feel sorry for those boys. What kind of father works his children that way?"

"Rob, that's who."

"I don't know how you put up with a man like that."

"I don't know what's wrong with him. He's always been demanding, but since we moved here, he's become obsessed. He's worse than his mother ever was. I'm going to try to get through to him tonight."

"Good luck! You've got your work cut out for you."

It was five thirty when Jane heard the car door slam. Rob's smoker's cough trumpeted his presence as he walked through the front door.

"Did the boys get all of their work done?"

"Rob, we need to talk."

"What about? Did the boys do their work or not?"

"It was too hot, so I let them…"

"You mean they didn't do what I explicitly told them to do? Where are they? Boys, get down here right now!"

"Rob, wait a minute, it's my fault. I told them it would be okay if they…"

"I don't care what you told them! I told them they had to do the weeding and watering! Boys, I'm not going to call you again! Get down here this minute!"

Robert had his belt off by the time Bruce and Freddy got downstairs.

"You two know better than to disobey me! Why didn't you finish your work?"

Bruce spoke up first.

"Mom said we could finish tomorrow."

"Your mother isn't in charge of this house, I am. When I tell you to do something, you do it. You don't go running to your mother."

Bruce tried covering up with his hands. Robert was swinging the belt wildly. Bruce received lashes all over. Robert moved his attentions to Freddy. After a few minutes he stopped.

"Are you two going to disobey me again?"

"No, sir."

"I better not come home tomorrow night and find your work half done."

Jane couldn't take anymore.

"Robert, how can you treat your sons this way?"

"I'm not hurting them! See, they're not even crying!"

Robert strapped them each again to demonstrate his point.

"I said stop hitting my boys! How do you like it?"

Jane had gone into the room armed with her own belt. She started lashing at Robert with a ferocity exceeding his. She swung, hitting him with the buckle. She was rewarded by the trickle of blood on Robert's cheek. Rob hit her with the back of his hand. Jane spun from the impact, hitting the floor with a thud.

"How dare you hit me, bitch! You better stay down, unless you want another one! When are you going to learn not to interfere?"

Jane tried to rise, but Robert used his foot to push her back to the floor.

"I don't know why I ever married you! You're an awful father and a worse husband! I wish you'd leave and never come back!"

"Fine, fine! I'm leaving now! Let's see how you do without any money!"

The next morning Louise came over to get Mark and Nicole. Jane appreciated having some time to herself. Before he left with Louise, Mark climbed onto his mother's lap, giving her a hug and kiss.

"I love you, Mommy."

"I love you too. Have fun playing with Lonnie. Do you know where we're going tomorrow?"

"To see Smokey!"

"That's right honey, to see Smokey. Now go with momma Louise and have fun."

"Bye, Mommy!"

Jane watched Louise take her two children across the street. Her eyelids fluttered and a single tear traced its moist path down her cheek, as she thought of her husband. *Maybe I should divorce him. I can start practicing my typing and shorthand. I could take the Civil Service Test. After last night, I don't care if I ever see him again.*

Jane finished her morning chores and decided to take a break. She found watching the children at play helped her relax. She sat on the front porch, listening to the song her little boy sang.

"Smokey the bear, Smokey the bear..."

PART THREE

Jane felt the impact of Robert's blow. Her eyes fluttered open, taking in her sterile surroundings. She remembered watching her children. Jane's scream pierced the hallway. Everything came back, the green car, her baby…the blood.

Nurses on duty rushed to Jane's room.

"Mrs. Misner, what is it? Are you okay, can I get you anything?"

"Get me? I don't want you to get me anything! Is my little boy alive?"

"Yes ma'am. He's in surgery now. Should I get your husband?"

Jane placed her fingers on the welt covering the side of her face.

The nurse diverted her eyes pretending not to notice the ugly bruise.

"Mrs. Misner, do you want to see your husband, or should I tell him you're asleep?"

Jane struggled with the answer, not knowing what she wanted from Robert.

*****

Robert looked at his watch. He had been in the hospital chapel for over three hours. He was scared. His legs were numb from kneeling. He placed his hands firmly on the pew in front of him and pushed up. His legs tingled as he tried to stand. He eased himself back into the pew, rubbing feeling back into his legs. He rose slowly.

As he stood in front of the cross, he nodded in thanks to God for showing him where he went wrong. Robert believed God had opened the door to the past and made him walk through. The result, he remembered every detail of his married life up to this point.

He remembered why he was in the hospital. His Scorch was at death's door. Robert's reflection on the past made him take a good look at the kind of man he had become. He found himself thinking of his father. He knew his dad would disapprove of a man that beat his wife and kids.

Something in Rob's mind snapped. For the first time he accepted responsibility for his actions. He especially remembered that night almost four years ago. The night he raped his wife. Their relationship started its downward spiral that night.

It was not all his fault. His mother had to shoulder some of the blame. Hilda poisoned him against his own family. Robert thought of his family and what they must be going through. The vision of his wife's blood mingling with that of his son's made him desperate to see her.

It's not too late for me. I can have my family back. I can change. I have to change. I will change! Please God! Don't take my wife and boy away from me!

Robert left the chapel with new purpose. He almost ran the doctor over as he exited the chapel.

"Doctor! Can I see my wife? Is she awake?"

"She just woke up, but the nurses are with her. Why don't you give it a few more minutes?"

"What about my son?"

"Mr. Misner, you need to sit down."

"He's not dead?"

"Your son is in surgery. That little guy is a fighter. By all reason, he should not have lived through that awful accident. X-rays showed a piece of his skull pressing on his brain. We need to relieve the pressure to stop brain swelling. The surgeons are finishing that up. If successful, his chances of survival will increase significantly."

"Doctor, do whatever you have to do to save my Scorch!"

"Scorch? The name fits him. We're doing our best."

"You have to do more than your best!"

"You realize, this isn't the only surgery he'll need?"

"What else is wrong?"

"He's got several broken bones, along with numerous internal injuries. By comparison, the rest are minor. We'll deal with them, once he gets through with this big one."

"I understand."

"I'll check back with you when he comes out."

"I'll be right here."

As Robert entered the waiting room, he saw two men looking his way expectantly. Rob approached them. One was just a boy.

"Mr. Misner, my name is Paul Layton, Jimmy's father."

"Do I know you?"

"We've never met. We live on the other end of the drive from you."

Robert's attention was centered on the boy. He couldn't have been more than sixteen or seventeen. The young man met Robert's stare straight on. Rob was a little unnerved by the steadiness. The boy's eyes were black and penetrating. All at once Robert knew who this was.

"Son, you're the one that hit my boy."

"Yes sir, I am."

"You've come to see how he is?"

"Yes sir, but sir?"

"Yes?"

"I wanted to tell you how sorry I am for the accident. It was my fault. I wasn't paying enough attention. It should have never happened."

Robert wanted to strangle the life from this kid. He could see the boy's resolve begin to weaken. His shoulders slumped and he bowed his head. Rob placed a hand on Jimmy's shoulder. For once, Rob's good side prevailed.

"Jimmy, I appreciate your coming here like this. It takes a real man to accept responsibility."

"Mr. Misner, is he...is he..."

"No he's not...dead. The doctors are operating. All we can do is wait."

"Thank God he's still alive. Sir, I'll pray that he'll pull through."

"The chapel is across the hall. It's a good place to think things out."

The boy and his father made their way across the hall. Robert found his wife's room. He was reluctant as he stood outside. What do I say to her? How can I convince her about my love for her and the kids? Does she still love me? I wouldn't blame her if she didn't. Rob gently rapped on her door.

The nurse opened the door to see Robert standing there.

"My goodness! Speak of the devil. Mrs. Misner, it seems I won't have to go far to find your husband, he's right here. I think he wants to see you."

*****

Jane noticed Robert tentatively squeeze past the nurse. He seemed unsure of himself. Jane could see his mouth moving. She was vaguely aware of sounds, but wasn't listening. His words didn't seem important. She was still deep in thought. How could my life turn into such a mess? We were happy once. I even forgave him for that night. I accepted blame for it. That wasn't good enough. I thought we found each other the night of the big snow.

Jane's fingers were tracing the outline of the welt. This didn't go unnoticed. Rob stopped talking. Jane was attracted by his sudden silence. She looked up at him. Robert shied back when he saw the uncertainty on her face.

Jane saw self-doubt in his eyes. He looked shaken, grief stricken...vulnerable. She had too much compassion to be angry. She reached a hand out. Robert rushed to her side. He gently kissed her hand.

"Jane, how can you ever forgive me?"

"Forgive you?"

"Yes, forgive me. I thought I lost you. God spoke to me and told me to change. I realized how much I love you. I couldn't bear losing you. He made me see that. He made me think about that night...that night I...I did that awful thing. Will you ever forgive me?"

Jane was not imagining this. Her husband was on his knees at her side, pleading for forgiveness. His sincerity seemed genuine, but she'd been fooled before. The best actor could not duplicate the emotions flooding from him. She took his hand and tenderly kissed it.

*****

The next day, Jimmy went back to the accident scene. Someone had tried to wash away the blood. He could still see the smears on the road. He would never forget those smears. He couldn't get it out of his mind. He put his hand up to the pocket holding the flower. He could feel it beneath the material of his shirt. He would keep it as a reminder of the debt he owed.

Freddy saw Jimmy from the front window and went outside.

"Jimmy, are you okay?"

Jimmy had to think who this boy was. He recognized him from yesterday.

"Freddy, right?"

"Yeah."

"Thanks for trying to make me feel better yesterday. How's your little brother?"

"My father called Mrs. Scolnik this morning. They operated on his brain. They're not sure what will happen. My father said he was in surgery for over six hours."

There wasn't anything for Jimmy to say, so he started back home.

"Jimmy!"

The teenager turned around.

"Yeah Freddy, what is it?"

"How come you're not driving your cool car?"

"I can't. I just can't. See you later, Freddy."

*****

His skull was fractured in three places. One of the fractures involved severe brain trauma. His little body was encased in plaster. Weeks turned into months, as his broken body mended. Jane spent every day at his side. Robert stopped by each night on the way home to pick his wife up. He marveled at his son's toughness.

At first, the sight of his atrophied limbs caused his parents great concern. The Scorch's body responded well to the physical therapy. It wasn't long before he was walking, then running down the hallways.

After six months of hospitalization, the Scorch was home.

The extensive head injury was the only concern. Monthly sessions with a neurologist and child psychologist would be necessary for several years. Brain scans could only chart Scorch's physical progress. Interaction with other children would be the real test. None of doctors knew what to expect.

After the first test, the doctor expressed his amazement at the test results.

"Mrs. Misner, your son seems to have had an amazing recovery. All of his brain functions appear normal. There are a couple slight abnormalities we need to watch."

"Are you saying he'll be retarded?"

"No ma'am. It might take him longer to grasp things than normal children."

"Normal children? You are saying he will be retarded!"

"I didn't say that. I said he might be a slow learner, that's all. Consider yourself very fortunate. It's a miracle he's even alive, not to mention normal."

"Then he is normal."

"Yes ma'am, he is quite normal. I am sorry if you misunderstood."

Jane and her son stopped by Robert's office on the way home to give him Mark's status report. They stopped at the security desk before going up to Rob's office.

"Hello, Mrs. Misner! How are you today? Who's that big fella with you, your boyfriend?"

"Good afternoon Sergeant Baxter, we're fine, how are you? You remember Mark. Say hello to the Sergeant, Mark."

"Hello, Sergeant Baxter. Is that a real gun?"

"It sure is, Mark. Doesn't your daddy have a real gun?"

"Yeeeah, but I don't get to play with it."

"Your daddy is right, a gun is not a toy to play with."

"I have guns and I shoot Lonnie with them all the time."

"Is Lonnie your friend?"

"My best friend. We play Roy Rogers everyday."

"I bet you're Roy, aren't you? Who plays Dale?"

Mark frowned not understanding what the man meant. He noticed his mother laughing with the policeman, so he laughed too.

"I'm here to see Rob. Is he back from lunch?"

"Yes ma'am. I'll call up for you."

The guard dialed the phone.

"Mr. Misner, you have a pretty lady and a fine looking young gentleman down here to see you. Should I send them on up? You'll come down? Okay then, I'll have them wait here for you. Ma'am, he says he's coming down."

"Thank you, Sergeant Baxter."

Five minutes later, Robert appeared at the foot of the stairs with his suit coat slung over his shoulder.

"Hi honey, I decided it's a perfect day for a ballgame. It's time I introduced the Scorch to baseball. If we hurry, we can make it before the first pitch."

"Mark, your daddy's going to take us to see the Senators. Who are they playing?"

"The Yankees, of course."

"Mark, you and I can root for the Nats. Your daddy can root for those nasty Yankees."

The three boarded the streetcar at 11th & 'E' and got off at Sixth and Florida.

The Scorch didn't know what to expect. He knew about baseball some. His older brothers played it in the yard with their friends. Mark knew his daddy took his brothers to games. He tried to sit with them while they watched on TV, but got bored quickly.

Seeing a major league ballpark for the first time was something he'd never forget. The P.A. announcer was introducing the starting lineups as they approached the portal. The field wasn't visible yet, but Mark could feel the excitement.

"Hear that Scorch? They're announcing the starting lineups. Did you hear them say Mickey Mantle?"

"Who's Mickey?"

"He's the best player in baseball."

Robert put the Scorch on his shoulders as they walked through the portal, giving Mark his first look at a big league field. In his excitement, Mark was pointing at everything at once. Nothing went unnoticed as he asked his father one question after another.

"Oooooooh, look Mommy! Look at the grass; it's pretty! Daddy, where are the cow pies?"

"Yes Daddy, where are the cow pies?"

Jane framed the question louder than she needed, knowing it would get the attention of others. It had the desired effect. In unison, everyone in earshot asked Robert where the cow pies were.

"Scorch, they only use cow pies in the Minors. This is the Big Leagues. They use real bases, see the white things that look like pillows?"

"Daddy, see the giant big bottle?"

Mark was pointing to the huge billboard of National Bohemian Beer towering over the green wall in left-center field. After about the fourth inning, Mark fell asleep on his father's lap. Robert nudged Jane with his elbow.

"Looks like I'll get to watch part of the game after all."

"This has been a big day for him, he's exhausted."

In the eighth inning, Robert caught a Mantle foul ball. He took the prize to the dugout where the 'Mick' autographed it. Robert had a big smile on his face as he showed the ball to Jane.

"You think Bruce will like it?"

"Are you kidding? Mickey Mantle is his hero, he'll love it!"

*****

Mark's curly blonde hair was back. Jane decided it was time to have an official 'welcome back' party for him. More than two-dozen friends and relatives showed up for the party. Jane was running around trying to get last minute details done.

"Robert, they'll be here any minute. Are you ready with the lights and camera?"

"Just about ready, where's the Scorch?"

"Nicki is getting him ready."

"Jane are you sure you want all of our friends gawking at him?"

"Are you kidding? All of his hair is back longer and curlier than ever! He's adorable! I can't wait to show him off!"

Ever since he'd come home from the hospital, Mark had gotten all of the attention. The only attention Nicole got from her father was when her little brother misbehaved. Then she got yelled at.

"Sit still, Mark! I'm supposed to comb your hair."

As Nicki ran the brush through his hair he kept squirming, trying to get away from her.

"Sit still Mark, I have to do this, or I'll get in trouble."

All her mother and father ever did anymore was talk about how cute Mark was with his curly blonde hair. Nicole had an idea of how to fix her little brother's hair.

"Jane, get the front door; I'm still fussing with these lights."

"Hi everyone, come on in. Robert is in the dining room fooling with his lights. We wanted to get a picture of Mark and his curly blonde hair. Wait until you see it!"

"Nicole, bring your little brother down!"

Nicki didn't answer, so Jane went to see what was keeping her. She opened her bedroom door and stared in amazement.

"Nicki, what have you done?"

"Jane? What's going on up there? Are the kids ready? What's taking so long?"

"We're coming!"

As Jane entered the room, she saw Nicole holding scissors. Mark's blonde curls lay in tufts all around him. Nicole's solution to all the attention given Mark, was summed up in one word...haircut. The hair that went where it wanted went where Nicki wanted. Jane scooped up the Scorch, took Nicki in hand and went down to her guests.

Robert was the first to speak.

"My God! What happened?"

"It seems someone was a little j-e-a-l-o-u-s of all the attention Mark has been getting."

"Jane, look at him!"

Robert gave Nicole a look that had almost been forgotten by the children. The little girl was suddenly petrified. She remembered the sound of the belt hitting her brothers.

No one knew who started laughing first, but it became contagious. Nicole shied from her father as he reached for her. Lifting her above the crowd, Robert proclaimed Nicki to be his new barber. She could be heard giggling above the din as her daddy placed her on his shoulders.

As fast as it started, the laughter stopped. Still in his mother's arms, his baldness revealed what his curls had hidden...scars. People stared in morbid fascination at the evidence of the accident. Jane broke the uneasy silence.

"Looks like a bad game of tic-tac-toe."

The cork had been removed. Months of bottled up questions came flooding forth. Nicki, having been set down by her father, looked up from among the forest of legs. She was puzzled as to why Mark was still the center of attention.

*****

Robert worked tirelessly with Bruce and Freddy. Their baseball talents came naturally. Bruce idolized all of the Yankees, especially Mickey Mantle. Robert took the boys to all of the Yankee games when they were in town. By the end of the season, Bruce had gotten the entire team to autograph his ball. It was his favorite possession.

Robert had found a common tie with his boys. His favorite memories of his dad were of baseball. The sport would bind his sons to him.

"Come on Dad, we're going to be late for the game!"

"You said we could get to the park early, for batting practice. Maybe Mantle will hit fungoes at the beer sign again."

"Give me a minute boys, I'll be right there."

"Robert, why don't you take Mark with you?"

"I'll take the Scorch next time. Besides, he's playing with Lonnie."

"He'll be disappointed."

"He'll be fine. I'll take him to the park tomorrow and let him hit some balls with his older brothers; he'll like that."

"Dad!"

"Okay Freddy, I'm coming. Honey, we gotta go, bye!"

As they drove away, Jane couldn't help thinking of the difference in Rob.

Louise was almost run over as they sped toward Rt. 123.

"Janey, how are you doin' this fine day?"

"Hi Louise, things couldn't be better."

"Where are your men folk off to in such a hurry?"

"A ballgame."

"I don't know what got into Robert, but he sure has turned the corner ain't he?"

"He's been wonderful; just like the man I married."

"What about his mother, any more problems?"

"After all these years, Robert has learned to stand up to her. Now she's even bearable, although, I keep waiting to see the old Hilda make a comeback. You know, a leopard never changes its spots."

"Well, let's hope that's an exception in Robert's case."

"Robert isn't like his mother. There was always good in him. Hilda was born mean and vindictive. Let's not talk about that. Those days are gone forever."

"Whatever you say sweetie. How about fixing old toothless here a cup of your good iced tea?"

"Okay, we can have it in the rose garden."

The rose bushes were planted around a square arbor. Under the arbor were chairs and side tables where Jane entertained her friends. It was a beautiful setting for afternoon chats with her friends. These visits gave her a chance to relax and catch up on neighborhood gossip. The only embarrassment was the dog pens.

The pens were impossible to ignore, if not their appearance, then certainly their odor. The smell hung in the air, especially on hot, muggy days. She tried mitigating the odor by planting peppermint around them. All this did was make her friends raise their eyebrows when they saw fresh peppermint in their tea.

"Girl you have a special talent for gardening. Your roses are beautiful!"

"Thanks Louise, they take a lot of care, much like children. Speaking of children…"

"Naw! You ain't pregnant again?"

"Yep!"

"You two sure did get it turned around. I'm real happy for you Janey girl, real happy!"

Robert was as tight as ever with money. This time, Jane knew it was because of the accident. Mark's medical bills were through the roof. Rob's insurance covered about 80% of the bills. Jimmy Layton had no money, being only seventeen. Mr. Layton sent Rob a few dollars each month, but bus drivers don't make much.

Now with four children and a fifth on the way, twenty dollars a week didn't come close to being enough. Rob allowed Jane to have a Washington Shopping Plate. The card was good at all nine DC department stores. An occasional argument would break out over her spending. She'd curb her shopping activity for a while, but it never lasted long. She didn't want money to come between them now that their life had changed for the better.

Jane was getting as big as a house. She noticed Robert wasn't too interested in having sex with her. Looking at her swollen belly, she could understand Rob's lack of interest. She decided not to worry about it, outwardly at least. Inwardly was another story.

*****

Robert's will power was all but gone. *I wonder what Brandi is up to.* He stopped by the Slipper after work one night. A familiar voice greeted him.

"Where have you been Marco Polo?"

"Off to the orient, my dear Brandi."

"We thought you must have expired. It's been a long time."

"I wanted to see if anything has changed. Everything appears to be in its right place, including you, gorgeous."

"Honey, you know I've got to take care of the equipment, it's all I got."

"Baby, it's just what I need, too."

"Come back with me, handsome. Let's see if you've still go it!"

As she led him to the curtained room, his mind was busy justifying his decision. *This will put some excitement back into my life. This one time won't hurt anything.*

Her body wore better than her face. The years of boozing and sleepless nights had taken their toll on Brandi's face. Robert couldn't take his eyes from the deep lines around her eyes and mouth. His stares didn't go unnoticed.

"What's the matter, honey?"

"Oh, nothing, nothing at all. You look terrific."

"Terrific! Well whoopty-do!"

"Really, baby, you look just like you did the last time I saw you."

"Thanks for trying honey, but your bullshit won't work on me like it does your wife. I can see right through you. Now…"

Brandi let the satin dressing gown drop to the floor. Robert noticed a few sags that were not there before but all in all the prostitute still looked sexy. At least she didn't have a big fat belly.

"I never could bullshit you, could I? Yeah baby, you're looking a little long in the tooth, but I'm sure you've still got what it takes."

Brandi undid Robert's belt and opened his pants. No preliminaries were necessary. She eased him down on the bed and straddled him. He slammed into her repeatedly, as if this was his first time. With his final thrust, Rob glanced at his watch and knew it was time to get back to work.

As Robert opened the door to exit the Slipper, he saw a group from work. They passed within ten feet of him. He let them get comfortably ahead before walking back to the office. His mind ran through possible scenarios as he shadowed them.

What if they saw me? What if they say something to Gordon? Rob had just made it back into Gordon Starling's good graces. He remembered Gordon's suspicions of a few years ago. Gordon never came right out and said he knew about Sheila, but Rob knew he did.

Robert had been back from his lunchtime rendezvous for a couple of hours. He thought he was in the clear. Mrs. Cassidy's voice chirped over his intercom.

His stomach knotted with tension as he listened.

"Mr. Misner, Mr. Gordon would like to see you in his office."

Before he got up, he reached in his drawer for the bottle, but thought better of it. *Gordon will smell it.* Robert knocked on Gordon Starling's door.

"Robert, come in and sit down."

"Sure Gordon, what can I do for you?" *Gordon seems to be in an okay mood. Maybe this is about something else.*

"Robert, were you at the Silver Slipper during lunch?"

Oh shit, I knew I shouldn't have done it.

"I have no idea what you are talking about?"

"Several people saw you. It's very unlikely they would be telling tales."

"Who said I was in that place?"

"No one, Rob. I overheard the conversation as they came in from lunch."

Now what? There is no pleasing this asshole! The guy puts me on probation, threatens to fire me, and now this. He's out to get me. I'm much more capable of running this department than he is. That's it! He's jealous and wants to find a way of moving me out.

140

"Okay Gordon, it's true. I was curious about the place and decided to go in and see what the big deal was."

"Why do you feel you have to lie to me Robert? I wouldn't have been nearly as upset as I am now. I'm really disappointed in you. I thought you had turned it around over the last several years. You had actually worked your way back to being considered for advancement. Now this happens. I don't know what to think. You have an absolutely beautiful wife and wonderful kids. Why would you need to go into a place like that? I don't understand you, man. What in the Hell is with you?"

"Gordon, I don't know what to say. I made a mistake. It won't happen again."

"Robert, career men at the Bureau are not allowed the luxury of making these kinds of mistakes. They need to be men of the strongest moral fiber. You know how the old man feels about this kind of thing. If he knew, your ass would be transferred to the biggest shit hole he could find."

"Come on Gordon, I said it won't happen again. What more can I say."

"Not a thing Robert. It's what you do that matters! I'm not going to put this in your file. You better see to it this never happens again, understood?"

"Yes sir. Thanks Gordon."

"Don't thank me, thank your wife and kids; that's who I'm doing this for! Now get out of my sight!"

Why me? Why me? One of these days I'll get that son-of-a-bitch for what he's done to me!

Mrs. Cassidy got Rob's attention as he left Gordon's office.

"Mr. Misner, someone named Louise called."

"Yeah, what did she want?"

His tone with his long time secretary was harsher than he had meant.

"I'm sorry Jean; I didn't mean to take your head off. What did Louise want?"

"You know, your wife, pregnancy, hospital."

"Oh lord, I've got to go. I'll call you from the hospital!"

Gordon stepped out of his office as Rob rushed for the door. He overheard the exchange with his secretary.

"Miss Cassidy, where is Mr. Misner off to in such a hurry?"

"His wife is in labor and on her way to the hospital."

*****

Irene Martha Misner was a carbon copy of her four older siblings. Jane had been home a week and decided to introduce her infant to the outdoors. Jane placed Rene on an army blanket next to her while she worked the flowerbed. Bruce and Freddy were playing in the locust tree. Mark and Nicole were helping their mother pull weeds. Jane's mind wasn't really on her gardening. She was being serenaded by the banter of her boys in the tree.

"Freddy, throw me that rope!"

"Why are you tying it on that limb? That's about thirty-feet up!"

"You know how far we can swing out on a long rope like this? It'll be great man, you'll see. We can launch off of the first limb and swing out over all those bushes. It'll be a blast, man!"

"I thought we were going to cut the rope in ten foot lengths and tie them to different limbs, so we could swing from rope to rope like Tarzan?"

"We can still do that. Besides, did you ever see Tarzan climb DOWN a tree? No man, Tarzan swings down…uuuuh-uuhuuh-uuh-uuhuuhuuh!"

"Man, you got his yell down perfect, you should play 'Boy.'"

"I'm the oldest! Me Tarzan, you Boy, you little twerp!"

Jane thought about interceding. She could see Nicole's attention riveted to her older brothers. She wasn't surprised when Nicole went to the tree.

"I'll be Jane. I can climb as good as either of you!"

Nicole's challenge seemed to offend Freddy.

"Nicole, who asked you anyway? Go play with Mark and leave us alone!"

Jane had to laugh as she saw Nicole stick her tongue out at Freddy. Frustrated, Nicole flopped down next to her mother.

"Momma, why is Freddy so mean to me?"

"He's not being mean to you honey."

"Yes he is. He won't let me play in the tree with him and Bruce."

"Honey, they're older and don't want to have to watch you."

"But he always picks on me, why?"

"Why do you always pick on Mark."

"He bugs me sometimes. He follows me everywhere."

"Maybe that's how your older brothers feel about you."

As if to prove her mother wrong, Nicole went over to Mark and sat next to him.

"Mark, when the boys finish, you wanna climb the tree and swing on the rope?"

"I don't know, it's pretty high, we might fall."

"You're not afraid are you?"

"I don't know."

"Mark, it'll be fun! There's nothing to be scared of. Look how high Bruce is!"

"He sure can climb trees. I wish I could climb trees like him."

"You will when you're as big as him. You'll be better than him one of these days!"

"Do you really think so?"

"Of course!"

Mark would be entering first grade in the fall. School weighed heavily on his mind.

"Nicki?"

"Yeah?"

"Do you think I'll like school?"

"You'll love it, especially if you have Sister Mary Catherine, she's nice!"

"Why do they call nuns sisters? They're not my sisters."

"They just do, I don't know why."

Their talk was interrupted by another triumphant yell.

"Uuuuh-uuhuuh-uuh-uuhuuhuuh!"

"Mark! Look how far Bruce is swinging, uh oh, he's going to hit the tree!"

Bruce swung out from the tree about forty-feet. It looked like he would smack into it on the return. At the last minute he used his legs like a spring, pushing away from it. He then released his grip on the rope and dropped to ground. Jane had been watching with her heart in her throat.

"Bruce! Swing the rope back to me! I betcha I can swing further than you did."

"You're full of it, Freddy!"

Jane could see Rene yawning and knew it was time to take her in. She picked up the baby and made for the house. On her way, she thought about Robert. *I hope he isn't up to his old tricks. Now that I'm not pregnant, maybe he'll want to have sex, maybe tonight.* Jane didn't want to give in to her gut. Deep down she knew what he was up to…again.

*****

Robert was feeling the pressure of having six mouths to feed. Jane had become very compliant as a wife but after five children, she was beginning to lose her figure. Robert had been after her to diet but to no avail. Jane wasn't fat, but her body was changing.

Rob had curbed his trips to the Slipper after the incident with Gordon. He needed to relieve the pressure he was feeling. *I need some excitement. Life is becoming too boring. This family man life is getting me down. I'll make a trip to the Slipper tonight well after work.*

A call from Jane interrupted his planning.

"Rob, Mother Superior called and needs you to pick Mark up."

"It's in the middle of the school day. Is he sick?"

"No, he had a problem in class and needs to come home. Louise is not home, otherwise I'd go."

"What did they say is wrong?"

"It seems he wet his pants in class."

"He did what?"

"He wet his pants. I have a feeling there's more to it than Mother Superior is saying."

"This is bullshit! I'll go get him. He better have a good reason for embarrassing me like this!"

"Just go get him, okay?"

"I'm leaving right now."

Robert got in the car and made his way to St. Peter's in Falls Church. He wasn't happy about having to change his plans. *When is he going to grow out of wetting his pants? I've got a six-year old son that still pisses his bed. What did I do to deserve that? Now he pees his pants in front of his class.*

Robert walked into the school office. Mark was sitting in the corner.

"Mark, did you pee your pants?"

"Yes sir."

"What happened?"

"I had to go to the bathroom but Sister Mary Catherine wouldn't let me…"

The story came flowing like a river from the boy's mouth. Robert listened to the whole thing without interrupting. Robert's face contorted with rage as he approached the counter.

"Who's in charge here?"

A woman that looked like she ate a persimmon came over. Mrs. Miller had been the school secretary for seven years. She'd heard all about Robert Misner's reputation.

"I'm Mrs. Miller, the school secretary. Mother Superior will be with you shortly. I've informed her of your presence, Mr. Misner."

"Mrs. Miller, I want you to go in her office this very second and tell her I refuse to wait another minute!"

Mrs. Miller did as she was…asked.

Mother Superior emerged from her office with Mrs. Miller. The mistake she made was in her initial demeanor. Robert Misner didn't care how mean she looked. He had plenty of mean in his own arsenal. Mother Superior was about to be taught a lesson in discipline herself.

"Mr. Misner! What gives you the right to speak to Mrs. Miller in that manner? You have…"

"I have what? I pay this school tuition for four children. I pay you…people to educate not humiliate my children. I want the boy's teacher to join us immediately, immediately do you understand me, woman?"

The nun had no idea how to deal with this man. Her haughtiness always worked on parents before, many of which she taught. She replied,

"Mr. Misner, that is no tone to take with me!"

Another mistake.

"Look, you're lucky I'm not throwing things. My son tells me this all started because of the school's gross negligence. Is that true?"

This made the principle think for a moment. Robert jumped in again before she could respond.

"My son is not a liar. He knows what the punishment is for lying to me. Lady, you have handled this poorly. Bishop O'Fallon is going to hear about this."

Sister Mary Catherine entered Mother Superior's office and sat next to Robert. Robert put the two nuns through the Misner version of the Great Inquisition. Sister Mary Catherine was close to tears. They didn't have a chance. He was in his element. He had years of pent up rage to get rid of and the two nuns were the benefactors.

While driving home, Robert looked at his son and winked.

"I guess I showed them, huh Scorcher boy."

Robert turned an embarrassment into one of his great personal triumphs. When he got home he proudly shared his big moment with Jane.

"How can we send him back to that school after this? How can Mark face all of those children. They'll tease him to death over this."

"He'll just have to learn to cope with it like anyone else. He needs to quit pissing his pants anyway."

"The psychologist warned Mark might not be ready for the rigors of school. We're forgetting how close we came to losing him. Do you think we should keep him out until next year?"

"I don't want people calling my son a dummy. What will that say about us? Hell, he'll be the oldest first grader in school. How do I explain that to people?"

"Why do you even care what others think? This is our son we are talking about. The only thing that should concern you is what's best for him. For goodness sake Rob, can't you think about someone besides yourself?"

"I guess my opinion doesn't count. You do whatever you want with the little dummy!"

"Rob, he's your Scorch, don't call him that!"

"What do you call it then? You know very well he isn't as bright as children his age. How many notes did we get from his teacher about him not being able to keep up with the other kids? Three in two months, that's how many!"

"Rob, it was his head injury and you know it. You're being very unfair!"

"You pick him up the next time he pisses his pants!"

Robert went back to work. During the heat of their argument, they'd forgotten Mark was sitting on the couch.

"Mom, what is retarded?"

"It's just a word."

"The kids call me that sometimes. Am I dumb?"

"Honey, you're not dumb. Don't pay any attention to your father. He's just upset with those mean old nuns."

"Will I have to go back there tomorrow?"

"You won't have to go back, I promise."

"Mom, does Daddy hate me?"

Trying to hold back her tears, Jane replied, "Of course your daddy doesn't hate you, sweetie."

Jane made an appointment for she and Rob to talk with the child psychologist the next day. The recommendation was for Mark to sit the rest of the school year out. A public school in Fairfax County was recommended. Jane would go talk with them the next day.

"So doctor, you think my son is retarded?"

"Mr. Misner, he is no such thing!"

"Then why can't he keep up in school?"

"Your son had an extremely serious head injury and is lucky to be alive. If he has to sit out a year of school then I think that's a small price to pay. If you send him back this year it will create more of a problem in my opinion."

"I'm not sending my son to a public school. He won't get a decent education."

"Mr. Misner, where did you hear that? You have a wonderful public school near you. Its reputation is excellent. Fairfax County has one of the best public school systems in the entire country."

Jane didn't win many arguments with Robert but she did win this one. A few weeks after the incident with Mark, Robert started getting home later and later. Jane had thought those days were well behind them. She made the mistake of asking why he was late one evening. His defense was to change the subject.

"Jane, do you have to keep running these credit cards up?"

"The boys are growing out of their clothes, as are Nicki and Mark. Now we have Irene. I don't need to tell you how fast she's growing."

"Why can't you go back to sewing their clothes?"

"I don't have the time. I have to take care of the baby, do the cleaning and cooking. When would I be able to find time to sew?"

"You need to find a way to do it. I can't afford these credit card bills!"

"Robert, you don't have to yell at me. I do the best I can."

"Damn Jane, that's NOT GOOD ENOUGH! You have to quit this spending!"

"Robert, why are you yelling? Is there something going on at work that you are not telling me?"

"No, of course not. Everything at work is fine. I'm simply tired of all these goddamn bills!"

"Did you stop by your mother's before you came home?"

"Why do you ask?"

"She called here about two hours ago, screaming at me over the credit card bills. Why were you late anyway? I can smell liquor all over your clothes."

"I'm not answering to you! If I want to stop by 'Harvey's' for a couple of drinks after work, that's my business. I don't need you nagging me! I don't ask you to account for your time do I?"

"No Robert, you…"

"No, that's right, so you don't need to know what I am doing!"

"A simple phone call saying not to wait on dinner is all I'm asking. Quit yelling at me."

"I don't yell at you enough! Look at this house, it's a mess."

"I cleaned today. It's not a mess."

Jane couldn't take anymore. She retreated upstairs with the rest of the children. Bruce and Freddy looked at each other. Yelling had always been the prelude to a beating. They stayed in their room…waiting.

Everyone heard the front door slam. Soon the car door shut. No one came down until they heard his car backing out of the driveway.

*****

Rob couldn't explain his mood. He was in the elevator. Euphoria overtook him as he started whistling. He got off on his floor. As he passed Mrs. Cassidy, he greeted her by her first name.

"Good morning Jean, how are you this morning? What seems to be the problem? You look like you've been crying."

"You haven't heard?"

"Heard what?"

"Gordon had a massive heart attack over the weekend. He's dead!"

Robert had a difficult time disguising how he felt. His wonderful mood just got better.

"That's terrible!"

"It's awful. I worked with him for over twenty years. It's so sad."

"Yes it is sad, very sad."

Robert turned to go into his office, as he was about to betray his true feelings. He was about to enter his office when Bill Hawkins, the Division Director, approached him.

"Rob, I assume you've heard the news?"

"Yes Mr. Hawkins, I have. What a terrible thing to happen. I'm going to miss Gordon."

"I'm sure you will Rob. Would you come into my office for a moment?"

Rob's imagination took control of him. This was his time. Life goes on at the Bureau. He was sure Bill Hawkins was about to promote him into Gordon's position. He eagerly followed the Director into his office.

"Yes sir, Mr. Hawkins."

Both men sat down. Robert did his best to maintain a serious demeanor while Mr. Hawkins' stare bore through him. Finally Mr. Hawkins broke the silence.

"You know, we have to go on despite this tragedy."

"Yes sir, it's a damn shame. I had no idea he was sick."

"No one did, Rob. His death comes as a huge shock to all of us. I've been struggling with the decision of who's best to fill Gordon's position."

Robert's chest puffed out as he readied himself for his promotion. Bill then pulled the rug out from under him.

"Do you know Stanley Collingsworth?"

"Uh…Stanley, sure, I know Stanley. I trained him when he first came into Headquarters. Hasn't he been in Identification?"

"Good memory Rob, yes he has."

What are you worried about Rob? He's going to suggest he take your job. That's it! Whew! Man I thought for a minute Hawkins might be talking about moving that 'wet behind the ears,' Collingsworth into Gordon's, oh, MY job! Settle down Rob. Here comes the moment you've been waiting for.

"I'm glad you remember him. He's going to need all the help you can give him in his new position."

"You mean he is going to replace me as assistant department director?"

"I'm sorry Rob, I should have been more clear. You'll be working FOR Mr. Collingsworth. I know this probably comes as a shock, but Gordon brought his name up months ago. There will be other opportunities for you Rob. We need you to help Stan get anchored into his new responsibility. Can we count on you Rob?"

Robert just sat there dumbfounded.

"Rob, I said can we count on you for your professionalism?"

"Oh…yes…yes sir, it's just that…well, it's just…"

"Fine, fine Rob. I knew you'd understand. I told Mr. Hoover you were a team player. You can go back to your desk now, we'll talk later."

*****

Robert had forbidden his boys to hang out with Danny Finchum. Danny wore a leather jacket and looked like a punk. The fact that his father disliked the boy was reason enough for Bruce to hang out with him.

Danny came to the house while Bruce and Freddy were watering the garden. It was a hot August afternoon and the boys were nearly done.

"Hey, when you guys are done, you want to go to the swimming hole?"

"I don't think so Danny. Freddy and me have a better idea...watermelons!"

"Yeah man. Look over there and tell me what you see."

"Just old man Barns' garden, so?"

"So it's full of those dark green watermelons. Freddy and me have had our eye on those things all summer. Have you ever had one?"

"No, are they good?"

"Man, they're about the best thing I ever tasted. Tell him Freddy."

"Yeah, they're real sweet and juicy, just the perfect thing on a day like today."

"When you guys are done, let's go snitch a few. What time does old man Barns get home?"

Bruce replied, "He doesn't get home until almost five thirty. We have almost two hours. That's plenty of time to grab a few melons. We'll sit behind his shed and have a feast!"

"Aren't you forgettin' something Bruce?"

"What?"

"Old lady Barns."

"She's visiting her sister in Philadelphia."

"How do you know that, man?"

"I deliver their paper. She told me last week to stop delivery for this week cause she wouldn't be home."

"What about old man Barns? Don't he read the paper?"

"No man, she's the only one that reads it. There's no one home right now. Are you ready?"

"Yeah man! Watermelons here we come!"

An hour later the boys had gorged themselves. Freddy took aim at Danny, hitting him in the head with a piece of rind. That started a spirited rind fight.

"Hey man, don't hit me with that slimy piece of shit!"

"I gottcha man, right in the head!"

"I'll show you man, take that!"

All three boys froze in place when they heard the car door shut.

"Who's back there? Goddamn it, you little delinquents, get out of my melons! Come out from behind there this minute!"

The three boys looked at each other. Bruce and Freddy immediately thought of the whipping in store for them. Danny was just plain scared. He was the first to bolt. The brothers followed suit. Bruce had the presence of mind to run away from home. Freddy, on the other hand, ran straight for the house.

"Freddy Misner, is that you? Wait until I tell your father what you've done!"

*****

Sunday morning was Robert's favorite time. He got to parade his family in front of the community, showing what a great family man he was. All seven Misners would file into one of the front pews of St. Peters Catholic Church. Mass wasn't until 10 o'clock. He had plenty of time to eat breakfast and read the paper. Robert was just thinking about getting ready for church when he heard the knocking.

"Jane, get the door."

"Robert, it's Mr. Barns."

Freddy was halfway down the stairs when his mother opened the door. He did an about face, taking the steps three at a time. Bruce was getting dressed when Freddy burst into the room.

"Freddy, you look like you've seen a…"

Their father yelled for them before Bruce finished his sentence.

"Bruce! Freddy! Get down here right now!"

The boys looked at each other in resignation. Freddy pulled on his pants and they went downstairs.

"Boys, you know Mr. Barns?"

"Yes, sir."

"Mr. Barns says you two were in his watermelons yesterday. Is that true?"

The boys knew the jig was up. As always, Bruce spoke for both.

"Yes, sir, but we only took two."

Robert was still in his pajamas. He barked his order to Mark.

"Mark, go get my belt from upstairs!"

The silence was deafening as Mark went for the belt. Rob could smell the fear on everyone, including the neighbor. A feeling of power surged through him like never before. Mr. Barns gave voice to a weak protest.

"I expected a spanking, but you're not going to beat them with a belt over two melons?"

Robert contemplated his reply.

"Hmm, only two melons?"

Feeling he diffused the situation, Mr. Barns began breathing easier.

"Mr. Misner, I have an idea. Why not make the boys help me around the house for a week as their punishment?"

"Mr. Barns, did they ask for those melons?"

"How could they, I wasn't home."

"Precisely! They took them without permission. That's called stealing."

"Really Mr. Misner, if I thought for one minute that you would…"

Mark returned, handing the belt to his father. Robert wasted no time.

SMACK, SMACK, SMACK, SMACK…

Jane's urgent pleas were ignored.

"Robert! Stop! They're only watermelons! Mr. Barns, can't you do something? Mr. Barns! Mr. Barns…?"

Robert fed on the neighbor's fear while he ignored the man's feeble protest.

"Mr. Misner, this is horrifying!"

Months of pent up rage were uncorked. Robert swung the heavy belt indiscriminately. The boys were driven to the floor. They curled into a fetal position and covered their heads. Robert pushed Jane to the floor as she grabbed for his offending arm. He swung at her. The buckle tore through the fabric of her dressing gown. Jane took more blows as she tried protecting her sons. Her eyes bore into the cowardly neighbors' pleading for his help. She would have to help herself.

Robert was taken aback by the surprise assault from Jane.

"What the…?"

"Stop! Leave them alone! They're bleeding! Stop! Get out of here! Get out of here! You're no father! Quit hitting them! Stop, I SAID STOP!"

Jane was screaming at the top of her lungs. Her fists were slamming into Robert's chest. He hit her with the back of his hand. Her blows ceased as she landed on the floor a second time. Something was wrong. Robert could feel blows against his thighs.

The Scorch launched his own attack, both verbal and physical at his father. *If you want some of this, you'll have it, by God!* Robert's response was immediate. The blow sent the little boy backward. His head hit the corner of the coffee table. Blood seeped from the cut behind Mark's ear. Robert knew hitting his Scorch was a mistake. Seeing his son's blood made him stop. Jane was holding Scorch. Everything went quiet except for his wife's voice.

"You son-of-a-bitch! Get out of here! Mark! Mark! Honey, are you all right?"

Robert's attention was focused on Scorch. The feeling of power he felt earlier was gone as he stared at the limp form of his Scorch. He discarded the belt and reached for Mark. His hand was slapped away by Jane.

"Get away from him! You don't deserve a family! Mr. Barns! Mr. Barns! Call an ambulance, my son is unconscious!"

Robert didn't stop Bruce and Freddy as they ran outside. He looked to Mr. Barns for a reaction. Robert could see the shock on the neighbor's face. Without warning, he felt the little blows against his legs again. The Scorch regained his senses and came at his father again.

"You hurt my mommy! I hate you! I hate you!"

The words cut through Robert like a knife. The belt fell to the floor. He let his little boy rain punches on his legs. Robert did the only thing he could do; he left.

What will I do now? The question reverberated in his mind as he drove to his mothers'.

*****

Hilda hid her elation behind a façade of sympathy. She could see remorse written all over her son. She had to do something to change that.

"What do you mean she kicked you out?"

"I disciplined the boys. She was screaming at me at the top of her lungs to leave."

"Robby, how could that woman kick you out of the house you paid for?"

"I didn't want to make a big scene in front of the kids so I left."

"She wouldn't even let you pack a suitcase?"

"No mother. I thought it best to simply leave. I have some clothes here, remember from the last time?"

"I remember. You can stay here as long as you want. That woman never has appreciated you anyway. I've told you before she doesn't deserve you. She's poisoned the children against you like she did with me. I swear! When are you going to leave her?"

"Mother, we've been over this before. The Bureau would have a fit. Plus, the church doesn't condone divorce. I can't get a divorce."

"The Bureau! What do they know? You should hear some of the stories I've heard about your director. Yours is nothing compared to what I've heard about him!"

"Mother, I have too much time invested with the Bureau. I'd have to start all over somewhere else."

"I never wanted you to go to work for them in the first place! If you'd have done what I told you to, you wouldn't be in this mess now!"

"Mother, I didn't want to be a lawyer."

"You didn't want to go to school for an extra two years. Robby, you're lazy just like your father was!"

"Okay mother, let's not go there right now. You can say 'I told you so' if you want."

"I will! I told you so. I told you that woman was no good for you too! But no, you wouldn't listen to your mother. You had to marry her and ruin your life."

Robert couldn't stand the thought of staying with his mother. He didn't see any alternative. Rob's finances were not in the best shape. His carousing with other woman had cost him. Rob didn't like it, but he had no real choice. He'd have to stay with her until he could convince Jane to take him back.

"Robert, I'm talking to you. Did you hear anything I said?"

Rob resigned himself to his fate.

"Yes mother, I heard everything you said."

*****

After three weeks, Rob pulled into his driveway. The curtain in the dining room parted imperceptibly, as Robert strode to the porch. The door was locked. He tried his key, but it didn't work. *The bitch changed the locks!* He banged on the door. The door opened far enough to reveal Martha's face. Martha was the first to speak.

"What do you think you're doing?"

"I think I'm coming into my house. What gives you the right to keep me out?"

"You should be horsewhipped! Those boys had cuts all over their bodies from that awful belt. What exactly was their crime?"

"Look Martha, I'm not answering to you. Get out of my way, I need to talk to my wife."

"She's not here. She had an appointment with an attorney."

"An attorney?"

"What kind of woman do you think my daughter is? Did you really think she'd let you get away with what you've done?"

"That was a mistake and I'm sorry it happened. Wait a minute! Why am I saying this to you? It's none of your Goddamn business!"

"Mister, if it concerns the welfare of my daughter and grandchildren I make it my business. In fact, I've given considerable thought to calling J. Edgar myself. I don't think he would like the way you treat your family."

"You wouldn't dare! How could I support my family without a job?"

"They'd be a whole lot better off without you, besides, I'd be happy to help them out! She was a good secretary before she married you."

"I can't talk to you. You've never given me a fair chance. I'm sure you're responsible for poisoning my family against me."

"Robert, you're delusional. You've done your own job of poisoning them against you. I used to pity you, but I don't anymore. To me, you're just scum."

"I don't care what you think old woman, now move aside I'm coming in and you're leaving."

"What are you going to do, use a belt on me? I'd like you to try that. You'll get a chance to see what the other side of a jail cell looks like."

Robert pushed his way past Martha into the house. He busied himself in the basement until Jane came home, an hour later. Martha pointed her to the basement.

"It's not enough you beat your sons but now you threaten my mother. How stupid are you, Robert?"

"What's this about you seeing a lawyer?"

"I see mother told you."

"You can't be serious about wanting a divorce...can you?"

"Robert, what happened to you? Everything was fine until you lost it that day."

Rob told Jane of his meeting with Mr. Hawkins.

"Jane, I don't know what gets into me. It seems like there is someone else inside of me that takes control when I'm under pressure."

"You can tell that someone he's cost you your family. I'm divorcing you."

"You can't divorce me. How will you support the children?"

"You'll continue to support the children. I'll be forced to show the photos of the boys to your boss."

"Photos?"

"Yeah, eight and a half by eleven glossies."

"I don't believe you?"

"I don't care whether you do or not. Try me and find out."

"Try you?"

"Yeah, try me. I took the boys to my lawyer the very next day. He had a professional photographer take the pictures. Mr. Callodney wanted to have you prosecuted. He's of the opinion you should be in jail. So, try me, I dare you!"

Robert tried a different tactic.

"Jane, look, I'm sorry. I don't know what gets into me. I've been miserable ever since the day Mr. Barnes came to the house. I don't know how I can make up for what I've done, but I'd like to try. Things had been so good between us since Mark's accident. Somehow I lost that person and this evil one took control for that one instant. I promise I'll never lay another hand on any of the children. But please forget this divorce nonsense. Let me be with my family?"

"What about your girlfriend?"

"Girlfriend? I don't have a girlfriend."

"Sure you do. You know, the one with the cheap perfume and pink lipstick."

"Jane, you know I interview secretarial applicants all day long. Some of these young women I suppose wear cheap perfume. It's no wonder that my clothes smell of it. I'm around it constantly. As for the pink lipstick, that's the shirt I wore the day Mrs. Cassidy told me about Gordon. She was upset and hugged me around the neck. I guess she got some of her lipstick on my collar."

"First of all, I don't think Jean Cassidy wears hot pink lipstick. It's just not her style. Second, I never said it was on your shirt."

"If it wasn't on my shirt, where was it?"

"Your boxers. Do you want to try another story or are you going to stick with that one? How about this one? Fifty-nine year old Mrs. Cassidy needed to blot her hot pink lipstick. There was no Kleenex so you gallantly offered up your underwear. Really Rob! You must think I'm a total idiot."

"No, as a matter of fact, I don't. This is a side of you I've never seen. I like this feisty behavior. I think it's sexy."

"You can get that notion right out of your head. Those days between us are long gone so don't even think about it!"

"Okay, I've been seeing a prostitute. There, are you happy? You got the truth out of me. You've totally broken me down. Does that make you feel good?"

"No Robert, it doesn't make me feel good. Nothing about this whole mess makes me feel good. Watching my maniacal husband strip the flesh off of his own sons doesn't make me feel good. Knowing that I lost the man I loved to a prostitute doesn't make me feel good. Just how do you think I should feel anyway?"

"Jane, believe it or not, I love you and the kids."

"I have to think about the children and what's best for them. You even hit Mark. He hit his head on the coffee table. The neurologist warned what could happen if he sustained another head injury. They said it could KILL him Robert."

"That's the first time I ever touched him. He was hitting me, his own father. I'm not supposed to discipline the boy for hitting his father?"

"You know damn well he was trying to protect me."

"Jane, you know I love the little guy. He's my Scorch. Don't you think I've been torturing myself over this?"

"No, I don't. I think you'd say anything at this point just to keep me from filing."

Robert put his hand on Jane's shoulder and stroked her arm.

"Robert, take your hand off of me. That's not going to work."

"What can I do to convince you I can change?"

"Get psychological help. Until you do, stay away from us."

"I'm not crazy!"

"No sane person does the things you do. Until you can prove you're not a danger to the children, you'll not go near them. Accept that, or I file for divorce tomorrow."

Rob's eyes watered involuntarily. He knew further talk was useless.

"How long do you expect me to stay away?"

"We'll have to see what happens."

*****

Three months went by. The phone rang.

"Hello, Jane, it's me."

"Yes, Robert, what do you want?"

"I did what you wanted."

"What's that?"

"I thought about what you said about seeing a psychiatrist."

"And?"

"I've been seeing a psychiatrist."

"I don't believe you."

"It's true. In fact, he suggested you come in for a talk."

"I'm not the one that needs help."

"I didn't say that. Dr. Kerns wants to meet you."

"Why?"

"I asked if he'd meet with you."

"Why?"

"Jane, you're not making this any easier."

"Robert, let's just say, you don't inspire trust."

"I asked Doctor Kerns to give you a report on my progress. He's helped me a great deal. I feel like a new person."

"All right Rob, I'll humor you. When does he want to see me?"

"How about this afternoon, after lunch. I'll come get you."

"That's not necessary, I'll get Louise to drive me."

"I don't mind…

"Louise will drive me."

Jane hung up the phone and turned to her mother.

"Jane, don't fall for it."

"Fall for what, mother?"

"I bet he hasn't seen a doctor. Let me call the AMA. They'll be able to confirm the existence of this Doctor Kerns."

Jane went along with Martha's idea. Martha made the call. There was a psychiatrist named Jonathan Kerns with an office at 22nd and P Sts. NW.

"Now that we know he exists, let's find out if Robert is one of his patients."

*****

Not having to pick Jane up worked in Rob's favor. He had some last minute coaching to do.

"Bill, remember, you're Doctor Jonathan Kerns"

"Right Rob, no problem. For what you're paying me, I'll be Pope Pius himself."

"Don't go overboard. Tell her enough of my sad story to convince her I've changed."

"Where's the real Doctor Kerns?"

"He's on vacation for a week."

"What about access to his office? How about his secretary, plus, the other doctors in the building? These guys all know each other."

"Bill, I've thought of everything. The secretary is also on vacation. Wilbur Pucket, the janitor, gave me the keys for fifty bucks. I'm not worried about the other offices. People are up and down these halls all day long. Quit your worrying."

"Okay, I should have known you'd have it covered."

The two men were in the hall, about to enter the doctor's office. Robert unlocked the door and they went in.

"Bill, here's my dummy file. Put it in the front of one of those file drawers. After we all sit down, make a display out of retrieving it. Make it look natural. I'll be watching for her from that deli across the street. I'll give her ten minutes before I come up."

While the men were talking the phone rang.

"Bill, get the phone before it rings again!"

"Hello, this is Dr. Kerns."

"You're Doctor Jonathan Kerns?"

"May I ask who is calling?"

"Yes, my name is Jane Misner."

"You're Robert Misner's wife?"

"I am. Have you been treating my husband?"

"Yes, I have. Robert said something about you coming in this afternoon. I really would like to meet with you. Will you be coming in?"

"I suppose so. Would three o'clock be okay, doctor?"

"Three o'clock is fine, Mrs. Misner. I'll see you then."

Jane looked over at her still skeptical mother.

"Jane, I don't trust him. I refuse to believe Robert is seeing a psychiatrist. He'd never admit to that kind of weakness."

"What if you're wrong, mother? The children need their father. I owe it to them to check this out."

"You do what you have to, honey. I'll remain dubious."

Jane went upstairs to get ready.

*****

"Bill, I'm sorry I doubted you. That was a great job!"

"Rob, I've played the con a long time. I think I can pull off the psychiatrist bit."

"I wouldn't have paid for your services otherwise."

"You were right about her checking this guy out."

"I had a feeling she would. Jane's not the naive little housewife she used to be. By the way, I told Wilbur he'd get the key back by four-thirty."

"Where do you know this janitor from?"

"He lives on one of the farms I hunt on. I let him hunt with me a few weeks ago."

"So, you found out what kind of tenants were in the building and their hours."

Rob looked at his watch; it was 2:30.

"It's time for me the leave. Put those pictures of the real Doctor Kerns in one of the drawers. All we need is for Jane to see those."

Rob's vigil at the deli across the street lasted only twenty minutes. He watched Jane get off the bus and enter the building. *I could always count on her to be on time.* He gave her ten minutes before he left.

*****

Jane found Dr. Jonathan Kerns' office on the sixth floor, room 607. As she entered the tastefully appointed office, a tall, good-looking man in his late fifties greeted her.

"Mrs. Misner?"

"Doctor Kerns?"

"Please, call me Jonathan. I feel I've known you and your children for years."

"Really?"

"Oh yes, Rob is very proud of his family."

Jane took a seat in a richly appointed leather chair. Dr. Kerns sat in one across from her.

"Robert said he was proud of his family? How much did he tell you?"

Jane inched to the edge of the chair, anxious for the doctor's response.

"Before we get into all of that, Jane, you don't mind if I call you that?"

"No, of course not."

Jane had the hook in her mouth, not knowing she was about to be reeled in.

"Good, good. Jane, can I get you something, coffee maybe?"

Jane's heart was racing. She wanted answers to her questions.

"I'm fine. You were going to tell me how much Rob told you."

"Let me get his file."

Jane watched the doctor go to the metal file cabinet and thumb his way to a thick manila folder. He pulled the folder out and returned to his seat. Just as he sat, Robert appeared in the doorway.

"Rob, you're late. Your beautiful wife and I were about to start without you."

"I had some last minute stuff come up at the office, sorry."

"Rob, I was about to go over your file with Jane."

"Do you want me to leave so you two can talk? I don't want to influence what's said."

Jane looked at Rob as if they'd just met.

"Don't be silly, Rob. We both need to be here."

Dr. Kerns broke in.

"All right. Let's see, where was I? Oh yeah, Rob's file. As you can see, your husband has prompted a lot of note taking. I could write a book about him."

"Doctor Kerns, what progress have you made? Have you been able to help him?"

"Jane, only time will tell. I will say we've spent almost all of our time dealing with his anger."

Rob sat back in his chair thinking this was the best two hundred bucks he'd ever spent. Bill Boles was a real pro. He could tell Jane was hooked.

"His anger?"

"Yes Jane, his anger. Rob and I spend time talking about where it comes from. I've been trying to help Rob come to grips with why he gets so angry and what he can do to mitigate it."

Jane's full attention was on the doctor as he took her through one session at a time. Rob smiled inwardly. *Bill, you did your homework well. She's falling for it hook, line and sinker.* Jane's next question put Rob on the edge of his seat.

"Doctor, what do you think about him coming back home? Do you think he can deal with the children without hurting them?"

"Jane, if I'm sure of one thing, it's this; Rob needs his family. He has deep seeded love for all of you, especially the youngest boy, The Scorch. His remorse is genuine. Ever since his father died, Rob has struggled with who he is. As you know, his mother has exerted tremendous influence over him. We agree this is where most of his anger originates. He understands and accepts that. He has taken responsibility for all of his mistakes. I am sure, you will find Rob has changed a great deal."

Rob looked Jane squarely in the eyes and said,

"Jane, I've worked hard at dealing with my demons. All I want now is to come home to my family."

Jane eased back into the softness of the leather, relaxed. This was all very convincing, however, she'd been taken in before. She noticed Rob squirming in his seat nervously as she contemplated her reply.

"Robert, I'm telling you this once; the first time you raise your hand against me or any of the kids, you're history."

"Jane you won't regret it, I promise."

"Another thing; you need to spend more time with Nicole."

"I've given Nicki a lot of thought. I know I've neglected her. I've finally come to grips with that entire situation. She had nothing to do with what I did that night. I'll make it up to her, if it's not too late. Do you think she'll forgive me?"

"I think she still needs her father."

"Does this mean you'll take me back?"

"Yes, Robert, it does. I had my doubts at first, but now I'm convinced you're sincere."

Robert turned to Dr. Kerns, alias Bill Boles and took his hand in gratitude.

"Dr. Kerns, thanks for making me see what I almost threw away. Thanks for giving me my family back."

"Rob, it's been my pleasure. My door is always open to you. Good luck, you two."

*****

Robert took Nicole shopping for back to school clothes the very next day. He still struggled with his conscience whenever he was close to Nicole. It had been thirteen years since that night. Nevertheless, he spent the day with Nicole and despite himself, enjoyed her excitement.

"Daddy, do you like this one. It's not too old for me is it?"

"No Nicki, you look very pretty in that dress."

"I do! You think I look pretty?"

"Yes, I do. I'm sorry I never told you that before. You look just like your mother."

"Daddy, Mom is beautiful. I'm not beautiful. My arms are too big. I'm stronger than most of the boys I know."

"Nicole, there is nothing wrong with your arms. You're a beautiful young lady. You're not going to give up your swimming are you? I love watching your meets."

"You like watching me swim, Daddy?"

"Very much, yes."

"You don't think my arms are too big from the swimming?"

"Of course not. You should be proud to be in such good physical shape."

"Thank you, Daddy!"

Nicki threw her arms around her daddy's neck, giving him a kiss on the cheek. They left the department store with their purchases hand-in-hand. From the corner of his eye, Robert caught the adoration in Nicki's eyes.

When they got home, Nicole ran into the house with her packages. Jane spent the next two hours checking out the new clothes in case they needed altering. She'd never seen Nicole so excited.

"Robert, Nicki told me everything you said. You're not leading our daughter on are you?"

"Jane, how can you say that? This is the first time Nicki and I have ever really connected. I owe this to Dr. Kerns. He helped me see everything I'd been missing. I meant what I said, about making it up to Nicole."

"I've never seen Nicole happier. She's always wanted your approval."

Robert knew where Jane's soft spot was. So far his plan was working. He'd been able to get back into her good graces by being nice to the kids. He did the best he could with Bruce and Freddy, but realized his relationship with them was done.

*****

Freddy looked in the stands and expected to see the usual audience, his mother, little brother and sister. To his surprise, his father was watching. What a time for him to show up. This was the worst he'd pitched all year. The game was in the fourth inning. He'd walked the bases loaded. Freddy could hear his father yelling at him from the bleachers.

"Why don't you walk this guy? You may as well finish what you started!"

"Robert, if you don't want to support your son, why don't you sit in the visitors section?"

"That's a good idea! Maybe that will motivate Freddy to start pitching."

Robert made a big show of getting up and telling everyone Freddy wasn't worth rooting for.

"You're a choke artist. Go ahead and walk this guy. Hey coach! If you want to win you better replace my son, he's stinks!"

Freddy didn't embarrass easily. His father had obviously been at the bottle and seemed intent on making a spectacle of himself. Freddy was determined to turn it around. His Legion team was down three to one in the fourth. Freddy's coach had already been to the mound once. One more visit meant the bench. There were two out and Roger Trumball was up. He was Annandale's big gun.

The two boys had been antagonists during Little League, Babe Ruth and now Legion ball. Freddy knew Roger. He was a bully. Many of the hits he got were because of his ability to intimidate the opposing pitcher. He didn't scare Freddy. Freddy was the one throwing the ball. He called time and Freddy's catcher Steve Lowry came to the mound.

"Come on Freddy, you need to throw a strike, you're down in the count three/one. You walk in another run and we may as well go home. By the way, what in the fuck is up with your old man? He's rooting for Trumball!"

"Don't pay any attention to him, he's just trying to get my goat. I'm going to strike this mother out but I'm not throwing him anything he can hit."

"Your crazy man, you'll walk him and the score will be four to one."

"He's just waiting for a nice juicy one down the middle. He knows I have to throw him a strike, but you know what?"

"What man?"

"He's too damn stupid to let a ball go by. He wants to crush one and be a big hero. I know this guy. Get ready for some Beethoven."

"Okay man, I hope you know what you're doing."

Freddy took his cap off and wiped his forehead on his sleeve. He turned to face his teammates as if to reassure them. Then he turned to face Roger.

"Come on you gutless little prick, show me what you got. Come on, put it in here and I'll put you out of your misery!"

"Come on Freddy! Blow it by 'em! Play him some chin music! He can't hit, no batter, no batter, blow it by 'em baby, blow it by 'em! Batter, batter, batter, batter...SWING!"

"Steeeriiike two!"

Roger stepped back and swung at the ball as it went whizzing by his chin. He swung so hard he fell backward. Roger got up without dusting himself off. Freddy looked over to where his father was and shook his head as he prepared his next delivery. Freddy looked at Steve and nodded his approval of the pitch.

"Hey Misner! You dust me off again and I'll kick your ass after the game. You don't have the guts to throw one in here. Come on man, don't be a pussy! Pitch to me, chicken shit!"

The count was full. Freddy had been right about Trumball. The batter inched closer to the plate, daring Freddy to duplicate his last pitch. Freddy knew the clumsy oaf waiting at the plate would swing at anything. The pitch was low and outside.

"Steeeeeriiiike!!!"

Roger threw his bat and helmet to the ground and started for the mound but it was too late. Freddy and his teammates jogged to their dugout with new purpose.

Roger became the goat. He never got a chance to redeem his last effort as he was left in the on-deck circle when Freddy struck out the last batter for a five to three win. All of the Maplesville players had swarmed their hero, carrying him from the field. Roger's threats fell on deaf ears.

"See, that's my son. I knew this reverse psychology would work. I just knew I could motivate him to do better!"

No one was listening to the man who had done everything he could to embarrass his son. Freddy got a ride home with one of his teammates.

*****

Nicole and Elizabeth Elgin had a scheme to get Bruce and Becky together. Both girls compared notes about their older siblings. Bruce was always pumping Nicole for information about Becky. Elizabeth said the same about Becky. It was apparent Bruce was too shy to make the first move.

Bruce had just finished weeding when he saw Nicole coming from Elizabeth's house. He wondered what Becky was doing. He thought about how the eighteen-year old looked in those lime green short-shorts and midriff top. He looked down realizing his excitement showed. He needed a cold shower.

"Hey Bruce, you wanna play kick-the-can with us?"

"I'm not playing little kid games, I'm nineteen!"

"Becky's going to play."

"She is?"

"Yeeeeaaah, she is. Soooo are you sure you don't want to play?"

Bruce couldn't let on he was dying to play, not the game, but with Becky. He remained as aloof as possible.

"I don't know, we'll see, maybe."

"I'll go tell Liz and Becky you're too busy."

Nicole started for Liz's house, but Bruce caught her by the arm.

"Wait a minute! I said I would see, didn't I?"

"I need a yes or no."

Bruce didn't want his excitement to be obvious. He hesitated before answering Nicole.

"I guess I'll play.."

"Great! I'll go tell Liz…and Becky!"

Bruce waited until his sister was out of sight and then hurried into the house to take a shower. The two conspirators were planning their next move.

"Hey Becky, come here for a minute."

"Elizabeth, you know I have to help Mom with dinner, what is it?"

"After dinner we're getting a game of kick-the-can together at Nicole's house."

"Oh really?"

"Yeah, we wanted to know if you'd play."

"You mean play a silly child's game?"

"Bruce is going to play."

"He is, or, I mean, we'll see, maybe."

Becky left the two girls as she made a beeline for her bedroom. Nicole and Elizabeth held their hands over their mouths to stifle the giggles. Nicole returned home to share the plan with her mother. Jane could hardly keep from laughing as she watched her oldest run around looking for something to wear.

"Mom, where is my stripped shirt?"

"It's on the line."

"Oh jeez, I don't have anything clean to wear."

"Bruce, what are you so worried about a clean shirt for? Not having clean clothes never bothered you before."

"I'd like something clean to wear every now and then. Is there anything wrong with that?"

"Of course not honey, I'll find you something else."

"No, I'll get something else, don't worry about it, jeez Louise!"

Jane finished peeling the potatoes. She thought about Bruce and how much time had gone by. *I remember my mother talking about how fast time goes by. I remember laughing. Ginny and I used to laugh at her stories about when she was growing up. She liked telling us to enjoy life while we could. Time doesn't wait for anyone. She was right. My children are going their own way. They won't be around for long. I need to cherish every moment. I wish Robert felt the same.*

Bruce heard the back door slam. He could hear Becky's laughter and gazed at her from his bedroom window. His heart quickened. How could he control his excitement? He was suddenly aware of it. He couldn't go outside like that! *Oh shit, man what am I going to do? I can't go out there with a boner. I need something loose. These jeans aren't going to cut it. I know, I know! I'll wear my gym shorts; they're real loose.*

*****

Robert was bent over the basement sink cleaning paintbrushes. He looked up when he heard the laughter from outside. Looking through the small window he saw Nicole with her friend and a pair of the most beautiful legs he'd ever seen. He recognized her as the eldest Elgin girl. God had she changed.

Robert loved young women. Their innocence excited him. His hand moved down to his crotch. He was getting stiff as he followed the lime green shorts. He imagined how much fun he could have with the girl in the basement. His pants were around his ankles as his ministrations to his manhood became more fervent. Robert shuffled from window to window as the legs moved around the house. Bruce came into view and it all made sense.

Bruce, I'll have to share some of my secrets about women with you. It looks like you need some help from the old master himself. Robert stood below the window staring at Becky while he masturbated. His perverted fantasy continued as he saw the kids scatter. He watched Bruce and Becky run off together. There were windows on every wall of the basement. He was able to follow them. Finally, Robert saw them crawl under the chaise lounge near the rose arbor.

They must be playing kick the can. Maybe Bruce isn't as dumb as I thought. I can have some real fun with him.

The lounge had a cover that went to the ground on all sides. Robert was the only one that knew where they had hidden. He would teach his son a lesson.

*****

Bruce took off around the corner making his way to the rose arbor. The chaise lounge was the perfect hiding place for him and Becky.

"Is there room for two?"

"It might be a little tight, but there's room for both of us."

"I don't mind that."

Bruce held the coverlet up as Becky crawled under. He squeezed in behind her. They were giggling like two little kids.

"Shhh, Becky, Nicole will hear us, shhh."

They were pressed together in such a way that Becky could feel his excitement against the back of her leg. Bruce had nowhere to put his hands except on her shoulders. He was in heaven. If he died at that moment, he would be content. Bruce could sense her heart beating in cadence with his. His hands caressed her shoulders. Nothing he had ever felt could compare to the soft silkiness of Becky's skin.

"I like it when you touch me."

She pressed her body into his.

"I...I like touching you. You make me feel..."

"Shhh, Bruce, would you kiss me?"

Bruce had never kissed a girl. He had watched movies and dreamt of how it would be the...first time. This was his first time and it was more than he ever could imagine. They explored the softness of each other's mouth. An urgency that had been too long suppressed screamed for its release.

Their hands explored each other. Becky's breath came out in short breaths as Bruce brushed his fingers over her nipples. Becky clamped a hand over his, urging him to knead her breast. His other hand moved up the smooth surface of her thigh. She spread her legs and groaned softly. Bruce was hopelessly lost. Becky's other hand was busy.

Their kissing became more frantic, primal. The coolness of the early evening breeze washed over them. Bruce had undone her shorts, finding the first wisps of pubic hair. Then it all came to an abrupt end as the coverlet was raised.

"What are you two doing under there? Young lady, I should call your father and tell him what you and my son have been up to!"

The youngsters were caught completely off guard. Bruce glared at his father as if looks could kill. Becky looked like a doe frozen in someone's headlights. She crawled out from under the lounge and ran home.

Bruce went into the house with his father on his heels, laughing at him. Bruce went into his room, slamming the door behind. Jane was puzzled. By the look on Robert's face, she knew he'd been up to something. Obviously it involved Bruce. She looked to Robert for an answer.

"What's that all about?"

"Not much. I just caught your son and the girl next door under the lounge together. They were having quite a time...under there."

"You mean you were spying on Bruce and Becky."

"I prevented them from making a big mistake!"

"Robert, I can't believe you'd spy on your own son!"

"He should have been more careful. Hey, he's nineteen. I can't tell him what to do anymore."

Jane let it slide. Bruce seemed more embarrassed than anything else.

*****

She had blonde hair and dark brown eyes. Her smile lit up the classroom. Miss Barrett welcomed her new third grade class. Mark Misner was much happier at Freedom Hill Elementary. This was nothing like St. Peter's. He got to go to school with all of his friends. He didn't have to take a DC transit bus either. The school was in easy walking distance, about a mile from home. There were some bright orange buses but most of the kids walked when the weather was good.

"Hey Mark, what do you think about Miss Barrett?"

"Man, I think she's beautiful!"

"Me too. I wonder if she has a boyfriend."

"It doesn't matter, I'm in love with her."

"I think she does. I saw some tall dude picking her up after school."

"Really?"

"Naw man, I'm only kidding ya!"

"You eat shit Carl, you know that."

"Yeah, but I only eat it once a day. You eat morning, noon and night!"

"Yeah, but at least I wash my mouth out afterwards. That's why we call you shit breath!"

This kind of conversation was normal for the four friends. Ronnie Colter and Lonnie Scolnik were laughing at Carl and Mark, happy not to be accused of fecal feasting. Mark didn't know many boys on the far end of the drive. He met Carl for the first time in second grade.

"Hey guys, what do you want to do after school?"

"I don't know Mark. Why don't you guys come over to my house? You guys have never been to my house before."

Mark was the only one to accept.

"Okay, I'll come, what about you two guys?"

"Na, I got things my mom wants me to do."

"Yeah me too, Mark. It looks like it's just you two guys."

"Okay Carl, I'll need to check in with my mom first."

After school, Mark said hello and goodbye to his mother. He noticed a funny look on her face when he told her where he was going.

Under a huge walnut tree in Carl's backyard was a massive green car. It looked like it had been there for quite a while. The grill was rusty and jammed with neglect.

"Cool man! Whose car is that?"

"Oh, that's my big brother's car. He doesn't drive it anymore."

"I didn't know you had a big brother. How big is he?"

"He's even older than your big brother. I don't get to see him very much."

"Why not, doesn't he live here?"

"Naw, he's in the Army."

"You mean he's a soldier?"

"Yeah, he's a soldier."

"Man that's really cool! What's that writing on the side?"

"Oh, you mean 'the green hornet'"

"The Green Hornet, what a cool name for a car!"

School in Miss Barrett's third grade class was a series of routines. Once the second bell rang, the children would all stand for the Pledge of Allegiance. Each week a new student won the honor of leading the Pledge. That same student got to help clean the erasers and wipe the blackboard. No matter how hard Mark tried, he had never won the honor.

Mark got bored easily in class. He had a hard time sitting still for even a few minutes. He was determined to get his gold star. If a kid made it a whole week, the honor of being Miss Barrett's helper was theirs for the following week. Miraculously, Mark had made it all week. It was Friday with only one hour of class left. He thought he was home free.

"Ow! Who did that?"

"Mark! Sit down and keep quiet! Mark, I am so disappointed in you. One more hour and you would have had your star."

Mark turned around and saw who threw the spitball. It was Joe Shipley. Joe had his hand over his mouth laughing, taunting Mark. Joe was the classroom bully. He had been held back twice. All of Mark's friends were laughing as well. Mark would have to challenge the bigger boy after school.

The last bell rang and Joe was waiting for Mark in the playground.

"Hey Misner! You wanna fight me, you little chicken?"

Mark's temper got the best of him. He was used to fighting with his sister. Nicole was a lot tougher than Joe Shipley.

"I'll fight you, you ugly butt wipe."

"Hey Misner, does your mother still change your diapers? I bet she still has to wipe your ass like a little…"

Joe didn't get to finish. Mark's temper exploded and he charged the bigger boy with his head down. He caught Joe by complete surprise. None of the other boys had the nerve to fight Joe before. Mark connected with his head. As Joe fell backward, he wrapped his arms around Mark's midsection, pulling him to the ground with him.

"You little twerp. Now you're really gonna get it!"

Joe started pounding on Mark's back with balled fists. Mark had Joe wrapped up in a bear hug, his head buried into the older boy's chest. Joe rolled around and finally freed himself. Mark came at him like a windmill, throwing one punch after another. Joe did not know how to defend himself. He took hits all over his body. Joe was backing up trying to protect his face. Finally Mark caught him solidly on the nose.

"Uncle, uncle, quit hitting me!"

Mr. Branscomb, the principle, with help from two other teachers broke it up. Parents were called and the boys were picked up an hour after school. Mark sat quietly in the back of Mrs. Scolnik's car. He knew his mother was angry with him. All she did was sit up front in silence until they got home.

"Mark, come over here and bend over!"

Jane used her bare hand to warm Mark's fanny and was immediately overcome with guilt.

"Now go to your room and stay there!"

Mark never thought his mother capable of issuing spankings. She gave it to him good, too. The realization that his mother spanked him angered him more. He felt betrayed. After a half hour, Jane couldn't stand it any longer.

What she saw in Mark frightened her. Mark had a violent temper. His brothers and sister thought it was real funny to egg him on until he lost his temper, usually with Nicole. Sometimes he'd go after one of his big brothers with whatever was handy, a bat, bottle, whatever. There was one other person in the family with that kind of temper.

"Mark, I want to talk to you."

"What do you want? Here's my belt so you can hit me like the old man!"

Jane was not prepared for that kind of rebuke. Of all her children, Mark was her favorite. She tried not showing favoritism, but Mark was her miracle boy. None of her other children had come close to death. This was a bond that would never change. Past tears were revisited as Jane sat next to her son.

"Mom, don't cry, I didn't mean it. I'm sorry, I didn't mean to make you cry."

Mark put his arms around his mother's neck and gave her a kiss on the cheek.

"Honey, I don't want you to be like your father. You have his temper and it frightens me. Please promise you won't fight anymore, please?"

"Okay Momma, I promise. I won't lose my temper anymore."

*****

Laura Lee Pike was a curvaceous twenty-eight year old applicant. This was her third interview. She had been trying to catch on with the Bureau for the last several months. Laura Lee's bright and attentive manner won people over quickly…especially men.

"Mr. Misner, your next interview is waiting."

"Fine Mrs. Cassidy, send her in."

Wonderful, she's probably an old prune like you. What happened to all the good-looking, young…

The door to Robert's office opened and in walked the sexiest woman he had ever seen as if in answer to his unfinished question.

"Hello, I'm Rob Misner. You are…?"

"Laura Lee Pike…Miss, Laura Lee Pike, very nice to make your acquaintance Mr. Misner!"

Laura Lee stuck out her hand confidently. Robert lingered with it longer than normal. Her hands were soft and pliant.

"Have a seat, Miss Pike. Can I get you anything, coffee, tea?"

Robert never asked interviewees if they wanted anything. He liked to watch them sweat. He never allowed them to smoke either, even though he daisy chained one after another. Robert would exhale right into their face, hoping to intimidate them.

"Can I offer you a cigarette?"

"Oh thank you, Mr. Mis…"

"Rob, call me Rob!"

"Oh thank you…Rob, that is so thoughtful. Chesterfields, what a manly cigarette, but I suppose I can handle it."

She crossed her Betty Grable legs as she made the last comment.

"I suppose I should try to quit smoking, it isn't very lady-like."

"Nonsense! Most everyone around here smokes. If they didn't when they started, it's not long before they pick it up."

Robert noticed the cigarette was on the verge of making Laura Lee gag, but she was determined.

"Now, let's take a look at your qualifications, hmm...I see you take shorthand at a reasonable speed. Your typing test results are excellent. The check we ran on your background is clean, your not a bank robber or murderer, heh, heh, heh."

"You mean they didn't find the bodies? I'm so relieved!"

"Let me make a note of that last comment. You are an accomplished murderer. What is your favorite weapon, gun, knife...poison?"

"None of those, I do my best work with an ax!"

"Oh my! Laura Lee, you left that off of the application and I'm afraid it was a terrible oversight."

"I left what off?"

She wasn't quite sure he was kidding now. The look on his face concerned her.

"The fact you were a Girl Scout."

"Girl Scout?"

"Yeah, you know, ax, camping...Girl Scout!"

"I see, that's hilarious Mr. Misner, uh, Rob I mean."

"I think you're going to work out just fine. The opening is in the typing pool. If you apply yourself and are diligent, I see no reason why you can't receive promotion within six months."

"Who's responsible for making that recommendation?"

"You're looking at him, Miss Pike."

"Well, Rob, I'll simply have to do everything I can to please you won't I?"

"Miss Pike, I am confident you will do just fine."

"Rob?"

"Yes, Miss Pike."

"It's Laura Lee."

*****

Jane knew Robert was seeing someone. In times past, the odor of cheap perfume permeated his suit coats. Another smell, an expensive one, adorned his clothes this time. *Rob, you must think I'm a fool. That, or you simply don't care if I know what you're doing.* Her reverie was broken by Mark's screams.

"Mark, my God! What happened? Your leg; the blood, my God, Nicole, Nicole, get me a towel quickly, quickly!"

Mark's entire tennis shoe was covered with blood that was gushing from a cut in his knee.

"Here, give me your leg. Let me wrap this around it. I'll just put some pressure on it. Does it hurt?"

Now that his mother was attending the leg, his cries stopped and he could talk.

"No, it doesn't really hurt that bad. I was more scared than anything I guess."

"Let's see what we have here. The bleeding is almost stopped. It's just a little cut. All it needs is a band-aid. You sure it doesn't hurt?"

"No, Mom, it'll be okay. I'll go out and finish cutting the grass."

Mark returned to his lawnmower, none the worse for wear. He was just finishing up when his father pulled into the driveway.

Robert got home at an irregular time, five-thirty. As he stepped into the dining room he saw the splotches of red all over the carpet.

"Jane, what in God's name happened in here?"

"Mark had an accident while he was cutting the grass."

"Are you going to tell me what happened?"

"Something shot from under the mower and cut his knee. I got the bleeding stopped and put a band-aid on it."

"Did he finish with the grass?"

Robert never got an answer to his question. Jane shook her head and left him standing in the dining room. He heard Mark come through the back door.

"Come in here and let me see your leg!"

Mark propped his leg on the chair so his father didn't have to bend over. Robert yanked the band-aid off in one clean jerk. A small fountain of puss and blood oozed from the open wound.

"Jane, bring something in here, he's bleeding again!"

"Why did you take that off? The bleeding had stopped."

"I wanted to see how bad it was. It's only a little cut, I don't understand what all of the fuss was about."

"Who was fussing? You're the one that's fussing about it."

"I can't say anything around here without you criticizing me! Why did I even bother coming home early? I'm going out, don't wait up for me!"

*****

Rob drove to Old Town Alexandria. He parked across the street from Laura Lea's row house, trying to decide what to do. He watched the dwelling, trying to summon the nerve to go knock on the door. Just as he was about to get out of his car, the door opened and a man about Laura Lea's age came out. She gave him a playful peck on the cheek. He got in his '55 Pontiac and drove off. Rob sat in his car trying to figure this out.

She should live in a better neighborhood. This place has got too many damn niggers. I wonder if that guy just fucked her? I should just go to the Slipper and get laid. Rob, you don't have a hair on your ass! Get out of the damn car and knock on the door!

Laura Lea saw Robert from the living room window and decided to play it cute.

"Who is it?"

"FTD man!"

The door opened and Rob's jaw dropped. All she had on was a towel.

"You must be new, I've never seen you before. You're kind of cute. Would you like to come in?"

Rob broke into a big smile as he entered Laura Lea's house.

"Did you have some kind of problem in the house today?"

"Problem, I'm not sure I know what you mean?"

"I saw a young guy leaving as I pulled up. I thought he might be a repairman or something."

Laura Lea flushed for an instant but did not lose her composure.

"That was William, my little brother! He's visiting from Pittsburgh."

"He's pretty affectionate."

"We've always been very close. Why, Mr. Misner! Are you jealous of my little brother?"

"Jealous? Why would I be jealous? I just represent the office welcome wagon. Now, where would you like me to put these roses?"

Laura Lea took the proffered flowers and dropped them on the floor along with her towel.

"I saw you walking up to the door from upstairs. I was wondering how long it would take you to visit me."

Robert took Laura Lea in his arms and guided her to the couch. He lay on the sofa, running his hands all over her body. Her nipples were surrounded by goose bumps. Rob knelt, cupping a breast with his hand as he lowered his mouth onto it. Laura Lea made soft mewling sounds.

"Mister Misner, you're sooo wicked! That feels sooo good."

Robert undid his pants and removed his shoes. This was the best looking one yet. Rob could hardly contain his excitement. He spread her thighs apart and entered her forcefully. Laura Lea let out a gasp and fell into a grinding rhythm with him. After only seconds Robert's seed exploded within her. He lay next to Laura Lea on the couch. The foulness of his rancid cigarette breath almost made her sick but she hid it well.

"Ooooh Mister Misner, is that one of the fringe benefits. You never mentioned that during our interview."

"Miss Pike, that is only one of them, there are more."

"I can't wait to see the rest of them. May I have another now?"

"Baby, I wish I could but Pepe is all petered out. If you're a good girl, maybe he'll feel like playing later."

"Ooooh I can't wait!"

*****

Two days later Mark fell trying to get out of bed. He couldn't bend his right leg. It ached the night before but he thought nothing of it. As he put his foot down, pain shot up his leg. He peeled the band-aid off and saw puss oozing from the wound. It also smelled. He went downstairs finding his mother in the kitchen.

"Mom! I can't bend my leg!"

Jane told him the raise the leg of his pajamas. When she saw the leg, she knew infection had set in.

"My God Mark! Your leg looks awful!"

"Jeez mom, don't touch it. It's really sore. Is it supposed to be that red?"

Jane saw the red lines radiating from the wound, confirming her first impression. She called Doctor Sterns immediately.

"Doctor Sterns, this is Jane Misner. I'm fine, Doctor, I'm calling about Mark."

"What's wrong, Jane?"

"He cut his leg yesterday. Now it looks infected. It's also swollen so much he can't bend it."

"Can you get him in here?"

"Sure, I'll get Louise to drive us right now."

Mark walked as if he had a two by four tied to his leg. By the time they got to Doc' Sterns' office, the leg was throbbing. It was very sensitive to any pressure. The swelling had also spread to his ankle.

"My goodness, I don't believe I've ever seen a leg that swollen before. Let me clean out that wound."

Doc Sterns pulled the cut open. Puss and blood erupted from it. He dipped a cotton swab in iodine and applied it to the cut. Mark hollered in pain, almost coming off the table. He put a fresh bandage around the knee and told Mark to wait out front for his mother.

"We don't have a minute to lose. Can Louise take you to Fairfax for some x-rays?"

"We'll leave right now. Where do we go?"

"Go to the emergency room. I'll call ahead. I'm also going to call a good orthopedic man, the best around."

"Thanks, Doctor. How serious is this?"

"Get Mark to the hospital as fast as you can. We'll know more when the x-rays are done."

They had been waiting for over two hours for the doctors to look at the x-rays. Both Doctor Sterns and Dr. Antonelli sat next to Jane in the waiting room.

"Jane, this is Doctor Antonelli. He's the orthopedic surgeon I told you about earlier."

"It's nice to meet you, Doctor. Do you know what's wrong with my son."

"Yes ma'am, we do. He has a foreign object wedged in his knee joint. It looks like a piece of nail or wire. How did this happen?"

"Mark was cutting grass yesterday. He came running into the house screaming. I got the bleeding stopped and put a band-aid on it. It just looked like a small cut. My kids are always getting cuts and scrapes, so I didn't think anything of it. He went back out and finished the cutting."

"This is considerably more than a simple cut. If you had waited any longer, gangrene would have certainly set in."

"Doctor, he's not going to lose his leg is he?"

"No, Mrs. Misner. I said IF, if you hadn't bought him in when you did. Now that we have him, we can fix him right up. We'll have to operate to remove the object as soon as possible."

"When?"

"We've already scheduled an operating room. Mark will be checked in and prepped as soon as possible. I hope to operate by 5 o'clock this evening."

"Will his leg be okay?"

"I'll know more once we open it up and remove the object."

Jane went into the exam room and explained everything to Mark.

"Mark, honey, looks like you're going to spend a few days here. Dr. Antonelli is going to operate on your leg tonight. You must have run over a piece of wire with the mower."

"Cool, can I keep the wire when they take it out?"

"I'll ask the Doctor. I don't think he'll need it once it's removed. They're going to check you into a room now. Mrs. Scolnik is going to drive me home so I can pick up some pj's for you. I'll be back in about an hour, okay?"

"Sure Mom, don't worry about me, I'll be okay. Mom?"

"Yes honey, what is it?"

"Dad's going to be here, isn't he?"

"I'll call him when I get home. I'm sure he'll come later."

Jane knew how important it was to Mark to see his father. It wasn't the question itself that stuck in her mind, but Mark's tone; it was almost pleading; "Dad's going to be here isn't he?"

"Robert Misner's office, Mrs. Cassidy can I help you?"

"Jean, this is Jane Misner."

"Oh Mrs. Misner, how are you? I haven't talked to you in such a long time."

"I know it's been a long time. Jean, is my husband there?"

"He hasn't come back from lunch yet. Can I give him a message?"

"We've had an accident at home. Mark's in Fairfax Hospital."

"My stars, I hope it's nothing serious."

"They're going to operate on his knee tonight. I wanted Mr. Misner to join me at the hospital. Could you have him call just as soon as possible?"

"Of course, Mrs. Misner. I'll have him call just as soon as he gets back."

When Rob got back to the office, Mrs. Cassidy gave him the message. Robert was to meet Laura Lea after work. *The Scorch doesn't need me there. Jane will be there. What good can I do anyway?*

Mark woke up eighteen hours after the operation. He was saturated with his own urine. Everything smelled of it. He tried getting out of bed but felt too weak. He felt like he had the flu only ten times worse. He gave up the effort, falling back into bed. Mark felt too sick to worry about being embarrassed.

The door opened sometime later. Mark saw his nurse, Dixie, standing in the doorway with fresh linens. He lay there hoping she wasn't going to change his pajamas for him. No matter how sick he felt, that's an embarrassment he'd never get over.

"I see you've finally woken up! Let's see if we can't make you more comfortable, shall we?"

A huge colored man dressed in white came into the room. He lifted Mark onto a gurney.

"Mark, this is George Kingsley. He helped prep you for your operation. Do you remember him?"

In truth, Mark didn't remember. There is no way he could have forgotten the biggest colored man he'd ever seen in his life. Although, the more he thought about it the more he remembered. He thought he was dreaming about the big nigger, er, colored man.

Mark knew his mother would be very upset with him if she heard him say that word. Jane insisted her children refer to them as colored. His father called them niggers all the time. It was hard not to call them that. Mark had never talked to a colored person before. He wondered what his father would think.

"Mr. Kingsley, did you come into my room before the operation?"

"Yes sir, Mr. Mark, I surely did sir."

Mark just stared at the man. No one had ever called him 'Sir' before. That's what he called his father. Mark had gotten slapped more than once for not calling him 'Sir.' Now here was a grown man calling him 'Sir.'

"Mr. Kingsley, why are you calling me 'Sir'?"

"I is just bein polite Mr. Mark."

To hear his father talk, Mark thought colored people were nothing but lazy thieves with little, or no brains. His father almost made them sound evil. Mark had formed the same opinion, even though he'd never met one. George talked to Mark during the entire sponge bath. George's mannerisms and huge white teeth fascinated Mark. Before he knew it, he'd been bathed and had fresh pajamas on.

"I guess that's okay if you're just bein polite."

"We's gonna git to know each other a whole lot. I'm gonna see you evera day until you check outa here."

"How come?"

"I'm an orderly." The man said this with a certain pride. "I gets to wheel you to x-ray, change your sheets, help you clean yourself evera day, all a that."

"Mr. Kingsley, I'm kinda tired."

"Sho nuf Mr. Mark, you get yourself some sleep and I'll check on you later."

"Mr. Kingsley?"

"Yes, sir."

"Do you know if my father was here last night?"

Mark watched George as the man contemplated the question before answering.

"Why Mr. Mark, I do believe I seen your daddy last night, yes sir I do recollect that."

The man's hesitancy made Mark suspicious of his honesty. *Why isn't Dad here? Doesn't he care about me?* Mark decided the man was only trying to make him feel better.

"That's okay, Mr. Kingsley. You don't have to fib. I know my father wasn't here."

With that, Mark closed his eyes. His sleep was not restive.

Robert hadn't come home at all that night. Jane was furious as she picked up the phone to call his office the next day.

"Good morning, Mr. Misner's office. How can I help you?"

"Mrs. Cassidy, this is Jane Misner, did you give Robert my message yesterday?"

"Of course I did Mrs. Misner. Didn't you see him last night at home?"

Jane didn't want to tell the secretary of Rob's absence the night before.

"Is he there now?"

"No ma'am, he's not. Do you want me to take another message?"

"That won't be necessary. Is Mr. Collingsworth in?"

"Yes, he is."

"May I please talk to him?"

"I'll send you right through."

Stanley Collingsworth thought what everyone else did; that Rob was at the hospital. He hadn't seen him for two days. He could understand Rob being gone. He couldn't accept not having Misner check in. Stan took the call from Jane.

"Hello Jane, what can I do for you?"

"Hi Stan, I hate to bother you like this but have you seen Robert this morning?"

"No Jane, we haven't. We thought he was with you at the hospital. By the way how's Mark?"

"Thank you for asking, Stan. He had surgery to remove a piece of wire from his knee two nights ago. There is still a lot of swelling and fever. Mark's been delirious with fever and been asking for his father. Rob hasn't even called. I didn't know what else to do. Can you find him and tell him to call?"

"Jane, this is the FBI, we can do anything. When I find him, I will have him call."

"Thank you, Stan."

Stan was furious. He checked with Rob's associates hoping someone had information as to his whereabouts. Not one person had seen him. All he could do was wait.

"Mrs. Cassidy, when he calls in buzz me immediately."

"Yes sir, I will."

Mark's fever persisted. Jane stayed near his room. It was now the third day after the operation and he was no better. Dr. Antonelli took Jane to the cafeteria for a cup of coffee.

"Mrs. Misner, I don't want you to be overly concerned at this time because we're still in a wait and see mode."

"Doctor, just tell me what you are apparently afraid to tell me."

"Hmm, does it show that much?"

"Yes Doctor, it does. I'm no fool. I've watched Dixie change his dressings. I've seen how swollen his leg still is, how angry it looks. Its still red and you're worried about the infection? That putrefying odor is impossible to hide."

"Ma'am, you should have been a doctor. Yes, you're right. His leg should have responded by now. His fever is at its highest. In fact, it's way too high."

"The cool sponge baths haven't helped much. What else can you do?"

"The problem is the infection. We have to get that under control. The leg appears to be getting worse by the hour. I'm not sure we got to it in time."

"Doctor, what are you saying?"

"We may have to go in again and clean out the infection if his body doesn't start winning this fight. If he doesn't show improvement in the next couple of hours, we'll have to go in again."

"What's the worst that can happen if you can't control the infection?"

There was one thing the doctor learned about Jane Misner; she wanted the unvarnished facts.

"It's possible we would have to amputate the leg."

Doctor Antonelli let those words sink in before he continued.

"Mrs. Misner, where is your husband?"

"I wish I knew."

"In his delirium, Mark keeps asking for his father. An appearance by him would certainly not hurt. It may be just what Mark needs."

Jane did not know how to answer and found herself making excuses for her husband. She had heard Mark's cries for his father, too. It broke her heart. The doctor continued with his rounds, leaving Jane to ponder his questions. *Rob you are truly a bastard! I'm done making excuses for you. If you don't care, the hell with you!*

*****

197

Robert walked into his office the next day.

"Good morning, Mr. Misner. How's Mark doing?"

"He's doing fine."

"Then you've been to the hospital to see him?"

"Of course I have, why?"

"Your wife called several times yesterday looking for you. She even talked with Mr. Collingsworth."

"She did?"

"Yes sir. Oh, Mr. Collingsworth wanted to see you the moment you got in."

"You mean right now?"

"Yes sir, immediately was the word he used."

Damn! He thinks I've been at the hospital for the last two days. Now he knows I wasn't. God damn you Jane! Why in the world did you call that son-of-a-bitch?

Robert knocked on his boss's door.

"Come in."

Robert stuck his head in the door.

"You wanted to see me, boss?"

Stan cut to the chase.

"Misner, get in here and close the door!"

"Stan, I can explain. I…"

"I said now!"

"Yes Sir."

"Don't play dumb with me Misner, sit down!"

"Stan I can explain."

"I don't want to hear it! There's no excuse for abandoning your family at a time like this. I want you to get your ass to that hospital right now!"

"Yes sir, I'm leaving now."

"There's something else Misner."

Robert had started to rise from the chair to leave but now sat back down.

"Yes Stan, I'm listening."

"Good, I'll only have to say this once. I know what you're doing on the side. Given your past, it's not too hard to figure out. Your family is the only reason you still have a job. I'm going to call the nurses station in forty-five minutes. You better be in Mark's room, or there will be Hell to pay!"

"Yes sir, forty-five minutes, I'll be there."

Robert didn't want to be in the office any longer than he had to. He should be able to make it in twenty-five minutes. He had enough time to stop for a bottle on the way. The fifth of Old Crow was a third gone before he had driven half the distance. *Damn you Jane. You'll pay for this! Why did you have to call him? What a stupid thing to do.*

Robert had to calm down. His mind drifted to thoughts of Laura Lee. He thought of the pleasure she gave him. Once he was done at the hospital, he'd go see her again. She had a sympathetic ear. Laura Lea was good at making Robert feel better about himself. She was a mature woman, not empty headed like Sandy or Sheila. Like Brandi, Laura Lea knew what Robert liked. *God she drives me crazy!*

Robert was standing over his son's bed. The odor from his leg was awful. Mark was sweating profusely and saying something unintelligible. It sounded like, yes, he was calling for his father.

Mark's eyes opened. Everything was out of focus. He'd been dreaming about his father. He blinked, to clear his vision. His father stood over him. He took his father's hand.

Rob squeezed his son's hand in response. He saw the muscles on Mark's face relax as he closed his eyes and fell asleep. He thought of breaking the grip so he could leave. Something made him stay; this was his Scorch.

Seeing his son's reaction to his presence, Rob realized he was needed. He wondered if it was the same with Nicole.

He was tired of walking on eggshells around Jane. Calling his office, looking for him was the last straw. He wanted to get back at Jane. A plan started to take form as he sat with Scorch. It was deliciously simple. *As long as the kids need me, Jane won't do a thing. I'll even spend time with Nicole. Jane's weakness is the kids. As long as the kids want their dad around…*

*****

Freddy and four of his teammates were at Black Pond celebrating their latest victory. The beer was flowing freely and the Fredster was holding court. He turned around and whom should he see towering over him but Roger Trumball.

"Hey punk, I've got your little wise ass now!"

Freddy had too many beers. Rather than run, he tried talking his way out.

"Roger, can't you take a joke, man. I was just messing around."

Roger advanced quickly. His friends cut off any possible retreat route.

"I'm just going to mess around with you, big mouth!"

Roger slammed a big fist into Freddy's mouth, knocking the smaller boy down. Freddy's hand came away from his mouth, smeared with blood. His tongue ran over a fresh gap that front teeth once occupied. He looked over to his retreating friends and knew he was alone. He lashed back at Roger as he rose to his feet.

"You big dumb son-of-a-bitch, you knocked my damn teeth out!"

Roger just laughed and swung at him again. This time, Freddy ducked under the swing and hit Roger flush in his groin. Roger was on the ground, holding his balls while gasping for breath. Freddy never knew when to leave well enough alone. He stood over Roger, taunting him.

"That'll teach you. Wait until word gets around that you let some little Maplesville punk get the best of you."

Freddy was grabbed from behind. He'd forgotten about Roger's friends. Roger was getting his breath as he came to his feet.

"You're not going to live to tell about it! Hold on to him guys while I get my breath."

Roger took a few deep breaths before renewing his assault on Freddy. While his friends held Freddy, Roger slammed one punch after another into Freddy. His friends released their grip on Freddy and he collapsed to the ground, bleeding from his mouth and broken nose.

"Who's gonna be talking now, big mouth!"

Roger gave Freddy a couple of kicks in the back before turning to his friends. Freddy wasn't about to quit. Within his grasp was a big stick. He clutched it in his right hand and stood on shaky legs.

"Hey fat ass, I'm not done with you!"

Freddy swung the stick with all his might. It met the bridge of Roger's nose just as he turned. This time, Freddy was like a rabid dog. He went after the other boys, viciously swinging the stick. Before they had a chance to recoup, Richard Selmer was pulling at Freddy, trying to get him to leave.

"Come on Freddy, let's get the hell out of here."

"I'm not done with these assholes, Richard."

"I sent the others for my dad. He'll bring a couple of his deputies. These guys will be sorry they were ever born when those dudes get a hold of 'em."

Suddenly, Freddy felt very tired. His adrenaline rush was dissipating. He hocked a mouthful of blood in Roger's direction and left with Richard.

*****

Louise had just dropped Jane off from the hospital when the phone rang.

"Mrs. Misner, this is Richard Selmer."

"Yes, Richard. If you're looking for Freddy, he's not here."

"No ma'am, that's not why I'm calling, we're at the hospital with Freddy."

"What happened? Is Freddy all right?"

"Well ma'am, you see, he's okay, but you need to come get him."

"Richard, just tell me what happened! Have you been in a car accident? Is Freddy hurt bad?"

"We weren't in an accident. Freddy got beat up by Roger Trumball."

"I'll be there as soon as I can. Tell Freddy I'm on the way."

Damn you Robert! Where are you? We have two sons in the hospital and you're nowhere around. I'm really getting fed up with this. Jane hated to impose on Louise again but she had no choice.

Just as she got to the emergency room, she saw Robert getting off of the elevator.

"Where have you been for the last three days?"

"I was upstairs with Mark when a nurse came in and asked if I had a son named Freddy."

"We'll talk about this later."

At that moment, Freddy stepped out of the exam room, his face put together with stitches.

"My God, Freddy! What happened to your face?"

"Mom, it'll be all right. I got a little beat up, but you should see the other guy!"

Freddy started to laugh but the effort pulled at his stitches. Freddy could see his father was about to say something.

"I see your big mouth finally got you into trouble. Who was the teacher?"

Nothing his father said anymore meant anything to Freddy.

"Why do you even care? You weren't even interested in watching me pitch the championship game. You don't even care if Mark loses a leg. You'd rather stay away from home and fuck some bimbo! Man, I got nothing to say to you except go to!"

"Boy, don't you talk to ME that way, I'll…"

"What are you going to do, hit me in front of all these people! Go ahead hit me. I don't give a shit what you do anymore, you no good bastard! Why don't you just do us all a big favor and croak?"

Robert was not ready for Freddy's challenge. His eyes were glued to the attractive nurse walking toward them with some urgency. He'd forgotten about Freddy for the moment as Dixie addressed them.

"Mr. and Mrs. Misner, I'm so glad I got you before you left."

Jane was the first to respond.

"Dixie, what is it? Is Mark worse?"

"Not at all. His fever has broken and he says he's hungry!"

Without another word, Jane followed the nurse to Mark's room. Her son was sitting up in bed. Jane turned around thinking Robert was there but saw only Freddy.

"Where's your father?"

"He left."

"Great! How are we supposed to get home?"

"Janey girl, remember me, ol toothless?"

"Louise, I'd forgotten you brought me here."

"That's okay darling, I'll be here when you're ready to go."

"Mom, Dad was here. I'm all wet, but I didn't wet the bed this time, honest."

Jane looked at Dixie.

"Mrs. Misner, his fever has broken! I'll get him some dry bed clothes and pajamas."

"Mom, I feel better. I'm hungry!"

"Honey, I'll have them get you something to eat. I'm so happy you feel better!"

Mark noticed his brother.

"Hey Freddy! What happened to you?"

"I had my face rearranged by a lard ass, but I fixed him."

Jane could see Freddy was anxious to leave.

"Freddy, if you want to go home it's all right."

"I'm whipped. Ha ha! I'll get Richard to take me home."

At about that time Dr. Antonelli walked in.

"Let's take a look at that leg, young man."

Dr. Antonelli cut the dressing away. He noticed a big reduction in the swelling and redness. Although the bandages still had that odor, once he disposed of them and cleaned the wound area the smell was gone.

"Mrs. Misner, this is wonderful. Not an hour ago my colleagues and I thought we were looking at more surgery. Your son is going to be fine! Of course, we want to keep him for a few more days just in case. That will also give us a chance to get him in some physical therapy."

"Doctor, thank you so much."

*****

Robert stormed from the hospital. He could add his next to oldest to his list of those to get even with. The scene at the hospital was a humiliation for him. Despite his son's defiance, he had to send a message that no one messes with Robert Misner.

Luke Selmer was sitting in his usual place, in the back of the Maplesville Tavern. A couple of his deputies were also there. His deputies were no more than high school dropouts. They were big dropouts. They followed all of Luke's orders, without question. No one in their right mind wanted to run into Luke's deputies.

"Hey Rob, over here. Richard told me what happened. Hell, the whole town knows. I can't have those Annandale punks thinking they can beat up one of our local heroes. I thought you'd like to know, my two able bodied men here, took care of things at Black Pond. The Trumball boy was drinking. He resisted arrest. He's in the county detention center infirmary."

"Thanks Luke, I appreciate that."

"Don't mention it. You owe me a hunting trip. You know what my two boys here like."

"I'll make sure they get their Christmas bonus early this year. How would that suit you fellas?"

The two officers shook their heads up and down in agreement knowing they had some extra cash coming their way. Robert finished his business with Maplesville's finest and returned to the hospital. He walked into Mark's room to find the biggest black man he had ever seen.

"Hey Dad, I didn't expect to see you this early. This is Big George!"

George extended his hand to Robert.

"Mr. Misner, I'm George. Mark here calls me Big George, it's nice to make yo' acquaintance!"

Robert ignored the proffered hand, dismissing George with a wave of his hand.

"I'd like to be alone with my son."

The smile was still there, but Robert didn't notice the change in George's eyes. It didn't escape Mark.

"Mark, what's that big nigger doing in your room?"

"George? He's helping me so I can use my leg again."

"You mean he's touching you! I don't want that black bastard touching my son! I'll talk to the doctors about it. I'll see to it he doesn't come back."

"Dad, I like Big George. He's really friendly. He has nine kids! When I get out of the hospital he said I could visit with him and his family. Do you want to go with me?"

"Boy, you're not going anywhere near that nigger's slum. You may as well know, niggers are no damn good. They'll smile and be nice to you one minute, and then turn on you the next."

"Dad, Big George isn't that way. He's nice. I like him."

"You're not to go anywhere near that nigger again, you understand!"

"Yes, sir."

*****

Jane wasn't convinced this version of Robert was better than no Robert at all. She knew Bruce and Freddy were done with their father. She also knew the word 'divorce' put fear in Robert. That combination gave her some control.

Jane needed to be prepared financially in the event they did split up. She found filching money from his wallet every few days was a good way to accumulate cash. These funds were placed in a savings account. Jane also started practicing her shorthand and typing. The dexterity in her fingers was still there. It wasn't long before she surpassed her old typing speed. She honed her shorthand by taking dictation from the TV.

The next thing she needed to do was take the civil service test. She took the test and passed with flying colors. Her application was now on file with the Government. There was a shortage of good secretaries. She soon found herself preparing for her first day of work since 1938. During those times, she was surprised Robert kept his emotions in check. She knew that he was up to something.

Over the last few months, Jane noticed Robert's wardrobe had grown. He had lots of snazzy new clothes. Her curiosity had gotten the best of her. She discovered where Robert kept his old bank statements. She found the box in the closet. She started going through the canceled checks, writing down anything unusual.

Well Robert, it looks like you're spending money on someone. It sure isn't your family. What are all these checks to the Ambassador Hotel? Jane took out a pad of paper and started listing check totals and dates. A pattern took shape. There was a check to the Ambassador each Wednesday for the last six months. Large checks to jewelry and department stores appeared within one or two days after his getting paid.

Robert you're being a bad boy on Wednesdays! Jane's mind was racing. She was suddenly consumed with the idea of catching her husband red-handed. Jane was tired of worrying about the future. It was time to develop a long-term strategy. She thought of Robert's infidelity.

I feel the beginnings of a great idea. I think I'll see if Louise wants to go downtown this coming Wednesday. Jane crossed the street to her friend's house and laid out her plan.

"Oh darlin' that is one good idea! I'd love to go with you!"

"Great! We'll take the bus down next Wednesday and get to the Ambassador Restaurant at about noon. His normal lunchtime used to be at 12:30. That will give us time to get a table in the back so we can see him come in."

"Oh Janey girl, I can't wait! Hey, I've got an idea!"

"What's your idea, Louise?"

"My cousin, Louie!"

"Your cousin Louie? What does he do?"

"I never told you cousin Louie was a private detective?"

"Really? Do you think he could come with us? Does he have a good camera?"

"Janey girl, I can see what you're thinking! Yeah, he's a good photographer. He has to be."

"He can pretend to be taking pictures of tourists. If Rob shows up with his girlfriend, then he can snap their picture and offer to sell them a print. You know, the happy couple on the town for lunch, that kind of thing. Do you think that would work?"

"Janey girl, you're devious. I love it! You know what would even be better?"

"No, what?"

"If he could somehow get us in the picture. You know, in the background. That way old Robert would be cooked, but good."

"That would be great! Maybe Louie could even get them to give him one of those lovey-dovey poses for the camera."

*****

Robert and Nicole returned home from shopping for Prom dresses. The happiness on Nicole's face gave Jane second thoughts about her scheme to catch her husband with his little floozy. Then she realized what her husband was up to. This strengthened Jane's resolve. He was staying in her good graces by being extra nice to the children, especially Nicole. Of course he had the children fooled completely. All they knew was that their father showed an interest in them.

"Mother, look at my new dress. Daddy bought me shoes, a matching evening bag, hose, everything. Should I call Timmy and tell him I can go with him?"

"It's never a good idea to let them know you're too anxious honey. Wait until he calls back, he said he would right?"

"Yes, he said he'd call me tonight."

"Let's go upstairs. You can try on your dress so I can see if it needs alteration."

"That's a wonderful idea. I can show Daddy how pretty I am in it!"

"Yes honey, you can show your father how pretty you are."

*****

Well Bruce, you are about to learn one of life's valuable lessons, you ungrateful whelp. I'm about to fix you good! Besides, I can't have my oldest son cavorting with the daughter of a mailman. How would that look?

Robert could see Gene Elgin's blue Buick in the driveway and knew he was home. Robert knocked on the door.

"Rob Misner! What do we owe this visit to?"

"Gene, I'm afraid I have some unpleasantness to discuss with you."

"Really? What would that be, Rob?"

"I would have hoped my son would have been man enough to do this but I can see by the look on your face Bruce hasn't talked to you, has he?"

"Does this have something to do with Becky running home in tears the other day?"

"Did she say anything about what happened?"

"No, she was too upset. What do you know about it?"

209

Oh I've got him now. I'm going to enjoy this!

"Gene, I want you to know I've always had tremendous respect for the way you have raised your family. I can tell you are very close to your girls. As you know, I have two girls myself."

"Rob, what are you trying to say? Did your son do something to Becky?"

"I'm only telling you this because I have daughters of my own. As a father, I'd want to know if a boy tried to take advantage of one of my daughters."

"Did your son try to take advantage of my Becky?"

"As much as I hate to admit it, he did."

"Rob, how do you know this?"

"I caught him fondling your daughter under the chaise lounge in our rose garden."

"Why would you tell me such a thing about your own son?"

"I've struggled with this decision. I was hoping Bruce would be man enough to tell you himself.

"He hasn't said anything to me!"

"I didn't think so. I'm disappointed in him, with his lack of courage. I prayed, given a few days, he'd come forward."

"He hasn't! I have some things I'd like to say to him!"

"I'm sure you do."

"I can't believe this. You're certain about this?"

"There was no mistaking it. Hasn't your daughter said anything?"

"Not a thing. She was very upset when she got home. I thought it best to let her cry it out, if you know what I mean."

"I do."

"Rob, if you'll excuse me, I have to talk with my daughter."

"Of course Gene, I understand. Again, I am sorry."

Without another word the two men parted company. *That was fun! Now let's see how you like that Mr. Bruce!*

*****

The two women got a table in the back of the restaurant. It had a clear view to the entrance. It was just before noon and the Ambassador dining room was filling up fast. There were no vacant tables around them. Even if Rob did see them, Jane could always use shopping as an excuse for being there. On the other hand, how would he explain his companion to her? At the very least, it promised to be an entertaining afternoon.

"Janey, there's Louie. I told you he was smooth."

"Maybe he ought to change jobs. It looks like he's doing well."

Right in the middle of their tuna salad, Jane saw them. Robert had a young blonde that appeared to be in her late twenties on his right arm. She was beautiful.

"My God! Janey girl, she's a looker!"

"She is quite…beautiful."

"Oooh wee, look at those!"

"Oh my! Now I see what attracted him to her."

"Honey, I've only seen things like that in magazines!"

"Louise, what magazines do you read?"

Robert had helped his companion out of her coat. The neckline of her dress was very low. This feature drew a lot of attention from nearby men. She came close to spilling out as she sat. Jane and Louise watched Robert fawn over her.

"Would you look at him? It's disgusting! He never showed me that much attention!"

"Janey, honey, you are one of the most beautiful women I know, but you can't compete with that! Just look at how she spills out of that dress!"

"Who says I want to compete with her. She can have him!"

"Honey, I love you to death, you know that? I also know you better than you know yourself. For instance, I know what you're feeling right now."

"What am I feeling?"

"You're feeling hurt and betrayed."

"Louise, that's ridiculous. I've known about his affairs for years."

"But this is the first time you've seen it up close and personal."

Jane realized Louise had her pegged as a tear tickled down her cheek.

"Janey, are you ok?"

Sniff..."yeah, I'll be okay."

"Honey, don't be cryin over that man! Look at all he's put you and your children through! Now is no time to shrivel up on me. You need to get mad, good and mad!"

"I know Louise...it's just that, well...I didn't expect to react this way. I didn't expect to be...jealous."

"Honey, that's only natural. It's okay to feel that way. You been married to that no good so and so for how many years...twenty?"

Sniff..."twenty-two."

Louise grabbed Jane by the arm to bolster her spirits.

"Look honey, Louie is moving closer to their table."

"Does he know that's Robert?"

"You gave me a picture, remember?

"I remember."

"Don't let this cloud your thinking. Get mad! Come on, he's talking to them."

The two women got up as if to approach the buffet. They made sure Louie had Robert's attention and circled behind his table.

*****

Robert and Laura Lea had just taken their seat when she noticed the photographer.

"Oh Rob, isn't that sweet! Look, over there. He's taking that young couple's picture."

"I've never noticed a photographer in here before."

"Oh Rob, can we get our picture together please, please?"

"I don't think that's a good idea."

"Robert, please for me? We don't have a picture together. What could it possibly hurt? It's not like you're going to take it home and put it on your mantle."

"All right. If he comes over we'll let him take our picture."

Robert and Laura Lea ordered their lunch and settled into watching the photographer. Something about him looked vaguely familiar to Robert.

"Laura Lea, I've seen that guy somewhere. I don't know where, but he looks familiar."

"Robert, you've probably seen him downtown somewhere else and just don't remember."

"I'd remember a guy taking pictures. He looks familiar I'm telling you!"

Laura Lea adopted a pouting expression, her lower lip protruding out.

"You mean you're not going to let him take our picture? Oh Rob, please? I'll be extra good to you tonight."

213

"If it means that much to you, I suppose it can't hurt. I'm probably mistaken about the guy anyway."

"Look at you two! What a handsome couple you make! Mister how about a keepsake for the little lady? It's only a buck for an eight and half by eleven."

"Yeah sure, why not?"

"Come on Mister, you can look happier than that. Take a good look at your girl! She's beautiful. Put your arm around her and give her a kiss for the camera. Oh, come on. I'll pay for you to take my picture kissing her! That's better! Show her how much you love her! Come on let her know you mean it! Perfect! Here's my card little lady. Give me a call in a couple of days and your picture will be ready. I can have wallet size made up also."

"No, now here's your buck, get lost."

"Robert, you didn't have to be mean to him. He's just trying to make a living."

"Yeah, right. I'll be real surprised if you ever see a picture from this. I think he's scamming people for dollars. Come to think of it, that would be a nice little racket."

"You always think the worst of people."

*****

Jane was staring at the back of her husband's head from about ten feet away. She had a tremendous urge to hit him with something. Jane felt the grip of her friend's hand on her arm when they kissed. When the flash went off, Jane blinked and almost gave herself away. Louise ushered Jane back to their table. As they sat, Louie continued to make his rounds through the dining room.

"Louise, I've seen enough for one day. I'm ready to go home now."

"Honey, we better wait until they leave. We don't want to tempt fate again. Let's order desert."

PART FOUR

Bruce knocked on the Elgin's front door and Mr. Elgin answered.

"Mr. Elgin, how are you sir? Is Becky here?"

"Son, you have a lot of nerve coming here like this!"

"Sir, I don't understand?"

"You're not welcome here, after what you did to my Becky. Turn around and leave right now!"

The door slammed in Bruce's face. He knocked on it again...louder.

"Boy, what did I just tell you?"

"Mr. Elgin, wait! Please? Why are you so angry with me?"

"You know very well! Now if you don't leave, this is going to get physical!"

"Mr. Elgin, Please, let me explain!"

"Your father already told me everything I need to know. Are you going to leave or do you need help?"

Mr. Elgin moved his six foot four frame onto the porch.

"My father? When did you see my father?"

Bruce's ire was raised and wanted answers of his own.

"Yesterday!"

Mr. Elgin moved closer to Bruce.

"Sir, do you know my father?"

Gene Elgin grabbed Bruce by the shirt and hauled him to his toes.

"Mr. Elgin, if it will make you feel better to hit me, I understand. Before you do, can I say something?"

Not releasing his grip, Mr. Elgin said, "Talk quick."

"My father hates me and would do anything to ruin my life. I don't know what he told you, but I am prepared to tell you what happened. First, I love Becky and would never do anything to hurt her. Second…"

Becky came to her open window when she heard Bruce's voice. She heard his last words and ran downstairs. Mr. Elgin released Bruce. Becky wedged herself between the two men she loved.

"Bruce, you love me!"

The look on his daughter's face spoke volumes. Mr. Elgin decided there was more to this story than Robert let on. He was willing to let Bruce have his say.

"Becky, stay out of this. Let Bruce talk."

Bruce started, once Becky stepped to the side.

"Mr. Elgin, I'm not going to try to explain my father. I'm not going to make excuses for my behavior either. We were playing kick the can with the younger kids and wound up under our chaise lounge. We started kissing and…touching each other. My father must have been spying on us, cause he lifted the coverlet and saw us. That's what happened."

"Why didn't you come sooner?"

I wanted to come here sooner, but my little brother has been in the hospital for the last few days. I've had to take care of my sisters, while mom has attended Mark. This is the first chance I've had to see you. Sir, I love Becky. I wouldn't do anything to hurt her."

Becky threw her arms around Bruce's neck, kissing him all over. Bruce broke free, turning red, as he looked Mr. Elgin in the eye. Clearly embarrassed, Becky's father shook his head and went into the house.

"Bruce, you love me, you really love me?"

"I do, but we have to be careful. Becky is your father going to be okay with us dating? I mean, he doesn't seem to like me."

"Daddy will be fine. Is your father going to be a problem?"

"We don't need to worry about him. I won't be living at home much longer anyway."

"I love you, Bruce."

"I love you too, Becky."

Bruce decided he'd not let his father draw him into an argument. *If he wants to think he's won some sort of battle, so be it. I'll let him think that.*

*****

Robert knew Bruce had gone next door. He watched through the window as he knocked on the Elgin's door. He went back to his chair, to his bottle of Old Crow, gloating over his triumph. *I bet he gets an earful. It serves him right; he's gotten too big for his britches. He needs to be taken down a notch. Hmm, maybe I could recruit her for the office. I need to find another young broad to fuck. I'd love showing her the ropes. Wouldn't that be something? .*

Robert could hear Bruce taking the back steps two at a time. Something wasn't right. Bruce was whistling when he entered the house. *Why is he whistling? What in the Hell happened? Don't tell me he talked himself out of it?*

"Bruce, come in here for a minute. I want to talk to you."

"I don't want to talk to you."

"Boy, you still live in my house. You better get in here."

Bruce went into the living room and stood over his father.

"I'm here, what do you want to tell me?"

217

"How's that little slut of a girlfriend doing?"

Bruce wasn't going to let his drunken father bait him.

"She's fine, how's your slut?"

"That's no way for you to talk about your mother. Ha ha ha!"

"We all know you've been screwing around behind mom's back. Do you think you've actually fooled her? She's had you figured out a long time!"

Robert tried to rise. As he put his hand on the buckle, Bruce did the same with his belt. Before Rob could stand, Bruce shoved him back, into his chair. Bruce had taken his belt off. He was waving it under his father's nose.

"Next time you come at me with your belt, I'll be ready."

"If I wasn't half drunk, I'd beat your ass right now!"

"That never stopped you before."

Jane could hear the commotion from the basement. She ran up the stairs to the living room. Bruce had his belt off and was threatening Robert.

"Bruce, that's enough! He can't hurt you anymore. "

"Mom, do you know what he did?"

"What?"

Bruce told her about his father's visit to Mr. Elgin.

"Robert, I thought your beatings were bad. You just went way beyond that. Why would you do such a thing?"

"He's turned into an ungrateful punk. I don't want him under my roof, if he can't show me proper respect!"

"I know all about your little liaison with the blonde at the Ambassador. Don't threaten to kick my son out of this house. You'll be the one leaving!"

"What are you talking about? What blonde?"

Jane left the room. She came back with Louie's freshly developed glossies. Robert recognized them immediately. The most damaging was the one of Robert screwing Laura Lea on her couch.

"Tell me that's not you and your bimbo!"

"Where did you get these?"

"What does that matter?"

Robert grabbed the photos and ran for the front door.

"Mom! Where did you...how did you...?"

"Bruce, what did I hear you tell your father? Oh yes, she's had you figured out a long time!"

"You were listening?"

"I didn't want to interrupt. You deserved to have your moment."

"What are you going to do? I'll tell you what you should do."

"Honey, I know what you're going to say. I don't care who he's screwing. The more he stays away the better."

*****

Robert had real problems now and needed an escape, even if it was just temporary.

It was late afternoon when Robert pulled out of the drive. The booze had slowed his reaction time as he came to a neck-snapping stop at the end of the street. Looking to the right, he saw the Elgin's blue Buick turn onto Chain Bridge Rd. from Old Courthouse.

It's that saucy little bitch that's causing all of my trouble. I wonder how fast she can hit the brakes.

Robert waited until the last minute. He whipped his car onto 123, in front of Becky. As he picked up speed, he heard the sound of squealing tires and crunching metal behind him.

As he sped toward town, he saw the long line of brake lights in his rearview mirror. He noticed something else. His back window ledge had a collection of dead insects. His family was like that; a collection of dead bees and dragonflies in the rearview mirror of his mind.

When he entered the tavern, Luke was there with his deputies. Rob noticed Whip in his usual place. He was mumbling incoherently to himself as Rob sat down with Luke. Suddenly, Luke's radio came to life.

"Luke! Luke! Pick up, pick up! There's been an accident at Chain Bridge and Horseshoe with probable injuries!"

"Linda, this is Luke, me and the boys are on our way!"

"Rob! There's a bad accident right at your intersection! Did you see anything on your way here?"

"No Luke, I didn't."

After Luke and his men left, Rob was alone with Whip. The two men spent the next four hours complaining about ungrateful women.

*****

Bruce had just gone upstairs to study when he heard the crash.

"Mom! What was that?"

"Bruce, I don't know. It sounded like a crash."

Jane's mind went back to another day when her thoughts were interrupted by screeching tires.

"Quick, go see what happened!"

Bruce was already out the door before Jane could finish her sentence. He had a funny feeling in the pit of his stomach. His legs propelled him toward the scene swiftly. Men were pulling at the driver's door of a blue Buick.

"Somebody bring a crowbar she's still alive, hurry!"

Bruce wedged his way through the growing throng of passersby.

"Let me through, let me through!"

"Son, get back, we're trying to get to her."

The sound of sirens could be heard, as they got ever closer. Bruce ignored the protests of the men trying to pry the door open. He moved to the passenger side of the Elgin Buick. Wedging his body through the broken glass, Bruce was able to reach Becky. She was trying to call to him. Her voice was barely a whisper.

"Bruce, Bruce, where are you? Bruce."

"Becky, honey, I'm here! I'm here! I'm holding you Becky! We'll get you out of here. You'll be okay. We'll get you out, can you hear me Becky? Becky I love you, don't leave me, please Becky don't leave me!"

"Bruce, there you are. My daddy's not mad at you anymore. I told him I love you. Bruce, hold me, please hold me."

"I am Becky, I'm right here, holding you. I love you. I want to marry you. Don't leave me!"

She found him through eyes that could not see.

Becky died moments later.

Strong arms pulled Bruce from the car. It was Mr. Elgin. They shared their torment as they embraced on the side of the road.

*****

Louise visited the next day. Jane and she talked while sipping tea under the rose arbor.

"How is everything with Bruce?"

"I've never seen him so low. Why did this have to happen? He was so happy. Now all I see is hopelessness."

"Has Robert said anything? Has he tried to talk with Bruce about the accident?"

Jane turned her face away, trying to compose herself.

"Jane, what's the matter? Did I say something I shouldn't?"

She took a long breath before answering.

"Robert was scheming to break them up. He went to Mr. Elgin with some crazy story about Bruce groping Becky in our backyard."

"He didn't?"

"Yes, he did. That's when I showed him Louie's pictures. He grabbed them from me and left. Shortly afterward, Bruce and I heard the crash. At first, I thought it was Robert."

"Janey, you don't think he had anything to do with the accident?"

"What could he have done?"

"I heard someone say they saw a car like Rob's speeding away from the accident."

"Oh my God!"

"I'm just putting two and two together. Robert would have been pulling onto the highway at about the same time as the accident. You said he was drunk. Maybe she was trying to avoid hitting his car."

"No! Louise, that's too terrible. Rob is rotten, but not that rotten!"

"I'm just saying it's a possibility."

"Louise, don't say anything about this to anyone, it's only your opinion."

"Whatever you say. Rob didn't say anything when he got home?"

"He never came home. He was probably with blondie."

*****

The next night at the dinner table, Rob spent most of his time sneering at Bruce. Bruce tried ignoring him, while he played with his food. Bruce had started to get up when Robert finally spoke.

"Luke Selmer says they figured out how that accident happened."

Jane looked from her son to Robert. She tried changing the subject.

"Let's not talk about that now."

Robert ignored Jane's request and forged ahead.

"You know old Luke. He hates women drivers worse than I do! That accident is another good reason why women shouldn't drive. The little slut is lucky she didn't kill someone else."

Robert's timing was impeccable. He knew exactly what button to push. Bruce's reaction caught him off guard.

"You miserable son-of-a-bitch!"

Bruce came to his feet swinging. The blow knocked Robert to the floor, dazed. Bruce followed up by straddling his father's chest, wailing away.

"Bruce! That's enough. Stop! You've done enough."

"Okay. He's out cold anyway."

The attack lasted less than a minute. Bruce looked at his mother with resignation.

"I guess I better go pack some things. I can't see myself staying here any longer."

"You're not moving out permanently, are you?"

"It's time for me to be on my own."

"Where will you stay? What will you do for money?"

"I've been thinking about this for a long time. I'll be fine; I've got it all worked out. I can live in the pool office. That's one advantage of managing the place."

"There's no heat. How will you keep warm?"

"Its warm enough. I'll only be there at night. I'll just use extra blankets."

"What about money for food?"

"Mom, you know I've been saving since I was twelve. I have plenty of money."

"I'm just worried."

"Don't worry about me, really, I'll be fine."

Jane followed Bruce to his room. She watched as he picked up the duffle he'd pre-packed.

"You were planning on leaving anyway?"

"I've been trying to tell you all day. I didn't know how too."

Jane's eyes watered as Bruce turned to leave. They both saw Robert at the same time. He had a gun. His speech was slurred as he stood pointing his nickel plated .38 at his son.

"I've called Luke. He and two of his boys are going to take you for a little ride. I told him you attacked me. I'm having you arrested. Drop that bag and sit on the bed until he gets here."

"Robert! What do you think you're going to do with that gun?"

When Robert turned to reply Bruce charged into him. They both hit the floor hard. The gun went off…BANG! The bullet just missed Bruce's head. Bruce and Robert grappled for the gun. Another shot went off. Jane was hysterical. Bruce hit his father with a hard right. The gun rattled to the floor. Jane snatched it up.

Bruce stood over his father and spit on him. He made a step to his door but turned around to get his prized possession. His signature baseball was no more. The last bullet tore its path through the 'y' in 'Mickey'. Bits of the ball were everywhere. Bruce dropped the empty cover on his father's chest as he stepped over him.

"Here's a souvenir of our relationship."

"You come back here. You're under arrest! Do you hear me?"

Robert looked up at his wife's face. He'd never seen such fire and determination before.

"Robert, I want you gone from this house. You're not spending another night under this roof!"

"You can't kick me out of this house, I own it!"

"Fine, if you don't leave, I'll have you arrested for attempted murder."

"You wouldn't dare! How will you support your precious children without my money?"

"I don't need you. The court will make you pay child support."

"You'll never make it on your own!"

"I've been on my own for years. I'll do fine."

Jane packed a bag for him and threw it down the stairs. Robert was about to leave when Luke Selmer knocked on the door.

"Luke, we won't be needing you tonight. Robert was drunk again and made a mistake. You might want to make sure he's okay to drive, he's had a snoot full."

"I haven't had too much to drink! My wife is kicking me out. What do you think about that Luke? The bitch is kicking me out of my own house!"

Robert gave Jane a searing look as he reached for the bag. All Jane felt was pity for the man her husband used to be. She bore into his drooping eyes and said,

"Goodbye Robert."

Robert woke the next morning to a tapping on his car window. It was Luke.

"Robert, wake up man. Have you been here all night?"

The world was out of focus. Rob held his head in both hands.

"I guess so. Me and Whip were uh, well I guess I had a little too much to drink."

"You need to clean up. Do you have a place to go?"

"I'll go to my mother's."

"Rob, why don't you go home? You and Jane have had fights before. She's always forgiven you."

"I think this time I've really done it. I'll go stay with my mother for a while."

"That's your hangover talking. Jane will take you back, you'll see."

"I think this time she means it. Hell, she's even getting a fulltime job."

"At least come to the station and take a shower. You'll feel better once you've cleaned up. Things might look a little better then."

Robert called in sick. He was contemplating how to get Jane to change her mind. Then he thought about Laura Lea. The hell with his mother, he'd stay with Laura Lea. The next thing he knew, he was knocking on her door.

"Robert, what's with the suitcase?"

"You've been after me for months to leave Jane."

"You mean you're finally going to do it?"

"That's why I'm here, happy? Why don't you call in sick today, we have a lot to talk over."

"Oh yes, I'll call in. I have some wonderful news for you as well!"

Robert stepped into the townhouse and shut the door behind him.

"What's the wonderful news baby?"

"I'm pregnant!"

"You're what? How can that be? You said you were taking precautions! We agreed there would be no babies!"

"Robert! Don't scream at me. Now that you've left your wife, what difference does it make?"

"What difference? It makes all of the difference! I'm not ready to broadcast this news to the world. Do you realize what you've done? You said you were taking precautions!"

"What about you, why couldn't you be the one to take precautions?"

"I hate using those things; it's like taking a shower with a raincoat on!"

"There's nothing we can do about it now. I'm pregnant. It can't be undone. We'll have to deal with it. Besides, I thought you loved me!"

"I do love you. But this…this is not what I wanted. This changes everything!"

"Robert, what does it change?"

"Everything! It changes everything! I didn't tell you to get pregnant!"

"Robert! You're not going to leave me are you? I couldn't bear that! Please say it will be okay! I couldn't stand being without you!"

Robert took Laura Lea in his arms to comfort her. She pressed her body tightly against him. Robert pushed himself away and held Laura Lea at arms length.

"I need some time to think. I'll go stay with my mother for a few days. I'll call you once I've worked this out."

Anguish showing on her face, Laura Lea tried to hold Robert to her. He stepped back. She became angry.

"Work what out? Mister you got me pregnant and now you have to pay. There is nothing else to work out. The only thing to work out is how you're going to live up to your responsibilities."

Robert kept backing his way to the door with his suitcase in hand.

"Laura Lea, I'll call you, I'll call you. I have to go."

By this time, Laura Lea was talking to Robert's back. He could hear her screaming through the closed door.

"Robert, Robert, come back! I need you, please come back!"

*****

Laura Lea watched Robert drive away before going to the phone. The line on the other end rang twice. A male voice answered.

"Well lover, I sprung it on him just a minute ago."

"How'd he take it?"

"The timing couldn't have been better! His wife kicked him out. He showed up with a suitcase."

"You're shittin me?"

"I wouldn't shit you, baby. You should have seen the look on his face."

"This is beautiful. We'll suck every dime we can out of that S.O.B. You have the doc lined up for the abortion?"

"I know how to play this. He'll call back here in a couple of days and want to talk about it. I'll get him in the sack and work him. I'll tell him I don't want to lose him and will give up our baby. He's about the horniest guy I ever met, next to you. We'll get a couple of thousand from him for the abortion. That's only the beginning."

"Baby you're a genius! How did you suck him in like this?"

"Why don't you come over and I'll tell you. I need a real man, one that can satisfy me before blowing his wad."

"Get ready for the screwing of your life baby. I'll be there in an hour."

"I'm getting hot just thinking about you, baby."

"Oh baby, one more thing?"

"What is it lover?"

"You're not really pregnant are you?"

"What do you think?"

"Just making sure, that's all."

*****

Robert's heart was pounding in his chest as he made the drive to Fessenden Street. *What else can go wrong? Pregnant! The little bitch is pregnant! What am I going to do?* He wasn't ready to face his mother. Robert went for a drive through Rock Creek Park. The scenery there always seemed to calm him. Something about this didn't feel right.

After about an hour, Robert decided to go back to Laura Lea's. He knew the right people. One advantage about being in law enforcement was the contacts he made. Doc Joynes was a good example.

Doctor Griffith Joynes had lost his medical license for performing abortions. He'd also done some time. *It won't even cost me that much.* As he walked toward Laura Lea's house, he saw her brother's car.

Instead of knocking on the door, he stepped off of the stoop and peered into the front window. They weren't in the living room. He moved to the back window looking into the kitchen. He was instantly rewarded.

Sitting with her legs wrapped around her brother was Laura Lea. Robert's hand moved down to his crotch. His excitement grew as he watched Laura Lea getting fucked by her brother. *Brother my ass. Miss Pike, it looks like you've been stringing me along.*

Robert couldn't pull himself from the window. He hated to admit it, but watching her with another guy excited him. Robert looked around making sure no one was watching him. Finally, he broke away from the window. Once he was back in his car, the scene kept replaying in his mind.

Laura Lea you never acted that wild when I fucked you. He wrote down the license number of her boyfriend's car. *I'll have a couple of Luke's deputies pay the brother a visit. They'll find out what Romeo is up to. Once lover boy is gone...*

Back through Rock Creek he drove, planning his next move. *Rob you're an idiot. You fell for one of the oldest scams around. I bet they planned on soaking me good. I wonder if she's really pregnant?* Robert would force her hand on that issue. He would use old Doc Joynes. If she balked in any way, her game was over.

Robert realized he couldn't simply dump her. He couldn't fire her either. Robert remembered Sheila. He would do the same thing with Laura Lea. *I'll get her transferred to the deepest shit-hole at the Bureau. There are areas in the identification division where the cobwebs have cobwebs.*

Rob called Luke, giving him the plate number. Luke assured him the boys would handle things from there. The next night Rob found the boys at their table in the Tavern.

"Hey Rob, we're over here."

"Luke, you have some news for me?"

"You know that little slime ball lives in town here?"

"No I didn't. Is he in the relocation program?"

"My boys found him banging Angela Corbett on his living room floor."

"Isn't she William E's little girl?"

"Yeah and only fifteen. This one was free Rob. My boys got a lot of pleasure rehabilitating the prick."

"Here's a little something anyway."

"Rob I said it's not necessary."

"I know, but take it anyway. You want another drink boys?"

"We also got all the scoop on their scam."

"Oh yeah?"

"First of all, the girl isn't pregnant. They were going to squeeze you good."

Robert received a complete report from Luke. He was assured the boyfriend was out of the picture. Robert could breath a little easier. He was free to address his bigger problem, Jane.

If she files for divorce, I'm cooked. I've got to convince her to let me hang around. Thank God I've been good with the younger ones. She wouldn't dare kick me out if she thought it would hurt the kids. That's her soft spot, the kids. All she's ever wanted from me is to be a good father. I can do that.

When Robert entered the house, he wasn't greeted with the usual, "Where have you been" from his mother. As a matter of fact, it was too quiet. He walked all through the house calling his mother. There was no response. As he entered the kitchen Robert looked out the back window and saw her.

He flung the screen door open and ran to his mother's side. Hilda was lying on the ground with the broom still clutched in her hands. *Well mother, it looks like you beat your last rug.* Hilda Misner was dead. Rob felt nothing, not even the slightest twinge of remorse. His mother was dead and that was it.

*****

Robert sat in the front row during the funeral service. He was wallowing in self-pity, or at least put on a good show of it. To his amazement, Jane sat down next to him.

"Jane! What are you doing here? You hated my mother."

"Hate Rob? No, I don't hate anyone, that's your domain."

"All the same, I didn't expect to see you."

"I guess you wouldn't understand something like compassion."

"Compassion, I have plenty of compassion."

"Rob, if you had any compassion, we'd still be together. This is not the place for this conversation."

"Can we talk after the service?"

Jane left Rob hanging on the last question. They had been apart for almost a week. To Robert, it seemed years since the showdown with Bruce. Lately, his life seemed to be one cataclysmic event after another. When the service was over, Robert walked Jane to Louise's car.

"Jane, why don't you tell Louise she can go. I'll take you home."

"That won't be necessary."

"Are you still determined to see this divorce through?"

Jane searched Robert's features, hoping to see some sign of feeling. There was none. His face had taken on the permanent mask of harshness. The young Robert she married over twenty years ago, the one full of hopes and dreams…was gone. She looked into Rob's eyes and saw Hilda.

"The children have been asking about you, especially Nicki."

This was the opportunity Robert wanted. He stopped in mid-stride. He looked intently into Jane's eyes. Robert didn't see the same naïve girl he married. He did see a woman to reckon with. He needed to choose his words carefully.

"I know I've made a mess of things. There are too many holes in the dike and not enough fingers between us. I accept complete responsibility for the failure of our marriage. I mistakenly thought by being tough on the kids, they'd grow to be strong men and women."

"You're right. Bruce and Freddy are both strong, but look at the cost. They are who they are despite your best efforts to break them."

"What about the others?"

"Now that is the problem isn't it?"

"What do you mean?"

"Nicki, Mark and Rene want their father. I'm not sure what to do about it. You had finally connected with Nicki. She was starved for your approval. Now that you're gone she's been very depressed. Mark misses you too. The thing is, every brain cell in my head, says, divorce him. I have to do what's best for my children and they want their father home."

"You mean you're going to take me back?"

"I mean you can move back home but understand this; there is nothing between us. You killed any feelings I once had for you. Your place will be on the couch, not in my bed. If you do one more thing to hurt my children, it's finished."

"Jane, I don't know what to say."

"You need to understand, this isn't for you or me. I am doing this for the children. If you lose them, there's no reason for your being around."

"All I've ever wanted is to be a better father to my children. I promise I won't do anything to ruin this chance."

Robert was dying to ask about Bruce, but thought better of it. He went back to his mother's house and packed his bag.

It occurred to him that Jane might be too willing to let him move back home. Hilda left him with a considerable amount of money. No, as much as he liked to think Jane was that way, he knew she wasn't. Now that the big problem was settled, he could focus again on the smaller one.

*****

Laura Lea had driven by her boyfriend's apartment. She'd used the spare key to get in. Everything was gone. More disturbing than that, were the bloodstains on the wall. A feeling of dread came over her as she walked to the office. She knew Leon's departure was not of his choosing. She had to find out where he was.

Laura Lea knocked on the landlady's door. An elderly lady with no teeth answered the door.

"I hate to disturb you ma'am, but I'm worried about my brother. Do you know where he is?"

"I wish I did honey, he owes me for a month's rent. Since he's your relative, you can pay me!"

"How much does he owe you?"

"Fifty dollars plus damages."

"If I settle with you, will you tell me what happened?"

"Money first, talk second."

"How much?"

"A hunerd should cover it."

"Here, now tell me what happened to him."

"If you don't calm down honey, I'll have to call my son, Luke Selmer."

"Who's he?"

"Your not from around here are ya?"

"No, I'm from Ohio."

"Luke, he's the sheriff. Want me to call him?"

"Okay."

"I didn't think you so."

"Mrs. Selmer, I'm sorry for acting impatient. I'm worried about my brother. Can you please tell me what happened to him?"

"Okay. Here it is."

The old lady told of the visit from her son's deputies.

"What did they do to my brother?"

"First of all dearie, he ain't no brother to you and you know it. That boy is lucky to be alive. The boys caught him having his way with little Angela Corbett. She's only fifteen. Anyway, they taught him a little lesson. Then they escorted him to the county line. Do you have any more questions?"

Laura Lea could hear the old woman cackling as she got in her car and drove back to Old Town. When she got home the phone was ringing. She had never felt so alone.

"Laura Lea, it's Robert."

She quickly tried to compose herself. Maybe all was not lost after all. All Laura Lea could think about on the way home was Leon screwing some little girl. She hoped the deputies killed him. Well, it just meant more money for her.

"Robert, I'm so happy you called. Where have you been? I've been so worried about you!"

"I've been around. You hit me with quite a bombshell last time we saw each other. Since then, my mother died so I had to take care of the funeral and so forth."

"Robert! I'm so sorry to hear that. Why didn't you call me?"

"That's not why I'm calling. Besides, you didn't even know her."

"Of course, we have other things to discuss. Do you want to come over?"

"I'll be there in twenty minutes."

Twenty minutes didn't give her much time. She looked a wreck. Laura Lea went upstairs to gussy up. Rob knocked on her door just as she finished.

"Robert, come in! I'm so happy to see you. I've been worried about you. I don't know what I would do without you."

Since the funeral, all Rob could think about was screwing Laura Lea one last time. Then he would leave her life in shambles.

"Oh baby, you look good enough to eat."

Robert hauled Laura Lea to the floor and ravaged her body. The feeling of power and control he felt over her was sublime.

"Oh, Oh Robert, you've never...I mean I've never had it so hard before. Please do it again."

"What about the baby? Aren't you worried about your baby?"

"Robert, it's our baby."

Robert penetrated her again as she was splayed on the floor. His thrusts were hard and urgent. Laura Lea's breaths came in short, rapturous gasps. Robert talked between his angry thrusts.

"You like it rough don't you? You little fucking slut! I'm going to give it to you harder and meaner than you've ever had...you...little...whore!"

"Oh, Rob...ert, what...oh, oh...are...you...oh, oh baby, baby...what...are...you...saying?"

With one final thrust Robert filled Laura Lea with his seed. He then stuck his penis in her mouth and made her clean it off. Standing above her, he reassembled his clothing and said,

"Well baby, I sure am going to miss screwing you. You are without a doubt the best lay I've ever had. What is it they say? Oh yes, all good things must come to an end."

Laura Lea scrambled to her knees, her breasts swaying in her agitation.

"Robert! What are you saying? Why are you talking to me that way? I thought you loved me? We're going to have a baby and get married…aren't we?"

"I got a call from my good friend Sheriff Selmer. He told me you stopped by your…brother's apartment. You know your brother was a bad boy. He had to be taught a lesson. That's the way things are done in the country. We don't have much use for courts. We take care of problems in our own way."

"Robert, I can explain. I can…"

Robert held his hand up to silence Laura Lea. Panic was etched in her every mannerism. His moment of triumph was at hand.

"I know all about your scam with lover boy. I saw you and lover boy in the kitchen about a week ago. I had my friends pay him a little visit. I can have them pay you a little visit if you'd like?"

"You'd let them hurt me?"

"Not before they showed you a real good time."

"You can't do this to me. I'll…I'll tell. That's right! I'll tell everyone about you! I'll tell Stanley how you pursued me at work, how you forced yourself on me. I'll tell them you threatened to kill me if I said anything. I'll call your wife and tell her too! I'll even call your priest. I'll tell him what a lecherous bastard you are! I'll tell…"

Laura Lea was standing now, pulling at his arm. She disgusted him. Her desperate threats were pitiful. She was hysterical, clawing at him, pleading with him to stay. Robert had finally had enough. He grabbed her clutching arm and pummeled her with his other fist.

Laura Lea sank to the floor on her back. Robert straddled her chest with a hand on her throat. He had the index finger of his free hand in her face as he issued a warning.

"I'll tell you what you're going to do! You will keep your mouth shut. If you say anything to anyone, my friends will find you. Are you getting this or do I have to draw you a picture?"

Laura Lea was petrified. All she could do was tremble beneath the weight of Robert Misner.

*****

November 1, 1963 was one of those crisp fall days. Robert loved this time of year. The cold weather signaled the approach of quail season. He had taken his two dogs, Prince and Patch out for late afternoon runs to help condition them. Prince was getting old, but at fourteen he could still hunt circles around the five-year old, Patch.

Jane watched Robert with the dogs the evening before the hunting trip. The submissiveness they displayed in Robert's presence reminded her of the children. *Better the dogs than her children,* Jane thought. It had been over three years since the blow-up with Bruce. Robert and she had been able to maintain an uneasy truce.

Jane was happy to see Mark excited about the hunting trip. This was proof she had done the right thing by letting Robert stay. But she was nervous. Knowing her son was going to carry a gun worried her. She remembered all the stories she'd heard about hunting accidents.

Jane knew her nagging Mark over being careful was one reason he turned in early the night before. Since Freddy moved out, Mark had the bedroom to himself. Jane could hear him throughout the night rummaging through his gear. She doubted he slept at all. When she opened his bedroom door at 4am, he was already dressed. Jane went to the couch and woke Rob.

She reflected on the undisturbed half of what used to be his side of the bed. *This is what our marriage has come to. You've got the whole couch and I've got the whole bed.*

It was four-thirty am when they pulled out of the drive.

"Mark, you wearing your long-handles?"

"Yes sir, but they're awful hot."

"When we get out in that cold mountain air you'll be glad I made you put them on."

Robert had permission to hunt on Mr. Ander's farm. Wildlife was in abundance on the dairy farm, nestled in the Blue Ridge. Shooting quail was the first order of business, however, it wasn't unusual to see other game, even bears.

Robert's relationship with the Scorch had its peaks and valleys. Currently it was at its highest peak. Robert looked on his son with fondness and pride. Mark would be bigger than either of his older brothers. To Robert, Mark was his only son. His relationship with Freddy ran the same course as with Bruce's. Mark would be the one to carry on the family name.

*****

Rob was pleased with himself. The confessional was a wonderful contrivance. He knew the priest was forbidden to break the sanctity of confession. Rob got everything off his chest to Father O'Fallon.

"Bless me father for I have sinned. It has been one month since my last confession."

"What sins burden you, my son?"

Robert dug deep to come up with his best pious demeanor.

"Father, my sins are grievous. How can God forgive them?"

"God will forgive, if your confession comes from the heart."

"Father, I have betrayed the sanctity of my marriage vows."

"You have committed adultery?"

"Yes father."

"Have you told your wife?"

"Yes father. I begged her forgiveness, but she has driven me from our bed."

"She refuses to perform her wifely duty for mother church?"

"Father, she doesn't even attend mass anymore."

"Her sins are for her to confess. You have confessed yours and will be forgiven. Is there more?"

"Yes father. I'm not sure, but I fear I may have been responsible for a terrible accident."

"What kind of accident?"

"A young girl was killed."

"Why do you think you were responsible?"

"I had been drinking. I knew I shouldn't have driven, but I was heartsick over my wife's refusal to forgive me. I wanted to buy her some flowers. I pulled onto the main road without looking and sped off. I found out later the girl hit a phone pole, trying to avoid a collision. She was killed."

"You can't be sure she was avoiding you, my son. Your willingness to accept responsibility is commendable but misplaced. Surely, there were witnesses to this accident?"

"Yes father, many."

"Had you been responsible, certainly witnesses would have reported this. Do not carry this guilt further, my son."

Rob went on with his confession. His list of sins included taking the Lord's name in vain on a few occasions as well as lying. To the latter, he added a couple for good measure. He walked away from the confessional with a clear conscience, having done his penance.

He had one other thought before hearing Mark's voice. *God is on my side. He has forgiven my sins. Jane doesn't even go to church, let alone confession. How can God forgive her?*

"Hey dad, dad? Are you ok?"

"Sure son."

"You looked like you were sick or something."

"No, I feel fine. You think you'll hit anything?"

"I hope so. I'd like to see a deer or bear! That would be cool!"

"A deer is one thing, but I don't think you want any part of a bear."

"I think it would be neat to see a bear. I can out run him if I need to."

"You think so?"

"Yeah, I have the school record for the fifty. I can run faster than any old bear."

"Can you outrun a horse?"

"I bet I could keep up with one for a while."

"A bear can run faster than a horse for a short distance. Did you know that?"

"Really?"

"Yep."

Mark wasn't so sure about seeing a bear after hearing they were faster than horses.

"I don't suppose we'll see any bears."

"You never know. Sometimes you just walk up on them. That's why I want you to put a slug in one barrel."

"Will a slug bring a bear down?"

"If you hit him in the right place it will."

"Where's the right place?"

"You want to aim just behind the shoulder."

"What if he's coming straight at me? I can't see his shoulder if he's coming straight at me."

"Well then, I guess you just run as fast as you can."

"But you said he'd catch me if I run."

"He will."

"Then what do I do if I see one?"

"Pray you don't see one."

That ended Mark's questions concerning the possibility of seeing a bear. Robert could see the nerves working on his son for the rest of the trip.

Robert was an excellent shot. He was all instinct and reflexes. He never showed excitement when the birds took wing. The gun seemed to be an extension of him. Everything was accomplished in one fluid blur of motion. The only excitement he displayed was when the dogs picked up scent and pointed.

The anticipation of firing his gun and killing something infused Robert with a sense of power. The drive took a little over an hour. Robert pulled the car off the narrow gravel road and into the entrance of the large open field. They had arrived and it was time to hunt.

"Scorch, when I open the trunk, grab Patch before he has a chance to get away."

"Okay dad, I'm ready."

"Get ready Mark. I'm popping the trunk."

"No you don't, Patch! I gotcha!"

Mark had the dog by the collar. Patch threatened to pull him off his feet.

"Hold onto to him son or he'll bolt for the wide open spaces."

"I got him dad, when can I let go?"

"Hang on to him until I get the guns and Prince out."

"How come Prince doesn't bolt away?"

"Son, his bolting days are way behind him. He's all business. Watch Prince work when we get into that field of lespedeza. Patch could learn from the old boy if he had any sense. He reminds me of the young bull standing on the hill overlooking the heifers with the old bull. The young bull says, *'Let's run down this hill and have at that heifer over there.* The old bull, he says, *'Nah, I'd rather walk down and have at the whole herd.'*

Robert could tell his son didn't understand his joke by his quizzical look. All was ready.

"Mark, turn him loose."

"Wow! Look at him go!"

"Mark I want you about thirty yards to my left. Make sure you don't get ahead of me. We give the dogs plenty of room to work in front of us. Watch old Prince. When his tail stops moving, you stop. Be ready for the birds when they flush. Pick one bird in the covey and lead him, like I showed you. That's the only way you'll hit anything."

"Yes sir."

"Mark, one more thing. Keep your safety on until the dogs find the birds. Then and only then do you take the safety off, understand?"

"Yes sir."

Mark couldn't take his eyes off of his father. It was like watching a stranger. He was tranquil, at peace with his surroundings, in fact, part of the surroundings. His steadiness fit the calmness of the outdoors like a glove. Mark was anxious for action. His father moved in rhythm with the dogs, the embodiment of harmony. Mark kept thinking about the man he was watching. *Why can't he be like this at home? Why does he always yell at home? It's almost like I just met him, never knowing him before. I like him.*

In a hushed tone Mark heard his father's excited words.

"Mark, Mark, stop! Look at the dogs. Prince is onto the birds, take your safety off!"

Mark fumbled for the safety. As he lifted his gun, he tried to remember everything his father told him. Suddenly there was an upward blur of beating wings to his front.

"Mark! Get ready! Any second now!"

FFFFWWWWOOOOOSSSSSHHHHH! BANG-BANG.

"They went that way!"

"Mark! Why didn't you shoot?"

"Man, they're fast! I saw where they went. They're down by that old stone fence about three hundred yards."

"Mark! Don't go running off after those birds. Prince will find them, that is, if hard head doesn't botch it up for him like he almost did this time."

"How many did we get?"

Robert had to laugh at his son's excitement. Not shooting his gun hadn't fazed him in the least. All he wanted to do was go after the birds he'd followed with his eyes.

"I got two."

Mark didn't get a chance to take his father to the birds. Patch took off at a dead run, disappearing into the woods opposite where Mark saw the birds land.

"Dad, the birds went that way. Why's Patch going the other way?"

"I don't know. Wait, hear that?"

"It sounds like a beagle chasing something."

"Mark, go after him. I'll get Prince and follow after you. Oh, and Mark."

"Yes sir."

"Remember to click on your safety. Get going before Patch gets to the next county."

Robert watched his son take off at a dead run after the dog. Mark entered the woods at almost the exact spot as the dog.

"Come on Prince ol' boy, I'll take you to the car. I'll make better time by myself."

Robert was about twenty minutes behind Mark. As he walked, he schemed. *I'll mold Mark in my image. By the time I'm done, he'll hate his older brothers as much as I do. It'll take more time to get him on my side, but given time, I'm sure I can accomplish that.* Jane would pay. He'd get even with her through the children.

Robert could hear two dogs barking now. One was definitely Patch. His staccato bark blended with the extended baying of the beagle. They seemed to be getting further away. Robert picked up his pace.

*****

After about fifteen minutes, Mark stopped to get his breath. *Patch, damn it! Where are you? Man I'm hungry. I wish I had a cup of hot coffee and some of those little Vienna Sausages dad packed.* All Mark could do was follow the barking of the two dogs. They were definitely chasing something. *I wonder what the hell those dogs are chasing?*

Mark remembered how he and his friends would spend hours in the woods with make believe guns, evading capture by wild Indians. *I wonder if Davy Crockett hunted this way. I feel like Davy, stalking big game in the forest with nothing but 'ol Betsy.* With that thought, Mark patted the side of his shotgun. He seemed to be getting closer to the wailing of the dogs…or they, closer to him. *Patch sounds like he's running right at me. It sounds like he's just over this next hill.*

All of a sudden, a ball of blackish fur came bursting over the hill with the dogs nipping at the stub of its tail. The cub was moving extremely fast. Mark was mesmerized, as he had never seen a bear in the wild before. This was really neat!

"Patch! Patch, get over here!"

Both dogs were hot on the heels of the cub. The cub didn't see Mark and almost bowled him over. Patch passed within a few feet of Mark. Mark grabbed for his collar and missed.

"Damn it Patch, come back here."

Something occurred to Mark, as he picked himself up from the leafy ground. *Oh shit! Where's the mother?*

The thought no sooner entered his mind, than he heard her approaching from over the rise. She was headed straight for him. Mark lifted the shotgun to his shoulder trying to steady his shaking hands. *I've got you sighted now!* Click! *Oh no, I didn't take the safety off!*

Mark was about twenty yards in front of the furious parent. He turned and made for a big rock that towered about eight feet high. As he ran, he saw the cub scamper up a big oak with the dogs closing in. Mama bear's attention was focused on Mark. She was almost on him.

Mark threw his gun to the side so he could grab the handholds on the face of the boulder. He didn't think the bear could scale the vertical face of the rock. He was right. Her back feet couldn't find an adequate foothold. Mark was staring straight into the mother's angry eyes. He hadn't noticed how the boulder sloped gradually in the back. *Oh Jeez, if she sees that I'm bear bait!*

"Patch, Patch, get over here!"

The beagle was intent on climbing the tree. Patch saw the mother and started nipping at her back legs. The bear turned on him, rearing onto her hind legs. She ambled toward Patch on two legs. The dog drew the bear away.

I think I can make it to my gun. If I go down around the back of the rock, she won't see me! I can get to my gun and put a pumpkin ball in her. Yeah, I'll do it! Mark made it to his shotgun. The bear never saw him, as he fumbled for the safety. Mark knew the slug would bring her down if he hit the mother behind the shoulder. That's what his father said, anyway. Aim behind the shoulder for a heart shot.

Mark bought the gun up and took careful aim. BANG. Nothing happened to the bear. All Mark saw was a few pieces of black fur rise. Then he realized what he'd done. *Oh man! I pulled the wrong trigger!* Instead of hitting the bear with the slug, he peppered her with birdshot. He might as well hit her with a flyswatter.

The bear turned on him again. Patch followed her, continuing to nip at her butt. Mark ran around the rock. The beagle still had the cub treed. Momma wasn't going to leave her baby. Mark was able to scramble up the rock again leaving the angry she-bear to growl her protest.

The bear attacked the unsuspecting beagle. One blow from the forepaw sent the feisty little dog reeling. Now, all of her attention centered on Patch. She again drew the setter away from her baby. Mark lay on the rock. He didn't move a muscle. He waited until the bear had her back to him. If he could make it off the rock without being seen, he could get a slug in her. Patch couldn't hold the bear off forever.

Mark positioned himself behind a big poplar tree and took steady aim behind her shoulder...again. He had a killing shot. He remembered the story his mother read to him. Smokey The Bear was orphaned as a cub. Mark didn't want to orphan this one.

He had another idea. He didn't like the thought of killing the mother bear. *What will the cub do if I kill its mother?* The bear was a good fifty yards from the cub's sanctuary. Mark put the tree between him and the cub. He heard something drop onto the dry leaves and scamper off. When he looked around the tree, the cub was gone.

He went back to his rock and called his dog. It was almost like Patch understood. Patch came back to the rock, tongue lolling out and sides heaving for breath. Momma bear didn't follow. He went over to check on the beagle. The dog was only stunned. Revived it took off again in the general direction of momma and her cub, down the hill.

Mark took a knee and held the dog's head in his hands, roughing his ears. The two always had a bond with one another. After today it would be even more special.

"Patch, dad's right! You are a hard head!"

The dog's response was to lather Mark's face with his tongue.

"You're a good old boy, Patch. You gave that old bear a fright?"

Mark put Patch on the leash and they headed back down the hill. The beagle's excited barking could be heard again.

Something occurred to Mark as he and Patch went down the hill. He stopped in his tracks.

"Patch! Dad will be coming up the hill. He's on a collision course with momma."

Mark took the two slugs from their chambers and replaced them with birdshot. He tied the leash to a sapling and fired off both rounds, reloaded and fired another two. He hoped that would be a warning to his father. He put the slugs back in the gun, untied Patch and moved quickly toward his father.

He thought about old Prince and knew the dog would die protecting his master from the bear. He hoped his father would see what was coming at him and get out of the way. Mark moved with urgency. In the distance he saw an odd looking sight. "Is that Dad in the top of that sapling? He looks like some kind of big lollypop."

*****

Robert was starting up a steep slope when he heard the shots. *What is that boy shooting at?* Robert had his head down, picking his footing carefully. *I'd sure hate to break my leg in the middle of nowhere. I can hear the beagle again. I don't hear Patch though. Maybe Mark caught him. Damn, that barking is getting close. What's that other noise I hear?*

As much as Robert had hunted he'd never seen a bear in the wild. He certainly didn't expect to see one today. The strange noise he heard was the crying of the bear cub being chased by the beagle. Of greater importance, however was the 300-pound mother bear close behind.

Robert didn't have much time to react. He looked up to see a bear cub running at him. They collided, rolling down the hill Rob had just climbed. He broke free as the cub kept going. He gained his feet just as the beagle dodged him. This time, Rob lost the grip on his gun. It slid down the hill about twenty feet, clanging on rocks all the way. *Shit, that's my new gun. It won't be worth a...*

Before he could make it to the gun, Robert heard the rumbling growl from behind. The mother bear was almost on him. He flew up the nearest tree like he had wings. It wasn't much of a tree. Robert's weight made the sapling sway. He watched the mother's rump disappear down the hill. He was too scared to move. All he could do was cling to the skinny trunk.

After about five minutes he saw Mark with Patch moving quickly toward him. *I can't let him see me up here. I've got to get down before he gets here.* Robert hit the ground with a hard thud. He'd lost his gun in the excitement and was frantically searching the area for it when Mark got to him.

"Dad, dad! Did you see that bear?"

"She almost landed on top of me when she came barreling down the hill."

"I was worried she'd get you so I came as fast as I could. What did you do? I didn't hear any shots."

"Help me find my gun and I'll tell you on the way back to the car."

They found the gun under some leaves and went back.

"Where's Prince?"

"I took the old boy back before coming for you. I'm glad I did. In his younger days he'd have been more than a match for that old bear…not now though."

"I thought the same thing. I'm glad he's okay."

They exchanged stories. By the time they got to the car that bear gained another 300 pounds. The beagle's now distant howling amused them for the rest of their walk. As the day wore on, they each wondered if the dog got the bear or the other way around. On the way home Robert tested the water with his son.

"That was some time huh Scorch?"

"Yeah, I thought that bear was going to get me for sure. It's a good thing that big rock was there. I thought you told me bears could climb trees?"

"I did, but that skinny little sapling was the only thing in sight."

"I guess it's a good thing that momma was more interested in that beagle."

They enjoyed a good laugh about their adventure. Robert took on a more serious tone.

"Scorch, you know your mother doesn't want me around don't you?"

"What do you mean, dad. I thought everything was better?"

"Son, as you get older you'll understand more about adults. I know I've made some mistakes. I know I'm not the most patient person around, but I'm trying. Since Bruce and Freddy left, your mother wants me out of the house."

"Dad I don't think mom wants you to move out. I sure don't want you to move away. We can go hunting and play tennis. You can come watch me play baseball like you did with Bruce and Freddy. I'm not as good as they were, but you can help me get better. Don't you see, you can't move? We're just now starting to do stuff like a real father and son should. I'll tell mom that you can't move away!"

Mark was getting agitated, like Robert knew he would. Robert knew Mark and Nicole were the emotional ones in the family. He was playing on those emotions now.

"Don't say anything to your mother about our conversation. I don't want her getting anymore upset with me than she is. Scorch I love you and I don't want to lose you. You've always been my favorite out of all the children. If you say anything to your mother, she'll know I said something to you and might make me leave."

"Maybe if you started being nicer to her she'd change her mind about you."

Mark's comment hit a little to close to home and Robert could feel the anger swelling within him. *Calm down. He's got a lot of nerve saying that to me. I should smack him good. No Robert, you're not going to smack him. Right now, you need all the support you can get.*

"Son, I've tried, but your mother hates me. Don't you hear the way she talks to me? I'm trying to be the best father I can, but your mom isn't making it easy for me. You love your dad don't you Scorch?"

"Sure I do dad! I don't want you to leave."

"Son, let's pray it doesn't come to that."

Mark was on the verge of tears, but didn't want to cry in front of his father. He took a deep breath and stared out of the window until the urge subsided. After collecting himself, Mark turned to his father.

"How can mom be so mean? You're trying your best!"

That was what Robert wanted to hear. The seed had been planted. Rob threw Mark a bone.

"Son, I don't want you being upset with your mother. She loves you very much and I'm sure she thinks she's protecting you."

"I don't need her to protect me from my own father."

The rest of the ride home was made in relative silence as Robert basked in his little victory.

*****

Robert walked through the front door one evening with a big smile on his face. Jane was in the dining room sewing on a dress for Nicole when he entered. He started giving Jane an excited account of the day.

"What are you so happy about?"

"You're looking at the new director of personnel."

"What happened with Stan Collingsworth?"

"He finally got what was coming to him."

"Come on Robert! Stan was a good man. You didn't like him because of jealousy."

"That's absurd!"

"It's not and you know it."

"Do you want to know what happened today or not?"

"You're going to tell me anyway."

"You remember his wife died."

"Of course I do. We went to the funeral. That was so sad. It was obvious he loved her very much. How are the children doing anyway?"

"Who cares about that? Let me go on."

Jane was disgusted by his shallowness.

"Robert, you're so insensitive! You don't care anything about your own family, so why should you give a damn about anyone else's?"

"Do you want to hear this or not?"

"All right, all right, finish."

"It seems Stan isn't much of a man. He buried himself in a bottle until something had to be done. He's not been around half the time to do his job. The boss finally got fed up with it and demoted him to some third level job in Identification. They needed a man who knew his way around and that was me."

"Congratulations Rob, you finally got the job you've wanted all of these years. Are you happy now?"

"Of course I am. You don't sound very happy about it. I'd think you could be a little happier for me."

"I'm ecstatic Rob."

"It means more money."

"That's good, why do you think I went back to work? You never gave me enough money to take care of the household needs or kids."

"I gave you more than enough. You just don't know how to manage money. All you ever did was put more pressure on me. You never supported me the way a wife should."

"Look Robert, I don't feel like getting into this with you. I could rehash a lot of things you did with your money, but frankly I'm not in the mood. That horse has been dead a long time."

"You know, I've tried my best to get along with you. But you've no intention of being cooperative. You could at least show me some respect in front of my children. I am their father!"

"You're right Rob. You're always right. I'm a terrible person for not showing you the proper respect. What respect have you ever given me? It's a two way street Rob!"

"I can't talk to you. I'm going to the tavern!"

Robert left, but he went the other way. He hadn't been to the Silver Slipper in several years. Brandi had come up in the world. Robert and a few other elite customers put a lot of money in her pocket over time. Apparently, Brandi was nobody's fool. The owner of the Slipper got into some financial problems and sold the establishment to her. Brandi was still a sexy woman but didn't have to earn her living on her back anymore. Rob and a couple other high paying customers were exceptions.

*****

Robert's affair with Laura Lea Pike had been over for quite sometime. After transferring her to the deepest dungeon of the Bureau he started on his next sexual conquest. Miss Jenette Wharton was performing a special service for her benefactor late one night after work.

"Oh baby that feels so goood. Ohh Rob you're too good to me. Give it to me Mr. Misner, give it to me!"

"Miss Wharton! You're so brazen. What would your daddy think?"

"Baby, I don't care just give it to me, harder! That's it, harder, harder!"

There was a knock on Rob's office door.

"For Christ's sake, someone's out there. Quick get yourself together! Sit in the chair, quickly and get your tablet!"

"Who is it?"

"Rob, it's Bill. What's going on in there?"

"Nothing Bill, come on in. Miss Wharton here is just doing some shorthand for me. I had some work to do and she agreed to stay late and help me."

"I just bet she did."

The boss's eyes drifted down to Rob's half open zipper, then his disheveled appearance.

"I think that will be all Miss Wharton, you can go home now."

"Certainly Mr. Misner. Are you sure there will be nothing else?"

The nineteen-year old left her shorthand tablet on the desk as she made a hasty retreat for the coat rack, runny mascara and all.

"That must have been some shorthand. Rob your barn door is still open."

Rob looked down and fumbled with his zipper.

"That's embarrassing, I wonder how long I've been walking around like that, thanks boss. Is there something I can do for you?"

"I can't remember, it mustn't have been important. Drive carefully on the way home Rob."

"Sure boss, you too. I'll see you in the morning."

Rob started to cross the office to open the door, but Bill Hawkins was already through it. *Shit, shit, shit, goddamn it and shit! Why does this kind of shit always happen to me? What was the old man doing here this late? Goddamn I'm screwed now. The son-of-a-bitch retires in a month and I got to go and pull something stupid like this. Damn it anyway, why me?* He pondered this latest fiasco as he pulled the bottle of Old Crow from his desk. It would be time to go home soon.

*****

Jane's savings account was growing due to her full time job at Agriculture. The days of pilfering cash from Rob's wallet were long over. Jane knew, even though their relationship was shot, her working drove him nuts. She was not the same woman he married. She wore her newfound independence like a badge of honor. Jane was constantly on her guard when it came to Robert. She knew he had another girlfriend; the perfume and lipstick had changed. Louise came over for some afternoon coffee and Jane filled her in.

"Louise, I think he's at it again."

"Do you know who it is this time?"

"No, that's why I need Louie again. Do you suppose he could spend some time following Robert like he did before? I can pay him this time."

"Darlin' don't you worry about that. He'll be happy to do it for nothing."

"I can't do that. I have some money, I WANT to pay him."

"If it will make you feel better, then fine, but he won't ask for much."

"How much does he usually get?"

"Fifty dollars should do it."

Jane wanted to be ready for the next blow-up when it happened.

"I can pay him more than that."

"Now darlin'! What did I say?"

"Okay, okay, I don't want Louie thinking I'm taking advantage of him."

"Look honey, don't worry about it. By the way, how's that boyfriend of Nicole's doing?"

"You mean Timmy Corrigan? It's a regular case of puppy love."

"That's so sweet. Robert hasn't given her any problems over dating?"

"No, Robert's been pretty easy to get along with lately. Its like he's always trying to butter me up."

"That's wonderful honey, but watch him!"

"I think it's disgusting. There's something else bothering me Louise."

"Tell old toothless about it!"

"It's Mark. He's been acting funny toward me lately."

"Funny, how do you mean?"

"Like he's mad at me for something. He's been downright surly at times. It worries me, because it reminds me of Robert."

"Honey, you better nip that in the bud. You should whack him one, you know?"

"Louise! How can you suggest such a thing? You know I'd never raise a hand to any of my children after what their father put them through."

Nicole came bursting into the kitchen, interrupting their conversation.

"Mom, when is dad going to be home?"

"Nicki, I have no idea, why?"

"Timmy wants to come over."

"He's been getting home about nine every night. That should give you and Timmy some privacy for a couple of hours. You going to be on the back porch?"

"Mom!"

"Honey, I wasn't a mother my whole life, goodness. I'll tap on the window when your father comes through the front door."

*****

Robert noticed the Corvair parked in front of the house, as he pulled into the driveway. He thought those things were a coffin on wheels. Before Robert left the office, he'd consumed a third of the Old Crow in his desk drawer. He was still wondering how much Hawkins saw. He thought about Jenette Wharton.

The girl was only nineteen, three years older than Nicole. He suspected she was using him, but he didn't care. *How many forty-eight year old men get to screw a nineteen-year old?* As he got out of his car, Robert had the urge to take a leak. His favorite spot was the big bush around the back corner of the house.

In mid-stream, Robert heard soft moaning from the back porch. It sounded much like the sexy mewling sounds emitted by Miss Wharton, earlier.

*****

Timmy and Nicole were oblivious to the man around the corner, peeing behind the bush.

"Timmy, no one has ever kissed me the way you do."

Tim had his arm around Nicole's waist as they sat on the porch swing. They had been dating off and on throughout most of their junior year. Their kissing became more fervent. Nicole was feeling sensations the nuns warned were forbidden for good Catholic girls.

She'd wondered if she had to confess this with the rest of her sins. *Why do I feel guilty? I love him. I won't push his hands away this time. I wonder if I should touch him, feel him. How would he feel inside me? No, no, I can't think that way! His hands feel so good. I didn't know it would be like this, oooh Tim!*

Nicole's hips were moving with the gentle caresses of Tim's fingers, which were probing the moistness between her open legs. Nicole's breathing was coming in quiet gasps as she searched him out with one of her hands. Their hands were exploring the depths of one another. Their explorations ceased abruptly with the sound of Robert's angry voice.

"What are you two doing?"

"Da…daddy, uh we were just talking."

Robert was feeling the effects of his drinking. He was unsteady as he made his way to the porch steps. He'd been watching and knew perfectly well what they were doing, as he worked himself over with his own hand. Robert realized this was his own daughter behaving so lustily.

Memories of his mother popped into Robert's head. He was still 'hanging out' as he approached the teenagers.

Realizing he'd overlooked something, he tried stuffing his erect penis back into his pants. He didn't bother zipping up.

"I can see how he was talking with you! Boy get your hands off of my daughter and get out of here!"

Robert took the last step up and was facing Timmy Corrigan. The boy was petrified. Everything he ever heard about Mr. Misner was revisiting him now. Timmy was trying to zip up his own pants.

"Yes sir, I'm leaving."

"Nicole, I'll see you in school."

"No you won't. I prohibit you from seeing my daughter again, now leave!"

"Daddy, you're hanging out!"

Robert reached down and stuffed his penis into his pants.

"I saw what you were doing with that little bastard!"

"Daddy, I'm sorry. We just…we were…"

"I don't want to hear anything from you!"

Robert slapped Nicole hard across the face causing her lower lip to bleed. That old feeling came back to him. He felt good. Nicole quivered beneath his verbal assault.

"You're just a little whore!"

He slapped her again. Nicole shoved past her father. She was not hurt physically. Nicole jumped from the top step to the ground and ran.

"Girl! Come back here! Don't run when I call you! Nicole, Nicole, get back here this minute!"

Nicole was gone from the yard. Tears were burning in her eyes as she ran across the highway. Drivers slammed on their brakes to avoid hitting her. *Let them hit me, I don't care, I don't care! I want to die, oh daddy I thought you loved me.* Nicole ran without paying attention to where she was headed. All Nicki knew was she had to get away from her father. She had the sensation of running over frozen ground and dodging things in her way. She lost track of time.

*****

Jane was in the dining room sewing, when she heard the yelling. She made it to the porch just in time to see her daughter running away. Jane screamed after her fleeing daughter, but there was no response. Jane turned on Robert.

"Robert, what is going on out here? What did you do to Nicole? Where's Timmy? Robert?"

"That little who…whore deserved what she got!"

"Whore! You called your own daughter a whore? Robert where is she? What else did you say to her?"

Without answering his wife, Robert got into his car and took off. His tires spun in the loose gravel as he backed from the driveway. Jane was left to wonder what happened. There was someone who knew. She went to the phone and called Timmy.

Mark heard the commotion and ran down the stairs. He listened to his mother's conversation with Timmy and knew something bad happened. His mother looked worried as she hung up the phone.

"Mom, what's going on? What happened to Nicki?

"She ran off. Can you find her? It's too cold for her to be out on a night like this."

*****

The stubbles of corn scraped at her legs, as exhaustion took its toll on her muscles. When her legs could no longer support her weight, Nicole collapsed at the base of a tree. The hour was late. The air carried the nip of approaching winter.

The coolness of her perspiration made Nicole shiver. She lost track of where she was. Nothing in her immediate vicinity was familiar. She was lost. She remembered running through fields and jumping fences. A thick, forbidding forest surrounded her. The dead leaves were slick with frost as she placed her body in the fetal position for warmth.

She knew she could not go home and face her father. Nicki cried convulsively before fatigue overtook her. She closed her eyes.

Nicole woke up to the cawing of crows. She found herself lying half buried in cold, damp leaves. Her body was beyond cold. Her feet were tucked under the skirt she had worn the night before. The night before, she remembered now. Her father's image played before her.

Nicole's feelings toward her father were in tatters. She remembered and was wracked with convulsions again. Until last night, she reveled at having her father's love and acceptance. That was all gone now. Old resentments resurfaced and Nicole was left with the bitter taste of hate. She wrapped Tim's sweater tightly around her torso, Shivering as she came to grips with her present situation.

There was no feeling in her feet. They would not support her body. Three times she tried standing, each time sinking to the ground. Finally, having stomped feeling back into her feet, she was able to stand. She started walking with no particular direction in mind. She had no idea where she was.

Wet leaves were plastered to Tim's sweater. Her hair was a tangled mess and dirt smeared Nicole's face and legs. The sun had not yet cast its warmth over the land. Through the trees, she could see the orange glow of sunrise in the east. For some reason, moving toward the warmth of the sun made sense to her. Movement of any kind was difficult. Her nose ran freely. A swipe with the sweaters sleeve removed the dripping mucus. She tried moving quicker to warm her muscles, as well as quicken her way home. *But which direction was home? What would be there greet her?*

She was suddenly at the edge of the woods. A cornfield with its brown whiskery stubble covered the landscape. There were no houses in sight, but she thought she saw something oddly familiar, yes a huge chestnut tree. It was the mistletoe tree her older brothers used to talk about climbing.

A man's voice was screaming as if from a dream, but it was not a dream. The old farmer was waving something toward her that looked like a rifle. Nicki sobered when she realized where she was. Any minute, old man Haskins would start shooting. The vision of her little brother's peppered butt materialized. Mark and Freddy had trespassed on the Haskins Farm a year ago, but Mark didn't escape the rock salt. She remembered how he screamed as her mother picked out the chunks of salt with tweezers.

"Hey! Get off of my property! Answer me or I'll shoot!"

She turned as if to run away, but her legs would not cooperate. Still numb from the cold, movement came slowly to her muscles. Before she could run, the old farmer was there. He was standing on the running board of his truck. The farmer's face was a roadmap of the harshness of farm life. Mr. Haskins stepped from the truck. A shotgun was cradled in his arm.

"Girl, who are you and what are you doing on my property?"

He got no response.

"Can't you talk? My God girl, you look like some wild thing from the forest!"

The man made a move toward Nicki.

"Nicki, Nicole Misner is my name."

"You can talk! What in Gods good name are you doing wandering around my farm at this hour?"

"I…I, ran away from home."

"A runaway huh? Where do you live? Wait a minute? Did you say your name was Misner?"

"Yes sir."

"I know where you live. I'll take you home. Go around the other side and get into the truck."

Nicole was seated in the ancient truck. The warmth of the heater thawed her mind as well as her muscles. Mr. Haskins drove Nicole to the farmhouse so he could call the Misners. As they pulled in front of the farmhouse, Mrs. Haskins was there to meet them. Nicole followed the older lady into the kitchen.

"You poor darling! How did you get into such a state? Sit down here and have some breakfast."

"Mrs. Haskins may I use your phone to call my mother?"

"Of course you can dear, it's over there, or better still, why don't you eat and I'll call your mother for you."

The smell of fresh bacon and eggs made Nicole realize she was starved. She went at the bacon and eggs as though she'd never eaten before. She heard Mrs. Haskins on the phone with her mother.

"Yes Mrs. Misner, your daughter is fine. She's eating some breakfast. Do you want to talk to her?"

"Nicole, your mother would like to talk to you."

Nicki wiped her mouth and went to the phone.

"Mom."

"Nicki, where have you been? We've been worried sick. Mark and Freddy have been looking for you all night! The police have been all over as well. Why did you run off like that?"

"Is daddy there? Did he look for me too?"

"Nicki, he left after you ran off and hasn't come home yet."

"He didn't look for me?"

"No honey, he didn't."

Her mother's words hit home. Nicki's tears matched her mother's on the other end of the line. Afterwards, Mr. Haskins took her home. Jane ran to the car just as Nicole opened the door.

"Mom! I'm sorry for worrying you."

"I was worried to death about you! Don't ever do anything that foolish again."

Jane turned to the farmer sitting in his truck.

"Mr. Haskins, I don't know how to thank you."

"That's all right ma'am. I'm glad your daughter is safe."

Jane waited until they were in the house before plying the story from Nicki.

"Nicki, tell me what happened. Timmy gave me part of the story."

"You called Timmy?"

"I didn't know what else to do."

"How can I ever face him again? It was so humiliating!"

"All right honey, calm down and tell me what happened."

"Daddy saw us last night on the porch. He slapped me! Mama, he called me a whore!

Nicole told her mother everything.

"Your father hit you!"

Jane didn't have to look hard to see the welt on Nicki's face. She was incensed.

"There's one more thing. His thing was hanging out of his pants!"

Jane tucked Nicki into her warm covers and went to Rob's closet. His clothes were pulled from their hangers and roughly thrown into a suitcase. An envelope fell from the pocket of one of his suits. A letter was inside. It was addressed, simply to, Jenette.

'My darling Jenette,

The softness of your skin makes my blood boil with passion.

Your warm smile and sparkling eyes never leave my mind.

When we make love I feel the world is at my feet.

Those times we are apart are an agony to me.

I am only whole again when I am with you.

Forever Yours, Robert

Jane would have puked if she hadn't been laughing so hard. *What do I need with a detective? I've got the best evidence in the world, a signed admission to his infidelity. Oh there is justice after all!*

*****

The week after Jane kicked Robert out she decided a talk with Mark was overdue. She noticed a distinct difference in Mark's attitude after the hunting trip. Jane knew for the first time in his life, Mark had his father to himself. The two had come through the front door laughing and exchanging their own versions of the bear encounter.

Jane tried to get the story from Mark. The look Mark gave her sent a chill down her spine. Rob's influence was having an affect on Mark's personality. She experienced the same transformation in Robert. *I have to get through to him. He's getting more like his father everyday. .*

"Mark, come sit with me for a minute?"

"Dad's coming to get me in a few minutes. What do you want?"

Mark sauntered down the stairs, stopping on the fourth so he towered over his mother.

"Mark, I'd like to know what has gotten into you the last few months?"

"What do you mean? Nothing has gotten into me."

"Yes it has. Mark, you act like you hate me! Please tell me what I've done to deserve that?"

"You kicked my father out of his own house. Just when he was taking an interest in me, you kicked him out!"

"Mark, he did that to himself. Your father had plenty of chances to be a father to you. Don't you remember all of the yelling? Don't you remember the beatings he gave your brothers?"

"He only beat them when they were bad. Dad tried to be good to them but they never liked him. They were never nice to me either. I remember they always talked mean about dad. They never gave him a chance, just like you. You're jealous of dad, so you kicked him out!"

There was venom in Mark's words.

"I hate you for that!"

Mark descended the last four steps and brushed past his mother. Jane wanted to go to Mark. She left him alone instead. She decided Mark needed time to sort through his feelings. His words continued to eat at her. She couldn't hold back the tears.

Jane watched Mark get into Robert's car. She wondered how low Rob was prepared to go.

Robert could read his son like a book.

"Son what's the matter, you look upset about something?"

"You were right. Mom IS jealous of you. She doesn't like all the attention you've been giving me."

"I'm glad you finally see the truth."

"Why did you have to move out of your own house? You own it. It's Nicole's fault! You have a right to yell at her!"

"Mark, I only yelled at Nicki because I love her. I don't want her to go to Hell. When I saw what that boy was doing to her I lost my temper and ran him off like any father would do. I have a right to protect my children don't I, son? Now your mother is trying to take you away from me. I don't know what I'd do without you, Mark."

Mark didn't know he was a pawn and thought his father's tears were real. He was unfamiliar with his father's ability to fake tears. He also couldn't see his father's internal jubilation.

"Don't worry dad, you're not going to lose me."

*****

Jane sat in the living room with her knitting. Nicole came in from working on her homework and saw her mother's tears.

"Mom, what's the matter?"

"Nothing, honey. Did you finish your homework?"

"Yes mother, I got it all done. Why are you crying?"

"Mark said he hated me. He blames me for driving your father away. I've lost my little boy!"

"Momma, you must be mistaken. Mark loves you. How could he ever hate you? What's wrong with him? Wait until I see him. I'm going to give it to him good!"

"Nicki, you'll do no such thing. Leave your brother alone. You'll just make it worse. He's upset because his father isn't here anymore. Let's give him time. He'll come around."

Jane knew Nicole wasn't about to accept that. It suddenly dawned on Jane what was going on. Mark was the most distant after spending time with his father. He also had fresh accusations to make about his older brothers and sister. Jane realized what Robert was doing. *How can I get Mark to see he's being used? If I say anything, the wedge will be even deeper. I'll call Bruce. He'll talk to Mark. Mark has always looked up to him.*

*****

"Mom, what do mean he hates you? All of us know you had special feelings for Mark."

"I love all of my children!"

"Mom, it's okay. Don't worry about it. We understand. Ever since his accident, you've been closer to him. We know you love all of us."

"When did you get so smart?"

"Living with that bastard made me grow up fast. I know what he's trying to do. He wants to turn Mark against the rest of us. The old man figures this would be a good way to get even."

"I'm afraid you're right, but I'm also afraid he's succeeded. Mark's attitude has turned hateful to all of us, except Rene. He treats her like his little princess. Bruce, I'm worried about him. I see your father in him. We have to do something to get through to Mark before it's too late."

"I'll talk some sense into him, mom. He'll listen to me. Don't you remember how he used to try and follow Freddy and me around? Where is he?"

"He went out sledding early this morning. He should've been home hours ago."

"Wait until I get hold of him. He's got no business worrying you like that!"

"It's okay Bruce, he'll be home soon."

No sooner had Jane said that, than they heard Mark enter through the basement. Bruce went down the stairs. Mark was taking off his ice-encrusted boots.

"I thought I heard you come in. Let me help you off with those boots, Mark."

"That's okay, I don't need your help."

"Listen, you might use that tone with mom, but not with me! I'll whip your little ass!"

"Why don't you leave me alone? I didn't ask you to come down here."

"You're a little bastard, you know that? You sound just like the old man! You don't want to turn out like him do you?"

"Who do you think you are, my father? I don't have to listen to you. You've never been worried about me before, so bug off!"

"You've upset mom with your bullshit attitude! Did you tell mom you hate her?"

"I don't have to answer to you! It's none of your business!"

"You've hurt our mother and that makes it my business!"

"Fuck you!"

All of the Misner children had a temper. All of them had become fiercely independent. None of them wanted to be told what to do. With Robert's departure, Bruce had taken on the role as head of the family. This wasn't the first time he tried imposing his will on Mark.

"You little bastard! I ought to whip your ass!"

"Come on asshole. I'd like to see you try!"

All Bruce could see was his father's image in Mark. He slapped him hard across the face. It didn't yield the result he had expected. Mark sprang at him like an enraged beast.

"You son-of-a-bitch! I'll kill you!"

Mark connected with a couple of sharp punches to Bruce's face. Mark didn't connect a third time.

"Goddamn you, I'll teach you to hit me!"

Bruce caught Mark's arm, as he was about to take another swing. He connected with his own right, knocking Mark down. Jane rushed down the steps.

"Bruce, what is the matter with you? I thought you were just going to talk to him?"

"There's no hope for that little bastard! He hit me! The little bastard hit me!"

"Look here Bruce! I don't want you calling him that. He's not a bastard. I don't want to here that word in this house again."

Jane took Bruce's attention away from Mark, who by no means was defeated. Mark picked up the nearest thing he could get his hands on. The snow shovel hit Bruce smack in the back of the legs knocking them out from under him. Mark raised the shovel over his head. His temper was out of control. He was ready to kill Bruce.

"Mark! Mark, put that down. You're going to kill him. Think about what you're doing! Put the shovel down! Please honey, put the shovel down?"

Mark looked at his mother, but still kept Bruce at bay with the shovel.

"He's not my father! He can't boss me around!"

Mark turned his full attention back to Bruce. He cocked his arms back, ready to bring the shovel down. Bruce inched back preparing to receive the blow. Mark was screaming at his older brother.

"You never cared anything about me and now you want to tell me what to do! You can go to Hell!"

Jane got between her two sons. She could see the terror on Bruce's face. Jane had never seen Bruce back off from anything. She saw Mark's expression and understood Bruce's fear.

"Mom, get him away from me. He's crazy!"

Something in his mother's look triggered a memory from long ago. Mark threw the shovel down and ran from the basement, into the snowy night. Bruce got to his feet.

"Whew, I thought he was going to kill me."

"Did you hit him?"

"Mom, I can't believe you're asking me that!"

"What did you do to set him off?"

"All right. I hit him, but he hit me first! He told me to F... off! God, he looked like the old man."

*****

Robert pulled in front of the house on Fessenden Street. Since his mother died, the house had been vacant. All of the furniture had been covered with sheets. Robert was glad he hadn't sold the place. The house was convenient for a number of reasons. It was a great place to entertain his young lady friends. The last thing he wanted was to have kids around. He saw Mark sitting on the stoop, shivering as the heavy snow cascaded down.

"Mark, what are you doing here?"

"Dad, I want to live with you. I don't want to go back there. Can I stay here, please?"

"You can't do that, son. Your mother has custody, not me."

"I have to stay there?"

"Yes son, you do. How in the hell did you get here?"

"Bruce came over and started bossing me around. We got into a fight. I ran out of the house and hopped on a bus."

"You fought with Bruce? Did he hurt you?"

"No, I sure scared the shit out of him though. Mom stopped me before I could whack him with the shovel."

"She's always interfering."

"I don't think he'll bother me again."

"You can't let him push you around. Did you punch him like I showed you?"

"I caught him good!"

"I'll have to call your mother and tell her you're here. You can stay for a while, but I'll have to take you home."

"Dad, I want to stay with you!"

Mark was determined. His adrenaline rose again, as he faced his father.

"I thought you wanted me to live with you?"

"Now Scorch, I never said you could live with me!"

"You did! You said if I wanted to live here, I could. You said we could go to ballgames on the streetcar. You told me I could go to the same school you went to. You lied to me!"

"Mark, I never lied to you. You misunderstood what I said. You're still upset from your fight with Bruce. Calm down and we'll talk about it."

"I don't want to talk about it. I want to live here."

Robert was losing his temper. The last thing he needed was to have his son living with him. He had done too good a job at swaying Mark over to his side. He struggled with a way of getting Mark to accept the situation without exposing his real feelings.

"I'll tell you what I'll do. When your mother and I get our divorce, I'll make sure I get 50% custody. You'll have to be patient. There's no way your mother will let me have you 100% of the time."

Mark's temper flared again as he realized his father really didn't want him.

"You don't love me! You're just using me to get back at mom!"

"Mark, that's not true!"

"It is true! I can tell you're lying."

Robert lost control of his own temper and smacked Mark across the mouth. He realized his mistake immediately.

"Mark, I'm sorry! I shouldn't have hit you! Let's talk this over like men."

"You hit me! I see it in your eyes! You don't love me! Now you're acting all sorry and everything so I won't be mad. Nicole and me used to listen from our room. You'd get into a fight with mom and she'd kick you out. You'd try and come back and make all kinds of promises to her. You never kept your promises to her and now you're breaking your promise to me! You can go to Hell with Bruce!"

Mark ran from the house and down the sidewalk until he got to Nebraska Avenue. He didn't know where he was. He looked behind, expecting to see his father. All he heard was his voice calling for him to come back. Mark slowed to a walk as his father's voice faded in the distance.

Mark walked aimlessly through the ankle deep snow. His feet were cold and wet from being out all day. He shivered as he thought of all the bad things his father said about his mother. His mind was working it out. All his father ever did was talk about his mother and siblings. The hour was much too late for Mark to be outside. Every body part felt frozen. As he started across an intersection, a police car blocked his path.

"Son, are you Mark Misner?"

Mark ran, but didn't get far. One of the officers took him down from behind.

"Let me go!"

"You're father is worried about you."

"I'm not going back there!"

"Settle down, or we'll have to cuff you."

The policemen deposited Mark at his father's.

Robert was waiting.

"Thanks officers, good work."

Robert closed the door behind his son. He started yelling at the top of his lungs about having to call the police and the embarrassment.

"You're just like all the rest, ungrateful. I do everything for you and this is how you show your gratitude! Boy, you don't ever tell me to go to Hell again!"

Robert grabbed Mark's arm so he couldn't run and smacked him several times with his open hand. Robert was in a fury. He stopped when he saw the first crimson trickle from Mark's mouth. Still gripping Mark's arm he then pulled him behind as he went out to the car. The snow was falling heavier by the time Robert ordered Mark from his car and into the house on Horseshoe Drive.

Jane heard the car door slam. She ran to the front door in time to see Robert's car pulling away. She put her arms around Mark as he walked through the door. He wrestled his way free and ran up the stairs to his room.

"Mark come back, don't run away. Can't we talk? Please Mark come down and talk with me."

All Jane got in response was the slamming of his bedroom door. She decided to leave him alone. The next morning Mark didn't come down for breakfast. Schools were closed because of the snow. Jane asked Nicole to check on him. She came back down a few minutes later.

"Mom, you better come upstairs."

"What's wrong, honey?"

"Mark's not in his room and the window over the side porch is open."

"What?"

Jane ran upstairs and sure enough, Mark was nowhere to be found. She ran outside into the foot of fresh snow wearing only a robe and bedroom slippers. She got to the spot where he apparently jumped the ten feet from the porch roof. Jane followed his footprints to the dog pen.

"Mark! Come out of there! Mark!"

There was no answer from within the doghouse. Patch came out wagging his tail, followed by Prince. Jane knew her son was in the doghouse. She opened the door to the pen and crawled into the doghouse where she found Mark unconscious and cold to the touch.

"Nicole! Nicole, call the ambulance! Hurry!"

Try as she would, Jane could not get Mark from the tiny enclosure. He seemed to be half frozen and she feared the worst. The two attendants from the ambulance entered the pen. Jane backed out and allowed them through.

"Please help my son?"

The men were able to extract the half frozen teenager. Jane was still dressed in her bedclothes as she got into the ambulance with Mark. This brought back an all too vivid memory of the car accident years before. They got to the emergency room and Jane waited.

Some time later a doctor came out.

"Mrs. Misner, Mark has hypothermia. We're pumping fluids into him and trying to bring up his temperature. Your son should not be alive. He was half frozen. What happened?"

Jane told the doctor all she knew.

"Ma'am, I'm afraid we'll have to inform social services about this."

"Doctor, please don't do that. Mark had a fight with his older brother and ran from the house. Somehow he got to his father's, in town. Something happened while he was there, I don't know what."

"Mrs. Misner, we have to be concerned with his welfare. We have already made the call. A representative from Social Services will be here within the hour. I suggest you call your husband. They'll want to talk to both of you."

"Okay doctor, I understand. Just help my son!"

"Yes ma'am, I'm sorry we have to involve them."

"I understand, doctor."

"Mrs. Misner, is there someone you can call?"

The doctor gestured to Jane's attire.

"Oh, you mean my clothes, yes, I'll call someone."

An hour later Louise and Nicole showed up with a change of clothes for Jane.

"Jane, honey, how is he?"

"He has hypothermia."

"What happened?"

"Louise, I really don't want to talk about it right now, okay?"

"Sure honey, I understand. Did you call you know who?"

"As soon as I got here."

"Well, where is he?"

"He said he'd be here later, whatever that means. Louise, why don't you take Nicole back, I'll be all right."

"Sure honey, if that's what you want. Call me at home if you need anything ya' hear."

"Okay, thanks Louise."

*****

Robert went into the office the next morning, not wanting to return the urgent call from his wife. He knew what it would be about. Jane would threaten him again. Frankly, he was to a point where he didn't give a damn. He felt betrayed by the Scorch. He showed Mark kindness he'd never shown the others. His way of rewarding him for that was to be told, "go to Hell!" Mrs. Cassidy's voice came over his intercom.

"Yes, Mrs. Cassidy, what is it?"

"Mr. Hawkins wants to see you in his office."

"Now, Mrs. Cassidy?"

"He said as soon as you get in."

Well Rob this is it. This is finally what you've been waiting for. He's retiring in a month and I'm going to take over as Director. When I'm Director, I'll put Collingsworth back in his old job. This time, he'll be under my thumb. I'll make his life miserable, like he made mine.

"Bill, you wanted to see me?"

"Rob, take a seat, we need to have a little talk."

"Yes sir."

"Rob, I'm going to cut to the chase. We're promoting Stan Collingsworth as Director."

"Collingsworth, that drunk! Mr. Hawkins, I deserve that promotion!"

"Rob, settle down and listen to me. You're lucky you still have a job."

"What do you mean? What did I do?"

"It's what you haven't. You haven't been doing a very good job. Hell man, drunk, Stan out performs you. Over the last several months Stan has rehabilitated himself and is getting married again. We feel he's the man to run things."

"We, who else decided?"

"The old man."

"I don't get it. I get along with him great. He led me to believe I would succeed you as Director of the department."

"Rob, do you think the old man is an idiot? He sees right through you and so do I. The only reason we made you the acting Assistant Director in Stan's place is we didn't have anyone at the time."

"That's not what you inferred when I took over."

"Whether it is or isn't doesn't matter. We need team players Rob. You've never been one of those. Your poison pen letters about Stan's lack of performance were examples of that. We didn't need you to point out that he was having a rough time. A good man would have stood by their boss and displayed some loyalty. You stabbed him in the back. If I were you, I'd worry about bringing your work up to Bureau standards. Stan is aware of your lack of loyalty too, so I'd walk lightly for a while."

"Is that it, Bill?"

"Not quite."

"There's more?"

"I understand you and Jane are getting a divorce? You know how the Bureau feels about that. If you can't manage your home life, how can you manage your work life?"

"We're working out our problems."

"I'll believe that when I see it. I'm transferring you to lobby security until you get your priorities in order."

"You mean you're making me a guard?"

"You won't have to wear a guard uniform, but yes, you will work with the guards. This will keep you away from the secretaries and give you time to think about your career."

"Bill, I don't know what you mean. Why do you want to keep me from the secretaries?"

"Don't play dumb with me, it's insulting. I'm talking about incidents like the one I saw with Miss Wharton...I'm sure you know what I'm referring to."

"When does this take effect?"

"I want you to clean out your desk today and report to Charlie Binkford in the lobby."

"The security guard?"

"We feel that's far enough removed from the female population so as not to be a distraction."

"I'll be the laughing stock of Headquarters! You can't do this to me Mr. Hawkins!"

"Rob, if you're smart, you'll take your lumps like a man and deal with it. Do I have to tell you what the alternative is?"

"No sir, I get the picture."

"Good, Charlie Binkford is waiting for you. He'll fill you in on your new responsibilities."

As Rob left Bill's office he thought, *this is the worst day of my life.*

*****

After work he went to see an old friend. Brandi was considerably different. She wasn't the ripe young temptress she once was. When he walked through the entrance of the Slipper, Robert saw her behind the bar taking inventory of the liquor. It had been a few years since he last saw her and could not believe his eyes when she turned around.

"Brandi, is that you?"

"What's the matter lover? You're not looking so young and virile any more either. What do you want?"

"I uh…I was thinking…"

"Look honey, I leave that up to the younger girls these days. I'm strictly management now. I've spent enough time on my knees. If you want your pizzle serviced, you better check with one of the girls on the floor."

Robert left the place. All of a sudden he didn't have the energy to bother. He had other things on his mind.

*****

He opened his front door and heard the phone ringing.

"Hello!"

"Robert, this is Jane, you might want to come to Fairfax Hospital to see your son. You may not have another chance."

"What do you mean, another chance? What happened?"

"Mark is near death. The doctors don't have a lot of hope for him."

"I don't have time for your goddamn games! Now what in the hell is going on?"

"After you dropped him off, he went upstairs to his room. He didn't stay there long. He jumped from the porch roof and spent the night with the dogs. Mark was half frozen when I found him this morning. It took both ambulance attendants to haul him out of the doghouse. The doctors have been trying to bring his temperature back up. They say its hypothermia. Now, do you have any more stupid questions?"

"Why don't you call me when he comes to?"

"Are you telling me you don't want to see your son?"

"What's the point if he's not awake?"

"You really don't care about anyone, do you Rob? All Mark wanted was to be with you. You even had me fooled. What did you say to him last night?"

"Me! Look at what you and that no good Bruce did to him. Oh yeah, Mark told me all about it. So don't go pointing your finger at me. You're as much to blame for his situation as anyone."

Jane stood in the phone booth accepting the truth behind Robert's words. He hung up the phone, leaving Jane to deal with the emergency on her own.

*****

When Jane got back to Mark's room, he had a visitor.

"Mrs. Misner, my name is Mr. Sheffield, from Social Services."

"Is there a problem, Mr. Sheffield?"

"Could I have a word with you in the hall, Mrs. Misner?"

"Of course."

Jane couldn't get passed the stern expression on the man's face as he closed the door behind them.

"Mrs. Misner, we're concerned about the welfare of your son."

Jane couldn't hide her anxiousness.

"I assure you, Mr. Sheffield I am too."

"Why don't you tell me what happened?"

"I don't understand why Social Services is involved."

"Calm down, Mrs. Misner. We're involved because of the unusual nature of this...accident. We have to be concerned about the welfare of your children."

"I'm their mother! I love my children! You needn't worry about their welfare!"

"Mrs. Misner, we are concerned. Not only is your son half frozen, his face is full of welts. It would appear he's been beat. That's why we're concerned. Now, what can you tell me about it?"

Suddenly, Jane felt very tired. She leaned against the wall.

"Mr. Sheffield, can we go somewhere more private?"

"Certainly, let's go get a quiet booth in the dining room. You look like you could use a cup of coffee anyway."

Five minutes later, they were in a corner booth.

"My husband and I are getting a divorce."

"What about the welts?"

"Robert has a bad temper and takes it out on the children at times."

"That's why you're divorcing him?"

"Yes, that and other things."

"Mark had always been Rob's favorite. Even so, Rob never paid much attention to him until recently. I guess Mark blames me for driving his father away."

"Tell me what happened last night."

Jane related the entire story, leaving out what she didn't know."

"That's pretty much it, Mr. Sheffield. You'll have to find out from Mark what happened at his father's, or ask Rob."

"I intend to do just that. I can tell, Mrs. Misner, that you are a very caring parent. When Mark is able, you may take him home. How can I get in touch with your husband? Will he be coming to the hospital?"

"No, he won't. I'll give you his phone number."

"You mean to tell me, his son almost froze to death and he's not coming to see him? What kind of man is he?"

Jane could see the understanding dawn on Mr. Sheffield's face. He excused himself and Jane returned to Mark's room. Jane walked through Mark's door. Mark was awake.

"Mom, I'm sorry for the way I acted. Is Bruce okay?"

Jane could not hold her tears back. Her little miracle boy had overcome yet another huge ordeal.

*****

Mark came home from the hospital after four days. He seemed to be the Mark of old. Jane was in the living room with Rene. She thought of something she needed from upstairs and called up to him.

"Mark! I have a pattern in my closet. Can you bring it down to me?"

"Sure mom, I'll be down in a minute."

No sooner had she made the request, than she ran up the stairs. Jane forgot the incriminating pictures of Rob were in the sewing box.

Mark opened the lid to the sewing box. He saw the large manila envelope. His curiosity got the best of him and he opened it. Inside the envelope were photos of his father having sex with a blonde woman.

Jane rushed into the room but was too late. Mark turned toward her with the pictures in his hands. Jane didn't know what to say.

Mark dropped the pictures to the floor and went to his room without a word.

PART FIVE

In early February of 1965 D.C. got hit with a huge snowstorm. Government offices closed early. Commuting was horrendous, especially for those relying on bus transportation. Jane walked through her front door at 7pm. Her feet were half frozen. High heels weren't much good in six inches of snow.

Just when Jane thought the day couldn't get worse, Freddy stopped by. It was apparent something was on his mind. He didn't even stomp the snow from his feet. Freddy stared blankly at his mother, not knowing how to break his news.

"To what do I owe this visit?"

"I got a letter today."

"A letter? From who?"

Freddy handed the envelope to his mother.

Jane didn't need to read it. The letter was from the Selective Service. It started,

Greetings,

"You are hereby ordered for induction into the Armed Forces of the United States."

"Freddy, you can't say you're surprised."

"I didn't think it would happen this soon. I only got the physical a month ago."

"There's no point in worrying about it now. If you spent more time studying than playing cards, you'd still be in school."

"Mom, do you think they'll be sending me to Vietnam?"

"I hope not."

*****

Two and a half months later, Freddy came home on a week's leave prior to shipping out.

"Mom, I've been thinking about something."

"Tell me."

"I don't want you getting all teary on me. I'm leaving for Hawaii next week."

"Do you know where they'll send you from there?"

"I've signed up for special training."

Jane didn't like the sound of this.

"What kind of training?"

"The kind that can save my life."

"Freddy! GI's with that kind of training will most certainly be in danger. Why did you do it?"

"Vietnam. The more I know about jungle survival, the better. That's the reason we're going to Hawaii. I'm to be trained by guys that have been there."

"You won't mind if I worry about you?"

"I know you'll be worried. I'll take care of myself."

"Promise you'll write as much as you can."

"I'll write at least once a week."

"Do you want me to say anything to your father?"

"He doesn't care anything about me, so what's the point?"

"He's your father."

"I can see him in the tavern now, bragging about his warrior son. He'll be a big man down at the tavern. Every one will buy him a drink. All I mean to him is a couple of free drinks."

"What happens when he finds out? You know he will."

"I really don't care."

"You're a full-grown man. He has to treat you as an equal."

"Mom, I love you, but you're naive as hell. He doesn't have to do a damn thing. Why do you still defend him?"

"I don't want you having regrets later."

"If I do, I do."

"I won't say another word about it. Just think about what I've said."

"Okay mom I'll think about it. Just don't be calling the bastard up and telling him."

*****

For Jimmy Layton, joining the Army was an escape from his feelings of guilt. Running over the little boy that day, thirteen-years ago changed his life forever. He had no idea how much the accident changed others. The memory of that day faded with each passing year. Now it was tucked in the deep recesses of his mind.

Jim had been in Vietnam for six months as an advisor to the Army of The Republic of Vietnam. He and his companions discovered their tactical training was of little use in this kind of war.

The jungle terrain dictated how this war would be fought. Hand-to-hand skills were more important than battle tactics. The enemy was expert at using the terrain. They seemed to spring from the ground, attack and vanish without a trace. Jim and his comrades became the students.

Experience proved to be the best teacher. Their newfound knowledge came at a steep price: the blood of his comrades. Jim had learned his lessons well. He learned to be one with the jungle. The enemy learned to fear him as a phantom that moved without detection through their territory. Such phantoms had a name, LRRP's (Long Range Recon Patrols).

Jim and his companions were in Hawaii to teach others what they had learned. He would not be prepared for what awaited him.

*****

Freddy recognized him immediately. He remembered the carefree teenager those many years ago. He remembered the boy's size. Even at seventeen, Jimmy had an imposing physique. More than anything else, Freddy remembered the eyes. Not many people could stand up to the intensity of those black orbs. They belied his age, making Jimmy Layton seem older.

When Freddy saw those eyes look in his direction he yelled out.

"Hey Jimmy, Jimmy Layton, it's me, Freddy Misner!

The big Sergeant approached the new arrival. The trainee looked vaguely familiar. He didn't quite pick up the name. One look at the black letters over the uniform pocket released the demons of his memory. Jim's eyes bore through Private First Class, Freddy Misner. There was no sign of recognition or warmth in them. There was only intensity, the intensity of the harsh reality of killing, a reality he would be teaching Freddy Misner.

Freddy felt dwarfed by this huge man with Sergeant stripes. He shrank from the stare of those eyes he remembered so well. There was something about them. They seemed...menacing. He tried once more to break through the silence of this hulking presence.

"Jimmy, don't you remember me?"

The Sergeants' response was anything but cordial.

"What did you call me you little puke?"

"I uh, Jimmy, don't you recognize me? I'm Freddy, Freddy Misner."

"I don't give a good God damned who you were back in the world. You address me as Master Sergeant or Sergeant Layton do you understand me you little dip shit?"

Freddy was astonished, but had heard the stories of guys brainwashed by too many years in uniform. He snapped to attention.

"Yes sir, Master Sergeant!"

"That's better, Private. Now get your ass into line with the other FNG's!"

Freddy turned sharply and stood in formation with the others. The Sergeant paced back and forth appraising his new trainees. He addressed them in a voice loud enough to be heard in LA.

"All right you ass-wipes listen up! You have volunteered yourself into six weeks of Hell. You're not in Hawaii to learn how to hula or surf. You are here because there is jungle here. This is the closest thing to jungle we have. This terrain is nothing like what you will encounter in the Nam. If you're not dripping in torrential downpours, you'll be dripping in your own sweat.

Make no mistake, for those of you that make it through this training, you will be going to the Nam. You will learn how to kill the enemy on his own turf! You are going to learn how to eat shit and love it!"

Jim paced back and forth, making eye contact with each trainee. When he was sure he had their undivided attention, he continued.

"The enemy is a little piece of shit named Charles Victor, Charley for short. Just because he's small, don't think for one minute you're better than him. He has no fear and is the smartest bastard you'll ever encounter. Charley lives for the opportunity to kill stupid pathetic pukes like you. Are there any questions?"

There was total silence.

"Good, Sergeant Hall will show you to your quarters. Dismissed!"

Later that night, Jimmy and Phil Hall were sharing a bottle of Scotch.

"Jim, did you know that kid back in the world?"

"It was a lifetime ago."

"How are you going to deal with it?"

"He's just another piece of meat. My job is to turn them into killers. Phil, you know Goddamn well we can't afford formalities. Hesitation in the bush means somebody buys it."

"You didn't answer my question."

"I'll treat him like the others. It's on him to make the cut."

Jimmy related the story of the accident 13 years ago to his friend. He couldn't hide the pain as he spoke. A brief silence followed.

"Jim, did his little brother make it?"

"He made it. Let's hope his big brother is as tough."

*****

Robert picked Irene up for one of his bi-weekly visits. When he took her back home two hours later, he was livid. Jane opened the front door. Robert started on her immediately.

"Why didn't you tell me Freddy was in Vietnam? Don't you think I had a right to know one of my sons is in danger?"

"I was following Freddy's wishes. Why should you care? Not once have you asked how he's doing!"

"I still have a right to know what's going on, especially when their lives are in jeopardy. When did he ship out?"

"Last week."

"He didn't want to see me or even talk to me?"

"Robert, why would he? All you ever did with Bruce and Freddy is find fault with them. You treated your damned dogs better than you did them! I don't blame him for not wanting to talk to you!"

Robert was angry but also down deep he was hurt. His whole life had been turned upside down and he blamed his family for it.

"Robert, did you hear me?"

"I heard you. What's his address?"

"Are you planning on writing him?"

"Jane, you never understood me at all, did you?"

"Rob, I don't want to hear how you were hard on the boys so they'd become stronger men."

"You can find all the fault with me you want. Those boys would be nothing if it weren't for me."

"You really believe that don't you?"

"I can't talk to you. You were always too soft on the kids, especially Mark."

"Are you finished?"

Robert left the house on Horseshoe and made his way home. He walked into a house filled with the aroma of roast beef cooking. Standing over the stove was Jenette Wharton, now Mrs. Robert Misner.

"How's my girl doing?"

"Hi honey, how was your visit with Rene?"

"She's the only one of my children I can still refer to as such."

"Your family is crazy not to appreciate you. Well, no matter, when I have our child you can start all over with a brand new family."

Robert had been married to Jenette for only a few months. He decided he didn't like being alone. He knew she really loved him. Robert would not make the same mistakes he made in his first marriage. All of that was in the past as if it never happened.

"I found out something interesting. Freddy is in Vietnam."

"You mean that woman kept something like that from you? How did you find out?"

"Rene. You know she can't keep a secret. She's my most reliable source of information. I've told you what I had to deal with married to her. The woman never told me anything. I always had to find out the hard way."

"I'd love to call her up. I'd give her a good piece of my mind. You're his father. You have a right to know. Did she at least tell you how to get hold of him?"

"Yes, but I had to pry it from her."

"You should write Freddy then. Who knows, now that both of you are away from that woman, maybe it will be different between you two."

"Hmm, you could be right about that. I'll write him tonight."

*****

The next day Robert was working security at the main desk. He'd not gotten over the humiliation of the demotion. Robert knew he was the brunt of numerous jokes throughout the building. He had been working the security desk for over a year. He wondered if he'd ever see an office again.

It was approaching lunchtime. He could hear the staccato sound of high heels on the tile floor. He raised his head from the paper. Staring down at him was Laura Lea Pike.

"What are you doing here?"

Laura Lea pretended not to hear him.

"Don't you look impressive behind your little desk, or is that a table? Do I call you officer Misner, guard Misner or just Misner like your little nameplate says?"

"Look you little slut, I don't have time for this."

"Tsk, tsk, Mr. Misner, I'm here to meet my husband for lunch."

"Your husband? What poor slob did you manipulate into marrying you?"

"I think you know him. I'm Mrs. Stanley Collingsworth. Now guard, if you would be so kind as to ring my husband and tell him I'm on my way up?"

*****

Jimmy was on his way back to Nam with his newly trained men. Much to his amazement Misner flew through the training. Misner rose to the top in every situation. Their assignment was to gather intelligence on enemy movement and strength. Of course they had to infiltrate enemy positions to do that. The VC and NVA had to be stopped. It was thought they were moving through a network of underground tunnels.

*****

Freddy and the rest of his recon unit had been at base camp for over a month. They had no luck finding any trace of the tunnel complex. They did however find several key trails used by the VC. The six-man unit awaited word on where they would search next.

Jimmy had taken Freddy under his wing. Freddy figured it was because he had proven himself in the bush. As he thought about this, Freddy studied the envelope in his hand. It was postmarked Washington DC with a return address on Fessenden Street. Freddy tentatively opened the letter from his father and began to read.

May 7, 1965

Freddy,

I'll bet you're surprised to hear from your old man. This isn't easy for me, but I wanted to write you anyway. I didn't know about your situation until after you left. I had to find out from Rene. That little girl misses her big brother.

I'm not writing you to make any kind of apologies or anything like that. I was hard on you boys for a reason. Life can be nasty. I wanted my sons to be able to handle it. Even with all of the disagreements we had between us, you're still my boy and I care about you. I would like to hear from you if you feel like writing. In the meantime, take care of yourself.

Sincerely,

Your Father

Freddy lowered the letter and stared at the clouds as they rolled by. His father forgot to mention one thing; life is full of surprises too. As Freddy lowered the letter, he remarked to the heavens,

"I'll be goddamned."

Jim came up from behind, as Freddy finished the letter.

"What are you goddamned about?"

"Would you believe it? My ass-hole father wrote me!"

"That's good. You need to write him back."

"Jim, I didn't grow up in the ideal family environment. My father was a real dick. He's writin' me because he feels guilty. I don't need this horseshit on my mind."

"What if he's writing because he really cares about you? I get letters four or five times a week from everyone in my family."

"Yeah, but that's your family. The only one in my family to write me so far is mom."

"That's not true anymore…your father. What's he say anyway, if you don't mind me askin?"

"Oh shit, it's only a few paragraphs, see."

Freddy held up the one page letter to his mentor and let him read it.

"Looks to me like your old man is trying to reach out to you. Come to think about it, I remember your old man at the hospital that time. He was cool, considering what happened. He had every reason in the world to let me have it, but he didn't."

Freddy sat there shaking his head. How could he get someone like Jimmy Layton to understand?

"Jim, you'll never get it. Let me ask you a question?"

"Okay"

"Did your father ever beat any of your brothers or sisters?"

"My father would never lay a hand on any of his kids."

"My old man made a weekly practice of beating me and my older brother. Now he says he did it to make us tough...bullshit!"

"You are a tough little bastard. I've never met anyone like you Freddy. Failure isn't a word you're too familiar with."

"Hell, if I fucked something up, the old man would kick my ass."

"There you have it."

"What do you mean by that?"

"Like it or not, you're who you are because of your father. You just said as much. I see how driven you are every day. Your father instilled that in you."

"You think so?"

"Man, this ain't a place for pussies, you understand? I'm here because I want to be. Most guys like you are here because your sorry ass got drafted and you HAVE to be here.

But, you're not like most of the other swinging dicks around here."

"How do you mean?"

"Success in the bush means you don't get to go home in a black bag. Most guys hit the bush scared shitless, not knowing what to do. You, on the other hand, understood your survival depended on how much you could learn. That's why you volunteered for recon. This deal isn't for everybody. You have to be both mentally and physically tough. Yep, like him or not, if you make it back to the world it'll be because your old man didn't raise no pussy."

"You sure do cut to the chase. Thanks for the fucking lecture professor."

"No charge dickhead. Cuttin' to the chase saves time. I tell it like it is, you know that."

The two men had become close. Dependence on one another in the bush did that. In their case however, they were bound to each other in another way. Freddy had something on his mind and had to get it out.

"Jim, do you mind if I ask you something?"

"No kid."

"No, don't ask, or no, you don't mind?"

"You sound like Perry fucking Mason. Ask your fucking question."

Both men laughed at Jim's rare display of humor.

"What happened to you that day?"

Jim knew this would eventually come up between the two. He'd asked himself that same question countless times. The answer always eluded him.

"You mean the accident?"

"Yeah."

"I don't know. Sometimes I think I'm still running away from that day."

"I look back on the way you used to be and see you now. Did the accident do that?"

"Do what?"

"You were always so happy. I remember seeing you in that big green car. I even remember the radio station you had on all the time."

"How could you remember that?"

"Because even then, I wanted to be you. Yeah, WPGC on your AM dial. You were always tapping your fingers on your door in time with the tunes. Now…well, you're different. You know what I mean?"

"I think I do. You want to know what I think?"

"Yeah, I do."

"The day I saw you jump off that truck in Hawaii brought it all back. I've spent thirteen years trying to forget that day and what happens?"

"I show up and bring it all back."

"Bingo. I thought God was punishing me. I think this is part of some big plan the man upstairs has for us. The accident was no accident. You showing up thirteen years later isn't any accident. All of this was supposed to happen. God knew we'd wind up in this shit hole together. He put me here to save your ass."

"Maybe he put me here to save YOUR ass."

"No, I don't think so. I'm the one that nearly killed your little brother. This is how he wants me to pay that debt."

"You've already done that a couple of times."

"Kid, the world is a funny place. I joined up as a kind of penance. I thought saving lives would make up for almost taking one. In order for me to do that I have to kill."

"I see what you mean. Having to kill to save lives carries a certain irony."

"No shit!"

There was a peaceful silence between the two men. Freddy got up and made for their hootch. Jim trailed after him. They had a patrol to prepare for. Before they left, Freddy had a letter to write.

May 23, 1965

Dear Dad,

I'm not sure how to respond to your letter. You weren't the best father a guy could have. But my Sergeant made a couple of good points. Oh, my Sergeant is Jimmy Layton. You remember him; he was the kid that ran over Mark. He's turned into the biggest, bad ass in the army. I owe a lot to him.

I didn't recognize him at first...the man is huge! The first time I recognized him was when he bored through me with those black empty eyes. I knew immediately who he was. He made it clear to all of us that he would ride our butts. We'd either make it, or we'd be history. He reminds me a lot of you.

Anyway, Jim's father never beat any of his kids. They all loved and respected their father. He gets letters all of the time from not only his parents, but also all of his brothers and sisters. Jim gets strength from his family. It's nothing like I've ever seen. His family is very close, not like ours. That's because of you. We all hated you. I can remember Bruce and I running upstairs each night when we heard your smokers' cough as you came up the porch steps.

What kind of father instills that kind of fear in his children? You are a mystery to me and I think you always will be.

Jim says I'm who I am because of you. He says I'm the most driven person he's ever seen. He thinks it's because of your constant pushing to make us the best at whatever we did. Bruce and I wanted to be the best so we could rub it in your face. We wanted to show we were better than you...and we did.

Just like you said you're not apologizing for anything, I'm not ready to talk about forgiveness. Maybe one day I'll be able to forgive you for being the biggest ass-hole in the world...I'll never forget though. I do know one thing. If I ever make it out of this hot, humid, awful place and have kids of my own; I'll be a better father than you were to me.

Freddy

*****

From their insertion point, it took the six men all day to hump to the enemy trail. The other guys were concealed in a cocoon of brush as Freddy looked at the night sky from his hidey-hole. He had the first watch and his mind drifted back to home.

This forest was not at all like those of home. There wasn't a single thing that even resembled home. It even smelled different. The forest loam of Virginia smelled rich and familiar. The forests of his childhood were home to all of his best memories. Even during the winter, there was a feeling of security. Freddy missed the snow. He missed the way it weighted tree limbs down until they touched the ground.

Here, the forest smelled of death and decay. The comforting warmth of home was replaced by the Hellish humidity of this triple canopy of vines and vegetation. The ground itself was never dry. There was no rustle of dry leaves as Freddy and his friends played soldier. At home the battles and enemies were imaginary.

The enemy here was not imaginary. The wetness and humidity concealed their quiet footfalls, threatening death. The density of the jungle was their armor and protector... their friend. They moved through it with the familiarity of home...their home.

*****

Robert sat at his kitchen table reading the letter from his son. He wasn't sure what he felt. It was a mixture of anger and pride. Jenette was fixing his dinner and turned to say something to Robert but waited until he finished reading the letter.

"What does Freddy say?"

"I'm sorry Jenny, what did you say?"

"I said, what does Freddy say in the letter. Did he get your letter?"

"Yeah, he got it. He says the jungle is a hot and humid place."

"Is that it?"

"He called me an ass-hole."

"Now that sounds like him."

"He's right, I was an ass-hole most of the time. I guess I rode them too hard."

"That's nonsense!"

"He did say it made him stronger."

"See, I told you."

*****

The phone rang while Jane was in the living room watching television.

"Hello."

"Mrs. Misner, this is Marvin Hill from across the street."

"Yes Mr. Hill what can I do for you?"

"I caught your son in some mischief and I'd like you to come over so we can talk."

"Mischief, what kind of mischief?"

"I'd rather not say over the phone. I'd rather you come over so I can show you."

"I'll be right there!"

Jane went over the small cape cod across the street. She didn't know much about Marvin Hill other than him being a widower. She did know his wife had died several years earlier of cancer. Eleanor Hill sold Avon to many of the women in the neighborhood and had lots of friends. Jane Misner was one of them. Jane brought food over to Marvin occasionally as a gesture of kindness.

Like most others, her attention seemed to focus on the way the man walked. Jane knocked on the door. Marvin answered. They stared at each other momentarily. She noticed the strong lantern-like jaw and penetrating eyes and felt goose bumps. He was noticing her as well. Jane stammered slightly before breaking the silence.

"Hi, uh good evening Mr. Hill. You said something about my son?"

"Thanks for coming over so quickly."

Sitting in the living room cleaning a pair of shoes…well, one shoe and what looked like another shoe but with the leg of a mannequin in it. As the man stepped aside Jane noticed the empty pant leg for the first time. She tried not to stare, but couldn't help herself. She saw Mark sitting uneasily on the edge of a chair.

"Mark, what have you done now?"

"Mrs. Misner, lets have a seat and I'll tell you."

"Please do and call me Jane please."

"Fine, Jane. Mark and a couple of his friends were up to some mischief. They thought it would be funny to light a bag of cow manure on my front porch and watch me stomp on it with my fake leg"

"Mark, that's an awful thing to do. You should be ashamed of yourself. Who else was with you?"

"I'm not rattin' on the other guys. I'll take my punishment."

"Don't think you won't be punished either!"

Jane returned her attention back to Marvin.

"Mr. Hill, I don't know what to say. Was anything damaged?"

"Other than getting some wet cow manure on my prosthesis, nothing was damaged."

"I'm so sorry for what my son has done. What can we do to make up for it?"

"I was just thinking about that after I called you. How about if you make Mark come over and do some yard work oh, say for about a week?"

"I think that's the least he can do. How about him starting tomorrow after school?"

"That'll be fine Jane. I'll see him around 3:30."

"Okay, Mr. Hill, again, I'm sorry."

"Jane, call me Marvin, okay?"

"Okay, Marvin it is. Mark get home, we're not finished talking about this!"

*****

Freddy and his recon unit had been back for a few days after being in the bush for over four weeks. They monitored Charley's movements up and down the network of trails. They made it back to their LZ and were extracted without a hitch. The mission yielded enough intelligence for the planning of a heavy ambush.

Freddy was trying to figure out how to tell his mother he'd gotten hurt. He didn't want to tell her it happened on the last mission. He propped himself up in his hospital bed and penned a letter.

May 30, 1965

Dear Mom

I don't want you to worry but I got hurt while on a mission. It's not serious so please don't worry about me. The good thing about getting wounded is, it gets you out of the shit for a while. I'll get a chance to chase some local girls around and see if I get lucky (only kidding).

I wish you could see this place. If it weren't for what was going on in this country, it would be a tropical paradise. The ocean and beaches are absolutely beautiful. We go surfing every chance we get. I can't hang ten yet but I'm working on it.

If you're worried about my wound, don't be. It was my own damn fault. I got a little careless in the jungle and twisted my ankle really bad. They have it in a cast and tell me I should be well enough to go back in a couple of weeks.

How's old Mark doing now that he's King of the Hill. I bet he's enjoying not having any big brothers around to boss him. Tell Rene I miss her and look forward to coming home to see her next year. Take care of yourself and write me soon.

Your Son,

Freddy

Marvin had become a regular fixture around the house. Jane was attracted to him the night Mark got in trouble. They spent almost everyday in each other's company. Both were lonely and far from being over the hill. There was a knock on Jane's door.

"Hi good looking what's cookin'?"

"Come in Marvin. I have a letter from Freddy. He got hurt and he's in the hospital!"

"What happened?"

Jane knew that military hospitals conjured up bad memories for her lover. Marvin told Jane the story about losing his leg to a mine in Korea.

"He's twisted his ankle and they have him in a cast. He says it'll be all right and they'll probably send him back to his unit in a few weeks."

"Well honey, that's good news. Hospital chow is a damned site better than field rations. Plus, look at all those gorgeous nurses Freddy will be around. He's one lucky GI."

"Lucky! How can you say that? When he told me he was wounded I panicked. I had visions of him lying in a hospital bed after being shot, or blown up."

"Jane, his buddies are having a good laugh on him right now. Freddy will have a hard time living down that sprained ankle. He's had the best training a combat soldier can get. Freddy will come through this."

"But in one piece! Marvin, I'm sorry. I didn't mean to…"

"Why don't you help this old one legged man out back for some of that tea of yours?"

Marvin Hill put his arm around Jane and they made their way out back to sit among the roses.

*****

In the house on Fessenden Street Robert opened his own letter from his son.

June 30, 1965

I've been thinking about home and how I grew up. Aside from the beatings, it wasn't that bad. If nothing else, it's given me a whole lot of stories to tell around camp. The guys can't believe some of the things I tried to get away with. They all agree that you were a prick, but the stories are funny at least looking back they are.

Little kids don't understand what kind of pressures their parents are under. For whatever the reason, you and mom just didn't get along very well. That's all in the past. It's all bullshit compared to what I've seen here.

We came upon a village the other day on our way into the bush. It was totally destroyed along with all of the people. Charley must have thought those poor bastards were helping us in some way. Everyone was killed, some tortured.

We got to our ambush site after humping in the bush from dawn to dusk. Granik and me set up a perimeter to our rear and front with claymores. We had Claymores facing the trail, away from us. We positioned ourselves well behind them. The back blast from those things can kill you just as dead as the hundreds of pellets inside. All we needed now was for Charley to show up. He didn't disappoint us.

We were arrayed for an 'L' shaped ambush. There were eleven of us. Six of us comprised the assault element. Four of us were lined up along the trail about fifteen feet apart while the other two covered the 'foot' of the 'L'. Charley had nowhere to go but forward or back. If he went back then our support element would take care of them. Those guys had M-60s. The last two guys were our security. They would plug up holes and keep Charley from getting away.

The waiting is the hardest thing. You have lots of time to think. Mainly all you think about are your weapons and ammo. I've seen guys get nailed because they didn't keep their shit wired tight. Jamming is the biggest problem. I keep my weapon clean as a whistle. Remember how you used to dog Bruce and I for not cleaning the guns after hunting? A dirty weapon here means you go home in a black bag. With all the mud and dampness those things jam all the time. I also picked up a 45 caliber for close encounters. We all had three or four frags each. All in all we were armed to the teeth.

There was a fairly wide stream paralleling the other side of the trail. Charley could wade that and get away but he'd leave himself exposed to our fire plus we set up a couple of claymores on the other side.

All I could think about during this waiting game was lighting up a camel when we got back to camp. Right in the middle of that thought, all hell broke loose. Somehow Charley knew we were there. It was like they sprung from the ground, all around us. Our perimeter didn't mean shit. Everyone was firing they're weapons at anything that moved. I looked to my left and saw Granik with one of the little bastards on his back getting ready to slice his throat. I just had time to nail him with the 45.

I'll never forget what happened next. Granik gave me the thumbs up just before his head exploded. The same gook leveled Granik's weapon at me but it misfired. He was only a few feet away when he charged me with his machete. I've never been so scared in my entire life. I didn't have time to shoot him as he landed on me. For a small guy he sure was strong. I had a hell of a time getting him off of me.

While I was occupied with him, another VC came at me. I let go with one of my hands so I could get to my 45, but before I knew it the first guy had the machete in his free hand ready to split my head open. The only thing I could get was my K-bar. I pulled it from the sheath and skewered the little bastard. As soon as I did that the other gook was on me.

I couldn't pull my knife free. It must have lodged in the guy's ribs, so I shoved his body at the second guy. That gave me time to make a dive for my 45 and plug the gook just as he raised his arm to hack at me. He fell on top of me. His mouth was moving but nothing was coming out but blood. I pushed him away from me and found my M-16. I rolled over on my stomach and started spraying and praying.

Before we knew it, the fight was over. We counted twenty-three enemy dead and we lost Granik. Those dudes just disappeared into thin air. Jimmy decided we needed to get the hell out of Dodge. We collected what we could and *got the hell out of there. The only problem was I twisted my ankle. It hurt like a bitch.*

It's amazing how you forget about pain when you're scared shitless. That brings me to the here and now. I tore the shit out of my ankle ligaments and am lying in a hospital bed in Saigon.

I don't know why I'm telling you all of this. I guess, in a way, I'm looking for your approval. I realized that's all I ever wanted from you. I've thought about the past. I remember the time you showed me how to brush the dog. I remember the way your big hand felt as it held mine while I guided the brush over Duke. That was one of the few times I can think of when you weren't raising hell with someone over some stupid thing.

Dad, what I'm trying to say is, I'd like to have a chance to start all over when I get back home. Our differences are squat compared to what I've been through here. I know I shouldn't have said anything about this firefight to you but I had to tell someone and I didn't want to tell mom. She would just worry. I'm asking you please not to mention this to her. I'll know if you do.

Sincerely,

Freddy

Robert read the letter in the privacy of his car. He felt alive, needed for the first time in years. His son wanted to start over. There was hope he could have an adult relationship with Freddy after all. Robert finished the letter and tucked into his suit pocket. He wouldn't say anything to Jane about it. *My son is a hero. He's killed the enemy's of his country in hand-to-hand fighting. I never thought I'd feel proud of him ever again.*

***** * *****

Jane and Marvin discovered one of the scenic overlooks of the George Washington Parkway. His visits to the house were always for coffee and chitchat. Their more romantic interludes were reserved for the backseat of Marvin's car. They had just made love in the back seat of his big Chrysler Imperial when Jane brought up the subject of Nicole.

"I'm worried about Nicole."

"What are you worried about?"

"She's been seeing someone I don't approve of."

"You mean that Jake guy."

"Jake Corning; he's a drop out. I don't want her dating a high school drop out. She's too good for that."

"Have you discussed this with her?"

"I've tried, but she won't listen to me. She gets mad and runs upstairs."

"Maybe you should give this Jake a chance. If Nicole likes him, he can't be that bad. Nicki has a good head on her shoulders. Besides, she's eighteen and is technically an adult. She can see whoever she wants."

"I know and that's what worries me. I feel like she's rebelling against me. I don't want her to make the same mistake I made."

"Jane, kids grow up to be adults. They move away from home and learn to make their own decisions. Maybe it's time you let Nicole do the same."

"Marvin, I worry about her."

"You're the prettiest worrier I ever saw. Now come here, I'm not finished talking to you yet."

"Oh Mr. Hill, I'm all ears."

They lay back down with the lightweight blanket providing a thin layer of privacy.

*****

Nicole was working full time now that she was out of school. She was also seeing Jake on a very regular basis.

This had been going on for months. Nicki knew her mother disapproved of Jake.

Nicole wasn't used to keeping things from her mother. This secrecy wore on her. Nicole wanted everything out in the open. Jake had forced the issue by asking Nicole to marry him. Nicole wanted to marry him, but was afraid of what her mother might say. Nicole waited on the corner of Chain Bridge and Old Courthouse Roads. Little did she know this was the secret rendezvous for her mother and Marvin.

It was a Wednesday night and Nicole was at the corner across from the ESSO station waiting for Jake to pick her up. Jake soon pulled up and off they went. Jake started every conversation with his girl the same way.

"Hey babe, what's happening?"

Jake leaned over and Nicole accepted his kiss like an old married woman.

"Jake, I've got to talk with mom. I'm really tired of all this sneaking around."

"Why don't we go to your house and we'll wait for her together?"

"I need to do this without you. I know you mean well, but this is between mom and I. Once she knows how much I love you, she'll have to accept you."

"You know, if she's worried about my not finishing high school, I am almost finished with my GED. Once she knows I have some ambition, she'll accept me all right."

"Who wouldn't love you Jake? You're such a good and decent man. I can't wait until we're married and have children of our own."

"Me too babe. Speaking of which, I found a new place for us"

"Where?"

"I'll show you."

Jake pulled onto Chain Bridge Road and made his way through McLean. He exited onto the GW Parkway from 123. They pulled into the overlook parking lot. The white Imperial was parked on the far end. Nicole couldn't place where she'd seen the car before.

"Jake, there's a another car here. Maybe we should go somewhere else."

"That's not necessary. Look at the windows."

"What about the windows?"

"They're all steamy. You know what that means?"

"Jake you're so bad."

The young couple had gotten out of the car and opened the doors to the back seat. Both doors slamming made the couple in the other car lift their heads and look out the window.

"Marvin, there's someone else here. We better leave."

Jane had to wipe off the moisture from the inside of the window in order to see from it. She used her discarded shorts for the purpose.

"Marvin, does that car look familiar to you? I swear I've seen it somewhere before."

Just as Jane got the words out, she saw Nicki. Nicole was pulling off her blouse when she happened to look out of the car window. Their eyes locked onto to one another's. Jane became aware of her naked state and fumbled for her blouse. Nicole did the same.

"Jane, what's the matter? You look like you just saw a ghost."

"It's, it's Nicole over there! She's taking off her clothes! She's with that Jake Corning! Oh my God!"

"Honey, seems to me you're in the same state."

"Quick! Give me my blouse and shorts!"

At the same time Nicole pulled the blouse back in place and went for the door handle.

"Jake, it's my mother! She's with that Mr. Hill from across the street!"

"You're kidding me right?"

"I wish I were! Look for yourself! Oh my God! Here she comes!"

Nicole got out of the car and met her mother halfway. All they did at first was take in each other's disheveled appearance and stammer at one another. Both men had gotten out and looked at each other. They couldn't help themselves and started laughing. That seemed to break the tension as both women looked at their men. Mother and daughter overcame their shock and joined the laughter. What else could they do?

They both blurted out at the same time,

"How long have you two…? You first mom."

"I want to know the same thing. Well I guess, given the circumstances there's not a lot I can say about your behavior."

"You're not upset?"

"Nicole, I'm too shocked by the coincidence to be upset. Why don't we all go back to the house and talk?"

The men let the girls talk in private.

"Jake, why don't you walk over to my house with me. I've got a cold six-pack in the fridge?"

"That sounds great. Uh, babe…Nicki, I'm going over with Marvin for a couple cold ones…Nicki?"

"Let's go Jake, she doesn't even know you're here."

Jane and Nicole had gotten past their mutual shock and were now into the nitty-gritty of the matter.

"Nicole, are you sure you love Jake?"

"Yes mama, I love him and he loves me."

"There's more to marriage than simply love. How is Jake going to support you?"

"Jake is almost finished with his equivalency test and will be able to get a job at the bank. They've already told him a job is his if he wants it. So you see, there's nothing to worry about. I know how you feel about Jake, but he loves me."

"When do you two want to get married?"

"Oh mama, I love you!"

*****

Freddy never thought he'd get a reply from his father. It had been three months since he wrote him detailing the firefight and his subsequent injury.

September 2, 1965

Dear Son,

I got your last letter and was happy to hear you're all right. I've only had to fire my service weapon once in my life. One bullet, one dead armed bank robber. I know the feeling. Killing another person leaves an empty, hollow feeling in the gut. It sounds to me as though you acquitted yourself very well. I'm proud of you, son. Your country is proud of you, despite what you may hear about the damned hippies.

We should round up all those dope smoking bastards and ship them out if they hate America so much! I haven't said anything to your mother. I like the idea of starting over with you. Why can't your older brother be sensible like that? I understand that both he and your sister are getting married soon. If it weren't for Rene I wouldn't know what was going on with my own family. I had hoped that, at least Nicole would have told me about her engagement.

Oh well, if they don't want me in they're lives, I don't have to want them in mine.

311

*I don't want to dwell on those things. How's your
ankle? Have you been out on any more missions? If you want
someone to talk to about it, I'm here for you son. Keep your
head down.*

Sincerely,

Dad

*****

Jane didn't know how to broach the topic with Mark.
She knew finding the photos of his father having sex with a
strange woman bothered him a great deal. Mark put on a
tough front when it came to his father. Whenever Robert
came to pick up Rene, Mark made sure he was no where to
be found. Her son had adopted Marvin as a father figure.
Marvin treated Mark like his own son. Jane asked Marvin to
talk to Mark that afternoon. When he knocked on the front
door Jane asked Mark to get it.

"Hey Mark, how's it goin today? I thought you'd be at
work?"

"I don't work on Tuesdays. Mom's upstairs, I'll go get
her."

"Mark, actually, I was thinking about going to
Woodside Lake for some fishing and thought you might
want to go with me."

"Sure Mr. Hill, I'd like to go fishing. Let me get my
rod."

Mark yelled up to his mother that he and Marvin were
going fishing. Jane tried to busy herself with aimless
straightening, but her mind was on Mark. *If anyone can talk
to Mark it's Marvin. He's so good with him. I hope he can
make Mark understand about the photos.*

They were in the Imperial on the way to the lake when
Marvin eased into the topic of conversation.

"Mark, I wanted to ask you something."

"What, you want to marry my mother?"

"No, no, not that, although, I have given it some thought. Why do you ask that? Has your mother said anything to you?"

"No she hasn't Mr. Hill, but I figured the way you've been coming around for the last several months that might be on your mind."

"Mark, I'd be lying if I told you it wasn't. How would you feel about that?"

"I think it would be all right. You treat mom well and she seems to like you a lot. I see the way she looks at you when she thinks us kids aren't looking."

"Mark Misner! Have you been spying on your mother and I?"

"No, I haven't, but if I had I wouldn't be the only spy around here."

"What do you mean by that, Mark?"

"I don't know if I should say anything to you about it. It's a family matter."

"Mark, does this family matter involve photos of your father with other women?"

"You didn't come over to take me fishing. You took me out to see how I feel about my father. Why can't adults just say what's on their minds? Why do they have to be so sneaky?"

"Mark, your mom is not being sneaky. She's concerned about you. I told her I'd talk to you about the pictures."

"Do you and my mother do what my father was doing with that woman?"

"You mean do we have sex together?"

"That's exactly what I mean."

"Yes, We have sex together. That's what a man and woman do when they love each other."

"All I can say is, my old man sure must love lots of women. I counted six different ones in the pictures. How did Mom come by them?"

"Do you remember how your parents got along?"

"Yeah, they fought all of the time."

"Do you think they loved each other?"

"They sure had enough kids. If you only have sex with someone you love, then they must have loved one another at some time."

"I can't argue with your logic. Somewhere along the line, your parents fell out of love. Your mother suspected your father was seeing other women. She hired a private investigator and he took those pictures."

"How long ago were they taken?"

"Your mom says the first ones were taken over six years ago."

"That's when he still lived here. He acted like he wanted to be a perfect father. He was always trying to butter mom up. That was all a lie, wasn't it?"

"I really don't know. I wasn't around then, remember?"

"If my father was having sex with all of those women while he was married to mom, then I really do hate him. After he left and moved into his mother's old house, he was always talking bad about mom and my brothers. He didn't have very nice things to say about Nicole either. I believed everything he said and actually hated Mom for a while. I thought she was trying to take my father away from me. I guess he took himself away."

"When you have a family of your own, you'll understand your parents actions better. You're not mad at your mother, are you?"

"You must love Mom an awful lot. Mr. Hill, do you love my mother?"

"I love her very much."

"Then why don't you marry her?"

"How old are you, Mark?"

"Sixteen."

"I thought I was going to be the teacher."

"What were you going to teach me?"

"Not to be afraid to express your feelings."

They fished for the rest of the day in relative silence.

*****

Jane hadn't gotten a letter from Freddy for quite a while. She maintained an anxious vigil over the mailbox each day. A few days after Christmas, a letter came.

December 29, 1965

Dear Mom,

I'm going to tell you a story and I'd like you to sit down. First of all, I'm sorry for missing a few letters. Something happened that I am going to tell you about. It prevented me from writing for a few weeks. I want you to know I am fine and I'm counting the days until I see all of you.

First of all, don't open the smaller envelope until you read this entire letter. Promise me that, okay?

All right here it is:

You know that Jim Layton and I have become best friends. We have saved each other's life a number of times. No matter how good you think you know someone, you find you really don't know him as well as you thought. My relationship with Jim Layton was that way.

One month ago we went out on recon to find Charley's tunnel complex. We'd been looking months for this. The VC and NVA were using these tunnels to infiltrate our camps. They've made life very difficult here. Jimmy was ordered to lead our six-man unit into the Iron Triangle to find the

315

tunnels and not come back until we did. Jimmy thought he knew where they were.

We were inserted during the night and laid low until the morning. We started our search at first light.

After a few days of covering our search grid, we arrived at a former ambush site. That's where I tore the ligaments in my ankle.

As the sun went down on the fifth day we were preparing for another night in the jungle when the VC attacked. It seemed they came from nowhere. This had happened before in the same sector. We took out quite a few before being captured. Four of my friends were killed. Jimmy and I were taken prisoner. The little bastards started marching us up north. I won't go into the details. Just remember I'm okay.

Before they started moving us, we were interrogated. They took us into their underground complex. These things were right under our noses the whole time. They kept Jimmy and me separate. They got all they could from us, which was nothing. That's when they decided to move us.

On the seventh day of capture, they marched us out blind folded with our hands bound behind our backs. I had a funny feeling they'd never get us up north. I knew Jimmy would escape and free me. He's the best there is.

As Jane read the narrative from her son, she noticed watermarks on the paper where the writing appeared smeared. There were only a few of these. She wondered if Freddy wrote this letter in the rain but then she saw the handwriting. Where the smears occurred the writing was very shaky. Jane knew the watermarks were tears. Freddy must have been crying during the writing of the letter. Jane's interest was peaked even more as she read on.

Jimmy did escape. The VC looked all over for him but to no avail. I knew he wouldn't leave me to them. One night Charley had his guard down. Jimmy was able to free me. We ran like a bat out of hell. Bullets were flying all around us as we hauled butt.

The VC started shooting in all directions. Apparently, they had no idea which direction we took off in because of the darkness. We crawled on our bellies during the shooting. When the shooting stopped, we stopped. Finally, we heard them beating the bushes for us. We slowly inched our way out of there. Once we were clear of the VC we moved faster.

I didn't know it at the time of the shooting, but Jimmy had been hit several times. I remembered he shielded me from their fire just before we hit the ground. I don't know how far we had gone when he collapsed.

Mom, I had no idea he'd been hit. I couldn't tell anything in that pitch-blackness. He seemed just as indomitable and strong as ever. The last person in the world I'd expect to get killed was Jim Layton. Mom, he died saving my life.

The writing was badly smeared here and Jane could tell her son must have been in anguish as he wrote this part.

Before he died he handed something to me. He must have been holding onto it the entire time. The thing was sticky with his blood. Jim opened his clenched fist and dropped it into my hand. Then he said the strangest thing. Jimmy said, "give this to your mother and tell her I'm sorry for the pain I caused. Freddy, tell her I'm sorry." That was the last thing he said to me. I put it in a plastic bag and included it with this letter.

It took me almost two weeks of crawling in the jungle dodging both vipers and VC but I finally made it back. I miss Jimmy something awful. I don't think I'll ever get over his death. The information that I took back enabled us to knock hell out of Charley's tunnels.

Jimmy Layton was responsible for saving the lives of a lot of GI's, including mine. After it was all over, I led a recon unit back to where I thought he went down. It was dark that night. I was scared and not paying much attention to landmarks. I think I found the right area but I'll never know for sure because we never found a trace of him. Jimmy is officially listed as KIA. I'm not so sure.

Love,

Freddy

Jane carefully opened the smaller envelope. She pulled out a plastic bag with a dried flower inside. The bag was smeared with a reddish-brown stain. She remembered the dandelion her little boy carried into the street when a young Jimmy Layton in his Green Hornet hit him. The flower was caked with blood but she knew it wasn't her little boy's. Jane sat with the painful reminder in her lap and cried for Jimmy.

*****

A month later Jane learned Freddy would be home in another week. She started making phone calls to all of his friends. She would have a welcome home party for him. Jane called Robert, as she knew the two of them had reconciled. Robert picked up the phone when it rang.

"Robert, this is Jane."

"What do you want, more money?"

"Robert, don't be ridiculous. I haven't asked for anything from you since the divorce. I also didn't need to take out a house loan and buy you out. The Judge would have given me the house if I'd wanted, so don't accuse me of being greedy. You got off real easy and you know it."

"You turned my children against me."

"We've been over this ground before. Rob, I didn't call you to rehash history. Your son is coming home from Vietnam. I'm planning a welcome home party. Do you want to welcome him home or not?"

"Freddy and I have been communicating all along. We're regular pen pals. I'll bet he didn't tell you how he really got wounded."

"Rob, I know all about it. Yes or no, are you coming or not?"

"I'll be there, when?"

Rob hung up the phone and Jenette walked into the living room.

"I heard you talking. What's going on with Freddy?"

"The old bag called to tell me he's coming home."

"That's wonderful! When is he due to arrive?"

"In a few days. I told her I'd come to his welcome home party at the house."

"Can I go with you?"

"It would be better if you didn't go."

"That's silly, Robert. You've been divorced and married for a while now. What are you worried about?"

"I don't want them staring at you. It's best you stay here. I'm going to see my son and then come right home."

*****

Rob hadn't seen Jane in a couple of years. Whenever he picked Rene up, he made sure she wasn't around. He pulled the car into what was once his driveway. He noticed the grass needed cutting. Jane obviously wasn't the disciplinarian he was. He wondered how much she'd changed. *She's probably let herself go. Most women did when they got into their mid-forties.* Rob stepped to the door and knocked.

Jane was giving last minute directives to everyone when there was a knock on the door. Without looking she knew who it was. She heard the smokers cough as he approached the porch. *That cough was always the warning for the kids to scatter each night when he came home. I haven't seen him in a couple of years. I wonder what he looks like.* Their eyes met when Jane opened the door.

"Rob, come in. I'm glad you could make it. Freddy will be happy to see you. You look…good."

Rob stepped into the foyer while looking around. He was hoping his ex looked dumpy. She didn't. The only thing hinting at her age, were a few gray strands.

"Thanks for inviting me. I wasn't sure I wanted to come."

"Our differences are behind us, Rob. I just want to get on with life, don't you?"

"Yeah, sure, get on with life. Where is Freddy?"

"His bus is due any minute. Most of his friends from his varsity team are here. Why don't you go outside to see them?"

Jane watched him make his way outside. Instead of going over to the boys, he sat down on a lawn chair, under the maple. She was shocked at his appearance. Rob's face had wizened. He moved stiffly, as if each step was a struggle. He seemed like a total stranger.

Jane was curious about what must be going through his mind.

Robert sat under the tree with a beer. All of his children but Freddy were there. They all saw him enter the house. They all ignored him. *Not one of them said a word to me. Those are my children, but they don't seem like my children. They seem more like strangers. You'd think they'd at least say hello to their father. At least Freddy has seen the error of his ways. Who needs the rest?*

Robert sipped on his drink as he tried to remember each of them. He couldn't remember their young faces. He couldn't remember the faces of the little children waiting for him at the door each night when he came home. They used to look forward to seeing their daddy.

Robert recalled the past with melancholy. His eyes watered as he thought of his own life passing by. He was no longer a young man. He was still bitter over the cards life dealt him. He drank his drink with a houseful of people buzzing around him, but he was alone.

Hurried conversations seemed to surround him. The sound of Jane's voice snapped him out of his reverie.

"Mark, you need to keep an eye on the bus stop. He was getting into Union Station at one-thirty. It's only a half hour bus ride from the train station. He'll be here any minute."

"All right mom, you've only told me fifty times. I'll go outside and keep an eye out for him."

"I don't want you getting into something else and forgetting your main job."

"All right, all right, I'm out the door!"

A short time later Mark came running into the house from his observation post in the backyard.

"He's coming! He'll be here any second. Everybody go out back!"

All of the guests with the exception of Freddy's family went to the back yard near the tables laden with food. So far, Robert had been the perfect guest. Jane knew he was nervous about the meeting. She couldn't help but feel a little sorry for him. Marvin decided to keep Robert occupied, as none of the children wanted anything to do with him.

"So you're the one-legged guy from across the street?"

"I used to own your house."

"Bullshit!"

"You don't remember the name?"

"I wasn't much for mixing with the neighbors."

"You bought the house from me."

"No I didn't. The only person at settlement was a woman."

"Her name was Rebecca Hill, my wife."

"All I remember was how we got screwed on the price."

"Screwed? You took advantage of a woman that was alone. We sold you the house below its market value and you know it."

"Come to think of it, I remember the real estate agent saying something about the owner going to Korea. So that was you?"

"That's where I lost this."

Marvin slapped at his wooden leg with his cane.

"That's a real shame."

"I can tell you're all broken up about it."

Robert didn't get the response he wanted so he changed tactics.

"How long have you been screwing my wife?"

"That's ex-wife and it's none of your business. How long were you screwing around on her before she caught you?"

"That's none of your goddamned business."

"Then I guess we're even. What else do you want to know?"

Just when their conversation was getting interesting the front door opened and Freddy was home.

*****

After an hour of banter with his drinking buddies, Freddy found his father sitting alone. He sat down next to him.

Freddy struggled with something to talk about. He realized his discomfort and shifted uneasily in the chair. Robert finally broke the ice.

"Do you remember the letter about the first ambush?"

"Of course I do. What about it?"

"I was proud of you. How did it feel, killing those little gook bastards?"

"Dad, if it's all the same to you, that's something I've been trying hard to forget."

"Okay. How come you changed your attitude toward me?"

"Someone made me realize how petty out differences were. I decided he was right and wanted to clear the air between us."

"You call your disrespect of your father petty?"

"No, I don't think it was petty by itself. It was petty by comparison."

"Comparison to what?"

"I don't expect you to understand. You weren't there."

"I've been in life and death struggles before. You forgot what I did for a living."

"No dad, I hadn't forgotten. The difference is, you went home every night and your struggles weren't constant."

"I've been in some intense situations."

"Okay dad, you were in more danger than me. Let's not talk about it anymore okay? Let's say we both made mistakes."

"The mistakes weren't mine."

"Okay dad, if you say so. It was entirely my fault."

Robert's need for confrontation was not being satisfied. Freddy's maturity was unexpected. He'd always been able to get the desired reaction in the past. Freddy just wasn't being very cooperative.

"Why aren't you defending yourself? I thought I raised a man?"

Freddy's patience with his father was wearing thin.

"I see now. Is that what you were doing when you beat me and Bruce?"

"I wanted you to be strong. Being hard on you two was the only way to do that."

"I guess that would make sense to you."

Freddy remembered what Jimmy had told him. He didn't want to admit it then, but he knew Jim was right after all. His father did make him who he was. He was alive now because of it, but the price, what of the price?

"I did what I thought was right."

"You won't mind if I choose not to raise my son that way...if I ever have one?"

"Was my way all that bad? Look how you've turned out. You get your strength of spirit from me."

Freddy was trying to keep his emotions in check. He wanted this confrontation to end. He didn't want to fight. His father wasn't listening to him.

"Actually, I get that from mom. I watched her put up with a lot from you. Most of my resentment toward you was because of the way you treated her. She overcame her situation and is stronger because of it."

"If you think I was that bad a father then why have me here at all?"

"Because you are my father. I don't want to go through the rest of my life hating you."

"When did you come to this?"

"Do you remember Jimmy Layton?"

"What does he have to do with any of this?"

"Everything. While in the Nam, all I could think about was making it back to the world. You never even called to wish me well when you learned I was heading over there."

"We weren't on speaking terms then."

"I'm you're son! That should have overcome our petty issues. We were both too proud to make the first move. I didn't want to die without reconciling with you."

Freddy's eyes were watering as he continued.

"Jimmy Layton showed me how important family could be to surviving. He was always reading letters from his family. Mom and Mark were the only ones to write me. Jimmy convinced me to swallow my pride. I want to be like him. Now that he's gone, I'll not tarnish his memory by holding on to hate."

Freddy was openly crying as he thought about Jimmy. Freddy's emotions were having an affect on Robert. Memories of snowball fights, hunting and baseball with his sons came back to him.

"Freddy, I've always had a hard time showing affection. I guess that's your grandmother's legacy to me. I don't think I'll ever be able to change that.

Freddy sensed the change in his father's demeanor and felt the anxiety melt away.

"Dad, I'm not asking for you to change. We are who we are. I just want a father."

"All I've ever wanted is to be proud of my sons. I guess I'll have to settle for just one."

Suddenly Freddy felt very tired. His anxiety over this meeting had worn him out.

"I'm glad to hear that dad."

"Okay son. We'll start over. Now, go back to your friends and have a good time. I've got to get going."

"Come on dad, you don't have to go so early. Come with me and we'll get shit-faced together!"

"No Freddy, I told Jenette I'd be home early. You'll have to come over to the house one day soon and meet your stepmother. She's quite a dish."

"Yeah, I heard you robbed the cradle."

Freddy laughed at his joke but Robert's earlier anger returned.

"You have no business saying that. You don't even know her. I should have known this wouldn't work!"

"Wait a minute dad! I didn't mean anything. I was just kidding with you. Don't go flying off the handle. I'm sorry. Stay a while and have a couple of beers with us."

Robert regained control, but was quietly seething at his son's flippant attitude toward his wife.

"All right, apology accepted. We'll get together one day at the tavern. I'm sure Luke and the boys would like to tie one on with us."

"Okay, if you need to go I understand."

Freddy moved over to his father, his arms spread apart for an embrace but Robert retreated a step and stuck out his hand instead.

"Hugging is for sissies and girls."

"Sometimes hugs work for men."

"Not for this man."

"You're wrong. I've been around men that kill without hesitation. I've seen these same men breakdown in tears hugging one another."

"Sounds like the Army's full of queers."

"You don't understand. Maybe one of these days you will."

"I've got to go. We'll meet for a beer sometime."

Freddy watched his father drive off, feeling the anxiety he remembered from childhood.

*****

It had been a while since Robert's last visit to the Tavern. Nothing had changed. The faces and voices were still the same. Whip Maples, Luke Selmer and his deputies were in their normal places. Robert sat down in his old place, a cold Hamms waiting for him. He wondered if he looked as old as they did.

"Hey boys, how's everything? Whip you still chasing all the women in town?"

"Rob, you always were jealous of my popularity with the ladies."

"I can see you're as full of it as ever."

For the first time that day he felt at ease. He realized his favorite memories involved getting drunk with these men.

"Hey Rob, you haven't been around here for a while. How's the Bureau treating you?"

"Luke, I told those worthless sons of bitches to kiss my ass about a year ago."

"What are you doing with yourself then?"

"I'm working as a consultant with the state police."

Whip couldn't resist a quip.

"Consultant for what, proper procedures for frisking young women?"

"I should have known an intelligent conversation was too much to expect from you, Whip."

"You know I didn't mean nothing by it, Rob."

Luke pulled Rob away from the others.

"You know, the county is looking to hire consultants. Why don't you give old Ernest Loring a call? I might be able to help you get that contract. There might be something in this for all of us."

Robert and Luke concluded their business and rejoined the others. Luke reminded his son Richard going to Freddy's welcome home party.

"So Rob, tell us about Freddy. How's he doing?"

"He looks good. You know he got a Silver Star."

"Rob, this is a small town; everyone knows about Freddy's Silver Star. We're actually planning a big parade for our war hero. What do you think about that?"

"I think my boy is a chip off the old block. I always knew Freddy had it in him. Why hell, he wouldn't be my son if he didn't. Did you say a parade?"

"I sure did. The town council is planning it now. You'll be sitting in the Mayor's big black Caddy convertible. You'll be the center of attention. The big papers want to cover the whole thing. You might even make the front page. What do you think of that?"

Rob never answered Luke. He only nodded in appreciation, while he thought of who would see his picture in the paper. *I bet those ass-holes at the Bureau will shit. Wait until they read about my son, the war hero. I'll bet they'll wish they treated me with more respect. Hell, I bet the old man even offers me another job. The first thing I'll do is fire Collingsworth.*

"Rob, Rob, you still with us old buddy?"

"Yeah Luke, I'm still with you. By the way, speaking about sons and chips off the old block, Richard was at the party pounding down the beers just like you. You would have been proud of him, Luke."

Luke beamed at this declaration of his son's drinking ability.

"Yeah, I'm proud of Richard. You know he's my newest deputy?"

"You mean Richard's a cop?"

"He just graduated from the academy. With any luck, there'll be a Selmer in charge of things around here for a long time."

Robert thought about Luke and his son Richard while driving back to Hagerstown. Luke and Richard had a special relationship. That's all Robert ever wanted. The old bitterness started to rise. *If it weren't for that damned ex-wife of mine, I'd have that kind of relationship with all of my sons. That woman set them against me. Maybe it's not too late for Freddy. After all, he's proved he's worthy.*

Robert pulled into his driveway at about eleven-thirty. He could see the silhouette of his young wife through the front curtain. His lust was rising as he massaged himself to rigid life. He knew what he would do when he got in. Jenette liked it rough and that's how he would give it to her.

I'll have new sons with Jenette. I'll have sons that will want to be like their father. If Freddy disappoints me again, who needs him? I have a new family. The old one can go to Hell.

*****

Jane knew her son's moods. Freddy's moping the last couple of weeks said something was bothering him. She finally sat down for a talk.

"Freddy, how's the job search coming?"

"I need to get on the stick with that. I haven't felt like dealing with work yet."

"You've been home over two months now. Its time to get going instead of hanging out with your friends all of the time?"

"You're right, I need to get serious. I've been thinking about going back to school."

"School? Well, I suppose that's something. At least you've been thinking about your future."

"Mom, there's something else I need to tell you."

Jane looked at Freddy expectantly.

"Elaine Becker is pregnant."

"My God Freddy, you've only known the girl for a couple of months! Are you sure the baby is yours?"

"The baby is mine."

"How could you be so careless?"

"It just happened. It's not like we were trying to have a kid!"

"Do her parents know?"

"We've got to tell them. They're going to shit! You know they're Orthodox Jews?"

"That's the least of your problems. How are you going to support a family?"

"We've been talking about that. Elaine wants to live with her parents, while I work part-time and go to school. The GI Bill will pay for school. The money from my part-time job will help pay expenses."

"You're welcome to stay here, Freddy. Her parents may not want you living there."

"Why do you think we've been putting this off?"

"Do you want me to go with you?"

"Thanks mom, but no. This is something I have to do."

The next day Freddy and Elaine were sitting in the Becker's living room watching TV, when Freddy broke the news.

"Why couldn't you stay with your own kind Elaine? Ve told you not to date this gentile boy! Ve vanted you to marry a nice Jewish boy. Vaat vill people think!"

"Mr. Becker, I know you're worried about your daughter, but I'll take care of her. I won't run away from my responsibilities. You have my word, sir."

"For gentile boy ve like you Freddy. Ve just not sure about liking you as a son-in-law."

"Sir, I fought for our country in Vietnam. I saw things that no one should have to see. I did things that no one should have to do. I love Elaine. I'd want to marry her even if she wasn't pregnant."

"Vat can ve do but say...okay."

Freddy agreed to move into the Becker home once he and Elaine were married. He would attend school full-time at American University, then teach. Freddy promised Jimmy he'd do something with his life. What better way to fulfill that promise than to help children? Freddy knew Jimmy would approve.

He had one more duty to perform. Freddy reluctantly agreed to the parade in Maplesville. He kept watching his father in the open car. Robert was beaming. It was the first time Freddy could remember his father showing his affections so publicly. *He'll understand. So what if Elaine isn't Catholic? Dad won't care she's Jewish. Shit, who am I kidding?*

The next day Freddy made the seventy-mile drive to Hagerstown. The rolling hills of western Maryland were very much like those of Virginia. The pleasant scenery wasn't enough to ease his nervousness. He turned on Antietem Drive and found number 4711.

As Freddy shut the car door he saw Jenette peering through the blinds.

"Robert, Freddy's here."

Jenette opened the door before Freddy could ring the bell.

"What a surprise! Did your father know you were coming today?"

"No, I just thought I'd stop by. I have something to discuss with him. Is he around?"

"He's out back with the dogs. Why don't you surprise him? I called him, but I don't think he heard me."

Freddy went out the front door and around the house. He stopped as he saw his father with the hunting dog. He was brushing the Setter. Freddy's mind went back to a time when he was little. He remembered his father showing him how to brush old Duke. That was one of the few peaceful times he recalled spending with his father.

"Hey dad, don't brush all the fur off of him."

"Freddy! What brings you all the way out here?"

"I need to talk with you."

"Sure son, what is it?"

"I'm getting married."

"Married! You've only been home a few months."

"Yeah, I know, but you see...I got this girl pregnant so..."

"You got what girl pregnant?"

"You don't know her."

"You're marrying her because she's pregnant?"

"I've got to do what's right."

"There are other solutions to this problem."

"What solutions?"

"I know a doctor."

"What kind of doctor?"

"The kind you can't tell anyone about."

It struck Freddy what his father was saying.

"Wait a minute. That's illegal. How can you suggest such a thing?"

"It's better than doing something you're not ready for."

"Who said I'm not ready to get married?"

"You don't sound very convincing."

"I think getting married is just what I need."

"How so?"

"For one thing, it will get me motivated. It'll get me moving in the right direction."

"Right direction?"

"Yeah. If I have a family to support I'll have to get serious about my future."

"That's why you're getting married?"

"Well, no. That's not the only reason. I love Elaine."

"You know Freddy, working and supporting a family is not all it's cracked up to be. Look at what happened with me. There's nothing wrong with partying and enjoying life. Don't get married for the wrong reason."

"I'm ready for it. Elaine's the right girl."

"As long as you're sure. I don't want you to look back ten years from now regretting your decision."

Freddy thought of all the lectures from his father about obeying the commandments. His father was a devoted Catholic, a hypocrite. He'd heard enough advice from his father.

"I'm not going to be a party to killing a baby…my baby. This is to be your grandchild. How can you even think about an abortion?"

"I'm only trying to point out some of your options. Of course I'm against having the thing aborted.

"That 'thing' is going to be your grandchild."

"Of course, I didn't mean anything by it. Once you get married, how are you going to support Elaine and my grandchild?"

"We're going to live with her parents while I go back to school. I'll get a part time job to help with expenses."

"Okay, if you're mind is made up. When is the wedding?"

"We're going to a Justice of the Peace next Thursday. Will you come?"

"Sure, We'll be there. You said you were going to move in with her parents. Where do they live?"

"Fessenden Street."

"Where on Fessenden Street? What is their last name?"

Freddy took a deep breath before answering.

"Becker, their last name is Becker."

"You mean those Jews at the end of the block! You're marrying a Jew?"

"What difference does it make?"

"It makes all of the difference in the world. You can't marry a Jew!"

"Dad, calm down. I'm sure once you meet Elaine you'll understand. She's really a…"

"She's a Jew bitch. I won't condone my son marrying a Jew bitch, even if she's pregnant. That's the best reason in the world to use my doctor friend."

"I can't believe what I'm hearing! I thought you changed. You're still a mean heartless bastard! Tell you what. Forget about everything. I guess it's too much asking you to think about someone else.

Freddy turned to leave and heard his father screaming at the top of his lungs.

"You marry that kike and you're no son of mine!"

Robert went into the house and turned on the TV. Jenette had his highball ready. Robert could tell his wife had something on her mind.

"What was that all about? I heard the two of you arguing. Is everything all right?"

"He's no son of mine!"

"What happened? You guys have been getting along so well."

"He's gotten some Kike bitch knocked up. The idiot is going to marry her. Can you believe that? A Misner getting some Jew knocked up. There's going to be a houseful of little kikes running around with MY NAME!"

"I'm sure it's not as bad as all of that."

"You better not be taking his side. You look like something is bothering you. What?"

"Were you serious when you said you wanted more children?"

"Of course I was. Are you pregnant?"

"Yes."

"That's wonderful!"

"I was so afraid you'd be angry."

"Angry, nonsense. I can start all over with a brand new family!"

Rob sat in his chair feeling self-satisfied.

Elaine Becker became Mrs. Freddy Misner on Thursday evening. The wedding included only immediate family. Robert wasn't there. Seven months later Daniel Misner was born.

Three days after Daniel's birth another Misner boy was born. Robert couldn't see any point in telling anyone about it. His old family was a thing of the past.

PART SIX

Robert needed a break from his game of catch with Jonathan, his seven year old. The shade of the maple was inviting. He sat under the tree lamenting the wasted years of his past. His relationship with his first family had completely disintegrated. All that remained was bitterness. His whole life was one frustration after another. He'd only been throwing a few minutes before the pain in his shoulder forced him to the shade. He felt old.

Just as he was starting to relax Jonathan came over and took his father by the arm.

"Come on, dad. You said five minutes. You promised you'd show me how to hit."

Jonathan pulled on Robert's arm, urging him to continue playing ball. As he struggled to get up he went into what was now a very common coughing fit. Robert turned, placing his hands against the maple and expelled gobs of yellowish phlegm. He then took a long pull from the glass of spiked ice tea.

None of this went unnoticed by Jenette. Robert knew what was coming as she approached, the familiar concern etched on her face.

"Before you say anything I promise I'll make an appointment to see the doctor tomorrow."

"You've been promising that ever since we got married. I'm going in right now and do it for you."

"I said I'd do it. Hell, all he's going to tell me is to quit smoking. I switched to filtered cigarettes for Christ's sake."

"You know my opinion on that mister. You need to quit period. Now are you going in to call Doctor Walker or am I?"

"Oh shit Jenette, okay make an appointment."

*****

Mrs. Marvin Hill was enjoying herself. The late July sun was hot. Her grown children didn't seem to notice as they argued over the game of kickball. Jane reflected on the past. It seemed like only yesterday. She closed her eyes visualizing that day. Jane could see Mark and Nicole rolling through fresh grass clippings with Lonnie Scolnik. She opened her eyes wondering where her youngest son was.

On her lap was her youngest grandchild, Kevin. The five-year olds' congenital heart ailment kept him a spectator. Jane knew her little grandson was itching to join the others. After all, he was a Misner.

"Grandma, how far do you think I could kick the ball?"

"I bet you could kick it over those bushes."

"That far!"

"You might even be able to kick it further."

"I wish I could play."

"Sweetie, I wish you could too, but you don't want to stay in that old hospital again, do you?"

"I don't like the hospital."

Jane could see that Marvin was busy at the grill.

"Kevin, look at grandpa trying to cook."

"Grandpa looks funny!"

"It looks like your grandpa needs some help."

"I can help grandpa!"

"That's a wonderful idea honey! Why don't you walk over and help your grandpa cook the hamburgers."

As she watched Kevin go to his grandpa, something from the past caught her attention. She turned to look. Jane's worst nightmare came back. The big green car approached the front of the house and stopped. Jane instinctively rose to her feet. Panic rushed through her. Exiting from the passenger side was the Scorch. He walked around the back of the car, waving to his mother. Jane could see he had something behind his back.

"Mom! Happy birthday! I bought you some flowers."

Mark handed his mother a fresh bouquet of daisies. Carl Layton sped off in a spray of gravel dust. Jane's eyes followed the big green car until it disappeared. Her mind snapped back to the present.

"Mark! Are you all right?"

"Of course mom, why wouldn't I be?"

Jane wiped perspiration from her forehead. It was hard to believe this strapping young man was that same bundle of bloody rags those many years ago.

"Earth to mom. Are you with me? Why wouldn't I be all right?"

"Oh, no reason. Who was driving that car?"

"Come on mom, you know Carl Layton."

"But where did he get that car?"

"Isn't it cool. That used to be his older brother's ride. You remember, his older brother was killed in Vietnam saving Freddy's life."

Freddy ran over to his mother having seen the car too. His own memory of Jimmy Layton became vivid in his minds' eye.

"Mom, was that…"

"Yes honey, it was…The Green Hornet."

"But how? Who was driving it?"

Mark interjected.

"Brother, don't you remember? I told you Carl was restoring it. It had been sitting under that big tree for over twenty years. Carl's a whiz when it comes to cars. Doesn't it look great?"

Freddy wiped the moisture from his cheek. His mother's reaction was similar. They each had a reason for remembering the Green Hornet.

"Freddy, did they ever recover Jim's body?"

"No bro', they never did."

"Do you think there's a chance he could still be alive?"

"I wish there was, but no, I know he's not."

"His parents have a regular shrine to him in their living room. Have you ever seen it?"

Jane gave Freddy an expectant look. Freddy reached for his wallet and pulled out a sheet of paper folded into a small square. He handed it to his mother and explained.

"Mom, I know what you're going to say. No, I've not gone to see his parents. Given what Mark just said, I think it's time I do it. They may like to have this."

"What is this, honey?"

"It's the last letter he wrote his parents. I took it from his breast pocket. I knew he'd want his mom and dad to have it."

"Why haven't you given this to them then?"

"I don't know. I guess it's my way of hanging on to him a little longer."

"Honey, why don't you take it to them now."

"You're right. I'll be back in a little while."

Before he left, Marvin came up to him with Kevin trailing behind.

"Your son wants to tell you something Freddy."

"Daddy, I'm going to help grandpa cook hamburgers. Can I make one for you?"

Freddy picked up his son.

"That would be great! I bet you're a real good cook. Can you put pickles and onions on it for me?"

"I'll make the best hamburger you ever had."

"I'll be back in a little while. You be good for grandpa while I'm gone. I love you son."

"I love you too daddy. Don't be gone too long. Your hamburger will get cold."

"All right, Kevy. I won't be gone long. Bye, bye!"

"Bye, bye daddy!"

Freddy watched his son walking side by side with his grandpa. He looked forward to having that burger. For now, he started for the house around the curve.

Freddy stepped up to the screen door and knocked. Mrs. Layton came to the door.

She knew who Freddy was immediately even though they never met. Freddy was the subject of countless letters from Jimmy.

"Mrs. Layton, I'm…"

"I know who you are, Freddy. I feel like you're part of the family after all the letters Jimmy wrote."

"He wrote about me?"

"All of the time. I think you gave him a way of finding peace with that horrible accident, years ago."

"I understand what you mean."

"What can we do for you, Freddy?"

"I don't know how to start. I'll just give you this."

Freddy handed over the letter. By this time Mr. Layton had come to the door. Freddy watched their anxious expressions as they read Jim's last letter together.

December 9, 1965

Dear Mom & Dad,

We're getting ready for Christmas here. I can just imagine what the family is doing back home. Have you finished Christmas shopping yet? I can always use socks.

This place is hell on socks. One of the biggest problems is foot rot.

Every time we get a crop of FNG's, that's new guys, we give them the skinny on hygiene, especially mouth and foot hygiene. The two things you don't want trouble with here are your teeth and your feet.

Dentists here don't fill cavities. You get a toothache, they pull it! Freddy didn't learn that lesson real well. The docs have yanked two of his teeth already.

Speaking of Freddy, he's turned out to be a first rate recon man. He and I are a team. It's like we each know what the other is thinking before anything is said. He'll be coming home before me and I've asked him to stop by and see you. I'm hoping this will be my last stint here, but you never know. This would be a beautiful place if it weren't for the fighting.

Well, I better close now. We're getting ready to move out early in the morning. Tell everyone I miss them and to have a Merry Christmas.

Love,

Jimmy

Mrs. Layton folded the letter and looked at Freddy with a question. Freddy knew what it would be before she voiced it.

"Ma'am, I'm sorry I didn't give this to you sooner. I think I held onto it because it makes me feel closer to him. I hope you're not too upset with me?"

Freddy was starting to lose his composure. Mr. Layton's scowl disappeared and he put his arm around Freddy.

"We would have preferred to have seen this seven years ago. I guess I can understand how you feel. We miss him. We have a lot more to remember him by than you."

"Thanks for understanding Mr. Layton. I have a lot of memories of him. I'll never have a friend like Jim again."

*****

Jane was watching from the kitchen. Marvin was cooking the burgers while Kevin sat at the picnic table, watching the other children play ball. Before anyone knew it, Kevin jumped from the bench and ran after the stray ball. Marvin wasn't quick enough to catch him. Jane ran out the back door and down the steps. The children were cheering Kevin's effort at chasing the runaway ball, not understanding the potential risk.

Kevin had been watching the game, yearning to be part of it. He didn't know why his mommy and daddy didn't want him to run. He didn't feel sick. Kevin seized his opportunity as the ball got by his big brother, Danny.

Kevin's parents couldn't watch him all of the time. In fact, there were times he would do everything his brother did. He liked climbing trees the best. He'd show everyone how fast he could run. Kevin chased down the big red ball. He stood in triumph, holding the ball high with both hands. The children cheered as he threw it back into play.

Just as Kevin threw the ball, he felt dizzy. He turned to see his Pom pom and Po po running toward him. Old people looked funny when they ran. He would show them how to run fast. Kevin suddenly felt very tired and sat down on the freshly mowed grass. His eyelids felt heavy. He closed them for only a moment.

In his dreams Kevin was playing baseball. *His whole family watched and cheered. The pitch came and he hit the ball. Kevin could see himself running around the bases with blinding speed. He made it to home plate before the ball even cleared the fence. The onlookers cheered as he rounded all of the bases. Kevin crossed home plate and was a hero.*

Jane had gotten to her grandson just as he collapsed to the ground. She held him in her arms, gently speaking to him.

"Kevin, wake up. Wake up Kevin!"

Marvin soaked a towel under the spigot. Jane bathed Kevin's face, pleading for him to wake. His face was pallid. Suddenly, his eyes came open to the relief of everyone. Kevin's expression was one of excitement as he recounted his triumph.

"Pom pom, did you see how fast I ran? Did you see me catch the ball? I can play ball just like Danny."

"Yes sweetheart, we all saw how fast you were. You can run faster than all the other children."

"I'm sleepy Pom pom. Where's my daddy?"

Freddy was just about there. He saw everyone gathered around something in the front yard. He saw Elaine being held by his stepfather. Reality hit him like a sledge. He ran the last several yards to the throng of relatives shouting his son's name.

"Kevin, Kevin!"

Freddy reached Kevin in time to hear his little boy's words.

"Pom pom, I'm sleepy now. Tell my daddy how fast I can run. Tell daddy I can catch the ball and run like the others. Tell…"

"No Kevin, don't leave! Daddy's right here Kevin, please don't leave me!"

Freddy cradled his son in his arms. Kevin's mouth was turned up in a smile. He looked happy.

*****

The doctors told the distraught couple it would happen sooner or later. Kevin wasn't expected to live much past the age of two. The fact he lived to the age of five was a miracle.

Of course, this was of no comfort to Freddy and Elaine. All they knew was their little Kevin was gone.

Freddy picked up the phone and dialed a number he had gotten from his mother. The phone rang four times and he heard the voice of a woman.

"Hello."

"Is my father there?"

"Your father? Who is calling?"

"This is Freddy. I need to talk to my father."

"Freddy, I don't think he wants to talk to you."

"Jenette, it's very important. Could you please tell him I need to talk with him immediately."

"What has happened Freddy?"

"Jenette, please!"

"Okay, I'll go get him."

She went out back to where Robert was brushing his German Short-haired Pointer with Jonathan.

"Robert, Freddy's on the phone. He sounds very distraught."

"So the little Jew lover wants to talk to me? Tell him to go to hell. I don't need to talk to him!"

"Robert, something is wrong. He sounded like he was about to start crying."

"Crying? Now I'm curious. Tell him I'll be there in a minute. Okay John, hold onto his collar and brush him like I showed you. I'll be back in a minute."

Robert's knees creaked as he stood. Jenette gave him the phone.

"Dad, are you there?"

"I'm here, what do you want?"

Freddy did his best to rein in his emotions but that was impossible. His voice quivered.

"Dad, my son...your grandson has died."

"My grandson? Which one. Don't you have two half-breeds?"

"Half-breeds! That's all you have to say? I call you up to tell you my son has died and all you can say is half-breed? What kind of human being are you?"

"The kind that wonders why his son is only calling him when he has a problem! You never called me when the little bastards were born. You never called me to congratulate me on the birth of my new sons! Why should I give a rat's ass about your half Jew brats?"

All Robert heard in response was a clunk as the phone on the other end fell to the floor. Freddy sagged into the living room chair and put his face in both hands, crying. His tears were twofold, for the death of his son and for the father he never had.

*****

Doctor Walker was one of the best EEN&T specialists around. Robert sat across from him waiting anxiously for the news he'd come to hear. Robert couldn't stand the silence any longer.

"Well doctor?"

"You have polyps in your throat."

"Polyps? What in the hell are those?"

"It's a serious warning sign that can't be ignored. They are the cause of your throat irritation. Your smoking certainly doesn't help either."

"I knew it, I knew it! I told my wife I'd get a lecture on smoking from you."

"Mr. Misner, this can be serious. You need to pay attention to what your body has been telling you. How long did you say you'd been coughing like this?"

On queue, Robert started hacking. Doctor Walker pushed a box of Kleenex over to him. Robert snatched one up and covered his mouth, coughing into it.

"I've always had a smokers cough ever since I can remember. It's been like this I guess for six or seven years."

The doctor was shaking his head in disbelief as he responded.

"I'm going to schedule you for a procedure at Hopkins as soon as possible. We need to do a biopsy."

"You mean I have cancer?"

"Relax, I'm not saying that. I am saying we need to do tests. Most of the time they're benign. Don't you think it's better to find out?"

Stunned by the possibilities, Robert stammered out his reply.

"Sure doc. Yeah, I'd like to get this over with. When did you say the procedure would be done?"

"I'll have to get you on the schedule. How about if I give you a call later this afternoon?"

With that, Robert left the office. His mind was in a daze as he drove home.

*****

Two days after his procedure the phone rang.

"Mr. Misner?"

"Yes."

"Mr. Misner, we got the results from the lab."

"So, what's wrong? Is it cancer?"

"Mr. Misner, can you come in tomorrow morning."

"Why can't you tell me over the phone?"

"I'd rather do this in the office."

"Look, I've waited long enough. All I want is a simple yes or no!"

"Okay. The tests were positive."

"Positive? Doctor tell me in English!"

"If that's what you want. Mr. Misner, you have cancer of the throat."

The news hit him hard.

"Cancer? Are you sure?"

"I know this is a shock. There are choices to be made. Come in tomorrow so we can talk?"

"What time?"

"We're here at eight."

"I'll be there."

Rob didn't say anything to Jenette. He'd deal with it on his own. All she would do anyway is nag him about the smoking. He didn't need that aggravation.

"Rob, was that the doctor? What did he say?"

"It's what I thought all along. My allergies are acting up."

"What a relief! I was worried it was something more serious. Now, will you quit smoking?"

"I've been smoking for over forty years. If it kills me, it kills me. Now get off of my back about quitting!"

The next morning Doctor Walker introduced Robert to his oncologist.

"Mr. Misner, this is Bart Henkles. Bart is one of the most respected oncologists in the country. Bart, tell Rob what we've been discussing."

"The polyps are cancerous as you know. They need to be removed. Unfortunately, your voice cords are involved. We'll do everything we can to save at least one of them so you can still talk."

"You sure didn't pull any punches with that."

"Mr. Misner, there is more. We may have to remove the entire larynx."

"Larynx?"

"Your voice box."

"Is this the operation where you have a hole in your throat for the rest of your life?"

"Yes it is."

"Jesus Christ, I wasn't expecting this! What happens if I don't go through with the operation? I mean, is there any other treatment?"

"This is the only treatment that gives you a chance to live."

"If I have the operation is there a guaranty that I'll live?"

"Mr. Misner, there are no guaranties. You will increase your chances for prolonged life."

"How prolonged?"

"There's no way of knowing for sure. It depends."

"Depends on what?"

"On if we get all of it."

"So, if you get all of it, I'll live?"

"It's more complicated than that, Mr. Misner. The cancer could come back somewhere else in your body. The thing is, there are no guarantees. We remove the cancerous tissue and hope for the best. We need to get moving as quick as possible."

"Define quick."

"I'd like to check you in now and do the surgery early tomorrow morning."

"That fast? What if I want a second opinion?"

"Mr. Misner, you could get one hundred opinions and each doctor will see the same thing we have. The sooner we get you into surgery, the better chance you have of beating this thing."

"I guess I don't have any choice. If you have to remove the larynx is there anyway I'll ever be able to talk?"

"Actually, yes there is. There are people that have learned to talk with the use of a resonator."

"A resonator?"

"Let's cross that bridge when we have to. The chances are good that we will not have to remove your cords or larynx. So we'll take one step at a time, okay?"

"I haven't said anything to my wife and kids about this. Why don't I check in tomorrow morning so I have a chance to talk with them before…"

"Be back in here tomorrow no later than noon. We'll prep you and operate around 2pm."

Robert's mind was racing. Jenette had no idea how to manage finances. Like his first wife, he kept Jenette in the dark when it came to money matters. Robert liked to keep her barefoot and pregnant. *Isn't that what they're for,* he thought. His thoughts along those lines continued. *They weren't even good for sex much past the third or fourth year of marriage.*

His old acquaintance Brandi still ran the best whorehouse in DC. She introduced her oldest customer to a couple of sweet young things. He could tell Brandi had instructed them on what he liked. They knew just what to do to please him. On his way home he would make one final stop.

Why am I always singled out? I'm never going to be able to talk again. I'll have to go around with a goddamn hole in my throat, sounding like some robot from Buck Roger's serials. God must be punishing me for the divorce. That's it! I'm being punished.

*****

Jane was cleaning up after dinner. Mark brought an unexpected guest over. When he walked through the front door with the black girl, Jane almost fell over. Mark seemed intent on shocking everyone with his taste in exotic women. For some reason, he seemed to like Asians. Jane asked him about his tastes one day. His reply was, "American girls are too demanding." He'd never brought home a black girl before.

"Mom, Marvin, I'd like you to meet Celia Kingsley."

"Celia, very nice to meet you. Are you from Africa?"

"Mom! Celia, I better explain my mom's question. I've bought home several girls over the last four or five years from different countries, the orient in particular. Now my mother thinks that's all I'm interested in. She's been after me to meet a nice American girl. Well mom, Celia is a nice American girl. In fact, she is a local girl. Don't you recognize her last name?"

"Kingsley...Kingsley, no honey I'm afraid to disappoint you, but I don't know any Kingsley's. Wait a minute! Are you related to that Mr. Kingsley that used to work at the hospital?"

"Yes ma'am. He's my father."

"My goodness, you must think I'm a terrible person. Come in the living room and have a seat. Would you like a cup of coffee?"

Celia looked to Mark with the question on her face.

"Yeah mom, we'll have some coffee. I was just bringing Celia home from work. Mr. Peterson hired her last week. Today was her first day at the store. Celia doesn't have a car so I offered to take her home."

A feeling of utter relief filled Jane as she took in that last bit of information.

"Oh, so you're not on a date?"

"No mom, we're not on a date. Celia, what do you think your father would say if you brought a honky home?"

"I think my father would surprise you. He used to talk about you all of the time."

Jane decided at once she liked this girl. Not everyone could make Mark stumble over his words. Jane saw the adoring look in Celia's eyes, as she looked at Mark.

"Celia, your dad would have a fit if we dated."

"I don't know Mark, I've dated other white boys. He never seemed to mind."

"You're kidding, right? I mean, that's just asking for trouble don't you think?"

"Mark, are you prejudiced?"

"No, of course not! That's my father's department."

Jane could see the need to change the subject quickly.

"Celia, why don't you help me with the coffee?"

"I'd be happy to, Mrs. Misner."

"It's Hill dear, but why don't you just call me Jane. After all, we're adults."

"Yes ma'am...er, Jane, I'd be happy to."

After dinner, Jane herded her son to the kitchen, while Marvin entertained Celia.

"Mark, Jenette called me today."

"Jenette? Oh, Jenette. What did she want?"

"She says your father wants to see you."

"If he wants to see me, why can't he call me instead of having his little slut do it for him?"

"Mark, that's way in the past. When are you going to grow up? If I don't have a problem with the woman, why should you? Besides, you're father CAN'T talk to you."

"What do you mean, can't?"

"Your father had a cancer operation. They removed his voice box. He can't talk."

"Is he going to die?"

"She didn't say what his prognosis was, but it's cancer."

"Did they get it all?"

"Jenette said they removed the tumors and feel they got all of it."

"It can come back though can't it?"

"Yes honey, it can come back."

"Did Jenette say how he's doing...you know, mentally?"

"Jenette says he came through the operation in surprisingly good spirits, considering what they had to remove. Your father wants to make peace with you. Will you go see him?"

"Is he still at the hospital?"

"He's at Hopkins."

"Yeah, I'll go see him."

*****

Mark walked into the room at about ten in the morning. His father was in a chair, looking out at the sidewalk. Robert turned his head when he heard the approach of heavy steps. Mark wasn't prepared for his father's appearance. Robert rose on shaky legs. They stared at each other briefly, before Mark approached his father and put his arms around him. When they finally looked at each other, they were both wiping at tears.

"Dad, I didn't know. Why didn't you tell me before the operation?"

Robert had to use one of those erasure boards little kids played with to communicate. He wrote his response.

"I only found out the day before the operation."

"What did they tell you about a recurrence?"

Robert raised the plastic sheet erasing his written words. The wooden stylus scribbled his reply. *They say they got it all. They say I can learn to talk again using vibrations.*

Mark noticed the waffle-like bandage around his father's throat for the first time. It had slipped down revealing a cavernous hole in the middle of his father's throat. There was moisture around the opening that looked like mucus. Mark turned his face away from the sight. When he looked back at his father, the bandage was back in place. Mark had no idea this was a test contrived by his father.

He's weak like his mother. He might be big but he has the squeamish stomach of his mother. The hole in my throat bothers him. I'm a better man than he'll ever be. With that thought Robert pulled the bandage back in place while Mark had his head turned.

"When can you go home? Is there anything I can get for you?"

"No, just sit with me for a while."

"I'll have to go to work in an hour or so."

He couldn't believe this bulky young man was his Scorch. He wanted to hate him but a battle was taking place inside him. The Scorch was always his favorite. *I've fought against myself my whole life. My Scorch is here. He's a man.*

Mark sat in silence next to his father. His eyes wandered to the window as he thought, m*y father is already dead. This whimpering person next to me isn't anything like my old man. He's weak and pathetic. How can I hate him? He's paid the price for the life he led.*

Mark broke the uneasy quiet.

"Dad, I've got to go. Have they told you when you can go home?"

The fluid in the I.V. tube jiggled as Robert scratched out his reply.

"No, they want to keep me here for a while."

"I'll check on you in a couple of days. See you later."

Robert watched the door close behind Mark. With Mark's departure, his thoughts turned malevolent again. *Mark doesn't care for me. All he cares about is making his guilt go away for the way he's treated me. They're all ungrateful. I can still get even. They think I'm done, but they'll find out different.*

*****

Several weeks later, while going through the mail, Jane opened an envelope from the Arch Diocese. Rob was requesting an annulment. That's not what shocked her the most. Robert accused her of infidelity. He was claiming the children were not his, that Jane's adulterous affairs produced them. It went on to say his marriage to her was never consummated.

Robert came across as the dedicated Catholic trying to save his marriage. In the end, his wife's sexual infidelities and perversions finally drove him away. He portrayed himself as the perfect martyr.

Jane didn't know what to do. *If I sign this, the children will be bastards in the eyes of the Church.* She wasn't too worried about the three oldest. Mark and Rene were another matter. She still thought they harbored strong emotions for their father. In the back of her mind, she knew she'd sign it. *What harm can it really do? He's dying and can't hurt us any more. Mark and Rene need never know about it. The least I can do is give him piece of mind.*

Jane was still pondering over the document when Marvin walked in.

"Hey you, let's do something dif...what's the matter?"

Jane handed Marvin the annulment. Marvin's mouth dropped open as he scanned the pages.

"What are you going to do? You're not thinking about signing this? This would devastate Mark. I've tried to be the father he never had. He has finally connected with his real father. This will destroy that!"

"You've showed Mark as much love as any father. I know you love him like he was your own son. I know how painful it must be not to have it returned."

"I understand. I don't begrudge his relationship with Robert. That's why he can't see this. Let me throw it away."

"No, I need time to think about this."

"After seeing this pack of lies, I now believe every evil story about Robert Misner. How can a man write off his children?"

"What can it hurt if I sign it? None of the children go to church anymore. If it makes Rob's last days go by easier, fine. I used to hold a grudge. Once I met you. That hate vanished."

"What happens down the road if one of your children decides to go back to the Church. They'll be viewed as illegitimate!"

"That won't happen. You're worrying about something for nothing."

"Am I? Are you willing to chance them finding out? Are you so sure of their true feelings? They deserve to know the truth."

"You're reading too much into this. This is merely a formality. The Church can't afford to lose members. If they excommunicated every member that divorced, they'd go broke. This is their way of bending the rules."

"How can you let him get away with the lies about you?"

"Marvin, the man is dying."

"What about the part that says you committed adultery?"

"That's not true either."

"Of course it's not, but how can you let the man get away with this?"

"Marvin, he's dying. Let him have his pathetic peace."

"He is denying the legitimacy of his children. They'll be bastards in the eyes of the church. How are they suppose to reconcile that with the Church?"

"I didn't say I was going to sign it. I just said I would think about it."

"This is the last thing I'll say. Your children are going to get hurt. You cannot prevent them from finding out about this."

Marvin handed the document back to Jane. She sat at the dining room table staring at the form. The phone rang. Rene needed a ride home. Jane grabbed her keys and left. Marvin went for his afternoon walk. Both forgot about the Annulment form.

*****

Mark was in a hurry to get home and change. He and Celia had started dating. It started with rides home from work. The seeds were planted the day Mark introduced Celia to his mother. Celia was on Mark's mind a lot. They started taking lunch and dinner together at work.

Before going to his apartment Mark needed to stop by the house. His father wanted the metal case containing some old slides. Mark promised he'd pick them up. Celia was expecting him at six and Mark was running behind. *Celia...how do I tell him about her? Man if he knew I was dating a black girl he'd flip out for sure. I can't tell him, it would kill him.*

Mark entered the house. The car wasn't in the drive. He went into the dining room. He was rifling through the buffet when his mother opened the front door and saw him. Mark raised his head when he heard the door open.

"Hey mom! Hey Rene, how's school?"

"Hi Mark, I'm in a play at school called <u>The Lottery</u>."

"Oh yeah, I know that one. What is your character?"

Before Rene could answer Jane took three quick steps over to the table, scanning it.

"Mom, what's the matter?"

Her eyes caught a glimpse of the form from the Diocese. Jane relaxed a little when she realized Mark hadn't seen it.

"Nothing honey, nothing is wrong. How was your day?"

"Fine, just fine. I'm kind of in a hurry. I have to pick Celia up at six and it's almost five-thirty. I told dad I'd get those old slides of the dogs."

"They're upstairs in the closet."

Mark closed the drawer to the buffet and started for the stairs.

"Mom, you seem on edge. Are you sure everything is okay? You're not sick, are you?"

As Jane tried to answer her eyes darted toward the table. Mark's eyes followed.

"Honey, I'm fine, really."

"What do you keep looking at?"

Before Jane could reach for the document, Mark beat her to it. He picked up the form with the fancy seal.

"Mark, let me have that!"

"Wait a minute mom. What is this?"

Mark saw the heading that said Annulment and scanned the paperwork. Jane watched the transformation take place. Mark's face went from mild curiosity to unbridled anger in the blink of an eye.

"Honey, please, let me have that."

"Is this what I think it is? Can the Church do this? Why would dad do this? You're not going to sign this, are you?"

"Mark, what difference does it make? You have no interest in the Church anymore. If it gives your dying father some peace, let him have it."

"I can't believe you. My feelings have nothing to do with the Catholic Church. He's claiming you aren't our mother. He doesn't love me. This whole reconciliation is a big lie. I'm some kind of tool to help him with his guilt."

"Mark, your father does love you. Of all the children, he always had special feelings for you. He's desperate and dying. The church doesn't recognize divorce. He really thinks he'll go to Hell if the church doesn't forgive him."

"As far as I'm concerned, he is going straight to Hell. I'm not letting him get away with this!"

Mark threw the papers to the floor and bolted from the house.

*****

Mark sat on his couch staring blankly at the wall. He picked up the phone on the fifth ring.

"Mark?"

"Celia, hi."

"Hi? You were supposed to be here two hours ago. What happened to you? Why didn't you call?"

Like his father, Mark felt a powerful need for vindication. Once he lost his temper, there was no room for rational thought. All he could think of was revenge. Not just revenge for this latest insult, but revenge for a lifetime of disappointment and deception by his father. *How can I get even? It has to be something he'll take to his grave.* When Mark heard Celia's voice on the phone, an idea took root.

"Mark, did you hear me? Are you all right?"

"Yes Celia, I'm fine. I'm just getting ready to leave now."

Mark was nervous when he knocked on the door. When it opened he saw Celia standing there in a halter-top. She was wearing pink hot pants. He could make out the lines of her breasts beneath the loose fitting top. Celia was lean and curvaceous. Her breasts strained at the confinement of the loose fitting top. She had the kind of body all men noticed regardless of skin color. Mark thought she was the sexiest woman he'd ever seen.

"There you are. I didn't think you were going to show up."

Mark couldn't take his eyes off the girl and it was obvious to Celia what had attracted his attention.

"My God Celia! You look beautiful tonight!"

"I thought I'd make our first real date special, know what I mean?"

Mark felt the touch of her gentle fingers as she reached for and took his hand in hers. Celia pulled him into her apartment. He followed the scent of jasmine as he sat next to her on the couch. He watched her trace the contour of her bright red lips with her moist tongue. Mark's breath quickened as he cupped her face in his right hand.

"Special, what did you have in mind?"

"You know, I really don't feel like going out tonight."

"Really, what do you feel like tonight?"

"Like this."

Celia undid the straps and let the halter-top fall around her tiny waist. Her breasts were pendulous with small dark brown nipples that formed erect little peaks. Mark bent his mouth over them in turn and traced their outline with his tongue. Celia leaned back while making soft mewling sounds. Her hands were pulling Mark's face into her harder and harder. She reached down and held Mark's erection, massaging it.

"I think I like this better than dancing."

"Mark baby, I've thought about this for a long time. Oooh keep it up, that feels so nice."

Mark slid a hand down her belly relishing the feel of her hard stomach.

"Further baby, reach in there and feel how wet I am. I want you sooo bad!"

His hand undid her belt, then her buttons. Tufts of her pubic hair were now between his fingers as he inched them closer and closer to the source of her wetness. Mark massaged her clitoris with thumb and forefinger, eliciting more groans from her writhing body. His fingers slid into her vagina and probed deeply.

"Mark, kiss me."

Their lips joined and their tongues sought out the deepest recesses of their mouths. Clothes were flung in every direction as Mark stood with her buttocks supported by his hands. Her legs were wrapped around his waist. He could feel the tautness off those delicious brown nipples against his chest. He maneuvered her onto his erection. She threw her head back in one long sigh as they moved to each other's rhythm.

"Mark, this is my dream come true. Oh, oh, ohhhh! I...I've always had a huge crush...oh, oh, oh...on you. Baby, that feels soooo good. Does it feel good to you?"

"You're, you're unbelievable. I want to do this all night long."

"Oh baby, yes all night and tomorrow. Who said white boys couldn't dance? Harder Mark oh yes baby harder!"

All night is exactly what they did. The next morning Mark drove back home but couldn't get Celia off his mind. He wasn't sure if his feelings were love or lust. Mark tried to imagine what his father's reaction would be. He tried working it out in his head as he drove.

What if the old man thought I was going to marry her? All Celia will be to him is a nigger. I'll introduce her as my fiancé. That will freak him out like nothing else could.

It occurred to Mark, that both white and black society might ostracize racially mixed kids should he and Celia marry. That could be asking for a lifetime of trouble. *I don't have to really marry her. Hell, we've only screwed once. All I have to do is make the old man 'think' we're getting married...interesting!*

*****

Jenette had been trying to call Mark for a couple of weeks. He picked up his phone one day and found her on the other end.

"Mark, where have you been? Your father is getting worse. You haven't been by for over three weeks. He wants to see you."

"I've been busy."

"Busy? Your father is on his death bed and you've been too busy to see him?"

"That's what he told me my whole life. He was always too busy for me. He'll have to deal with some disappointment of his own."

"Mark! What's happened to you? I thought you loved your father?"

"I know all about his deal with the Church."

"Deal? Church? What are you talking about?"

"I see you don't know. You wouldn't believe me if I told you, so what's the point?"

361

"What did your father do?"

Mark gave her the Readers Digest version. There was a long moment of silence before she reacted.

"I can't believe he would do such a thing."

"Well believe it or not, he did. My mother signed off on it too."

"Mark, your father is just looking for peace. Your mother put the past behind her, why can't you?"

Mark played her like a fish on a line.

"I can't forget as easily as my mother."

"Mark, please? Just think about it."

"Oh Christ Jenette! Okay, tell the bastard I'll be there. He might as well meet my fiancée."

"You're getting married?"

"Yep. Her name is Celia Kingsley. He met her father."

"Mark your father does love you. He talks...or writes about you all of the time. He wouldn't do that if he didn't love you."

"We'll see. Tell him we'll be by tomorrow."

"Thank you Mark. You're doing the right thing. He'll be excited about meeting Celia."

*****

That night Mark went to Celia's for another session of torrid sex. Fully spent, he rolled over on his back while running a finger around her nipples.

"Baby, that feels gooood. You keep that up and I'll be ready to go again."

Mark had decided this might be the last time he'd have sex with Celia so he may as well make the most of it.

"Come here baby. I didn't think I could go anymore but..."

"Yeah baby! I know, so let me take care of you."

Celia rose to her knees and straddled Mark.

"Celia, ease yourself down…ahhh that's it! Now ride it baby, ride it!"

Mark had both hands around her waist lifting her up and down. Celia bent down and kissed him deeply, her nipples brushing his. She finally collapsed over him, the orgasm draining her of all strength. They lay there, looking into each other's eyes. Celia was the first to get a breath and speak.

"Mark, you make me feel so good. I've never, ever had anyone make me feel this way before."

"Baby, you're just saying that. What about all those stories about black guys and how heavy they're hung?"

"I don't know where you white boys come up with all that. I've had me some black guys. You're different. I've never had anyone make me come the way you just did."

"You're just trying to make me feel better because you know I'm worried about my father."

"Your father, oh yeah, well I'm sorry about him being sick, but that's not what I was thinking about. I was thinking I'd like you to move in with me. We could do this everyday."

"Are you talking about marriage, Celia?"

"Not marriage, well, maybe later. That is if we get along once we live together for a while."

"Celia, you know I see other women. I also told you not to quit seeing other guys. Marriage is no damn good Celia. I watched my mother and father fight my entire life. The only thing that came out of their marriage was us kids. Most of us, except for Rene, are screwed up. No, marriage is definitely not for me."

"My parents still love each other and they had nine kids. You can't think all marriages are bad just because your parents weren't happy."

"I suppose you do have a point."

"You know I do. Besides, you couldn't make love to me the way you do if you didn't feel anything for me."

"What do you mean by that?"

"I think I'm falling in love with you. You are all I think about every minute of every day. You feel something for me don't you?"

"I'd be lying if I said I didn't. I've never met anyone like you before. I'm not sure what to do."

"Is it because I'm black and you don't want your family to know about me?"

"You know better than that. If that's the way I felt, would I go out with you in public?"

"You worried what your family would say?"

"Well, you've got me there. I'll tell you what I'll do."

Celia's eyes brightened in the darkness of the dimly lit room. Mark could see the anticipation in them.

"What baby? What are you going to do?"

"Tomorrow we'll go see my mother. I'll tell her all about us. Then we'll drive to Hagerstown and see my father."

"Your father? But he's a bigot, at least that's what you told me."

"What are you afraid of? He can't even talk. I want him to meet the girl I love. Say you'll go with me."

"Mark, you said you love me."

"Come here and I'll show you how much."

"Mark, I'll go anywhere you want. Make love to me again! Make love to me hard!"

He did just that.

*****

After stopping by his mother's Mark and Celia made the drive to Hagerstown Maryland. On the way Celia said, "Mark, I changed my mind. I don't want to do this. I thought I could face your father, but I'm scared."

"He's mellowed a lot since he got cancer. He's more worried about going to heaven than whether I'm seeing a black girl."

"Did you tell him about us?"

"Celia, he can't talk. I told Jenette I was bringing you by to meet him."

"But, did you tell her I was black?"

"No."

"No! Your father's going to shit when he sees me! You should have told him like we discussed!"

"I'm gambling, once he meets you, he'll become enchanted, like me."

They pulled in front of the house and made their way up to the front porch. When Jenette answered the door she could barely speak as Mark introduced Celia. Her mouth was moving, but nothing came out.

"It'll be okay, Jenette. Why don't you stay here, while I introduce Celia to dad."

Jenette found her voice.

"Mark, I can't let you do that! You know what it will do to your father!"

Celia was frozen in place.

"Mark, I'm scared! I can't do this!"

"Celia, settle down. I need him to know about you. I need him to be okay with it. If he accepts you, then I'll know he really does love me. Please Celia, come with me!"

Mark took her hand. She reluctantly followed him down the narrow hall.

*****

Something had happened to Mark while driving to Hagerstown. He kept looking at Celia. For some reason, he couldn't take his eyes from her. The worried expression on her face gave him second thoughts. He didn't want to hurt her. He realized a change had taken place the night before. *She's scared to death, but willing to do this for me. Maybe I do love her.*

Mark took a deep breath and stepped into the room. Celia was at his side. The look on his father's face was pure shock. Mark brought Celia's hand to his mouth and tenderly kissed it. He looked at his gasping father and spoke in a quiet tone.

"Dad, this is Celia Kingsley. Do you remember her father? I called him Big George, do you remember? He was the physical therapist you had fired when I was in the hospital."

Robert's eyes were bulging. Mark was sure his words were getting through because he could see his father's chest heaving with the effort to breath. A spray of moisture and mucus erupted from the hole in Robert's throat.

"Dad, what do you want to say...oh I'm sorry, you can't talk. Do you want your tablet and little wooden pencil?"

Mark reached for the pad on the nightstand. As he extended the tablet, Robert gripped his wrist.

"Damn dad, that's a pretty strong grip for a dying man."

Mark pried Robert's hand from his wrist. He laid the pad on his father's chest and patted it reassuringly.

"Dad, don't get excited. I don't want you having a heart attack. I brought my fiancée to meet you. There's no telling how long you're going to be around. I thought you might want to meet the woman that's going to be the mother of your grandchildren."

Celia found her tongue and lashed out at Mark.

"I can't stay for any more of this. I'm going to the car!"

Celia turned on her heel and left. Mark turned his attention back to his father. His face was inches from Robert's for his final statement.

"My goodness, she seems a little upset. Oh well, I'm not worried. I'm a chip right off the old block. I know just what to do to calm her down. The fact is dad I do love her. She is without a doubt the best lay I've ever had. I think Celia's beautiful don't you? Our kids should be exotic looking, don't you think? I'll name the first either Robert or Roberta. Just think of it; the world will have a little brown Robert Misner running around."

By this time, Mark felt Jenette pulling at him. Robert was having trouble breathing.

"Mark, leave my house or I'll call the police! You're killing him. He can't breath."

"Okay Jenette, I'm leaving."

Mark turned to go, but stopped and said one last thing.

"Dad, has your latest marriage been consummated, or are you planning to annul it too?"

Mark took in the pitiful sight of his father one last time and left without another word. Mark barely noticed Celia as he backed from the driveway. Celia was in tears. Mark pulled over before entering the ramp to I270. He slid across the seat. Celia pressed herself against the passenger door not wanting Mark to touch her.

"Stay away from me, Mark! I hate you. How could you? How could you do such a thing?"

She covered her face up with her hands and cried. Mark was able to get one arm and then another around her.

"Shh, shhh, it's okay Celia. I love you. I'm sorry I hurt you. I didn't mean to. I don't expect you to understand."

"You're right! I don't understand!"

"My father had his marriage to my mother annulled by the Church. You should have read the accusations against her. He said she had been unfaithful the entire marriage. He said we weren't his children."

"Mark, how could he get away with that?"

"He has. Mom signed the thing. She said, *What difference does it make?*" She says, he's dying and looking for peace."

Now Celia was looking at him with a curious expression.

"I've struggled all of my life over whose son I am; my mother's or father's. I guess, after this, I have more of my father in me."

They'd been in the car for about an hour and Celia had gotten over her initial shock. She could see the torment on Mark's face. Mark was crying freely now. Celia moved over to comfort him.

"Don't end it this way with your father. Let's go back. For your sake as much as his."

"You're right, Celia. He is my father. I do love him despite the pain he's caused. I need to tell him that face to face. I need to show him I'm not like him. The best way of doing that is to forgive him. We're going back!"

Mark whipped the car around and headed back to his father's house.

As he checked for traffic in the rearview mirror he saw his own collection of dead bees and dragonflies in his window well. He hoped he wouldn't be too late.

*****

His Scorch was saying awful things. Why was he doing this? He loved the Scorch. He desperately wanted to make his son understand what was going through his mind. *No, no, Scorch you can't marry this nigger! You are going to ruin my good name! I'm going to have nigger pickaninnies for grandchildren. You're going to ruin the blood of our family because you're mad at me. Don't do this son. Think about what you are doing. I've fucked niggers. I can understand that, but don't marry one Scorch. Please oh God don't let him marry one. I can't breathe. Scorch, please don't leave like this. Come back, come back, you're my boy don't leave like this! Jenette, Jenette, don't let… him…leave.*

Robert heard the sound of the ambulance as it pulled up. His eyes were staring into space, non-responsive. His last thoughts were of Griffith Stadium, baseball and the father he loved.

The End